Highland Rebel

TESS MALLORY

BERKLEY SENSATION, NEW YORK

THE BERKLEY PUBLISHING GROUP
Published by the Penguin Group
Penguin Group (USA) Inc.
375 Hudson Street, New York, New York 10014, USA
Penguin Group (Canada), 90 Eglinton Avenue East, Suite 700, Toronto, Ontario M4P 2Y3, Canada
(a division of Pearson Penguin Canada Inc.)
Penguin Books Ltd., 80 Strand, London WC2R 0RL, England
Penguin Group Ireland, 25 St. Stephen's Green, Dublin 2, Ireland (a division of Penguin Books Ltd.)
Penguin Group (Australia), 250 Camberwell Road, Camberwell, Victoria 3124, Australia
(a division of Pearson Australia Group Pty. Ltd.)
Penguin Books India Pvt. Ltd., 11 Community Centre, Panchsheel Park, New Delhi—110 017, India
Penguin Group (NZ), 67 Apollo Drive, Rosedale, North Shore 0632, New Zealand
(a division of Pearson New Zealand Ltd.)
Penguin Books (South Africa) (Pty.) Ltd., 24 Sturdee Avenue, Rosebank, Johannesburg 2196,
South Africa

Penguin Books Ltd., Registered Offices: 80 Strand, London WC2R 0RL, England

This is a work of fiction. Names, characters, places, and incidents either are the product of the author's imagination or are used fictitiously, and any resemblance to actual persons, living or dead, business establishments, events, or locales is entirely coincidental. The publisher does not have any control over and does not assume any responsibility for author or third-party websites or their content.

HIGHLAND REBEL

A Berkley Sensation Book / published by arrangement with the author

PRINTING HISTORY
Berkley Sensation mass-market edition / March 2009

Copyright © 2009 by Tess Mallory.
Cover art by Phil Heffernan.
Cover design by George Long.
Cover hand lettering by Ron Zinn.
Interior text design by Laura K. Corless.

ISBN: 978-0-425-22635-3

BERKLEY® SENSATION
Berkley Sensation Books are published by The Berkley Publishing Group,
a division of Penguin Group (USA) Inc.,
375 Hudson Street, New York, New York 10014.
BERKLEY® SENSATION and the "B" design are trademarks of Penguin Group (USA) Inc.

PRINTED IN THE UNITED STATES OF AMERICA

10 9 8 7 6 5 4 3 2 1

This book is lovingly dedicated to the real Angus, Dennis Thomas, whose generosity of heart and spirit was largely responsible for the completion of this book. Angus, my dear friend, you are so terribly missed, but how lovely to know that where you are now, you are truly "Never better." Thanks for every kindness and every smile.

acknowledgments

I would like to acknowledge some special people who gave large quantities of love and support during the creation of this book. Thanks so much to: my sister, Jewell Dean, for being my Head Cheerleader; Jan Miller, BFF and Brainstorm Buddy; Sharon Carolan, Coffee Pal and Fwiend for Life; Terry Carolan, All Around Good Guy; Mary Lou DeVriendt, Pom-Pom Girl!; Kathy Mehalko, Queen of Crayons; Denise Broussard, Earth Angel; Roberta Brown, Amazing Agent Extraordinaire; Ellen & Greg, Melissa & Steve, Kerrville Klub; Erin, Heather, Jordan, Mackenzie, Bringers of Joy; and Bill, N.C.M. Hubby I Adore.

To all of you, and the rest of my family and friends, near and far, who have rejoiced with me and for me, prayed for me and hoped for me, cheered for me and wept for me, please know that you are the sweet and precious blessings of my life. May the road rise up to meet you, always.

one

Celtic music sensation Ian MacGregor flashed his now-famous smile at the thousand or more cheering fans as he took his place center stage at the Glasgow Royal Concert Hall. He wore a traditional MacGregor kilt, knee-high suede leather boots, and nothing else except a burnished gold band around his upper arm, skimming the lower edge of his Trinity tattoo.

As he grabbed the wireless mike from its stand and welcomed the suddenly hushed crowd, offstage Ellie Graham tossed her dyed black hair back from her shoulders and narrowed her eyes.

His bare chest could be seen beneath the bagpipes strapped around his torso, his ragged hair grazing the top of his broad shoulders, his burning gaze promising pleasure to all who gazed up at him.

The pipes' leather "halter" was Ian's own creation, fashioned to leave his hands free for grabbing the microphone—or any willing woman who might fling herself in his direction. And there were a lot of willing women in Ian's life. He was the epitome of a Highland Bad Boy, a Celtic Casanova, a Scottish Scoundrel, a—

Oh, stop, a little voice inside her head ordered. *You know that Ian is one of the nicest, humblest guys you've ever met. It's not his fault that he's gorgeous and, well, a man.*

Ellie folded her arms across her chest. It was true. Ian was darn near perfect. Then her mouth went dry and her brain functions faltered as Ian took center stage. Dazed again by the sight of him in action, she watched as he raised both fists into the air and gave the sea of adoring fans what they'd all been waiting for with bated breath.

"*Ard Cholle!*" he shouted.

The crowd went wild. Hundreds of women rushed the stage, screaming like banshees. Ellie shivered. She couldn't deny that she still got goose bumps when she heard Ian give the MacGregor war cry. His rough, rich voice resonated across the vast hall and she took a deep, steadying breath.

Ian grinned widely as his backup band, Outlaw, launched into a rock-and-roll version of "Donald, Where's Your Trousers?" Ellie couldn't help but smile. The song was an old one, written as a slur against Scotsmen, but Ian had taken it and made it the national anthem of sexy men in kilts. It had become an instant hit in the United Kingdom.

With a loud whoop, he danced across the wide platform, his kilt whirling above his knees, exposing lean, hard thighs. He sang into the microphone, his deep, rich voice seducing every woman in the hall. He moved his trim, muscular body like a man possessed, working the crowd into its usual frenzy, and Ellie knew, with a sinking heart, that she had made the right choice.

There was no way around it. As soon as this last show on the UK tour was over, she had to dump Ian. Until then, she had no choice but to watch the man she loved do his best to give a thousand other women musical orgasms.

Ian sang. Women screamed. Ian shouted. Men shouted back. Ian rocked the crowd, enticing every person there, daring them to dance, to sing, to lose every inhibition they'd ever had. And as he did, the walls of the auditorium seemed to tremble with an intense, frantic energy, with Ian at the center of the maelstrom, inviting everyone to join him, love him, embrace him, as he reached the last verse of the song.

> *The lassies love me every one*
> *But they must catch me if they can,*
> *Ye canna put breeks on a Highland man, saying,*
> *"Donald, where's your trousers?"*

Ellie closed her eyes at the thought of Ian without his trousers. The crowd whistled and cheered as Ian took a bow and gestured to his band; then the mood changed as the music shifted into something soft and mellow.

She opened her eyes, her throat tight, knowing what came next. She steeled her heart not to feel, not to share the stark emotions that slid across Ian's face as he raised the microphone to his lips once again. It was one of his own songs. One that filled Ellie—and probably every other woman in the hall—with an indescribable longing. He called it, "Lass o' My Heart."

"Ah, bonny lass, I dinna know yer name," he sang, "but someday I will find ye . . . Ye are my heart, though we have never met . . . my love forevermore . . ."

The words swept over Ellie painfully, and when he reached the end of the second verse and slid the mouthpiece of the pipes between his lips like a lover's tongue, her heart beat faster and she ran her own tongue across her lips. What would it be like to be the woman of Ian's dreams? What would it take to capture his heart so completely?

A hush fell over the audience as the haunting melody shuddered through the air, bringing first sighs and then tears to those who watched and listened.

Leave Ian. She'd have to be crazy.

Just six months ago Ellie's visa had expired and she'd started packing her bags to leave Scotland, when her sister Maggie told her Ian was looking for an assistant for his upcoming tour. She'd ignored the idea until Ian had shown up on her doorstep, irresistibly adorable, and she'd found herself agreeing to take the job.

The prospect of touring the UK with the hottest Celtic band on the planet—a combination of bagpipes, bodhran, tin whistle, drums, electric fiddle, and electric guitar, not to mention Ian MacGregor—had seemed like a dream come true. And it had been, for a while. For the first few weeks, Ellie thought she'd died and gone to heaven, if she believed in such things.

Ellie had been a natural at her new job, her ability to shut out any and all emotion turning out to be really helpful in the day-to-day machinations of booking the popular band. It had been a thrill to watch the Scottish lads dazzle their fans and know that she had a large part in making it happen. With Ian as the charismatic lead singer, he and the band had taken the UK and Europe by storm, and now there was talk of a U.S. tour. Ellie would be a fool to turn down the opportunity.

That was the problem. She was a fool.

About a week into the tour she had fallen, flat-out, face-down, slam-bang in love with Ian. She'd hid her mounting frustration, along with her growing love, as best she could, cloaking it with an aloof negativity that generally kept Ian at arm's length. Before each show they met to go over the details of the gig, but that was thankfully the extent of any personal time she spent with Ian.

Oh, they had traveled together in the tour bus, Ellie hidden behind her book, seemingly oblivious to the playful banter around her; they ate together sometimes, and went to after parties held in his honor. But she was always careful to keep everything professional between them, never personal. Which was hard, because Ian had such an easygoing, flirty, likeable nature. He had made her smile more in the last six months than she had in the last six years.

He was dangerous.

Ellie took a deep breath and tried to slow the pounding of her heart. On the other side of the stage, his current girlfriend—Tiffany? Brittany? Something with an *ee* sound— stood, looking bored and impatient.

One thing about Ian, he had a knack for picking the most

vapid, selfish, shallow women for his arm candy, which had helped Ellie harden her heart toward him as the tour continued. The sight of Ian with his arms slung around two European models, or groupies, or actresses, had made her realize, again and again, that her crush on the piper was absolutely ridiculous.

Then, to her horror, Ian had actually turned his attention to her, teasing and flirting with her, insisting on talking to her into the wee hours after a gig, alone in his or her hotel room. He'd even taken her hand at times and kissed it. She'd almost fainted.

Terrified that she would succumb to his charm, Ellie knew she had to switch gears and move from being standoffish to becoming completely cold. Once she'd overheard one of the musicians in the band call her the Ice Queen. At the ripe old age of twenty-four she'd been easing out of the goth persona that had protected her from the world since she was twelve. She'd kept her hair dyed black, if only to keep her separate from her twin, but had mostly given up the layers of black she'd worn through high school and college, and toned down the harsh makeup. But as soon as there was a chance her heart might be in danger, Ellie ran back to the shelter of that disguise as fast as she could.

It was easy to revert. Even easier to send Ian careening for the nearest supermodel. Clad in her favorite black clothing, black boots, wearing lipstick so dark it looked black, with her dyed black hair and heavily outlined eyes, Ellie knew she looked fairly formidable. Not that Ian knew a war was going on. He'd just shaken his head at her "new" style and, as she had intended, retreated from the fray. Oh, he was still sweet to her, but the flirting had stopped . . . just in time.

Ian began to sing again and glanced offstage, his face brightening at the sight of her. Then he tossed her that rakish grin she had come to both love and fear, and her face grew warm as she fought to keep from smiling back.

Her fingers tightened in the pocket of the overly large black sweater she wore. Paper crackled. Her resignation letter was short and concise. It didn't give away even one little bit of her true feelings. If she let down her walls for one instant, Ian would use that amazing smile and those burning eyes to convince her to stay. She would give in and go on loving him from afar, a little bit of her heart shattering daily like the last note of a faulty pipe. Better to fake disdain than to take such a risk.

The lush, poignant notes skirled from Ian's pipes as if they had a life of their own, and Ellie clasped her hands together, caught in the magic only Ian could create. Tears threatened to fill her eyes and she took a deep breath and willed them away.

She didn't cry. She hadn't cried when her parents died, so she sure wasn't going to cry over a song, even if this *was* the last time she would ever see Ian like this—eyes closed, face radiant, caught in the throes of the love that meant more to him than any woman probably ever could.

Then he opened his eyes and Ellie's throat tightened. He was looking at her again, his gaze tender as he sang the last lines of the song directly to her.

"And when the lass o' my heart I find . . . in the heather soft, in yer arms entwined . . . I will love ye, lass, 'til the end of time . . ." He held the note, his liquid voice hovering in the air above a dazzled audience as Ellie held her breath, the ache in her chest almost unbearable. Then he turned away, and she felt the loss down to the core of her soul as he sang again to his audience.

"Och, my bonny lass, my bonny lass . . . oh, the bonny lass o' my heart . . ."

The final note filled the auditorium like the swelling breath of an angel, and she inhaled sharply as the crowd went crazy and their roar filled the auditorium. Ian spread his arms and faced his fans, his eyes closed, as if he would take them all into his arms, if only he could.

Ellie took a step back, feeling stunned. She'd made the right decision. She had to get out while she was still alive.

But everybody has to die sometime, right? The thought danced through her mind and she pushed it brusquely away.

As soon as the show was over, she'd give him the letter

and leave. She'd head back to Edinburgh, to the cozy little apartment she shared with her twin sister, and forget the last six months had ever happened.

Suddenly Ellie realized the music had stopped and the crowd was going wild again. She looked up, aghast to see Ian running toward her, his face alight with happiness.

"Ellie, d'ye hear that?" he cried, grabbing her by the shoulders and jarring her out of her reverie. "Isn't it grand, lass? Och, to think this could happen to me—to me!"

Before Ellie could speak, Ian lifted her into his arms and with a cry of joy, spun the two of them around in a circle. The unexpected movement made her clutch at his shoulders as her heart pounded in her chest, and when her feet touched the floor again, he grinned down at her, the way he always did. She gazed up at him, absolutely terrified.

Something quickened in Ian's sky blue eyes and his smile faltered as his gaze searched hers. Then the smile was back and he stepped away from her, accepting the towel she automatically handed him. He wiped the sweat away from his face as he continued to look at her, his expression gentle, quizzical.

Ellie tried to turn and walk away, but he held her with his eyes, motionless, frozen. Her throat tightened as need and desire swept over her, and to her horror, tears burned into her eyes. Ian frowned in concern and slid his hands up the sides of her arms. She shivered. From far away the sound of the crowd in the auditorium screaming and shouting for an encore could be heard, but the two of them stood there, oblivious to their demands.

"Ellie, darlin'," Ian said, his hands moving to caress her shoulders, "what's wrong?"

She closed her eyes, lost for a moment in the warmth of his voice.

"Ian!" His lead guitarist cried from onstage. "Get back out here afore they tear the place apart!"

Ellie's eyes flew open. She took a step back. "Nothing's wrong," she said, her voice cool, collected. "I'm fine. You'd better get back out there."

One corner of Ian's mouth lifted in a quizzical half smile and he shook his head. "Aye. Wait for me. We'll ride to the party together." He touched the end of her nose with one finger and then turned and ran back onstage. The rising shouts of the audience coalesced into one gigantic roar, and she watched Ian take another bow, his blond hair illuminated in the spotlight.

The party. Her sister Maggie was hosting an end-of-tour party at her cottage in Drymen, not too far from this last concert in Glasgow. The thought of riding with Ian alone for even as long as it would take to reach the party suddenly overwhelmed her. Gritting her teeth, Ellie jerked the letter from her pocket and crushed it between her hands. It dropped from her nerveless fingers as with one last desperate look toward the stage, she turned, and ran.

Outside his posh hotel in Glasgow, Ian MacGregor got into the plush interior of the limousine and leaned his head back against the seat. Dragging one hand through his hair, still damp from a quick shower, he tried to convince himself that he wasn't upset at all about Ellie's letter crumpled into a ball and left backstage where she'd been standing. She had every right to quit being his manager. Lord knew she hadn't seemed happy during the last few months.

He checked his cell phone, half hoping she'd left him a message, but there was only a text from Maggie and Quinn asking where in the world he could be and why wasn't he at the party yet? He quickly texted back, asking if Ellie had arrived yet, explaining he'd stopped at his hotel to take a quick shower. Maggie answered within seconds, her message back to him short and succinct.

"El here. U smell fine. Hurry up!"

Grinning in spite of himself, Ian closed the phone, and then frowned as the strange sensation that always hit him when he used modern technology swept over him. He'd been in the future for almost a year now, and he still couldn't believe, not fully, that he had traveled with Quinn and Maggie from his own time of 1711, ending up in the year 2008. The thought of the three "magical" spirals in the floor of the cairn near Drymen, and the dead man he and Quinn had left behind in the past, was always disconcerting, but Ian pushed that memory away in favor of others less disturbing.

After their arrival in the twenty-first century, Quinn had introduced him as an old friend, and Maggie's family had opened their arms to him as easily as they had her new fiancé. The couple's wedding had followed before long, and now his best friend and his wife were expecting their first child. He was glad he'd been able to plan the end of the tour to coincide with the delivery date of the bairn. Somehow they already knew the baby would be a boy. More technological wonders that he didn't understand.

The first months in this world had been strange, but with Quinn and Maggie there to guide him, he'd found his way. Falling in love with modern music had led to the creation of his own sound, a blend of traditional bagpipe music with added instruments that gave it a decidedly modern sound. The formation of a band of musicians with the same fervent passion for performing had followed. Ian's sudden rise to fame had caught him off guard, but he had plunged into the opportunity with both feet, grateful for something he could understand in this strange new world.

Quinn had found his own niche, giving private lessons on the bagpipes, as well as aiding Alex MacGregor, head of the excavation of the Drymen Cairn, where the tri-spirals were located, by researching Scottish history. Ian smiled, wondering what Ellie would think if she knew her sister's husband and Ian himself were both throwbacks from a distant time.

Ellie. The girl was a mystery; that was for certain. During the first couple of weeks of the tour, she'd seemed thrilled to be his manager. In fact, for a time he'd thought she fancied him. He had been attracted to her from the moment they first met, her blue gray eyes like a cod, fathomless ocean beneath long black lashes, mesmerizing and intriguing him in the best possible way. Ian often wondered what her real hair color looked like. Red, perhaps, like Maggie's.

Still, the shoulder-length, straight black hair falling loosely to her shoulders, curving in places against her creamy complexion, gave her an exotic look that had immediately sent a surge of heat through him, and continued to do so every time he glanced her way. Besides the physical attraction, he felt he'd really begun to know her in the first weeks of the tour, had made her laugh, had found her to be good company.

He had approached her gently, flirting innocently enough, kissing her hand in thanks for bringing him a beer, simple things. But before he could take it any farther, the camaraderie between them had turned suddenly cold, with Ellie becoming aloof and distant. Her looks had changed as well. The trendy clothes she had begun to wear had disappeared, replaced by loose, black clothing, and her blue eyes, newly lined like Cleopatra's, seemed to grow icier with each new layer she donned.

From that point on, Ellie had avoided him as much as possible, still doing her job with excellence, but treating him as if he were a stranger. When his attempts to bridge the gap were met with stony indifference again and again, he finally decided that somehow he had hurt her feelings. He'd approached her, armed with an apology, but she cut him off midsentence, bluntly stating that he had done nothing to offend her but she simply wanted to keep their relationship on a strictly business basis.

When he asked cautiously if they couldn't be friends as well as business associates, she had stared at him with her blue gray eyes for a long moment before shaking her head.

"I don't need friends," she'd said shortly, and walked away.

Confused, Ian had nonetheless honored her wishes, though it had been hard to tour with a beautiful woman who so obviously didn't want to be in the same room with him. Not only did he regret the loss of their budding friendship, but her rejection had actually made a dent in his admittedly healthy ego. He was used to the lassies throwing themselves at his feet, and here was one who wanted nothing to do with him.

Until tonight. Tonight, Ellie had stood in the wings, her eyes huge in her face as she stared up at him, the black eye makeup she wore slightly smeared beneath her eyes and her usually porcelain skin flushed. She looked like she was about to cry. Ian couldn't imagine Ellie crying. After spending six months on the road with her, he was sad to say he couldn't imagine that she could feel anything deeply enough to weep.

And when he'd rushed offstage and encountered the soft and wistful look on her face, he'd felt something stir inside of him. Some *need* that he hadn't really known was there. There hadn't been time to examine the unexpected feelings, and when he returned from doing his encore, she was gone, a wadded-up envelope left where she'd been standing.

Ian glanced down at the paper he held. He'd pulled it from the envelope, smoothed out the wrinkles, and then stared in disbelief. Ellie's resignation. He read it again, now, still dismayed at the succinct two lines that said so little, but said so much. She'd quit. Quit the tour. Quit him.

The limousine was making good time out of the city, headed for Maggie's party, but Ian tapped his fingers against his thigh, wishing the car could go faster. He'd called Ellie's hotel room, and her cell, but there was no answer at either number. Would she still be at the party? And if she was, should he try to talk her out of her decision? He shook his head. Why should he bother? If the lass didn't like him, why should he care?

But he did. Maybe it was time he let her know just how much.

two

Ellie reached for another brownie and leaned back against the headboard of one of the twin beds in Maggie's guest room. She held the brownie up to make sure this one had plenty of pecans in it. The last one had only had two. *Stupid brownies.*

When she'd fled the auditorium after that strange moment with Ian, she'd slammed into her rented car and driven the thirty or so miles straight to Maggie's cottage. She wasn't surprised to find Allie already there. Being on time was just one of her annoying habits.

Now as she shoved the brownie into her mouth, Ellie watched her sister gazing at her reflection in the full-length mirror attached to the back of the bedroom door across the room. She gave the outfit she wore a critical once-over, turning this way and that. She wore a dress of pale pink silk that clung to her slim body, caressing each slight curve and flaring out above the knees. The dress was low-cut, modestly short, and innocently flirty, perfectly matching her pink stiletto heels. Her strawberry blonde hair hung in perfect, luxurious waves halfway down her back and her perfectly made-up face was, well, perfect.

In contrast, after arriving at the cottage Ellie had shed her clothes and pulled on the same ratty black bathrobe, now sort of gray, that she'd had since her junior year in high school. She'd piled her dyed black hair haphazardly on top of her head and knotted it into a bun by sticking a pencil through it. Her trademark black eyeliner was smudged and there were brownie crumbs in her lap.

Ellie sighed and thrust her hands into the pockets embroidered with pink skulls as she watched her twin. You'd think she'd be used to it by now. Allie was coq au vin, and Ellie was Kentucky Fried Chicken.

By choice, she reminded her more jealous side.

The sound of voices drifted up to them from the first floor of the cottage, letting her know that people were beginning to arrive for the party. Ian could be there at any moment. Her throat tightened.

"So," she said, continuing an explanation postponed by her third brownie, "I decided to quit."

"Just like that, you quit," Allie stated, her voice deceptively mild. Ellie knew better. She waited for her sister to pounce.

As she watched Allie turn this way and that in front of the mirror, Ellie suddenly wondered why she'd spent most of her life trying not to look like her twin. Allie was more than beautiful—she was dazzling. Throughout high school and college, men had thrown themselves at her feet, begging her to walk all over them, and with a smile, she did, while Ellie hid her then-plus-sized figure underneath layers of black.

"Yep. Just like that," she said, pulling the edges of her robe together more securely with one hand, while picking up another brownie with the other.

When Maggie had gone missing the year before, Ellie had stopped eating, certain her sister had met an untimely fate, just like their parents. Maggie had returned safe and happy, with Quinn MacIntyre in tow, and Ellie had actually cried a few tears of relief. And then she'd met Ian.

It was at that moment she'd made her decision. With a head start loss of ten pounds, caused by Maggie's disappearance, Ellie resolved to lose the rest of the extra fifty pounds she'd packed on when she was twelve. The second ten came off pretty easily, after Ian offered her the job of managing his band, partly because she was too besotted with the handsome Scot to worry about such mundane things as eating, and partly because she'd entertained a faint, bright hope that if she was slender, she might have a chance with the sexy piper.

She'd gone on the road with him and more pounds melted away. Strange how the smaller she became, the bigger her fear of showing Ian how she felt grew.

Ellie stared down at the brownie. She put it back on the plate and pushed it away.

"So let me get this straight," Allie was saying as she turned and faced her twin, her hands on her hips, a glint in her eye. "You love your job, you love the band, you love traveling, and—oh, yeah—you love Ian, but you've given up the opportunity to be around the man 24/7 because—oh, yeah—you love him. Do I have this right?"

Ellie scowled. "Do not even go there. And who said I love the job? I don't love the job. I hate the job! It's a pain in the butt! You don't know what you're talking about."

"I notice you don't deny loving Ian."

She glared at her sister and clutched her robe a little tighter. "I do not love Ian. Are you kidding? That's ridiculous. He's not my type. No way. Ha. You're crazy." She ran out of words, and Allie gave her a knowing grin.

"Methinks thou dost protest too much," she said.

"And methinks thou dost butt into my business too much," Ellie retorted.

"Don't you ever get lonely?" her sister asked. "Don't you ever get tired of running away?"

"'I recognize my destiny . . . now hath my last lonesomeness begun,'" Ellie said flatly, then added, "I am not interested in Ian."

Allie rolled her eyes and then crossed the small room to plop down on the bed beside her. "Oh, Lord, not Nietzsche again. I thought you got over all that gloom and doom in college."

"I didn't finish college."

"Oh, come on, Ellie!" Allie's voice went up a notch. "You've been crazy about Ian ever since he showed up with Maggie and Quinn at the cairn. You are hopelessly in love with him. Why don't you just admit it?"

"Am not."

"Are too."

"Am not."

"Are *too*."

Ellie glared at her twin. "Oh, just—just—shut up."

"Well, you are," Allie insisted. "And now you've done the dumbest thing in your life—and believe me, that's saying a lot—by quitting your job." She shook her head. "At least you'll see him again tonight and you can tell him you changed your mind."

Ellie took a deep breath. Okay, she'd been wrong. She wasn't completely numb inside. Not as long as her sister was around to antagonize her. She'd have to work on that. She released her breath and tried to release the anger as well.

"I have not changed my mind," she said, forcing a note of calm into her voice. "I'm through with Ian MacGregor and his stupid band." She leaned back against the headboard. "Believe me, I will not be missed."

Allie's gaze softened. "*Aha*. So that's the problem."

"What's the problem?" Ellie demanded.

"You think he hasn't noticed you, so you, of course, being you, think he's not interested in you anyway, so why not just give up?"

Ellie counted to ten silently. "What do you mean, 'me being me'?"

"I mean"—Allie leaned toward her—"you give up too easily, El. At the first sign of a challenge, you tuck tail and run." She waved one hand in dismissal as Ellie tried to sputter her reply. "No, don't try and deny it. You know it's true. Oh, you may look all tough on the outside, Goth Girl, but this is me, remember? Inside you're still just a marshmallow. Time to grow a backbone, kid."

"You don't know anything," Ellie said, feeling about twelve years old even as she said the words. She slumped back against the headboard and folded her arms across her chest. "I'll have you know that I've negotiated every gig the band has played, so don't go talking to me about backbones! Mine is made of steel!"

Allie's brows darted together above her calm blue gray eyes. "I'm not talking about your ability to rip the skin off of a man at thirty paces." She laughed and waved one hand as if to dismiss that thought. "Believe me, you've got that kind of backbone down pat. I'm talking about the kind of courage it takes to actually dare to let someone inside that stone castle you call your soul." She shook her head. "Did you even tell Ian you liked him?"

Tell Ian I liked *him?* The woman had to be crazy. Ellie lost what little hold she had left on her temper and shot out of bed to stand glaring down at her sister.

"Are you out of your *mind*?" she asked. Have you *seen* this guy? He's gorgeous, talented, sexy, got a body like a god, women throw themselves at his feet, and you think I would just walk up to him and tell him I *like* him?"

"Oh, so he's not a very nice guy, then?"

"Of course he is!" Ellie said as she stomped over to the wardrobe and slammed the door open to expose the clothes inside. She might as well get dressed for the party. Between Allie and Maggie there was no way they'd let her get away with missing it. If she did, Allie would probably tell Ian how she really felt. She closed her eyes, feeling helpless. Maybe Ian would decide not to come. Maybe she could fall down the stairs. No one could expect her to come to a party if she had two broken legs.

"So he's nice?" Allie went on.

Ellie opened her eyes and jerked a blouse out of the closet, pretending to look at it. "He's the sweetest guy in the world!" she retaliated.

"Uh-huh."

Oops. Ellie glanced back at her sister and scowled at the smirk on her face. She'd forgotten how easily Allie could foil her. Turning back to the closet, she put the blouse back and started rummaging through the clothes she'd hung in it when she arrived. Being on the road with the band and losing weight along the way had forced her to buy some new clothes. At least she had something to wear that was halfway decent—if you liked black.

"But he's shallow, right?" Allie insisted. "And kind of stupid?"

"What?" Ellie pulled out the dress she had considered wearing, before her impromptu resignation, and turned around, shaking her head in disbelief. "Are you kidding? He's one of the smartest people I've ever met. You should hear him talk about history! And shallow? I've seen him actually get tears in his eyes when he sees those commercials about orphaned children."

"So then, *you* must be mean, shallow, and stupid, right?" Allie crossed her legs and smiled, looking as smug as a cat with a mouse in its grip.

Ellie narrowed her eyes. "Okay, where are you going with this?"

Her sister stood and smoothed her dress. "Look, if he's such a great guy, then why do you think he wouldn't be interested in you, unless, as usual, you're wallowing in that old tub of low self-esteem that you carry around with you?" Ellie didn't answer, and Allie moved to her side, her voice softening. "Honey, you just don't see how amazing you are. You're smart, sweet, intelligent, beautiful—"

"Oh, please," Ellie cut her off. "I repeat—have you *seen* this guy? *He's* beautiful. Next to him I look like—like—"

"I hate when you act this way."

"What way?"

"Like you're ugly or something. Like no man in his right mind would want you." She pressed her lips together in a tight, flat line. "You know, when you act that way, you're insulting *me*."

Ellie frowned. "How do you figure?"

"Hello? We're twins! If you're ugly, I'm ugly. If you're undesirable, so am I."

"I think Mom lied to us about that," she said sullenly. "I think I was adopted."

Without warning Allie grabbed her by the arm, spun her around, and marched her over to the full-length mirror on the back of the bedroom door. "I want you to take a good look, missy. Do you even see yourself? How beautiful you are? Even with all that glop on your face."

Ellie stared at the still-unfamiliar reflection. Her weight loss had left her with cheekbones and a softly curved body, but her blue eyes still looked the same. Haunted. Lonely. She drew in a deep breath.

"Well, since I've lost the weight I guess I look a little better."

Allie rolled her eyes at her sister in the mirror. "Even with the weight you were beautiful, El, and more important than that, you're a great person, when you aren't hiding behind these layers of black!"

Ellie turned away from the sight of her own face. "I don't think I'm going to the party."

"Oh, yes, you are." Allie's voice was like steel and it sparked Ellie's own temper. She spun around.

"Look, you aren't my mother—" she began, only to be cut off.

"No, I'm not, but Maggie is!" Allie said, then glanced away and back again, her eyes a little softer. "Okay, she's the nearest thing to a mother either of us has, and you are not going to let this pity party you're having wreck this night for her. She's gone to a lot of trouble *and* she's really worried about you."

Ellie shook her head, truly confused by her sister's words. "Worried? Why?"

Allie sighed with exasperation. "Uh, because you look like death warmed over?"

"I thought I was beautiful," Ellie said sullenly.

"You are, usually, but right now you have no color in your face, you're skin and bones, and you're obviously depressed! Have you forgotten that Maggie is pregnant? *Very* pregnant? Or don't you care?"

Tears burned suddenly into Ellie's eyes and she turned away from her twin, aghast. What was wrong with her?

Get a grip, Eleanor.

Allie was right. She was being selfish. She owed Maggie more than she could ever repay. After their parents died she had stepped into the breech, giving up her own dreams for her two little sisters. Maggie had saved her life.

So what if my heart is breaking? I'm not going to cause Maggie more stress. The answer? Turn off whatever stupid feelings I think I have for Ian.

Ellie took a deep breath and turned around. Her sister's eyes were filled with an uncharacteristic sympathy.

"Look," Allie said, "I really do understand. I do. I just get frustrated with you because I want you to be happy. You've got to let go of the past—"

"I know," Ellie cut her off, more uncomfortable with her twin's compassion than her anger. "I won't make Maggie worry any more. I promise."

Allie frowned and searched her face carefully. "Just like that, huh?"

"Just like that." Ellie forced a smile. "You're the evil twin, you know that, don't you?"

Her sister relaxed slightly. "Of course," she agreed, "but I only use my evilness to make sure some good comes your way." The iron came back into her voice. "Now get dressed and come on."

Ellie move back to the bed and sat down, narrowing her eyes as she gazed up at her twin. " 'Ye see me troubled, driven forth, unwillingly obedient, ready to go—alas, to go away from *you*!' "

Allie shook her head. "I never should have given you *Bartlett's Familiar Quotations* that Christmas. Five minutes," she added as she headed for the door, then paused and looked back. "Oh, and do *not* wear *anything* black, do you hear me? I hung up a dress for you in the bathroom." With that, she fled the room before Ellie could react.

" 'They mocked me when I found and walked in mine own path . . . ' " she muttered. She glared after her twin for a moment, then, too curious not to look, got up and walked down the hall to the small bath that served the second floor of the cottage.

Hanging on a hook on the back of the door was a filmy, slightly longer, electric blue version of the dress Allie was wearing. Allie didn't wear blue. She must have bought the dress especially for her, like she was a little kid who couldn't make the right decision.

Ellie leaned her head against the beautiful garment, letting the silk caress her face. A sudden memory of running to hug her mother, crushing her face against the soft dress she wore, darted through her mind and for a moment she couldn't breathe. Carefully she lifted her head and backed away from the garment. She sucked in a trembling breath.

"To paraphrase Nietzsche," she whispered, "no freaking way."

Turning away from Allie's choice, she headed back to the bedroom, suddenly determined to prove once and for all that she could take care of herself.

Ian stood at the bottom of the stairs, holding his second drink in his hand, watching Ellie Graham walk slowly toward him. His breath caught in his throat. For the last six months he'd seen her wear layer after layer of black—black trousers, black blouses, black jackets, black boots, black coat—she'd seemed bent on covering herself, hiding her skin from any and all gazes. Now she still wore black, but like no garment he'd ever seen on her before.

As she moved down the stairs, he had to fight several unchivalrous thoughts. He was still shocked by the amount of skin young women revealed in their everyday clothing— a holdover from his eighteenth-century ways, though he'd never admit his puritanical thinking to anyone else. After all, weren't modern men supposed to encourage women to wear less clothing whenever possible? But at the moment his ideas of propriety were forgotten as he watched Ellie move.

Cinched up the front with red ribbons, the black leather bodice seemed in dire peril of falling off of her body at any moment. The matching skirt was so short he had to restrain himself from pulling the tablecloth from Maggie's table and wrapping it around the lass. Sheer black hosiery caressed her long legs, making his heart thud in his chest as his gaze swept irresistibly down to bright red shoes almost more provocative than her dress.

Backless, the shoes had four-inch heels, and he marveled that she could even walk, let alone navigate down the stairs. Her toes peeked out the front of the flirtatious footwear to entice him, her toenails painted bright red. As she stopped on the step just above him, bringing his head almost level with hers, Ian saw the front of Ellie's dress was even lower than he'd first thought, revealing a lacy red strapless bra beneath.

After six months on the road, with women throwing themselves at him nightly, Ian had become acquainted with the strange underwear of the future, but he'd never quite gotten used to seeing it exposed like an ordinary piece of clothing. And he certainly wasn't used to seeing Ellie's bosom, thrust up by the red underwear, practically bursting out the top of the sultry outfit she wore.

"Hello, Ian," she said, her voice cool.

He jerked his attention back to the matter at hand. "Ellie, darlin', I need to talk to ye." He stepped up to stand beside her and found the view had improved even more. He forced his gaze back to her face. "I dinna understand what I've done to make ye want to quit being my tour manager, but whatever it was, I apologize."

Her dark-lined eyes swept over him, down and then up again, meeting his gaze.

"It was purely a business decision," she said. "Good luck with the American tour." With that, she glided down the last step and into the large living room, where the rest of his band let out a loud cheer. Ian tightened his jaw and with fists clenched, followed Ellie.

After an hour spent watching the lass flirt with every member of the band except him, Ian was ready to call it a night.

What had he ever done to make her dislike him so much? For in spite of her words, he knew an angry woman when he saw one.

Still, if she refused to discuss the matter, what was he to do? He dragged one hand through his hair and felt inexplicably tired. After this night he'd probably only see Ellie on holidays when the family gathered. He frowned. As grateful as he was to be considered family by Quinn and Maggie, the thought of spending holidays in the company of someone who so obviously disliked him held little appeal.

Rising from Quinn's favorite easy chair, he tossed back the rest of the whiskey in his glass and decided to find Maggie and make his excuses.

"She's got a lot of guts, don't you think?" said a voice at his elbow. He turned to find Allie staring across the room at her sister, who was currently leaning against the drummer of the band and laughing at something he'd said.

"Is that what ye call it?" he said, shaking his head. "In my world, she could be arrested for dressing like that."

Allie's brows knit together as she looked up at him. "In your world? What do you mean?"

Ian ran his tongue over his lips. He was always putting his foot in it, saying the wrong thing. Quinn had cautioned him about that. He cleared his throat and shrugged.

"I was raised by my grandmother," he said, "and I suppose she taught me to be what in this day and age would be considered prudish."

Allie's brows darted upward and her eyes danced with amusement. "You? Voted the Sexiest Man Alive for 2009 by *Musician's Magazine*, a prude?"

Ian couldn't help but smile back at her. The honor she spoke of had embarrassed him, but that was the way the music business operated in the twenty-first century. Sex always seemed to enter into the equation no matter how hard he tried to keep it about the tunes.

"Aye. Hard to believe, I know."

Allie's gaze swept over him, but there was no flirtation in

the gesture, just a frank appraisal. "You are pretty yummy," she said matter-of-factly, "in spite of your lack of style."

Ian glanced down at the worn jeans he'd changed into at the hotel, along with a well-worn, long-sleeved black T-shirt. He smiled in perplexity. "Thanks. I think."

"So you don't approve of the way Ellie's dressed?" Allie asked.

Ian stared down into his empty glass, gathering his thoughts. This was Ellie's sister. Likely anything he said would get back to her twin. Strange that they were twins. Not only did they look completely different to him, but their personalities appeared to be totally opposite.

"'Tis no' my place to approve or disapprove," he said. "But if I were her husband—" He broke off and then glanced at Allie. The amusement had vanished from her eyes. She gave a quick look in the direction of Ellie across the room, surrounded by the band, and then laid one hand on his arm.

"Your glass is empty," she said. "Let's get a drink and talk. I heard Ellie went nuts and gave you her resignation tonight."

He nodded. "Aye 'tis true, and I havena got a clue why."

Allie frowned. "I'm not surprised. Come over here. Let's talk." She led him to the refreshment table set up at the end of the room and poured him a fresh whiskey. "I've been anxious to hear how things went out on the road. I was so shocked when Ellie took the job at all. She's really a home-body, you know."

"Is she, now?" Ian mused. "She seemed totally in her element, wheeling and dealing with booking agents and the like. We used to call her the Maid of Steel." *And the Ice Queen,* he added silently. "She doesn't seem—" He stopped, hesitant.

Allie crossed to a small sofa a little farther away from the crowd. She sat down and patted the space beside her. Ian glanced over at Ellie, still laughing and drinking, and with a sigh, sat down beside her twin.

"Now," she said, "my sister doesn't seem what?"

He took a deep breath, released it, and plunged in. "She

doesn't seem to feel very much, if ye ken what I mean. Nothing seems to faze her, neither joy nor grief."

Allie arched one brow. "Did she ever tell you about our parents?"

"Aye, and that's what first made me draw this conclusion." He frowned, trying to phrase his words in such a way that it wouldn't sound critical. "Maggie had shared the calamity with me and Quinn, and I was saddened. One night on the tour, 'twas just Ellie and me alone in the bus, going over some matters. She'd been acting more and more cold to me and I was trying to draw her out, to get to know her better, ye ken?" Allie nodded. "I asked her about that sad time." He frowned again and took a drink from his glass.

"What did she say?"

"Oh, she told me about it, as matter-of-fact as ye please. But she never shed a tear; her voice never quivered. Ye'd have thought that she was discussing our next gig, so empty of emotion was she." He shook his head. "I'm sorry ye all lost yer mother and father at such young ages."

"It was really tough, at first," Allie said, her voice growing softer, "on all of us. But it was especially hard on Ellie. Ever since then she's been waiting for someone else to die. You know, the proverbial 'other shoe to fall.' That's why she's obsessed with death and this whole goth, nonemotional thing." She sighed and leaned her chin on her hand. "I'd hoped that going on the tour with you would have helped her leave all of that nonsense behind."

Ian leaned back and blinked. "This explains why she says the strange and dismal things she does sometimes."

Allie grinned. "You mean her Nietzsche quotes?"

He shook his head in confusion. "Things about dying and nothingness and God being dead. Terrible things. She's a young woman to have such a jaded view of life."

"It's her wall."

"Pardon?"

"To keep people out."

He shook his head. "I dinna understand. She has experienced so much loss. Why would she not seek out friendship with others?"

Allie shot him an indefinable look and arched one brow. "Friendship? Is that all you wanted?"

Ian felt his face grow warm. Allie was a perceptive woman. "Well, that would have been nice to start with," he said, "and aye, I was attracted to the lass, But she let me know in no uncertain terms that she wasna interested in more than a business relationship." He shook his head. "But it was more than that. She seems to truly dislike me."

Allie took a drink from her glass and then looked at him appraisingly. "So you and Ellie never—you know—when you were on the road together?"

The thought brought a sudden image into his mind, one he couldn't honestly say hadn't been there before, in his dreams, in his daily meanderings: Ellie in his arms, her mouth hot against his, his hands caressing her—

"Ian, you okay?"

Allie's amused voice brought him back to reality. He blinked and then frowned. "Aye. I mean, no, we never—you know—on the road."

Allie sighed. "I'm sorry to hear that," she said, and then leaned toward him, her blue gray eyes, so much like Ellie's, narrowed. "Look, my sister needs to get laid in the worst way. So what are you going to do about it?"

three

An hour of the party was all Ellie could stand, especially after Allie decided to monopolize Ian in the corner. Not that she doubted what her sister was up to—no, she knew exactly what Allie was doing. She was building her twin up to him and digging for information at the same time. By the time the party was over, Ian would be running for the hills of Scotland to get away from Allie and her obviously desperate sister.

As soon as she could, Ellie slipped out of the large "great" room that Quinn had remodeled from three smaller rooms that originally made up the downstairs of their cottage, and headed up the stairs to the bedroom she shared with her twin. She shed the tight, uncomfortable clothing she'd worn to show Allie that she couldn't control her, threw on her jeans, a tank top, sweater, and jacket, and pulled on her Doc Martens. Sneaking back down the stairs without being seen took some patience, but she was finally able to make it and zip out the back door.

The moon above was full and bright and as she paused, shivering in the cold Highland air, she gazed up at the awesome starry spectacle above her. Scotland was almost at the top of the world, and the stars and moon seemed so near, so brilliant, she felt sometimes she could reach out and touch them. For a moment her heart lifted, then her cynical side thumped her in the side of the head.

They're just balls of gas in a vacuum. Don't go getting all mushy about it.

"I'm sure I saw her go this way," said a voice behind her. Ellie ducked behind a bush and peered out to see her twin near the back door. The masculine rumble that responded was surely Ian's.

She bolted before they could see her and ran around the cottage to the front where her rented car waited for her. Ellie hated to make Maggie worry, which she no doubt would do once she realized her sister was gone, but she had to get away, at least long enough to clear her head. Slipping quietly into the front seat of the little car, she took a deep breath, wishing she could cry.

Soon Ian would be leaving for his American tour, and after that, who knew what his future held? She wouldn't be surprised if he ended up in Hollywood. Oh, sure, she'd see him when he came to visit Maggie and Quinn, if she made a point of coming to the cottage when she knew he'd be there, but other than that, her time with Ian was over.

By your own choice. She could hear Allie's accusing voice inside of her head and it made her furious. It wasn't by her own choice. She had no other choice, not if she wanted to survive. Ellie started the car, gunned the motor, and peeled out before anyone could rush outside to stop her.

Davey Ferguson adjusted another knob on the intricate conglomeration of equipment he'd arranged in front of him, pushed his glasses up on his nose, made another notation on the pad in front of him, and smiled.

Amazing.

A few months ago, when his friend Alex MacGregor had asked him to come and take a look at an ancient cairn he'd discovered, Davey had reminded Alex that he was a physicist, not an archaeologist. That was when Alex told him exactly why he needed him. There was a curious energy beneath the carved tri-spiral, his friend said. He'd "felt" it. Would Davey come and bring his computers and equipment, and see what he thought?

Knowing Alex's tendency to con any- and everyone around him, including his friends, Davey'd been prepared for what would probably amount to an elaborate practical joke or some kind of scam. So when he had reached the cairn, he'd been shocked to find that for once in his life, Alex had been telling the truth.

Now, after three months of intense testing, investigation, and mathematical calculations, Davey was in total awe of what Alex had discovered. The three spirals, carved into the floor of the ancient cairn, joined in the middle, lay directly on top of one of the strongest magnetic fields he'd ever encountered. Not only that, but at night, most nights, the power below the earth grew even stronger. Exactly why or how, he hadn't yet ascertained.

And there was something else—it might mean nothing at all, but his watch, his computer clock, and any other time-keeping devices inside the cairn always ran three minutes slower than normal time. No matter how many times he reset them, within minutes, they were off by three minutes once again. An anomaly caused by the magnetic field? Possibly. And twice before when he ran the generators late at night, the clocks had done something just as peculiar. They had completely stopped.

Davey frowned and made another adjustment on the machine that measured the amount of energy pulsating underneath the cairn. He had decided to stay all night, keeping his equipment running off the portable generator in order to record anything that might happen. He'd expected to have to light the inside of the artifact, but that had been unnecessary.

Glancing over at the glimmering shafts of moonlight illuminating the artifact through holes in the ceiling, something suddenly clicked inside his brain. Hastily he scribbled down a word on his notepad. *Moonlight.* Could something so simple be the added element increasing the power beneath the stone spirals? And what was the power for? An ancient electric company? He smiled.

Determined to discover exactly what mysterious power lay within the confines of the large bowl-like structure, built hundreds, perhaps thousands, of years ago, Davey was prepared to camp there for the next three months if necessary; but he had an idea that might just speed things up. Luckily, Alex had agreed to meet him there and help run some of the equipment while he tried a few experiments within the spirals themselves.

Davey glanced at his watch. Alex was late, as usual. He strode outside to the windup clock he always left outside and checked it against his watch. His heart began to beat more quickly. Alex was even later than he had thought. According to the outside clock, his watch was ten minutes slow in comparison!

He glanced up at the full moon, shining like a huge copper penny above the distant Scottish horizon, then rushed back inside to his computer, where he typed in the documentation of this new time phenomenon. When he finished, he glanced at his watch again and widened his eyes, half in astonishment, half in excitement.

It was impossible! Just a moment before, outside the cairn, his watch had shown the time to be 2:07 a.m. Now it was 1:57 a.m., ten minutes earlier. Davey grinned and went back to his computer, working feverishly over a new equation that had just occurred to him. Time was going backward.

Ellie trudged up another rise, cursing all machines and rented cars in particular. She'd driven around aimlessly for a couple of hours, tense with unspoken frustration, when suddenly the dumb car had coughed, sputtered, and died. No amount of coaxing could get it to start again.

She'd started walking, thankful for her sweater and her thick, down-filled jacket against the cold October night.

Luckily there was a full moon, and she could easily see her way. At this time of year in the Highlands, the night sky was completely black unless the clouds and mists cleared enough to reveal the stars or moon.

She'd hiked for half an hour, growing progressively colder and more anxious. The Highlands at night were wild and strange, and unsuspecting travelers had gotten lost before.

Like Maggie, she thought.

Just a year ago, on a dig with Alex MacGregor, Maggie had fallen off a steep hill and hit her head, resulting in amnesia. She'd wandered in the Highlands for weeks, living off springwater and berries, before stumbling across Quinn MacIntyre, who had taken care of her and brought her back to civilization. Thankfully her memory had returned along with her.

Pausing to rest at the top of the rise, Ellie pushed away the familiar anxiety thinking about Maggie's disappearance always brought. Her own guilt over taking off without telling anyone kicked up a notch. As she scanned the countryside, she caught her breath at the sight of bright lights in the distance. A cottage? Maybe someone there would have a phone!

After another fifteen minutes of walking, following the lights, she reached the top of another craggy hill and stopped, staring at the light pouring out of the opening to Maggie's cairn. She must have driven in circles, eventually ending up close to her sister's cottage, since the cairn was only a few miles from Maggie's backyard.

Who in the world could be working there so late, with what looked like dozens of lanterns lighting the inside? She crossed to the open rounded doorway of the ancient artifact and ducked to look inside, then blinked in surprise.

Inside were three or four long, flat tables lined up facing the spirals in the middle. On top of these was a plethora of electronic equipment—boxes with wires coming out, machines humming and whirring, several computers with screens showing incomprehensible symbols and mathematical equations.

What must have been a generator hummed near one of the tables, and a couple of space heaters made the inside of the cairn rather toasty. Extension cords crisscrossed the floor and Ellie stepped over them carefully.

In front of one of the computers sat a man with dark red hair. Ellie coughed and he turned halfway around in his chair, his hands laced over his chest, his auburn brows knit together in concentration.

Breathing a sigh of relief, Ellie bent under the doorway and crossed the round room. "Davey?" she asked, stopping a few feet away from him.

He glanced up, a vague look on his face. Ellie took a tentative step forward. "You're Davey Ferguson, aren't you?" she asked, pretty sure she was right. "I met you once at my sister Maggie's house."

The man nodded, his eyes clearing a little. "Aye, aye. Ye're Elaine? Or is it Alice?"

"Eleanor. But I go by Ellie." She moved to one of the space heaters to warm her hands. From what Maggie had told her, Davey was an eccentric genius. At the age of twenty-two, he had two PhDs and was doing some kind of internship at a prestigious hospital in Edinburgh.

Belatedly he stood, patting his pockets and finding a pencil, turning and jotting something down on a piece of paper before he turned back to her and extended his hand. "Glad to see ye again, Ellie." He sat back down and turned to his computer as if she weren't there.

"Uh, sorry to interrupt, but what are you doing here? And do you have a cell phone?"

"Hmm?" He glanced back at her. "Oh, experiments. Energy fields. And such."

"Right." Ellie gazed around at the cairn as he turned back to his work again. What she had taken for dozens of lanterns from her vantage point on the other hill had turned out to be something much more amazing. The roof of the cairn had dozens of holes in it, and the inside of the domed structure was entirely lit by streams of moonlight.

"Wow," she said, moving to stand beside Davey as he

scribbled furiously on another piece of paper. "This is really something."

"Hmm? Oh, aye, aye. I think I've figured out that it isn't the moonlight powering the spirals, but something much more complicated."

"Really?" Ellie sat down in the empty chair beside him. If she waited to be asked, she'd be old and gray. Her stomach growled and she blushed. "Sorry. I missed supper." Davey simply reached into a sack beside the computer and handed her a granola bar. "Thanks. So the spirals have some kind of power?"

After Maggie's return, and before Ian's tour, Ellie had spent several hours one day with her sister inside the cairn. After all, the tri-spiral in the floor of the ancient building was an incredible discovery, and when Alex MacGregor had finally admitted that Maggie had been integral in the discovery of the artifact, her name had been in all the papers, and Alex had offered her a job.

Ellie had been fascinated by the triskele on the floor, and the mysterious "ogham" carved into the standing stone embedded in the wall. According to Maggie, the ogham spelled out a curious phrase: "Ages lost, ages found, follow forward, follow back." What it meant was anyone's guess.

Strangely enough, Maggie had seemed very uncomfortable while they were there, and the next day, when Ellie asked to go again, her sister said that there was a new rule about allowing visitors.

"Aye," Davey said, bringing her back to the question she'd asked. "A great deal of power, though I canna tell ye exactly how much, nor what its purpose might be." He scribbled another notation, talking as he did. "But I can tell ye this: it is doing something to time inside the cairn."

Ellie tore her gaze from the brilliant streams of moonlight painting circles of light on the floor, and turned to Davey. "*Time?* What do you mean?"

"I mean, inside this cairn, time is going backward!" He glanced up at her, the vagueness in his gray green eyes gone, replaced by intense excitement. He dragged one hand through his hair, making it stand on end. "It's incredible!"

Ellie shook her head. "It's also impossible. You must have figured something wrong, Einstein."

He frowned. "I'm no Einstein, but my calculations are correct." He held up his arm and pointed to his watch. "My watch is running backward."

She shrugged and yawned, glancing at Davey's watch. One thirty. The party was surely over by now. "Then there's something wrong with your watch. Listen, this is all fascinating—really it is—but do you have a cell phone? My car broke down, and I need to call my sister."

But Davey was lost in thought again, writing madly and muttering to himself. Ellie sighed, and then brightened as she saw a cell phone lying on the other side of his notebook. She stood and circled around his chair, grabbed the phone, and punched in Maggie's number.

No signal.

She sighed and ducked through the opening to the outside and tried again. Maggie picked up the phone, and after reassuring her sister she was fine and promising to stay where she was until someone could pick her up, Ellie snapped the phone shut and went back inside the cairn, only to stop in her tracks, stunned.

Maybe it was a trick of the imagination, or maybe it was real, but the moonlight seemed even more intense now, the narrow shafts of light shooting down through the small holes in the roof, appearing thick and brightly opaque. She walked forward with her hand extended, half expecting to touch a solid surface. Her hand passed through the light and she released a breath she hadn't known she was holding. Nope, just moonlight. She stared at the dancing, glittering glow on her palm, and then squinted up at the holes above, surprised by what she saw.

Stars. Walking along the middle spiral, she could see a star in each of the holes. She moved to one of the other spirals and looked up through the moonlight at the holes above it. *No stars.* Frowning, she walked over to the third spiral and looked up again. *No stars.* Maybe this was important.

She walked back to the spiral she'd been standing on first and tried to get Davey's attention.

"Davey, did you know that you can see stars through these holes, but not through the ones above the other spirals? And the moonlight seems brighter over the middle spiral."

"What's that, lass?" he said, erasing something on the paper in front of him and frowning in deep concentration.

"I said that—"

"Hey, Davey, lad, sorry I'm so late."

Alex MacGregor ducked through the opening and hurried over to Davey, then noticed Ellie.

"Elise, isn't it?" he asked with a charming smile.

"Ellie." She sighed as he turned back to Davey and began reading over his shoulder. Another handsome blond Scotsman. Did they clone them in the Highlands or what? Alex was almost as cute as Ian, but according to Maggie, he was little more than a con artist.

Too bad Davey wasn't her type. He was a little geeky with his auburn hair and glasses, but not bad looking. And he seemed nice. His inquisitive gray eyes behind horn-rimmed glasses were long-lashed and definitely noteworthy. He glanced over and gave her an absent smile, and Ellie smiled back.

This was good. She was thinking about other men, even if this one did have a pocket protector. She could forget Ian, no problem.

"So how is it going?" Alex asked Davey, turning toward his friend and giving Ellie another reason to sigh as he bent slightly, his tight jeans molding over every muscle of his backside.

"Och, there is no doubt about it, Alex." Davey flipped another switch on the machine next to his computer and then punched a few keys on his keyboard. "'Tis a strange energy emanating from this place, and it's making time run backward!"

"What?" Alex bent to look over his shoulder at the computer screen. "Ye're joking!"

"Nay," Davey said in delight. "Look, ye can see the arc right there. As the energy increases, the time on the computer goes backward faster!"

Ellie moved to stand behind the two, curiosity drawing her in. "Energy?" Ellie asked, jarred from leering at Alex's butt. "What kind of energy?"

"I'm not quite sure," Davey said distractedly. "There is magnetic energy here, beneath the stone spirals, but there is something more that I can't quite isolate." He fiddled with several knobs and typed a little more before shaking his head.

"Ye said before that there might be a way to record the energy," Alex reminded him.

Davey looked up, a light in his eyes. Ellie had to reassess her observations of the man. He really was attractive, for a geek.

"Not the energy exactly, but any frequencies that might be about. I've got the machine recording them right here." He patted the top of a big metal box with knobs and switches, and a row of buttons lit up across the front of it. "It will take a few days to process, but it will tell us what we want to know."

"How long will it take you to do the recording?" Alex asked.

"Oh, the night, I would say. 'Tis a meticulous process, if we want to get it right."

"Let's get it right," Alex said. "I'm going to stay and help ye."

Davey bent to open a box on the floor of the cairn, digging through wires and gadgets. "What? Oh, aye, that would be grand. I'm particularly interested to see how the energy increases or decreases with the amount of moonlight shining through the holes in the ceiling." He turned back to his machines with a glazed look on his face.

"Is he always like this?" Ellie asked.

Alex laughed. "Always. He's a genius, and they walk to the beat of a different drummer."

Ellie risked a smile up at the Adonis. "I thought it was 'dance to the beat of a different drummer.'"

Alex feigned a look of horror. "Davey does *not* dance. Back at university, we wouldn't allow it."

Ellie frowned. "Why not?"

"Och, the flailing arms, bowed legs askew—" Alex shook his head and shuddered. "Trust me, 'tis not a pretty sight."

"The two of you went to college together?"

"Aye, the University of Edinburgh, then he went on to Oxford for a time."

"Alex, look at this," Davey said.

"Excuse me, lass."

While the two conferred, Ellie congratulated herself. See, she was even talking to hunky, handsome men now. Ian had no claim on her emotions or her libido. She could feel just as hot about Alex MacGregor or any other man as she could the stubborn Celtic music miracle!

As she thought about how easy it was going to be to forget Ian, Ellie suddenly realized she had drifted over to the huge spiral in the floor and was walking around the middle one, tracing its curved surface with her footsteps. The sudden sound of Alex's angry voice startled her out of her reverie.

"Ye're walking on the spiral!" he yelled. "Get off, ye careless girl!"

Ellie lifted her chin. *Great.* Someone else telling her what to do. "It's my sister's cairn as much as yours," she told him as she continued to walk the spiral.

"It isn't either one of ours, ye daft lass," Alex cried. "It belongs to Scotland! But if ye damage it, I'll be the one to catch hell for it with the Society. Now get yer big clodhopper boots off or I'll—"

"Look, Indiana, I can walk on this if—" She broke off as a wave of dizziness washed over her and the room seemed to spin. Ellie tried to move forward another step, but couldn't. She couldn't move her arms either. Her throat tightened in panic.

"What's wrong with ye?" Alex demanded.

"I can't move," she whispered.

"Oh, for the love of—" Alex started forward, only to be

stopped by Davey bolting out of his chair. He pushed his friend backward and rushed across the room.

"Alex! Stay back!" he cried as he threw his arms around Ellie and tugged. She didn't budge. "What is it?" Ellie cried. "What's happening?" she asked in terror, as the scientist clung to her even tighter. "What are you doing?"

"Davey!" Alex shouted. "I canna approach! Something is pushing me back! Bring the girl, and let's get out of here!"

"Now I canna move," Davey said, and Ellie could feel him trembling. She took a deep breath and looked down to make sure her legs were still there, because she sure couldn't feel them anymore. Her breath caught in her throat.

"Davey," she whispered, "look."

He didn't speak. The spiral carving beneath their feet had begun to turn.

Ellie's head was spinning—no, the spiral was spinning—and as she clung to Davey, the carving spun faster and faster, the moonlight shining down through the holes above growing brighter, sharper, almost painful, like shimmering knives stabbing into her brain. From very far away, she heard a woman screaming. As the spiral turned faster and faster beneath their feet, she realized she was the one shrieking at the top of her lungs, as Davey clung to her, somehow just as trapped as she.

"Hold on!" he cried, and the moonlight shattered into a billion shimmering shards of radiant energy and all of earth and sky and stars and stones disappeared into a blinding blaze of light.

four

Ian hated driving. He'd never quite gotten used to the fact that horses were obsolete in this brave, new world, and giant metal boxes were used to transport people and goods from one place to another. But when Maggie had asked him to drive to the cairn and pick up Ellie, he couldn't refuse.

After talking to Allie for an hour, he had a vastly different understanding of Eleanor Graham than he'd had before, and he was determined to talk her into keeping her job. He glanced up through the windshield at the stars glimmering in the sky.

A beautiful night. Perhaps the stars and the moonlight would help him convince the lass that he needed her. For the tour, of course.

Well, maybe for more than just the tour.

Allie had seen through his denials of wanting only a friendship with Ellie, and made him realize that he had been attracted to her from the moment they first met. Armed now with more information, and a better understanding of what the loss of her parents had done to the lass, perhaps he could talk her into giving the job another chance. If she agreed, maybe he would get a second chance, too.

He made the turn onto the dirt road leading to the cairn and stopped at the base of the steep hill. Killing the motor, he was about to turn off the headlights when suddenly Alex MacGregor came half running, half sliding down the steep incline, stumbling out in front of Ian's car, wild-eyed with terror.

His heart pounding, Ian jumped out of the vehicle and ran to the man's side, catching him as he sank to the ground.

"What is it?" he cried as he knelt beside him. "Is Ellie all right?"

"They disappeared from the cairn," he whispered, staring straight ahead, the headlights lighting one side of his face. "Just disappeared into thin air."

"What are ye sayin'?" Ian asked, his voice hushed with fear. "Who disappeared?"

"Ellie and Davey!" Alex clutched his hair between his fingers, practically curling into a ball on the ground. "I was lookin' right at them, and—" He shuddered and then spoke again. "Ellie was walking on one of the spirals—" Alex paused in the story, his voice suddenly irate. "She should know better than to do that; 'tis a priceless artifact and—"

"Get on with it, man!" Ian commanded.

He nodded and took a deep breath. "Ellie was walking on the spiral, and I told her to stop, when all at once Davey rushes over to her like she's on fire! He grabs hold of her and"—his face paled again—"the two of them disappeared!" He shook his head, his gaze fixed. "Am I losing my mind, laddie?"

Ian's heart began to pound and a terror seized him unlike any he had ever known. Ellie. Ellie had been swept into the spinning vortex of time.

"No," he said grimly, "ye are not."

When consciousness returned, the blackness was all consuming. Ellie spun through it, careening head over heels in an endless void so terrifying she thought her heart would stop beating from fear. Perhaps it already had and she just didn't know it. Perhaps one of Davey's machines had blown up in the cairn and she was dead, headed for the hereafter.

She wasn't sure she believed in the hereafter anymore, but if heaven and hell did exist, she had definitely ended up in the wrong place. Maybe she should have listened to Allie about quoting Nietzsche so much. When it came down to it, running around saying "God is dead" might not have been the smartest idea she'd ever had.

She tried to cry out but couldn't make a sound. Her throat was as paralyzed as the rest of her body. Was Davey with her? There was no way to tell. She could only see the blackness in front of her, nothing else. Then suddenly, the spinning stopped, and she was rising upward. Trying to get her bearings, she looked down, and though her vision was clouded, blurry, she could finally make out something below. No, someone.

A body. Ellie tried to take a deep breath, but couldn't. When her vision cleared enough to see the person, she understood why.

The body below . . . was hers.

Before she could process this revelation, there came a rush of sound, like white noise, into her ears, and then she was falling, slamming back into her body, breathing in sharply, feeling her lungs expand and her heart begin to pound again.

Ellie opened her eyes. Above her, hundreds of small stones were intricately mortared together with mud, and intermittent bright streams of light seemed to pierce through the rocks and dance upon the floor around her. She was still in the cairn. She lay flat on her back, dizzy, slightly nauseated, but alive.

Davey.

She sat bolt upright and just as quickly lay back down again. The cairn spun around and around, and for a moment she feared she was being thrust back into the terrible vortex she had just escaped. After a few seconds she regained her equilibrium, and realized she just needed to lie flat.

Craning her neck from her prone position, she managed

to take a look around the cairn. Davey was nowhere in sight. After a few minutes more, she cautiously sat up again and this time experienced only a slight vertigo.

What in the world had happened? There was no evidence of an explosion—no damage, nothing. Ellie's frown deepened as she realized that all of Davey's equipment had disappeared. Even the tables were gone.

She dragged one hand through her tangled hair and groaned aloud. Every bone in her body ached as if she'd been twisted into a pretzel and back again, and her head throbbed with pain. Finally stumbling to her feet, she walked around the cairn, looking for a clue or a trace of Davey and his equipment—a forgotten disk, a paper clip, *anything.*

There was nothing, just the bare bones of the cairn as it had probably looked before Davey moved his equipment inside. Something, however, had been added—the opening to the cairn had been blocked with stones, effectively sealing off the only exit. As she stood there, considering her situation, Ellie suddenly realized that the light inside the small space had grown dimmer. She rushed over to where the small holes above allowed in the bright streams of moonlight.

The moon must be setting, she thought. *Another few minutes and I'm going to be left literally in the dark.*

Ellie shook her head in dismay and as she did, a pale strand of hair drifted across her face. She tucked it back behind her ear and then froze. Slowly she reached up and pulled a fistful of hair down past her forehead and stared at it in disbelief. Her hair was no longer black. It was too dark in the cairn to tell exactly what color, but it was definitely a light color now. Had her experience made her hair turn white?

"Or am I just going nuts?" she whispered.

The sound of her own voice was somehow comforting, and propelled her back into action. This was ridiculous. Of course she wasn't losing her mind. Davey and Alex were playing some kind of joke on her. Well, guess what?—it wasn't funny! And when she got out and found them, she was going to make them rue the day they had messed with Ellie Graham!

Buoyed up by her anger, Ellie marched over to the opening, and, thankful for her Doc Martens, began kicking the stones.

"They were standing in the middle of the center spiral," Alex said, sitting at Davey's computer, finally a little bit calmer.

When Ian had finished explaining that the two had likely been sent to another time through the mysterious workings of the triskele, Alex had thought he was joking. It had taken time to convince the man that it was true, time Ian didn't have. Ellie and Davey were in serious trouble, and whether or not they got back alive—or at all—might hinge on how quickly he could follow.

Ian walked over to the center spiral and looked down at the carving, his throat growing tight at the thought of how frightened Ellie must have been—must still be, wherever she had ended up.

"Time travel," Alex said for about the third time in as many minutes. He shook his head. "This could make me millions," he said. "Imagine if—"

"Aye." Ian cut him off, his voice harsh. "Imagine if this power fell into the wrong hands. Imagine the enemies of the civilized world going back in time and changing things to give them the advantage over their foes, or barbaric men from the past traveling here!" He stalked over to Alex and grabbed him by one arm. "This must remain a secret, and I am willing to do anything to ensure that it does."

"Fine, fine," Alex said hastily. "I willna say a word to anyone."

"And ye willna try to use it, either," Ian stated flatly. "Promise me that."

Alex's eyes widened. "Ye do not have to worry about that, laddie."

"And ye will go directly to Quinn and Maggie's from here and ask to speak to Quinn, alone, right? Make sure Maggie doesna hear of this. The worry could harm her and her bairn."

"Aye, I will only tell Quinn."

Ian hated to leave such a powerful secret in the hands of Alex, but there was nothing he could do about it. He had to go after Ellie and Davey, and waste no time doing so. Every minute he delayed was another minute that could possibly take the two farther away from the cairn, and his help.

"Give me yer coat," he ordered, and Alex shed his thick overcoat and handed it to him. Ian pulled it on over his jacket and then glanced around. "Look around and gather up anything that could be useful—food, water, weapons."

The two hurried around the circular room, gathering up bottles of water, the sack of granola bars, a couple of candy bars, and a blanket. Alex dumped some electrical cords out of a canvas satchel and, with Ian's help, began stuffing the supplies into the bag. When the two men straightened, Alex hesitated, then nodded toward the coat Ian wore.

"Reach inside the right pocket," he said.

Ian shoved his hand into the pocket and pulled out a small knife encased in a leather sheath. The entire knife was about six or seven inches long.

"A *skean dhu*," he said, removing the knife from the sheath. The handle was carved with Celtic symbols and the blade was exceedingly sharp. "I havena seen one of these in a long time."

Alex shrugged. "It's a souvenir I bought for my nephew." Ian's brows went up and Alex smiled. "He's eighteen and lives in the States. Anyway, there is yer weapon, for what it is worth."

"Worth more than ye might wager," Ian said, remembering a few fights when a small knife secreted in the top of a man's boot meant the difference between life and death. "Thank ye, lad. All right, then, there is no more time to be wasted." He turned to walk back to the spiral, but Alex stopped him, one hand on his arm.

"Are ye sure about this?" he asked. "About going alone?"

One corner of Ian's mouth quirked up. "Are ye offering to go with me, then?"

Alex visibly shuddered and shook his head. "Hell, no. I'd

be more of a hindrance than a help to ye. Ye'd have three to take care of instead of two. But I could drive quickly and bring Quinn back. I know he would—"

Ian shook his head firmly. "No, no, lad. Quinn belongs here with his Maggie." He clapped the man on the back. "I'll be fine, and be back with the two adventurers before ye know it."

"So ye know how it works and all?"

"Aye. 'Tis a simple thing, too simple apparently." He frowned at the man. "Remember, this remains between the two of us, and Quinn. I will be back, and if ye have shared this secret with anyone else—"

"Ye have my word," Alex said, standing a little straighter. After gazing into the man's eyes for a long moment, Ian finally believed him.

"All right, then. Ye'd best leave the cairn. I dinna know how far the magic reaches."

"Magic?" Alex laughed. "'Tis not magic, but some kind of science we dinna understand."

Ian smiled. "I havena time to change yer mind, but trust me, 'tis magic, pure and simple." To his surprise, Alex held out his hand. Ian shook it, laughing a little. "I'm coming back, ye know," he said.

Alex's tawny brows pressed together. "Aye," he said, "but just in case." He gave his hand another firm shake. "Godspeed and good luck."

Ian frowned as the archaeologist ran across the cairn, paused at the opening to toss him a salute, and then disappeared into the night. He walked toward the spiral, trying to prepare himself for what lay ahead, trying not to think of what might have happened to Ellie, and Davey as well. They could have ended up anywhere in time, he supposed, or perhaps the spirals all led to 1711, though why they would be stuck on that period of history he couldn't imagine.

What if he couldn't find them? What if something terrible had happened to Ellie? The past was no place for a defenseless young woman, and now that he knew her tough girl façade was just that, a façade, he was all the more worried.

What if he never got the chance to tell her that he cared for her, more than she might suspect?

Today's date was October 24, and according to Alex, Ellie and Davey had traveled back in time at around 2 a.m. If the ways of the time spirals were the same as when Maggie and Quinn had traveled them, then the date and time of day should remain constant no matter what time period was reached. He could only hope that the two had stayed at the cairn and waited for help.

Taking a deep breath, Ian stared down at the spiral and began to walk, but as he took each step, he felt as if he were forgetting something.

Oh, the words, aye, the ancient words—damn! He'd forgotten about that silly rhyme. How did it go now?

"Follow, follow, something . . ." he said out loud, new anguish rushing over him. "I canna remember," he whispered, as he continued to walk around the spiral. "But I must remember; I must reach Ellie, wherever she is!" He reached the center, his heart thudding painfully in his chest. Ian sank to his knees and closed his eyes.

"Take me to her, take me to Ellie, wherever she is." He opened his eyes.

The spiral began to turn.

Ellie sat on the top of a very tall hill, on a very hard rock, and stared down at the vast Scottish countryside below, feeling cold, exhausted, thirsty, and half-starved. Mid-October, fall was starting to creep across the hills and dells, brilliant golds and reds through bushes and foliage, bleeding into the bright green left over from summer. It was beautiful. She didn't care.

After breaking out of the cairn, she had decided to wait until daylight to make her way back to Maggie's. The last thing she needed was to trip and break something, like her neck. And the way her luck was going, that's probably exactly what would happen.

At dawn, after a near-sleepless night on the cold, hard

ground, she'd struck out for her sister's house. After walking a million miles—okay, at least ten—she had to face facts: She was lost.

How that could be, she didn't understand. She and Allie had walked to the cairn from Maggie's cottage many times, and had even driven the distance to measure how far they were walking. The ancient mound, now known in archaeology circles as the Drymen Cairn, measured 3.8 miles from Quinn and Maggie's home.

She shaded her eyes with one hand and looked up at the sun, filmy and vague behind fleecy gray clouds. It was maybe around ten o'clock in the morning? She'd left her watch on the bedside table in her room at the cottage, right beside her cell phone.

With a sigh of exasperation, Ellie lifted her right foot, propped it over her left knee, and began unlacing the heavy boot she wore. With a groan of relief she pulled it off and bit her lip at the sight of the huge blister on the back of her heel—proof that she'd walked a lot farther than three miles.

Her hair blew across her face, reminding her of the other anomaly in her adventure. She still hadn't figured out the sudden change in her hair color, but there had to be a logical explanation for it, just as there had to be a logical explanation for what happened to Davey and Alex and all the equipment in the cairn. Oh, yeah, and the crazy trip through that black, terrifying void. But maybe that was just a dream.

Of course. There'd been some kind of explosion in the cairn, some glitch with Davey's equipment, and she'd blacked out and had a weird dream. So why wasn't there any evidence of an explosion? And where were Davey and Alex? And why couldn't she find Maggie's house? And—

"Oh, stop," she said aloud. With a sigh, she started pulling on her boot again, wincing as it scraped over the blister beneath her sock. No matter how she tried to figure it out, she just kept going around in circles. The best thing to do was to find a house, a road, anything that would help her get back to civilization.

"Why the hell didn't I grab my cell phone before I left Maggie's?" Ellie muttered, as she stood and surveyed the distant horizon. The land was totally unfamiliar. She sighed and clasped her arms around herself, glad to have her jacket, wishing Davey had given her a bottle of water to go with that granola bar. She crossed to the edge of the craggy hill and looked down, hands on her hips.

"Okay, this is it," she said, her breath making soft clouds in the air. "I give up. I'm going to sit right here until someone finds me. That's what I should have done in the first place. I should have stayed at the cairn. How dumb was I to—"

The sudden rumble of thunder made her turn in alarm and hurriedly search the sky. So far that day she'd been incredibly lucky. It had rained twice, and then only a fine mist that she managed to escape both times by huddling under stone outcroppings. The sun had miraculously come out afterward, drying her clothes and keeping her from freezing to death in the chill Highland air.

She frowned up at the sky. No storm clouds. Then what had made that noise? Her breath caught in her throat as suddenly a dozen or more men on horseback pounded across the glen below, riding straight toward her. In Texas the phrase was "riding hell-for-leather." In Scotland it was probably something like "riding heather for leather," but either way they were coming fast.

Ellie watched as the horses continued to rush toward her. Maybe she was still asleep, still trapped in the bad dream. Her next thought sent a cold chill down her spine. Maybe she wasn't. For as the horsemen thundered toward her, she could make out more details: The men wore dark kilts, black shirts, and rough leather boots. Each man had a sword at his side.

A sword?

Sure. Why not? This is Scotland. During the six months she'd spent on the road with Ian, Ellie had seen all kinds of interesting customs. So this was all natural and normal, right? At least she wasn't alone anymore, and hopefully one of these men in kilts would have a cell phone, or would take her to someone who did.

"Hi!" Ellie called out, waving her hands as the first Scotsman made it up the hill. The man reined his mount in with a rough gesture, causing the horse to rear back on its hind legs before coming to a stop. Then the rider simply sat and stared at her.

His face was partially covered by a well-kept beard, and the part she could see was as lined as a map of the Highlands. His dark, bushy brows furrowed together over dark eyes that flashed angrily at the sight of her. Ellie's smile faded as he was joined by the rest of the riders, each and every one of them looking just as grim and forbidding as the first. She stood, her heart pounding, wondering what she should say.

The man spoke first, thank goodness, but Ellie couldn't understand him until he repeated the same words several times over.

"What are ye doin' here?" he said. "Whose protection are ye under?"

Protection? She shook her head. How was she supposed to answer such a question?

"Yer clan!" he shouted, his face growing red from the exertion. "What is yer clan?"

Ellie's eyes widened. *Wow.* People often said that things hadn't changed much in the Highlands during the last few hundred years, and she was beginning to think it was true. Her clan? Was there a Graham clan? She hadn't kept up with that kind of thing the way Maggie always had.

She did know that the MacGregors were still a viable clan, revered by the Scottish people. Maggie had dragged her to that movie—what was the name? Oh, yeah, *Rob Roy*—and then bought the DVD and forced her to watch it again.

"MacGregor," she said loudly, to be heard over the growing sweep of the wind and the jingle jangle of a dozen horses and men's movements.

Everything went suddenly still. Even the wind died down as if the weather had experienced the same shock evident on the faces of the men staring down at her. The man who had asked the question swung down from his horse and walked slowly toward her, stopping a few feet away. Then his face contorted, and Ellie collapsed to the ground again as he drew his sword and roared loudly enough to shake the rocks in the hill beneath them:

"*MacGregor?!*"

Coming through the time portal had once again been a terrifying experience. Wrenched from his body, Ian had floated in a black nothingness for what seemed like eternity, until he finally joined himself again and arrived in the past. He hoped Ellie hadn't had the same nightmarish occurrence. He had awakened outside the cairn, flat on his back, and now lay staring up at the sun trying to gather his thoughts.

The sun? But he'd left in the middle of the night! Had he been unconscious all night? Ian tried to sit up, but an intense dizziness overcame him. He waited a few minutes, and then cautiously rose to his feet and looked around. He recognized a large stone nearby, tall and curved at the top, and knew it stood at the base of the craggy hill on which the cairn sat.

Dragging one hand through his hair, he pushed the thoughts from his mind. Wherever he was, as long as it was the same place that Ellie had arrived, that's all that mattered. He remembered then that on one of her trips back in time, Maggie had ended up outside the cairn. Perhaps the separation of body and mind had something to do with that, he didn't know, but it was just more proof that the spirals were unpredictable, and exceedingly dangerous.

After taking several deep breaths, Ian felt ready to tackle the hill. From the top, he'd be able to see a good distance. As he climbed up the hill, he tried to decide what Ellie and Davey would have done once they reached the past. Maybe they hadn't realized they had journeyed to the past and were still in the cairn, waiting for someone to come and explain what had happened.

Before embarking on his band tour, Ian had gotten to know both Alex and Davey a bit. His impression of Davey had been that of a very intelligent young man who lived primarily inside his own head. The man often came to work with two different shoes on or with his shirt on inside out, and once without any shirt at all. When anyone mentioned such things, he would just smile and shrug. Davey had a brilliant mind, but apparently was easily distracted.

The thought of Ellie having only the naïve scientist to depend upon in this dangerous time made Ian's chest tighten with fear. No matter how tough and independent she might be in her own time, she was ill-prepared to handle the eighteenth century. A muscle in his jaw twitched. He had to find her.

Ian continued up the hill until he reached the rock-strewn pinnacle. There the cairn lay, as deceptively innocent as always. As he approached, he saw a pile of stones in front of the curved opening, and more halfway up. He knelt down beside the stones, noting that where the rocks had hit the ground, the earth beneath them was freshly disturbed.

Hope sprang up inside of him. The freshly broken soil proved that he had traveled back to the same time period as Ellie and Davey—didn't it? That the two had arrived inside the cairn and then broken their way out? Perhaps. He ducked inside the cairn and his spirits sagged at the sight of the empty structure.

Where in the world had they gone? He was about eight hours behind them, because of lying unconscious after his arrival, and in that amount of time, they could be anywhere. It was then that he heard a scream like a banshee being twisted in a vise. Ian ran out of the cairn to the edge of the hill. In the near distance, a dozen or more horsemen rode. He could make out that one of the horsemen had something flung across the saddle in front of him, and another scream pierced the glen.

Ellie?

Ian half slid, half climbed down the hillside, and then took off at a dead run. He had no horse, but would follow on foot. In his own time, he'd been a good tracker. He would find Ellie Graham if he had to walk the length and breadth of Scotland.

five

The men were fierce, ugly, and extremely smelly, but Ellie thought it better that she didn't mention any of those descriptions aloud. Not that she could. After the bearded Scotsman had bellowed the name "MacGregor" at the top of his lungs, he'd seized her, thrown her over his saddle, and galloped down the hillside, shaking her insides to Jell-O.

It had taken her several miles before she could catch her breath enough to scream her own lungs out. As a result, now she could barely whisper, let alone talk.

And what was the use? These men were obviously crazy—escaped lunatics from an asylum that specialized in Highland battle reenactments. It was the only semilogical explanation she could come up with—the only thing keeping her from becoming completely hysterical, though she couldn't stop her hands from shaking.

Once they had reached their destination—a camp with about ten or twenty more crazy Highlanders—she had been flung to the ground. Before she could try to run, one of the other men grabbed her and tied her arms behind her back. Slinging her roughly over his shoulder, he carried her to a huge campfire in the center of the gathered men, where he dumped her roughly on the ground.

At first, she'd been terrified, then furious, but her fury was turning quickly to terror, as the big Scot who had kidnapped her lumbered forward. He began ranting and raving, and though she couldn't understand half of what he said, she managed to get the gist of it.

She was in trouble. For being a MacGregor.

"I'm not a MacGregor!" she tried to tell him, but her voice wouldn't cooperate. To get his attention, Ellie began kicking her feet against the ground until he stopped yelling long enough to look at her. "I am *not* a MacGregor," she said, finally managing to make herself heard. "I'm a *Graham*— not that it's any of your business!"

He gave her a long, sweeping look from head to toe, and then threw back his shaggy head and laughed.

Why? Who knew? The man was nuts.

Nuts enough to kill her?

Ellie's heart began to pound. She'd been keeping the panic at bay, telling herself there was no way that a group of men this large could be roaming the Scottish countryside, pilfering and plundering like in the days of old, without someone knowing about it. The police, or sheriff, or someone, would be there soon to save her. Maybe the Scottish equivalent of a SWAT team. They had those, right?

"Look," she said, her voice trembling, "my sister is going to be looking for me and she's going to call the police when I don't show up. So you'd better just let me go and—" The words died in her throat as two men came trudging up to the campfire, dragging someone between them.

The man's face was bloody and battered, and Ellie stared at him and then screamed, but her throat was too raw, and the sound died away just as he raised his head and looked at her, blood dripping from his mouth. He wore glasses.

It was Davey.

* * *

The big Scotsman finally listened to at least one thing Ellie had to say. She'd cried out that Davey was her brother, and after muttering to himself and then a couple of other hairy Scotsman, he led them to a kind of makeshift tent, tied them together back to back, and shoved the two of them inside. A guard was posted outside and they were finally left alone.

"Your face looks terrible," Ellie said. She'd begged a drink of water from her captor for both of them, and could finally speak a little louder. "Are you all right?"

"It looks worse than it is," he said, his voice faint. "I'm just grateful my glasses aren't broken. What happened to your hair?"

"I have no idea," she said. "What color does it look to you? I can only see the ends."

"Before the blood dripped into my eyes, I thought it looked reddish blonde. Like yer sisters."

Ellie shook her head. "Then it's like I never dyed my hair at all. That's my natural color. Something very strange is going on." She ducked her head and let her hair fall over her face. Davey was right. Her hair was back to normal. How in the world had this happened? She shook her hair back and tried to shift into a more comfortable position. "Why did they beat you up? What is this all about?"

"I dinna know," he said, sounding as weary as she felt. "I somehow came to be outside the cairn—I dinna ken how exactly—actually a distance away. I walked back to the hill just as the men were riding away with ye. I followed and hid outside the camp, trying to figure out what to do, but one of their guards saw me and dragged me in. They asked who I was and I said my name and"—he shook his head—"they cried 'Jacobite!' and started in beating on me!"

Ellie nodded. "That's what happened to me, sort of."

"Did they hurt ye, lass?" he asked, his voice rough with concern.

Nice guy. Too bad he was so young. "No," she said, "but they asked me what clan I belonged to, and I didn't know if the Grahams still had a clan, so I said the first one that popped into my head—the MacGregors. The big guy kind of roared at me and before I could do anything, he picked me up and threw me onto his horse!" She took a deep breath and winced. "On second thought, they did hurt me. My ribs are killing me."

"I dinna ken what's going on here, but we've got to get away. I'm going to try and untie yer hands."

After thirty minutes, he gave up and let Ellie try to untie his. Whatever the Highlanders had used to bind them with was thin and impossible to budge. They would need a knife to get free.

"Don't have a sword on you, do you, laddie?" Ellie asked, trying to sound casual as she fought the fear raging inside of her. Unemotional Ellie had disappeared along with her black hair. Allie was right—underneath the black garb she was nothing but mush.

"Dinna worry," Davey said softly. "I won't let them hurt ye."

Ellie leaned her head back against his and smiled. She suspected that Davey was scarcely able to take care of himself, let alone look out for her, but she appreciated his attempts at reassurance.

"Thanks," she said.

"Try to get some sleep."

She shook her head. "I'm afraid to go to sleep," she admitted. "What if they come when we're asleep and slit our throats?"

"I'll stay awake," he promised. "Come on, lass, we'll take turns."

With a look toward the closed opening of the tent, Ellie closed her eyes, sure she was too scared and too cold and too hungry to sleep. She drifted into sleep more easily than she could imagine doing under the circumstances, welcoming unconsciousness like a drug.

Dream after dream barreled through her mind, until finally she was dreaming about Ian. He was there, inside the tent, his face close to hers, his mouth hovering above her lips, his hand warm against her cheek. He kissed her, gently, lovingly, but the kiss grew suddenly intense and she was frightened and—

Her eyes flew open. It was pitch-black except for a shaft of moonlight coming through the opening of the tent, giving her just enough light to see that a man was crouched in front of her. She started to scream and he clamped one hand over her mouth, the other gripping the back of her neck as he glanced toward the tent opening, his chest pressing against her knees. When he turned back, with her heart just about slamming out of her chest, Ellie saw it was Ian.

"*Shhhh,*" he whispered. She nodded, to show she understood. He lowered his hand from her mouth and stared at her. "Ellie?"

"What the hell?" Davey said, craning his neck around to look at him.

"Yes, it's me," she whispered. "You scared me half to death!"

Ian shook his head. "What did ye do to yer hair?"

"It's a mystery," she muttered. "Now, come on, let's get out of here!"

A blade flashed in Ian's hand and Ellie swallowed hard as he moved to cut the ropes binding them. They were free in seconds and Ian slipped the knife back into his boot and took her hand.

"Follow me," he ordered, drawing her to her feet. He led the two of them to the back of the tent and lifted the edge of the hide, motioning for them to crawl under. Once outside, Ellie stifled a scream as she almost stumbled over a man lying on the ground. Their guard? There was no time to wonder. Ian grabbed her arm and propelled her into motion, as Davey followed close behind.

The moon glimmered high above the horizon, shedding a dim light across the countryside. The horsemen's camp was just outside a forest, and the three slipped easily into the darkness that the huge pine trees provided, and crouched down.

"What the bloody hell is going on?" Davey demanded, his usual taciturn nature apparently blown out of the water by their experience.

"No time to explain," Ian said. "Come on!" He started to stand, but Ellie gasped and pulled him back down beside her.

"Too late," she said, shrinking against him. Directly in front of them were four hulking figures, all with swords drawn. One of them was the man who had thrown her atop his horse.

"Stay down," Ian whispered, "and wait here for me."

He stood, and Ellie's heart beat faster as moonlight streamed through the trees and illuminated his face. His jaw was set, and his eyes, darkened by the shadows, flashed with an anger she'd never seen before. A sword was buckled at his waist. From their guard? Likely, else he had decided to take a stroll to the cairn with it.

"By what right do ye draw yer swords against me?" Ian asked, his eyes narrowing as he folded his arms over his broad chest.

"By the right of those named by General Wade to watch the Highlands, and protect it from Jacobites like the three of ye," said the tallest man.

Ellie's gaze was fixed on Ian's face and she saw the slight flicker in his gaze, and then he laughed, lowered his arms to his sides and shook his head.

"Three? There is only myself, and I am no Jacobite."

"Where are the others that ye set free?"

Ian's voice grew sharper. "I said there is only me. Do ye no' ken who I am, laddies?"

"Nay," said the one who had spoken before. "I only ken ye are the one who set the traitors we captured free!"

Ian's hands clenched into fists and Ellie held her breath. If he attacked the four men, they would surely kill him.

"*Traitors?* Ye dare to call my friends *traitors*? Who is yer leader? Where is yer chief? I demand to see him at once!"

The man laughed. "Who are ye to demand anything, ye Jacobite scum?"

Ian took a step forward, and Ellie's heart almost stopped beating.

"I am the son of Fergus Campbell," he said, his voice low

and hard. "If ye know that name at all, ye know that I am no Jacobite. And if ye know that name at all, ye know that by taking his son captive, ye are courting disaster."

Ellie almost laughed at the way the puffed-up leader of the four faded into uncertainty right in front of them, his shoulders sagging. "Fergus Campbell is yer father?" he asked, his voice hushed.

"Aye, and if ye dinna release me this minute, I can promise that there will be hell to pay for this insult."

Ian's rock-hard gaze bored into the man facing him. Apparently the name Fergus Campbell held some weight in this part of the Highlands. *Campbell?* But Ian's last name was MacGregor. Ellie shook her head. Who knew? A few hours ago she'd been a brunette.

"Whist, now," another man said, stepping forward. "Three of the laird's sons are in our unit, and the other is at home, taking care of the laird's business during his illness." The man shook his head. "Ye are not Tavish."

Ian glanced away and then back again. "I am his eldest son. I've been away, in France."

The Scot's black brows crashed together. "France? Ye mean that country that harbors the Jacobite spies we have driven from our shores?"

With an oath, Ian coldcocked the man and wrenched his sword from his scabbard as the tall Scot fell to the ground. He put one foot on the man's chest and balanced the point of the sword at his throat.

"Ye willna question my loyalty to the king again," Ian said. He glanced up at the three stunned men, now looking at him with more respect. "Drop yer weapons, or pay the consequences."

Ellie stared at him, dumbfounded. This side of Ian was one she'd never seen before; one she'd never even believed existed. The Ian she knew was easygoing, kind, and generally soft-spoken. Of course, the Ian she knew wouldn't be wearing a sword, let alone holding it to a man's throat!

The other men backed away from him, and one of them

spoke up. "We'll take ye to the captain," he said. "Just let Duncan live."

Ian held his gaze for a long moment and then nodded and took his foot from the prostrate man's throat. The big man stumbled to his feet with his hand to his neck and backed away toward his comrades.

"Start walking." He glanced back at Ellie and Davey, still hidden in the brush. "Ye can come out now."

The two rose slowly, exchanging glances as they did.

"Ian," Ellie said, "let's just get out of here! These guys think they're on the set of *Braveheart* or something!"

"Aye," Davey agreed, and thrust his thumb over his shoulder, "let's go this a way."

Ian shook his head. "I must speak with this captain and learn of my father's house. We are in no danger now." He gestured to the four men with his sword, and grumbling, they turned and made their way out of the forest, with Ian close behind.

Ellie looked at Davey and he shrugged. "What choice do we have? I have no idea where we are."

"Okay," she said, "but I hope William Wallace up there knows what he's doing."

The four men led them back to the camp. As they approached, a tall man wearing a dark cloak stood next to the fire with his back to them, what looked like a traditional Scottish "bonnet" garnished with feathers, on his head.

"Captain!" the man called Duncan cried out as they drew near. "This man is the one who released the prisoners, and he demands to talk to ye."

"Demands? He *demands*?" the tall man said. He turned toward them, his face twisting with anger at the sight of the sword Ian held. "Seize them!"

Men seemed to come out of nowhere, from every corner of the darkness, and the three were suddenly surrounded—again.

"Oh, yeah, this was a great idea," Ellie said from behind Ian's broad shoulders.

"We are no' Jacobites!" Ian shouted, slashing his sword in front of him to keep the other men at bay.

The captain strode forward, and then stopped, looking as if someone had punched him in the stomach, his face ashen in the moonlight.

"We are no' Jacobites," Ian repeated, his voice like steel. "Now tell yer men—" He stopped speaking, and Ellie's throat tightened as she watched the blood drain from his face. Without thinking, she moved to his left side and slid one hand through the crook of his arm, her fingers tightening against the thick texture of the coat he wore.

"Ye are dead," the captain said, no longer blustering but shaking his head, his voice trembling. "That scoundrel Rob Roy told us ye died—and that was twenty-three years ago."

"Hello, Angus," Ian said softly. "I'm glad to see ye."

"And even if it wasna true"—he shook his head again, ignoring Ian's words—"ye were four and twenty when ye died. Twenty-three years ago. And here ye stand, looking no more than when last I saw ye. Ye have not aged."

His face twisted again, this time with fear. "Ye have not *aged*." He drew the sword from the scabbard at his side and backed away, his other hand held out as if to keep the other man back. He looked around wildly at his men. "'Tis my brother's ghost!"

"Ian," Ellie said, her voice hushed and taking on a sing-song quality, "this is freaking me ou-ut."

Ian squeezed her hand and took a step forward. "Aye, Angus," he said, "I have come back to set what is wrong, right again. Now release my friends, also spirits from the netherworld, or I must call upon the good God to rain His wrath down upon ye all."

Ellie turned and stared at Ian in disbelief. What in the world was he doing? And what did Angus mean, that Ian hadn't aged? That he'd died twenty-three years ago?

"Release them!" Angus said immediately, his eyes widening.

"Just tell me one thing, and I will leave ye in peace—for now," Ian said. He took a step forward and his brother backed away, raising his sword once again.

"What?" he cried roughly. "What is it ye want?"

"So ye are fighting against yer own people, are ye?"

Angus narrowed his eyes. "I am fighting against those who would usurp our king," he said.

Ellie frowned. *King? I might be out of touch, but I'm pretty sure England is still ruled by a queen. Ian's brother appears to be a few bricks shy of a load.*

"I am the captain of one of the Highland Watches," Angus continued, still watching Ian warily.

"Och, and what is it ye watch?" Ian demanded. "Yer fellow Scots? Why did ye accost my friend when she said she was under the protection of the MacGregor clan?"

"Ye know the MacGregors are outlaws."

Ian nodded. "Ye mean, like me."

The man looked away, uncertain. "We are bound to uphold the law," he said.

"Tell me, brother, who is the high commander of yer 'Highland Watch'?"

"Why, the king."

"The English king?" Ian prodded.

Angus's eyes turned to stone. "*Our* king," he said.

"Perhaps yers, but never mine. How are the rest of my brothers?"

"Serving the king," Angus said briskly. "Part of the Watch."

Ian's mouth flattened. "All of them."

Angus nodded. "Except for Tavish. He is home with Father."

"What ails him?"

"The doctors say he has a malady," Angus said. "That is all I know. Tavish is running the estate," he said, "and Kate is there as well."

"Kate? So Tavish is married?" Ian asked. Angus shook his head, a little less terrified.

"Nay. Father remarried. That wife died in childbirth, but her bairn lived. A girl, named Kate. She's sad comfort to the old man. An outspoken brat, she is."

Ian's eyes grew shadowed and he was silent for several long moments. "How ill is the laird?" he said at last.

"Dying," Angus whispered.

Ellie stopped breathing for a moment. Poor Ian. She knew what it was like to lose a parent. He must feel devastated. Ian lifted his gaze and his eyes were as hard as sapphires. Ellie raised both brows. *Well, maybe not.*

"We will leave ye then, for the present."

He turned, taking Ellie with him, Davey following as they moved away from the campfire.

"Wait!" Angus cried from behind them. "Please, wait!"

Ian kept walking, until finally Ellie dug her heels in, forcing him to stop.

"Ian," she whispered, "he's your brother!"

His grim expression softened the slightest bit, and he turned back toward the other man. "Aye?"

Angus stood trembling. Every other man in the camp had faded into the darkness. "Do ye have any words for our father?" he asked. "Any last comfort?"

Ian's hand tightened on hers so intensely that Ellie gasped. She looked up at him, startled by the thunderous look on his face.

"Aye," he said, his voice like the crack of a whip. "I have a word for him. Tell him that when he dies, the devil will be waiting at his bedside to take him to the lowest level of hell!"

He turned on his heel and walked away, leaving Ellie to stare after him in complete astonishment.

six

Ian soon left Ellie and Davey behind, but he couldn't slow down, not even for the two of them. As long as he kept them in sight, they would be fine, and he had to work off this anger, this rage that was filling him. He feared what he might do if he did not.

When just a child, he had learned to bury his anger, put on the persona of an obedient boy who wanted only to please his father. While inside, he had burned. His days with Quinn had lessened that fury, and at his side he had finally found some semblance of peace. After traveling to the twenty-first century, the easygoing man he had once feigned to be for so long had finally become real, and the demons that drove him had been laid to rest. Until now.

"Ian! Ian, wait!"

Ellie's furious voice pierced through the red haze around his brain, but he couldn't stop. Her footsteps pounded out behind him and then she was at his side, keeping pace with him, her breath coming hard and fast. He stared straight ahead and didn't slow down. Finally she gave a scream of frustration and jerked him to a standstill.

He looked down into her irate blue gray eyes, and some

distant part of his mind registered how much softer and approachable she looked now that her hair was a lighter color.

"For pity's sake, will you please *stop* for one *minute*?" she demanded.

Maybe not softer.

"What?" he said, his control breaking. "What do ye want?"

"I want to know what the hell is going on! For starters— why are you being such a jerk? That was a terrible thing to say! What if he tells your father? And why did you pretend to be a ghost? And why the hell are you walking like we're in a freaking race or something?"

Ian put his hands on his hips and released his pent-up breath as he tried to gain control over his emotions. It wasn't Ellie's fault, any of this. He had no right to take his anger out on her.

"I'm sorry," he said. He dragged one hand through his hair and shook his head. "There is much that I must tell the two of ye, and none of it is good."

Davey caught up with them in time to hear Ian's last words. "What do ye mean? I thought ye were familiar with this part of the Highlands. Are we lost?"

Ian rubbed the back of his neck and looked up at the sky so he wouldn't have to see the fear in Ellie's eyes. "Aye, ye might say that."

Angus's camp had been in the heart of a glen, and if not for the moonlight, they'd have been stumbling in the darkness trying to find their way to higher ground. He glanced out at the distant mountains, black against the sky where the moon shimmered behind a dark bank of clouds, and watched a light mist rising up from the valley. He knew exactly where they were; it was *when* they were that was disturbing. Twenty-three years, his brother had said.

"Look, I'm dying of thirst," Ellie said, interrupting his thoughts. "Are we a long way from Maggie's house?"

"And is Alex all right?" Davey's gray eyes were filled with concern. "I haven't had a chance to ask ye."

"Aye, Alex is fine."

"What caused the explosion?" Ellie's warm hand clutched at his arm. "Did we cause it somehow?"

"Did it ruin the cairn?" Davey asked anxiously.

Ian held up both hands. "Stop!" Ellie's face fell and he felt immediately contrite. "I'm sorry," he said. "Just wait, please. I'll answer all yer questions." He glanced up at the moon and started walking again. "I have a place for us to camp for the night. Come on."

"Camp?" Ellie said from behind, obviously not following him. "Don't tell me you don't have your cell phone either!"

With a sigh he stopped again and turned. She had her hands on her hips, ice in her eyes, and her chin lifted. It was a look he well knew, one that, when they were touring together, had sent him hurrying to make right whatever had caused the deep freeze.

When she'd had her hair dyed black, she had exuded a tough, no-nonsense aura, but now, with her tousled reddish blonde curls, it was as if a mask had been ripped away, revealing her true self. And her true self was adorable. Not that he hadn't been attracted to the band-manager side of the lass, but now she was infinitely more approachable.

"I dinna think we can get service here, lass," he said with a smile.

Ellie scowled at him. "Why are you smiling like that? Is this some kind of weird joke? Did my sister Allie put you up to all of this?" She glanced over at Davey and her eyes narrowed. "Are you in on this charade?"

Davey shook his head, his eyes widening in panic. "Nay, lass, nay! I wouldn't do such a thing, and surely yer sister wouldn't do such a thing either!"

"Ha. I wouldn't be so sure about that." She glared up at Ian. "She and Ian were awfully chummy last night at the party. Were you planning this nightmare?"

Ian's smile disappeared. "There's a spring not too far from here, and nearby a cave. We'll camp there tonight and I'll explain everything."

"A cave." Ellie's brows rose. "You have got to be kidding. I am not sleeping in a cave. Scotland isn't that big, and the kidnappers didn't take me that far away. We have to be close to the cairn and Maggie's house."

Davey moved a step closer. "There's something wrong, isn't there?"

Ian glanced at Ellie and then nodded. "Aye."

The lass seemed to crumple in front of him, clutching her hand to her chest. "Maggie . . ." she whispered, as she sank toward the ground. "Something's wrong with Maggie! The baby? Oh, please, God, no—" Her eyes fluttered shut as Ian caught her in his arms.

"Och, no, lass!" he cried, as he lowered her slowly to the ground, his arms still around her. "Maggie is fine, I promise ye. She's fine."

Ellie's eyes flew open and her skin, pale in the moonlight, seemed to darken a bit, regaining some of its color as the two men helped her sit up. As soon as she had taken a few deep breaths, she doubled up her fist and punched Ian in the arm.

He jumped from the blow and then nodded ruefully. "Aye, I deserved that. I'm sorry. I never meant for you to think there was something wrong with yer sister."

She folded her arms over her chest and stared him straight in the eye. "I am not moving another step until you tell us what's going on."

Ian stamped down on his temper, remembering he had just almost sent her over the edge with his insensitivity. "Ellie, darlin', I promise I'll tell ye what's going on, but first let me take ye to a safe place, one where I have stored some provisions."

"Food?" Davey said eagerly. "Aye, we can wait, can't we, Ellie?"

"Fine," Ellie said, after glaring at Ian for a moment. "But as soon as we get there—"

"I'll explain everything."

"And just for future reference—don't call me 'darlin'!" She turned and started stomping across the rocky ground.

"Uh, Ellie, dar—I mean, Eleanor?"

She stopped and whirled around, the look on her face murderous. "What?"

Ian sighed. It was going to be a damn long night. "Ye are going the wrong way." He gestured to the right of him and led the way, not looking back to see if she and Davey followed.

The cave wasn't far. Finding it along the trail of the horsemen's tracks and being able to stash the supplies he'd brought back with him had been a break. It didn't take long to reach it, which was both bad and good. Bad because it was so close to the horsemen's camp, and good because surely they would not think to look in such nearby proximity, if his brother decided to pursue his ghostly sibling.

Once inside the cave, he made a fire, grateful for the lighter Alex kept handy to light the emergency kerosene lanterns at the cairn if the generator ever failed. Soon he had a roaring fire going, and had distributed a bottle of water each to Ellie and Davey—cautioning them to make it last and to save the container—and one candy bar and granola bar apiece, and then sat down, ready to face the two of them with the truth.

"All right," he said, taking a seat on one of the stones near the fire. "I'll tell ye what has happened to ye. Ye will not believe it at first, so please, let me speak until I am completely finished, aye?"

Ellie and Davey exchanged glances and nodded. But suddenly, Ian didn't know what to say. How in the world could he explain this insanity? He was silent as he tried to decide the best way to begin.

"Ian," Ellie said at last, "you'd better start talking, and I mean *now*." As she spoke, her voice went higher and higher until it broke on the last word, sending Ian into a panic.

"All right, lass, all right!" He dragged one hand through his hair and released his breath explosively. "Here it is, then. We have traveled back in time. I'm not sure exactly what year, but I figure it to be around 1733 or 1734."

Silence greeted his words and he steeled himself to face their hysteria. Davey and Ellie stared back at him blankly, then looked at each other and burst into laughter, fair fit to split their sides.

* * *

They didn't laugh for long.

Ellie had been truly terrified twice in her life—twelve years before, when she learned her parents were in the hospital and not expected to live, and a year ago, when Maggie disappeared from the cairn and went missing for a month.

She had supposed that outside of losing someone she loved, nothing could ever make her as frightened again as those two events had. Now, as she sat staring into the fire, she had to reconsider. Ian said they had traveled back in time.

It was laughable. It was insane. It was . . . terrifying.

At first she had argued with Ian, accused him of trying to scare her, but the more he talked, the more she had to believe that either what he was saying was true or that he was crazy. And Ian wasn't crazy. She'd spent the last six months with the man and he was the poster boy for common sense.

When he told her that Maggie had gone missing because she'd accidentally gone back in time, met Quinn, and then returned, suddenly it all made perfect sense. Quinn had definitely been an odd one when they first met him, and now she knew why. Davey had added his scientific approval to the idea of the spirals powering some kind of time vortex. As far as he was concerned, it was entirely logical.

Logical it might be, but that didn't take away the fact that, if what Ian said was true, *they had traveled through time.*

On the other side of the fire, Davey lay snoring, wrapped in Ian's overcoat, since he didn't have one of his own. How could the man sleep if he really believed he had traveled three hundred years into the past? Ellie closed her eyes and then jumped as she felt a hand on her arm.

"I'm sorry," Ian said as he knelt down beside her, a metal cup in his hand. "I dinna mean to startle ye. I grabbed a couple of tea bags and a cup before I came after ye," he said, handing it to her.

She took it without speaking, too numb to talk anymore.

She glanced over and saw the sword Ian had taken from the guard propped at his side.

Who was this man in Ian's skin? This guy who wielded a sword with ease and had survival skills that would rival those of an Eagle Scout? He was certainly not the easygoing, fun-loving, irresponsible musician she had known in the twenty-first century.

"Are ye all right, Ellie?" he asked, easing down beside her, his face bright with the golden light of the fire.

"Maggie," she said faintly.

"Maggie is all right," Ian said. "I promise ye, she is fine."

She shook her head. "No, I mean, I was just remembering, when Maggie was missing, and the first day after she came back, she told us that she had traveled through time. We didn't believe her; we thought she'd lost her mind, and then she laughed and said it was a joke." Ellie lifted her gaze from her lap to Ian. "It wasn't a joke," she whispered. "It's true, but how can it be?" She shook her head.

"I know 'tis hard to accept," he began, then fell silent for a long moment before turning back to her. "Why don't ye try to get some rest? We have a long walk ahead of us tomorrow."

She frowned and then nodded. "Oh, right, right. The cairn."

After making sure she and Davey understood and believed him, which took some time for Ellie, Ian had said he would lead them to the cairn in the morning and somehow—he didn't explain how—help them return to their own time.

As if he had read her mind, Ian spoke. "I will make sure ye get home again, Eleanor."

"You said we would get back through the power of the spirals, and Davey seemed to understand what you meant," she said, "but I don't." She sipped the tea. It was bitter, without sugar, but somehow the taste comforted her. "How could a stone spiral from the Dark Ages send us through time?"

"Och, lass, I wish I knew. All I can tell ye is that it did, and that Maggie was able to return to her own time, and so shall ye."

Ellie lifted the cup to her mouth again, but it trembled so violently in her hand that the hot tea splashed over the edge. She set it down on the stone beside her, knocking it sideways, spilling the precious tea on the ground. Covering her face with both hands, she fought the hysteria welling up inside of her. Ian wouldn't tell her a lie like this. He was too kind, too compassionate. And if it wasn't a lie, that meant it was true. And what Maggie had said was true.

Feeling suddenly claustrophobic, Ellie rose to her feet and stumbled past Ian, out of the cave, into the cold night air, running as fast as she could, tears pouring down her cheeks. Then she was falling, but strong arms caught her, Ian caught her, and pulled her against his broad, warm chest, and she cried; cried out her fear and her panic and the loss of normalcy and perhaps her sanity; cried for long-ago sorrows, her parents' deaths, the loss of innocence when she watched them die; cried for Allie and Maggie and for herself, for their family that had been, and could never be again; cried because she was a fake, a phony, a cardboard image of the person she wanted to be, and she no longer had the strength to maintain the façade.

More than anything, she cried because she wanted to trust Ian and his promise that she would be able to return to her own time, her own world, but she was too afraid.

"Ah, lass, lass," Ian said, when her tears were spent and she was fighting simply to breathe, "dinna make yerself so ill." He tilted her face up to his and Ellie tried to turn away, ashamed to look into his eyes, but he cupped his hands around her face and she had no choice but to face him.

His eyes were midnight in the shadows, and in their depths, instead of pity, she saw understanding. "Eleanor," he said, "I promise I will get ye back to Maggie and Allie. I swear it upon my life."

She let the last tear trickle down her cheek. He brushed it away and his touch was gentle, warm. "Thanks," she whispered. "I'm sorry. I guess there's no coming back from a meltdown like that, is there?"

He looked at her quizzically and she pulled away from

him, stumbling to her feet, clasping her arms around herself so that maybe he wouldn't touch her again. Ian rose slowly beside her.

"Lass, if anyone deserves to have a meltdown, 'tis ye."

Ellie shrugged and laughed, shaking her hair back from her face. "So now you know my secret."

"Secret?"

"Sure. I'm a big fake." A sudden wind swept up from the dark glen below and she shivered. "Not a tough girl, just a frightened little mouse pretending to be a lion, or maybe in my case, a vampire bat."

Ian circled around to stand in front of her. She refused to meet his gaze.

"Ye are more courageous than ye suppose," he said.

She stared at the ground. "I used to be. Not anymore. I've lost any shred of courage I ever had."

"Ellie, look at me." Unwillingly she lifted her head. "Why do ye think such a thing?" he asked, his voice rough with concern. "Ye are a strong woman, but ye've had a shock. No one could fault ye for feeling scared and half-crazy."

She gave him a hesitant smile as the wind made her hair dance around her face. "I was trying to hide the crazy part from you."

Ian grinned and lifted his hand to brush a strand of hair back from her face and then lingered on her shoulder. For a moment their gazes met and she didn't feel awkward or strange or frightened.

"Ye are too hard on yerself," he said. "Remember, I watched ye wrestle club owners and stadium managers down to the mat, always getting the best money and best contract for me and the lads."

Ellie stepped back and his hand fell away, a shadow crossing his face. "That was just a part I played. Like I said, a façade."

"Ye must believe in yerself."

She moved a few steps away, trying to put some distance between them, pausing to look down at the glen that stretched beyond the cave, which was halfway up a mountain. She

hadn't asked how Ian had found the shelter, but he seemed
pretty familiar with the area.

Ellie shook her head. "You sound like a greeting card.
That's just a platitude."

He didn't say anything for a few minutes, and just when
she was sure she had offended him, he spoke up again. "I
like yer hair," he said.

She smiled into the darkness. "Thanks."

"But I miss yer dark side."

Ellie laughed in spite of herself. "My dark side. I like that."
She dragged one hand through her bedraggled hair, tangled
from the wind. "I still don't understand how it changed." She
sighed and took another step closer to the edge of where they
stood. "Not that I understand any of this, least of all the
changes in you."

"Me?" Ian raised both brows. "I havena changed."

Ellie shook her head. "Oh, no, you just started flashing a
sword around, sounding like Mel Gibson's clone, that's all."

In the near distance was a loch, and the moonlight shone
upon the smooth waters so brilliantly that it looked like
black glass. She'd never forget the first time she'd seen one
of the dark lakes of Scotland. Staring down into the inky
depths, she had felt as if she were meeting some strange
natural metaphor of herself.

"I'm just finding it hard to believe all of this," she said.

"Do ye know what I believe?" Ian asked softly, too close
to her again.

"Another platitude?" She smiled to take some of the sting
out of her words. "I warn you, just because I'm having a nervous breakdown, that doesn't mean you can try out Hall-
mark's best on me."

"Perhaps it is a platitude, but it has always held me in
good stead." He frowned thoughtfully. "Everything happens
for a reason."

Sadness attacked her again, a two-fisted grip around her
throat. "My mom used to say that."

Ian turned her toward him, his hands on her shoulders,

his brows knit together. "I'm sorry ye lost yer parents, lass. I lost my mother when I was young, so I know how it hurts."

Ellie gave him a searching look. "I didn't know. I'm sorry, Ian."

He shrugged. "Aye. I miss her, but life goes on."

She frowned. "I don't think mine did. Not really. I was twelve years old when my parents died because some drunk decided to go down the wrong side of the road, and somehow I couldn't go forward. And now I'm stuck in the past," Ellie said, wishing she could laugh at the irony.

"At least ye are alive," he reminded her.

"Alive in the *past*, right when Maggie needs me. And Allie won't remember to pay the rent on our apartment if I'm not there, and Quinn definitely won't remember to pack Maggie's bag for the hospital, and—"

"So everything will fall apart without ye, even though ye've been on tour with me for the last six months?"

Ellie frowned at him. "Hello? Cell phones."

Ian nodded and walked a few feet away from her, his hands thrust into his pockets. "So it is all up to ye."

"Of course not. Don't make it sound so—so—stupid. They're all adults, but feeling so out of touch, so unable—" She broke off, feeling the tears surge up again, and there was no way she was giving in to that another time.

"No, they aren't," Ian said.

"No, they aren't what?"

"They aren't adults."

Ellie rolled her eyes. Great, now he was going to give her some kind of psychobabble about how her sisters were like her children or some such garbage. "What do you mean?"

"Your sisters don't exist yet." He frowned. "I'm not so sure about Quinn."

She whirled around, her mouth open. "What?"

He lifted one shoulder in a half shrug. "Sure. Just think about it. This is the eighteenth century. Allie and Maggie haven't been born yet, so ye don't have to worry about them at all. I mean, it's not like they're hovering out in space somewhere, living their lives as we are living ours here. They don't exist."

Ellie swallowed hard. "Gee, thanks. That makes me feel *so* much better."

"But it doesn't matter," he said. "I will get ye and Davey home again."

"I know you're trying to make me feel better," she said, turning the collar of her jacket up against the brisk breeze. "The problem is, Maggie and Quinn may have traveled back and forth through time, but you're just as new to this as we are, so how can you say with any certainty that we can make it back?"

She took a deep breath and released it slowly, hoping he didn't take offense at her words. It wasn't that she didn't think Ian would do his best to help them, and since he knew of Maggie and Quinn's journey, he definitely was one-up on the whole—suddenly she realized he hadn't answered her.

Ellie turned to find him staring into the distance, a decidedly guilty look on his face. Something was up.

"Wait a minute." She took a step toward him, the cold air stinging her face. "Why are you so calm? Why aren't you more upset about traveling to the past? I mean, now that I think of it, you were really brave to do that, jumping right into some vortex in time."

He dragged one hand through his hair and his jacket fell open, revealing a long-sleeved T-shirt and a worn pair of jeans. Ellie hadn't noticed before what he'd been wearing. Good thing he'd had on the overcoat Alex had lent him, or Ian's brother Angus would have seen his strange clothing and . . .

Ian's brother.

"Good. Freaking. Grief," she said, hitting each word distinctly. Her mouth sagged open. "What is wrong with me? I guess I was just in shock after hearing that we were stuck in the past, but how did I forget that you were talking to *your brother* at that camp?"

He shrugged again and looked up toward the moon. The wind lifted his shaggy blond hair into the air, the moonlight making the lightest hues seem to almost shimmer. But even the amazing way the Scot looked, standing there on the crest of a mountain, his rugged face lit by the moon, his jaw unshaven and solid, couldn't distract Ellie from the truth, which was presently hitting her squarely in the chest.

"You're from this time!" she said, one hand flying up to her throat. "You aren't freaked-out because you've done this before!"

Ian closed his eyes briefly and then walked closer to her, his long-lashed blue eyes steady as he gazed down at her. "Aye, lass, ye are right. I was born in the year 1685."

seven

Ellie couldn't seem to form any words. Ian scrutinized her face for a moment and then went on.

"We came through time with Maggie, Quinn and I both, from the year 1711, to escape being hanged."

"Hanged?" The word was a whisper.

"Aye. Quinn and I were highwaymen, wreaking havoc upon the Duke of Montrose for murdering Quinn's father and brother."

"Oh, sure, of course," she said faintly.

He took another step closer and slipped his arms around Ellie's waist, turning her toward him. "Now ye can believe me, can't ye, lass? I traveled to the future, and now I have traveled once again to my own time. Believe me when I tell ye that ye and Davey will be returned to yers."

"Davey and me," she said, too stunned to even think about the fact that his arms were around her, and not in just a friendly way. "Davey and me," she repeated, knowing there was something there she was missing, something—

She drew in a sharp breath. "You aren't going back with us, are you?"

Ian gazed down into her eyes as if he never wanted to

look away. "No, lass, I am not." Then he sighed and gently released her, pushing her slightly away.

"A year ago, I turned my back on my past and my family, escaping into your time. Now I have returned, and in this world it is twenty-three years later and my brothers have become loyalists, fighting for the English king." He shook his head and looked away. "My father is ill. I canna leave."

Everything he said made perfect sense, in a surreal kind of way, but selfishly, Ellie didn't care. She'd known her love for Ian would always be unrequited, but she'd never dreamed she would someday have to face the fact that she would never see him again. Her heart constricted and without another word, she turned and walked back into the cave and lay down beside the fire again.

On the other side of the cave, Davey shifted in his sleep. "No," he muttered, rolling his head back and forth, "Dr. Einstein, ye had it all wrong. Let me expla—explai—explainnzzz . . ."

The stones under her back were cold and hard, but they were a feather bed compared to the thought of life without Ian. She closed her eyes and for the first time, in a long time, began to pray.

"Good-bye, Ian," Ellie said, clenching her fists at her side. Ian stood across from her and Davey at the opening leading out of the cairn. She wanted to curse, wanted to scream at him to come back with them, and she fought to keep her emotions under control.

He had roused them at daybreak and kept them moving at a fast pace for most of the morning, until they finally reached the cairn. Where they would travel home. Without him.

When Ellie had filled Davey in on the news that Ian was over three hundred years old, he didn't blink an eye. His exact words were, "Cool," and then he and Ian talked about the eighteenth century and how the MacGregors had lost the rights to their names and wearing kilts and such, while Ellie stewed.

Now she and Davey stood in the center of the same spiral that, according to Ian, had sent them back in time, and her heart was beating so hard she thought it might burst out of her skin. She was about to travel through time again. Now *there* was a sentence she never thought she'd utter in her life.

"Good-bye, Ellie," Ian said, his voice echoing against the stones creating the curved ceiling. "I'll ne'er forget ye, lass."

Her lower lip trembled and she sucked in a quick, steadying breath. "Any message for Quinn or Maggie?" she asked, willing her voice not to quaver.

"Give them my love and thanks," he said, "for all they've done for me."

"Right," Ellie said, anger making her sarcastic, "that will take care of everything. I'm sure Maggie and Quinn won't expect anything more. Oh, weren't you supposed to be their baby's godfather? Oh, well, no big deal."

Ian's eyes were shadowed by sadness. "Quinn will understand. And I will still be the bairn's godfather, in my heart."

"A fat lot of good that will do!" Ellie cried, then her next words tumbled out of her mouth without warning. "Come back with us, Ian! You don't belong here!"

He shook his head, his blond hair brushing his shoulders with the movement, his blue eyes unwavering. "I canna do it, lass. My brothers are following the wrong master, and I must set them right again."

"So it's all up to you, huh?" Ellie demanded, throwing his own words back in his face. An amused smile curved his lips.

"Aye, lass, I suppose it is." His blue eyes twinkled. "No cell phone here."

The blood rushed to Ellie's face. He was laughing— *laughing* about leaving her forever! But why not? She had no claim on him. She was nothing more than Maggie's sister. Davey put a restraining hand on her arm as she took a step forward. "Don't you even care that you'll never see your best friend again?" she demanded. "Or Maggie? Or their baby?" *Or me?* she added silently.

The stalwart expression on his face faltered and his gaze was suddenly filled with regret, as if he knew what she wasn't saying aloud. "I'll miss ye, Ellie."

Ellie felt the pain hit her, the same way it had so many years before when she'd lost her parents. All at once she realized that when she reached the future, Ian MacGregor would have been dead for almost three hundred years. She swallowed hard. It was getting difficult to breathe.

"Apparently not enough." She turned toward Davey. "Let's go," she whispered, "before I lose my nerve."

"Aye," Davey agreed. "I must confess that while from a scientist's point of view this is verra exciting, I am no' looking forward to the journey again."

"Good-bye, Davey," Ian said. "Have a good life." His voice softened. "Good-bye, Ellie."

Ellie felt the warmth leave her heart, perhaps her soul, as she and Davey began walking around the spiral toward the center, as she cast about in her mind for something—*anything* that might convince Ian to go with them. She walked in front, with Davey close behind, repeating the words Ian had remembered and made them memorize.

"Follow forward, follow back, ages lost, ages found," they said in unison.

Ellie felt a kind of panic begin as she took one hesitant step after another around the spiral. When they reached the apex of the giant carving, she glanced up quickly at Ian, wanting to see his face one last time before they disappeared into the twenty-first century. She steeled herself for the strange sensation she'd had before, waited for the whirling vortex to sweep them into its maelstrom.

Nothing happened.

"Are we there yet?" Davey asked. Ellie turned to find him standing beside her with his eyes squeezed shut. She could feel him trembling.

"No," she said, surprised to find she felt like she'd been given a reprieve. "We aren't. It didn't work."

Davey's eyes shot open. "Didn't work?" He reached into his back pocket and pulled out a small notebook and pencil, then made a notation in it. "The first of my hypotheses has been proven true," he said with satisfaction. He replaced his notebook and took out a calculator, tapping frantically upon it for several minutes before nodding to himself, and then putting it back in his pocket as well.

"Hypothesis?" Ellie asked.

"Hypotheses, as in more than one."

Ian crossed the round chamber to stand beside them. Was that relief Ellie saw on his face, or was that just wishful thinking on his part?

"I dinna understand," he said. "Why didn't it work?"

Davey adjusted his glasses and spoke eagerly. "My research on the carving had nothing to do with time travel, you understand, but it did yield some information that we might find useful. Ever since you told us our situation, I've been formulating several possible scenarios that may affect our attempts to return home."

"And you waited until now to tell us?" Ellie said, giving vent to her exasperation so that the pure joy she felt over still being with Ian wouldn't be so obvious.

Ian frowned at Davey. "Such as?"

He smiled, so obviously happy to be asked that Ellie almost forgave him for keeping important information to himself. He couldn't help it. He was a geek.

"One hypothesis," he said, "is that there is no guarantee that anyone who travels through time by using the spirals will be able use them in the same way to return to their own time."

Ellie stared at the grinning man, her heart beginning to race. "You mean, not ever?"

Davey frowned and glanced down at his notebook, turning a few pages as he did. "Aye, that is one hypothesis. Another is that there are factors at work in the actual shifting of the space-time continuum of which we are unaware, but if they are known, travel to a particular time period is assured." He tapped his chin with his pencil. "I will have to go over my notes."

"But they're back in—in our time," Ellie said.

He shook his head. "Not those notes." He tapped the side of his head with one finger. "These."

Not return home. Ellie felt the panic flood through her body with the strength of a hurricane. *Not return home.* "But Maggie and Quinn were able to return!" she blurted.

"Aye, but they dinna journey to this time in history." Davey wrote something else in the notebook and then snapped it shut and shoved it and the pencil into his back pocket again. "Quinn and Maggie went back to the year 1711. This is not the year 1711."

"How do you know that?" Ellie asked. "Those guys sure looked like eighteenth-century Scots to me."

"Aye," Ian said, "they were. But not from the year Quinn and I left. Not 1711. My brother said that he hadn't seen me in twenty-three years."

Davey tilted his head toward the ceiling of the cairn and then down toward the spirals, apparently working out something only he was privy to. Ellie frowned at his complacency.

"So it's 1734 instead of 1711. So what?" Ellie said. "What difference does that make?"

Davey turned and gave her an even wider grin, spreading his hands apart in apparent ecstasy. "None! Isn't that fascinating?"

Ellie whirled away from the man and stumbled toward the opening of the cairn, needing to get out of the enclosure and into the sunlight. She needed to breathe. Ducking under the low entry, she ran to the edge of the hill and stood dragging in deep, ragged breaths as she hugged herself tightly.

Not to return to Maggie and Allie. Never to see her sisters again, or hold Maggie's newborn baby in her arms.

But wait. Maggie and Allie and the baby didn't exist. Not yet. *She* didn't even exist. It was like she was a—a—hidden file on a computer. If you didn't know it was there, it didn't really exist. It was the old "If a tree falls in the forest with no one to hear it, does it still make a sound?"

A new thought flashed through her mind. Her parents hadn't been born yet either. Her parents had never been

killed in a car wreck by a drunk driver. Allie and Ellie and
Maggie hadn't grown up fatherless and motherless.

Slowly, very slowly, a smile spread across her lips as a
sensation like bright, cold water dancing through her veins.
Ever since her parents' death she'd been trapped by fear—
fear of dying, fear of someone else dying, fear of losing anyone close to her, fear of the unexpected. Now the most
unexpected, most fearful thing in the world had happened to
her, and she suddenly felt . . . free.

Ellie took a trembling breath, laughter bubbling close to
the surface, when all at once she was in Ian's arms and he
was holding her, his warmth sure and solid and all she
needed.

"Dinna panic," he murmured against her ear. "I will get
ye home again."

Home. How could he take her home, when home was
suddenly right there in his arms? She wanted to stay entwined in them forever. He slid his fingers gently up the side
of her face and into her hair, tilting her head back, forcing
her to look at him. His lips were so close she could have risen
up on her toes and touched them with her own. He stroked
her cheek with his thumb and his sky blue eyes glimmered
with compassion.

"I promise ye, lass, I'll get ye home to Maggie and Allie
again."

Ellie continued to gaze into his eyes, caught by the tim-
bre of his voice and the touch of his hand, until his words
finally sank in. She smiled at him, realizing it was probably
the first real, honest-to-goodness smile she'd ever given him.

"It's okay," she said. "I don't want to go home."

Ian blinked. "Ye don't?"

"I mean, maybe someday, when you want to go, too, but
right now I'm perfectly happy here."

He frowned down at her. "What did I miss?"

"Nothing! I just decided that you're right. Everything
happens for a reason, and guess what? I don't even exist!"

She danced away from him, lifting her arms into the

air and spinning around until she felt giddy and dizzy. Ian rushed to her side and caught her, and she laughed, no longer on the edge of hysteria, just happy to be alive. How long had it been since she had really been alive?

"Ellie, darlin'—Eleanor—" he said, correcting himself. Ellie pulled herself up straight and saluted.

"From now on, sergeant, you are allowed to call me darlin'. The more the merrier!"

"No one told me there was whiskey," Davey said from behind her.

"No whiskey," Ellie said, whirling around playfully. "Just high on life! Except I'm not alive! Go figure!"

Ian and Davey exchanged glances and Ellie made a pouty face at the two of them. "Ah, come on, guys, can't you get into the moment? This is a good thing! I'm free!"

Exuberant, she danced back and forth in front of the cairn, until Ian suddenly picked her up in his arms and carried her back inside.

"Hey!" she cried, folding her arms over her chest. Just when she was finally breaking loose, somebody had to rain on her parade.

"Sorry, lass," Ian said, shooting Davey a look that she didn't understand. "But my brother may realize at any time that I'm not a ghost. He could be scouring the countryside for me. We're too vulnerable here. Besides that, we need food and sleep. I need ye to stay inside with Davey until I come back for ye."

"Where are we going, Ian?" Davey asked.

Ian dragged one hand through his thick hair. "We're going to Drymen, to the Clachan Inn. Once there, we'll figure out what to do next."

Ellie spun around in a circle, laughing, and then sat down in the dirt abruptly, feeling dazed and suddenly a little ill. "I think I need to lie down for a few minutes," she said, and with that she stretched out on the ground and closed her eyes. As she drifted off to sleep, she could hear Ian and Davey arguing.

"Ye aren't going to leave me here alone with her, are ye?" Davey was saying, his voice filled with panic. What was his problem?

Then Ian spoke, sounding apologetic. "Sorry, lad, just keep her inside the cairn. I'll be back with a horse or mule or *something* for us to use for transportation as soon as I can!"

"Great," Davey said.

Ellie opened one eye and peered at him. He sat a few feet away from her, cross-legged, his arms folded over his chest, his face twisted into an uncharacteristic scowl. Her stomach rumbled and Ellie gave the scientist what she hoped was a captivating smile, and batted her eyelashes.

"Got any more granola bars?" she asked.

Davey held the reins of the small, shaggy pony and led it as he trudged behind Ian across the meadow thick with grass. Winter was coming, and a fine mist covered them, making it hard to navigate as the sun dipped lower in the sky. A loud snore from the direction of the horse made the scientist stop and make sure Ellie was all right.

Sagged across the saddle, she had been sound asleep for a couple of hours after three hours of nonstop talking, dancing, and laughing. He'd never seen it, but he'd studied how people faced with traumatic situations stayed sane by finding an overly idealistic view that sent their adrenal glands into overdrive. Now she was sleeping like the dead, her snores getting louder with every mile they walked.

As for himself, he was having a grand time. Since he'd long ago resigned himself to the fact that one day one of his wild experiments would likely kill him, he had nothing to fear, and as a scientist, everything to gain.

He was still in awe of what had happened. He had traveled through time. Amazing! When he thought about what that could mean—what power might be harnessed from the spirals! Why, it could mean the end of the world's dependence on oil!

"Well, at least now ye know that she snores," Davey

said, diverting his attention back to Ian, walking in front of him.

The Scot had been fairly quiet as they headed toward Drymen and the Clachan Inn. He glanced back over one shoulder and grinned.

"Aye. And that she can dance!" He rubbed the back of his neck with one hand. "Now that's something I would have never guessed."

"Well, now when the two of ye get married, ye'll know what ye are in for, both in and out of bed, eh?"

Ian slowed and waited for Davey and his burden to draw alongside. "What?"

Davey gave him an innocent smile. "Ye and Ellie. When ye return to our time and get married. Now ye'll know that she snores. Personally, I wouldn't kick her out of bed for it."

Ian frowned at him and started walking again. Davey hurried to keep up.

"What makes ye think that Ellie and I are getting married? I barely know the lass."

"Barely know her? Ye traveled with her for six months!"

"Aye," Ian acknowledged, "but we dinna spend much time alone." He shook his head and smiled. "Unfortunately for me."

Davey glanced at the still-sleeping Ellie and decided that things were too uncertain to waste on taking the tactful approach. The lass would thank him later.

"Surely ye must know the girl has feelings for ye," he said.

Ian lapsed into silence again, his brows pressed together. "Ian?"

"Och, Allie told me some nonsense about Ellie liking me. And I willna deny that I am attracted to the lass, but it doesna matter. Not now." He cleared his throat. "It won't be long now 'til we reach Drymen."

"Why not?"

"Why not what?"

"Why doesn't it matter now?" Davey insisted.

Ian stopped walking and lifted one hand to shield his eyes from the sun, setting over not-so-distant mountains.

Pointing to a trail just ahead of them, he seemed determined to change the subject.

"This road will take us to the inn. Come on, then; 'tis just a wee bit farther."

"This is not a road," Davey said. "This is a rut, and how much farther is 'a wee bit'?"

Ian shrugged. "Five to ten miles."

"Right. So why not now?" If he was going to have to walk another ten miles, Ian was going to have to make it interesting. The two men walked together in silence for a few minutes as the pony trailed behind with Ellie.

"Ye have a one-track mind," Ian finally said, his voice grim.

"Aye. So why not now?"

"Bloody hell!" Ian whirled on the man and Davey held up one hand, pointing at Ellie with the other. She wiggled in the saddle, obviously trying to find a more comfortable spot, yawned, then settled back into sleep. Ian started walking again and Davey followed.

"So why not—"

Ian cut him off with an oath and a glare. "Not now because I am not going back to the twenty-first century! There, are ye satisfied?"

Davey shook his head, half running now to keep up. "Not even a wee bit. I understand that ye need to help yer family into doing things yer way, but why can't ye return to our time afterward?"

"Because I'm the eldest son. My father is ill and when he dies—" He broke off.

"Ah," Davey said, the pieces of the puzzle coming suddenly together. "When yer father dies, as the eldest, ye will inherit all of his estates."

Ian nodded. "Aye. But dinna be thinking that I want it for myself. My father owns a wealth of land and is powerful in the Highlands. If he were to throw his support behind the Jacobites, it could change the outcome of Scottish history!"

He trudged on, his jaw set, a gleam in his eye that was disturbing. Davey pulled on the horse's reins to make him walk faster. "And that is what ye want to do—change history?"

Ian frowned down at him, hesitation in his eyes. "Aye. I know enough about what happens in the future to know that there are bad times coming for the Scottish people, especially those who dinna back the king."

"And ye think ye can change that?"

He nodded, his fists clenched at his sides. "Aye."

This could mean real trouble. If Ian was able to exact a change in Scottish history on a mathematical level equal to or beyond that of any other major event in Scottish history— he retrieved his little notebook and pencil from his pocket and looped the reins over his arm as he scribbled down an equation. After a moment, he pulled his horse to a stop and took out his calculator.

"Take away three, add the decimal, divide by the hypotenuse of the second set—"

"What are ye mumbling about?" Ian said, sounding cranky. He released his breath in irritation and put his hands on his hips. "What's wrong?"

The scientist looked up from his calculations, feeling a little nauseated. "Everything," he said. "If ye do what ye're planning, ye could cause an event that could destroy the world as we know it!"

Ian gazed at him, his blue eyes suddenly hard, unyielding. "Yer world or mine?"

eight

The Clachan Inn looked very nearly as it had in the twenty-first century—whitewashed stone walls, black roof, shuttered windows—but newer. As Davey led the pony past the sign on the front of the building, Ellie saw the words, Licensed 1734.

They came to a stop at the rear of the building, and feeling a little dizzy, Ellie slid off the back of the horse and yawned. Her jacket was tied to the back of the saddle. Funny, she didn't remember doing that, but it was awfully warm for a change.

Ian tied the pony to the ring on a post near a set of stairs and nodded to her. "Stay here," he cautioned, "and I'll see about getting us a room for the night."

Yawning again, she closed her eyes and stretched her arms above her head, aching in every bone in her body. "Oh, wow, that would be so wonderful," she moaned. "A bed. *Yum*. A real bed."

She opened her eyes to find Ian and Davey staring at her, the younger man's mouth hanging open.

"I'll—just—see—if—the horse—wants—anything," the scientist said, gesturing toward the pony as he began to sidestep past Ian, his eyes still fixed on Ellie. Ian thumped him in the head as he walked by and Davey ran the last few steps, no longer looking her way.

"Dinna do that," Ian said, his lips curving up in a rakish smile as he took a step closer to her. He brushed a lock of her hair back from her face. "We are only human, ye ken?"

"Dinna do what?" she asked. Now what had she done wrong?

Ian blinked and then shook his head. "Never mind. I'll be back in a minute. Stay here."

"Anyone ever tell you that you're really bossy?" she asked, and then yawned.

"And dinna start acting like ye did before, spinning and laughing and such," Ian said. He gave her a bemused smile. "Not that I don't appreciate certain aspects of yer, er, new outlook on life."

Ellie stared after him as he headed up a steep flight of stairs attached to the back of the building. What was he talking about? Her new outlook on life? She yawned again, feeling so, so groggy. Like she had a hangover or . . . something. Her eyes sprang fully open as the memory of her epiphany on life came back with ramming force.

"Oh, shoot," she muttered. What had happened to her? Even now she felt different somehow. More relaxed. Less afraid. Lingering euphoria, as if she had just had really great sex. Or at least how she imagined she would feel, since she'd never had any great sex.

She waited for guilt, embarrassment, and shame to tromp up the stairs to her brain and invade whatever lobe regulated emotions, but the three were no-shows. Nothing. No remorse, no feelings of humiliation, just a slight buzz, like she had imbibed of some particularly fine champagne.

Huh. Well, what do you know about that? Who knew discovering that you didn't exist anymore could be so liberating? She crossed over to Davey, who gave her a nervous glance.

"How is Ian going to pay for the room?" she asked, wondering what was wrong with him.

"Uh, with a silver coin he carries for luck, he said."
Davey turned his attention back to the pony.

"Lucky for us," she said, smiling. Gee, she just felt like
she couldn't *stop* smiling. "Are we going to flip for the bed
or what?" The thought of sharing a bed with Ian brought the
euphoria back, and Ellie tamped down on her urge to start
spinning around again.

At the word *bed*, Davey's face turned scarlet. "Oh, well, I
think, that is, I'm sure, that Ian and I will let ye have the bed
and we'll sleep on the floor."

Ellie frowned and peered closer at him. He kept his eyes
fixed on the mane of the horse. "You okay?"

He glanced over at her and smiled, shakily. "Oh, sure,
sure, fine, fine."

Ellie closed her eyes as a wave of dizziness swept over
her again. She opened them again and Ian was standing in
front of her.

"Wow. How did you do that?" she asked, swaying a little.
"You're, like, the fast guy, the speedy cartoon guy." She
frowned. "What's his name?

"Speed Racer?" Davey said.

She shook her head. "No, the other speedy guy, the one
who wears red."

"The Flash?"

She snapped her fingers and swayed toward Ian again.
"That's the one. The Flashy Flash man." She poked Ian in
the chest. "You are just like him, only much, much cuter."

Ian drew in a sharp breath, and Ellie wondered what was
wrong with his eyes. They were very hot. Sparkly. Intense.

"Let's get ye upstairs, lass," he said softly.

"Wait, I want to say something." What did she want to
say? *Oh, yeah.* "I'm sorry if I acted kind of—weird before.
I'm not sure what's wrong with me."

"Do ye feel ill?" Ian asked.

Ellie draped her arms around his neck and leaned
against him. "I feel . . . wonderful," she said, and promptly
passed out.

When she awoke, probably much, much later, from the

way she felt, she could hear the two men talking. They were in another room that opened onto the one she was in. A further peek showed her she was lying on a bed, on top of the covers. Yawning, she stripped off her clothes, leaving only her bra and panties on, and tugged on the thin blanket and sheet, too tired to care if they were dirty or not.

"What do ye think is wrong with her?" Ian was saying, his low voice making a soothing rumble. Ellie snuggled down under the covers and smiled. There must be a Mrs. Innkeeper, because there was a faint, sweet smell to the sheets.

"I'm not sure. At first I thought it was just her way of coping with the realization we may never get back home again, but now I'm not so sure." Davey sounded very, very serious. Ellie yawned. He needed to lighten up.

"Could it have something to do with the time travel?"

"Possibly," the scientist agreed. "Did Maggie or Quinn mention anything like this happening to them?"

"No."

There were a few minutes of silence and Ellie almost fell back asleep, then Ian's voice jarred her awake.

"It may be my fault."

"Why would ye think that?"

Ian coughed. "Ellie was very upset, about being stuck in the past. She was worried about her sisters and Maggie's baby. Ye see, ever since her parents died, she has lived in fear of losing anyone else that she loves."

"So what did ye say?"

Another silence. Another cough. "I, er, told her that Maggie and Allie hadn't even been born yet, that they didn't even exist. So she didn't have to worry about them."

"Uh-oh."

Ellie frowned. What "uh-oh"? It was the most amazing thing that had ever happened to her. She was free, now, free of worry and fear and doubt.

"What do ye mean, 'uh-oh'?" Ian asked, sounding worried. Ellie smiled and closed her eyes. *Don't worry, be happy,* she thought.

"Well, the trip through time, coupled with Ellie's already

fragile id and yer suggestion, could have caused her to have some kind of identity breakdown, ye ken, to sort of, disassociate from her normal personality and create this new one."

Gee, Davey sounded really worried again. She needed to tell him that she had never really had a *normal* personality, so the loss of the old Ellie was not really a loss at all. Maybe another rumba lesson would help him have a better attitude toward life.

"So what do we do about it?"

Ian sounded worried, too. Now, goshdarnit, those guys weren't going to spoil her good time. She was going to have to straighten them out. She yawned. *Tomorrow. Definitely tomorrow.*

The men's voices faded to a comfortable rumble, and then there was the sound of another voice, graveled and uncouth.

"Ye are responsible for any damages," the gruff voice said. "And I dinna tolerate noise or drunkenness."

"All we want is a good night's sleep," Ian said, "and yer discretion. I need to send a message in the morning. Do ye have a lad that can be trusted to take a wee ride for me?" There was the sound of coins chinking together and Ellie wondered sleepily if Ian had gotten change from his lucky coin.

"Aye," Gravel Voice said. "I'll send him up before breakfast, which is served at half past six and only for half an hour."

Ellie drifted off to sleep wondering if there was such a thing as room service in the eighteenth century. She was dreaming about pancakes, when the bed dipped down with the weight of someone sitting beside her. She opened her eyes and smiled to find Ian gazing down at her.

"Hello, love," she whispered, sliding her arms up around his neck. "Coming to bed?"

"Davey and I are sleeping on the floor. He's gone down to check on the pony." He smiled. "I think he's getting attached to her."

Someone had lit a candle on the rickety table next to the

bed, the flame soft and luminous, painting Ian's face with a golden light.

"And I think," he said, "that I'm getting attached to ye, Eleanor."

Her smile widened. "Are you comparing me to a pony?"

He ducked his head and laughed, then leaned down and brushed his lips against hers. "Good night, Eleanor," he whispered, "sweet dreams." He pulled away, but she drew him back down, suddenly longing to be held.

"Don't go," she said. "Stay with me."

Ian hesitated, then he kissed her again, and she arched against him, loving him so much she ached with it. His arms tightened around her as he deepened the kiss, his hands sliding beneath her, lifting her against him and then gently laying her back on the bed. She trembled in his arms as he lay down beside her, turning her toward him, making her gasp at the hard length of his body touching hers.

He drew back from her and smiled at the sight of her low-cut, pale pink bra. "This isn't black," he whispered, stroking his fingers lightly between the full, curved flesh, then leaning down to kiss the spot where they met, plump and full. Ellie gazed at him, overcome with her need to touch and be touched.

"Make love to me, Ian," she whispered.

He lifted his head and closed his eyes, the yearning on his face unable to mistake. Ellie felt giddy, light-headed with power, then he straightened, easing away from her.

"Davey will be back any minute," he said softly.

"Send him back to his horse," she said, reaching for him again.

Ian caught her hands in his and kissed each one before shaking his head.

"That isn't the only reason that I canna make love to ye, lass." His eyes were hot as they stroked over her, over the soft curves she had offered him, over her mouth, her eyes, her hair, until finally he rose from the bed, dragging one hand through his own hair, rumpled and sexy and everything she'd ever wanted. He blinked and then shook his head, like a man who had been under a spell for a moment, but who, just in time, had pulled himself free. Ellie felt an ache in her heart, and her head spun with his rejection.

"I'm sorry," he said. "None of this should have happened at all."

"I thought you liked me," she whispered, pulling the sheet up around her, feeling suddenly exposed, naked. "I thought you cared, that you—" She looked away.

Ian slid one knee across the bed and pulled her back to face him, his gaze soft with regret. "Och, I do care, lass, more than ye know. That's why I can't make love to ye tonight. Ye are not yerself, Ellie darlin'," he said. "Ye have had a terrible shock, and I willna take advantage of ye."

He leaned forward and kissed her on the forehead. She closed her eyes beneath his touch as he lingered there, his mouth against her skin. Then he sighed and kissed her on the cheek. "Go to sleep," he said, his breath soft against her ear. "There will be another time, a right time, for ye and I."

Then he was gone. Moving like a shadow across the room and out the door. Ellie sat stunned for a moment, then lay back down, staring into the darkness. A few minutes later someone knocked on the door and it opened. Davey stuck his head inside.

"Ellie? Ian said to tell ye we're sleepin' in the stables, so ye can have the room all to yerself. Good night, lass." He closed the door softly.

"All to myself," Ellie said aloud, and flung one arm over her head, against her pillow. Then she smiled. He had said there would be another time, and one thing she was beginning to learn about Ian MacGregor—he tended to keep his promises.

She turned over on her side, planning a way to make him realize that while it was true she wasn't herself, that wasn't necessarily a bad thing.

Ellie awoke the next morning and wondered where she had slept. She rose up on one elbow and looked around, her memory slowly seeping through the fog around her brain. The whitewashed room was about twelve feet wide and fourteen feet long, with a high ceiling and a floor made from wide weather-beaten boards. One tiny window above the bed let in a modicum of sunlight, and a few stray sunbeams danced across a rickety wardrobe, two chairs with peeling paint, and a wooden pedestal holding a huge bowl and pitcher.

She glanced around at the headboard of the double bed in which she'd slept, a ramshackle affair, unpainted, the original shabby chic. The bedspread was gray and dismal, and she decided not to look at the sheets now that it was daylight. All in all, the bed felt as if it might fall apart at any minute, and so it was probably a good thing she and Ian hadn't started bouncing on it.

She closed her eyes and groaned aloud. Had she really asked Ian to make love to her last night?

"Oh, no," she said with a groan, dragging herself to a sitting position, one hand to her head. The room spun and she closed her eyes, wondering what in the name of Timothy Leary had happened to her.

The door opened, and Davey stuck his head in cautiously. "Ye decent?" he asked.

She pulled the sheet up over her near-nakedness. "That's a matter of opinion," she said. "Come on in." His arms were full of what looked like clothing, and he pushed the door closed with one foot. "My, you're looking very swashbuckle-y today."

He wore dark trousers that looked like loose leggings, a long wheat-colored shirt belted with a wide piece of leather at the waist, and roughed-out boots that came to his knees.

"Ian thought we should dress more inconspicuously," he said. He put the pile of clothing at the end of the bed. "Here are some things for ye to try on. How are ye feeling?"

"Kind of weird," she said, frowning. If the things she remembered were just a dream and she asked Davey about them, he'd know how she felt about Ian. She hesitated, and then sighed. If she'd really been acting like an idiot, she needed to know.

"Uh, hey—did I really do all the things I remember doing? Spinning around? Laughing like an idiot? Kissing—" She broke off, warmth rushing to her cheeks.

Davey gave her a sympathetic look. "Aye."

Ellie groaned. *Great. I have an epiphany about my life and right off the bat I make a complete fool of myself. Good start, Ellie.*

"Close your eyes," she ordered. He obeyed and she quickly rummaged through the clothes, finding a cream-colored blouse and a dark brown skirt, faintly musty smelling. She pulled them on. The skirt fit her perfectly, but the blouse was too big, peasant style, and hung like a sack.

Remembering pictures she'd seen in Maggie's history books, Ellie looked through the clothes again, suspecting there was something more to the outfit. She found the olive green checked vest and slipped it on. It laced up the front and tamed the blouse. She slid her hand over her now-trim waist, feeling decidedly feminine.

"Can I open my eyes yet?"

"Oops, sorry. I'm decent."

Davey opened his eyes and smiled at her. "Lass, ye look so cute."

Ellie laughed. "I never thought I'd live to hear that word used to describe me. I am not cute."

"Aye," a deep voice said from the doorway, "ye are." Ian stood there, his gaze traveling over her, his smile reminding her of what a fool she had made of herself the night before.

However, in the vast scheme of things, what difference did it make? Amazing how traveling through time could give a person a different perspective. She smiled back at him.

"I need to apologize to both of you. I don't know what got into me yesterday, but I'm better today."

The two men relaxed visibly. "We were worried about ye," Davey said. "And by the way, ye snore."

Ellie's face grew warm, but for some reason his teasing didn't bring any of her old insecurities to the surface. "How would *you* know?" she shot back at him. "*Your* snoring would put bagpipes to shame."

"So ye feel better now?" Ian asked, shoving the scientist gently to one side and then draping his arm around Ellie's shoulders. She leaned into his embrace, just a little, and nodded.

She moved away from Ian and spun around, the skirt she wore billowing out around her. "Can you believe I'm wearing something so feminine?"

Ian's blue eyes suddenly quickened and Ellie suddenly remembered he had seen intimate evidence of her femininity the night before.

"Och, I have a suspicion there was always a secret femininity under those black clothes," he said soberly. The tension between them hovered in the air and Ellie wished he would put his arm around her again. Or kiss her. Or ask her to lie down and take off her clothes.

"Oh-kay," Davey said, clapping his hands together, breaking the silence. "Breakfast is ready downstairs and I dinna think they are going to wait for us. Shall we?"

Ellie pulled on her Doc Martens and they headed downstairs. The open room below apparently served as a dining hall in the daytime, as well as a pub at night. The walls were covered with dark wood, giving the place a dank, depressing ambiance. Not that the patrons were the type to worry about ambiance.

She glanced around at the few people sitting around the rough-hewn tables scattered around the large, open room. Most were large, gimlet-eyed men with beards, all concentrating on their breakfast and their ale, not necessarily in that order.

Bowls sat atop each table, along with a large plate of bread and mugs filled with foaming drink. Davey took his place at one of the tables and stared down into the wooden bowl. He looked up when she reached him, and pointed at the lumpy gray mixture.

"Porridge," he said mournfully.

"Stop yer whining," Ian ordered, smiling as he dug into his own lumpy mound with a wooden spoon. Ellie stood hesitant beside him. He glanced up and scooted over. "Sit down, love, and eat. It looks worse than it tastes. In fact, it doesn't have much of a taste."

"Don't listen to him," Davey said through a mouthful of porridge. "This stuff is bloody awful."

Ian laughed and winked at her, reaching up to tug her down beside him. Ellie took a tentative bite of the porridge and found Ian was closer on the taste. It was sort of like ground-up cardboard. She was thinking longingly of the granola bars they'd polished off the night before, when Ian took his last bite and put his arm around her, speaking low. "I've got a meeting." He nodded toward the doorway.

A heavyset man sat at a table near the door. There was so little light in the place it was hard to make out anything about him, save that he had a bushy beard.

Ian kissed her lightly. "I'll be back. Dinna go anywhere without me, and try not to draw attention to yerself." He stood and his gaze swept over her, and she was suddenly reminded of the low-cut blouse she wore. There were definitely drawbacks to wearing a dress. Was she going to blush every time a man looked at her?

No, she thought, a little thrill running through her veins, *just Ian.*

"Och," he said, "what am I saying?" He glanced around and Ellie followed his gaze. "All ye have to do is breathe to draw the eye of every man in the place."

Several men were, indeed, staring at her, lechery in their eyes. Ian's smile disappeared and he leaned over the table, startling Davey, who had been lost in some scientific thought, no doubt.

"Davey, lad, when ye finish eating, take Ellie upstairs and lock the door."

Ellie bristled "I'm not a child," she said. "I can take myself upstairs."

Ian didn't answer, but continued to stare at Davey. "Lad?"

Davey pushed his bowl away. "Aye, aye. I'm ready now. Are ye ready, Ellie?"

Fuming, she nodded, and without another word to Ian,

followed Davey across the room. Once there, she glanced back. Someone opened the door to the inn and light poured inside, giving her a better view of Ian's mysterious stranger. He had a full, florid face, gray hair and beard, and sad eyes. But when Ian stopped at the table, the man looked up and his eyes filled first with disbelief, then a wonderful joy.

He practically lunged for Ian, sweeping him into his arms and pounding him on the back. Ellie saw the man's face over Ian's shoulder, tears on his cheeks, his broad mouth split with laughter. Warmth flooded through her and her irritation at Ian disappeared.

Was this another brother? A lost uncle? In any case, it was someone who loved Ian and had missed him very much. A shadow crossed her thoughts. If Ian stayed in the past and she and Davey found a way, somehow, to return to their own time, she would be the one missing Ian, forever.

She shook the thought away, forcing herself to focus only on the here and now. But as she followed Davey up the stairs, the first prickling of doubt had begun.

nine

"Ye're alive," Bittie muttered, as he held Ian in a fierce bear hug.

"Aye, old friend," Ian said, touched by his demonstrative greeting. "I'm alive."

The beefy man shook with his tears and Ian felt a sudden shame wash over him. He and Quinn had made their escape from the Duke of Montrose's dungeon by taking herbs that made their bodies simulate death. Those who had aided them had been sworn to secrecy, but they'd dared not take Bittie into their confidence.

He wasn't a stupid man, but if he had a drink or two, he was known to talk a little too much. Ian stepped back and extricated himself from the bigger man's grasp.

"I'm sorry," he said sincerely as he clapped Bittie on the shoulder. "Let's sit down. 'Tis been a long time."

Bittie obediently sank back onto the bench and stared at the pewter mug sitting on the table in front of him. He shook his head, his gaze dumbfounded. "A long time? Aye, it's been nigh onto twenty-three years since last I saw ye! When I got yer message this morn, ye could have knocked me down with a feather!"

Ian shook his head, guilt heavy on his heart. "I thought ye would know by now, that Rob would have told ye."

"Och, he tried to tell me that ye had feigned yer own deaths, but I couldna believe it!" He shook his head, looking puzzled. "I saw ye dead, cold and dead, with me own eyes. If ye had planned such a thing, ye would have told me."

"Bittie," Ian said, "ye know that we would have told ye of our plan, but we dinna want to place ye in danger. I never thought ye would go all these years thinking we were dead." He shook his head. "I am so sorry."

Bittie's perplexed look disappeared and his broad, bearded face broke into another beatific smile. "Well, 'tis what I get for doubting Rob Roy MacGregor, eh? And I should have known ye dinna tell me because ye feared for my safety." He chuckled. "Ye and Quinn always did look out for me." He took a deep drink of his ale and then leaned forward.

"And Quinn? He's alive? And sweet Maggie?"

Ian nodded again. "Aye. They married and Maggie is expecting their first child."

Bittie sat back in his chair and for the first time since seeing Ian, appeared to relax. "Och, I'm that glad to hear of it. Are they in Scotland?"

Ian hesitated. "Aye. But I canna tell ye where. 'Tis their request." *Another lie.*

Bittie's amber eyes swept over his friend as if to assure himself again that he was real, and then he frowned. Suddenly Ian remembered that his looks had not changed since last the man had last seen him. In the year 2009 it had only been a year since Ian left the Highlands. In 1734, it had been twenty-three.

"Yer family always did wear their age well," he said at last, and Ian released his pent-up breath. "Ye look the same as when I last saw ye."

"My brother thinks I'm a ghost," Ian said, and laughed halfheartedly. "I was afraid ye might think the same."

"Yer brother?" His smile faltered. "Which one?"

"Angus."

"Och, so ye know, then, about him joining the Black Watch?"

"The *Black* Watch?" Ian frowned. "Angus told me 'twas called the *Highland* Watch."

Bittie scowled. "Aye, 'tis what those who run with the enforcers of King George's wrath call themselves, but to us they are the Black Watch, for the dark plaids they wear that enable them to skulk about in the darkness, and for the soulless acts of mayhem and treachery that are part and parcel of who they are."

He shrugged. "They've taken over, pure and simple. They're in league with the devil."

"King George," Ian said softly. "How did it begin?"

"It started in '24. Ol' George the first sent an Irishman, General Wade, into the Highlands to build roads."

"Roads?" Ian frowned. "I dinna suppose that was to aid the Scottish people."

Bittie laughed, a short, harsh bark. "Nay, was to make it easier to bring English troops into the Highlands in case there was another uprising, like the Battle of Sheriffmuir."

"A Jacobite uprising?" Ian asked. Bittie gave him a strange look, and Ian remembered that even in France, the news of such a monumental event would have been common knowledge. He hurriedly spoke to cover up his mistake. "Aye, 'twas a sad day for the rebels."

In truth, he had no idea what the man was talking about and Ian silently cursed himself for never being willing to listen to Quinn tell him of how Scotland had fared since they'd been gone. After arriving in the twenty-first century, his friend had immersed himself in Scottish history and was quite knowledgeable, but Ian hadn't wanted to know much. If he knew how Scotland had suffered, he feared, he would have to go back and fight. And selfishly, he hadn't wanted to return.

"Go on," he said.

Bittie took another long drink of ale and then continued. "With George's blessing, Wade created troops made up of Scots from the gentry, those loyal to the king."

"The king!" Ian said. "As if a true Scotsman could remain loyal to any save the Stuarts!"

Bittie reached across in alarm, his hand closing around Ian's wrist. "Whist, lad, not so loud! His agents are everywhere in the Highlands!"

Ian nodded, realizing he should have known better. He was out of practice at this game. It had been a long time since he teased the English lion with Quinn and Rob Roy.

Rob Roy.

"Has Rob struck back at the Watch?" he asked, his voice hushed now.

Bittie was silent for a moment, and then shook his shaggy head. "Och, no, lad. In the beginning, when Wade first came, one of the first to give in was Rob Roy."

Ian stared at him. "I dinna believe ye. Rob would never give in to such as they."

"Rob had been through hard times for many years. After ye and Quinn, er, died, Montrose cracked down on the reivers and the MacGregors in particular, and Rob turned outlaw. Remember the money he owed Montrose?"

Ian nodded. "It was stolen from him."

"Rob would have paid it back, ye know it as well as Montrose did, but the duke used the situation to have Rob arrested. He escaped, was captured again, escaped again, always on the run, and so, when Wade offered pardon in return for ceasing his outlaw ways, Rob's wife begged him to agree, and so he did." He lifted the big tankard in front of him and took a long drink. He lowered it and wiped the back of his sleeve across his face. "I suppose he just wanted a little peace, ye ken?"

Ian leaned his head against his hands for a moment. "And I wasna here to help him."

"Dinna fash yerself, laddie," Bittie said, clapping him so hard on the shoulder he almost fell off the bench. "If ye'd been here, ye'd likely be dead by now. Ye and Quinn were rash laddies. Rob Roy has always been a shrewd man, and that's why he's still alive."

"So Wade came to the Highlands ten years ago," he said, urging Bittie to go on with his story.

"Aye, and it's grown worse every year. Do ye know that we canna wear the kilt anymore, and are no' allowed to play the pipes?"

Ian swore softly under his breath. "So we are back to that."

"Some of the patrols act in a more lawful fashion. Yer brother's is one of them, but there are others that are nothing more than outlaws!" Bittie's jaw tightened, and Ian grew still at the sight of the anger in the easygoing man's eyes. "Men suspected of Jacobite leanings are arrested under one pretext or another and thrown in jail, often to be dangled at the end of a rope; women have been molested; children have been taken and pressed into what amounts to slavery; houses have been burned; sheep and cattle have been killed.

"Now, Wade's roads are nearing completion, opening the Highlands to the English. The MacGregors and their allies have had their very spirits trodden down to the point that they dare not rebel in any way." His dark eyes filled with despair. "They have given up."

Ian scowled. "I dinna believe that. There must be men left who are willing to fight for what they think is right."

"Perhaps," Bittie conceded thoughtfully. "But once Rob put down his arms, there was no leader here to raise up the standard once again." His gaze flashed over Ian and then away. "Every battle needs a leader, lad."

Ian laced his hands together on the tabletop and stared at his clenched fingers. "Do ye know these men who would follow such a leader?" he asked. Bittie stirred in front of him and he looked up to find a smile on his friend's face.

"Aye," he said. "I do."

A faint, familiar thrill ran through Ian's veins, and thoughts of his days as a highwayman flashed through his mind. "Then bring them here in two days' time." Ian dropped his voice to a whisper. "Bring them at dawn, and we shall talk of King George and his laws that seek to destroy the Scottish people."

His old friend's eyes were bright with suppressed hope, and Ian had the sudden realization that he might just be the death of this man. But like any Scot, he knew Bittie would rather go out fighting than die with the bootheel of the English on his throat.

"I'll bring them, lad. Ye can count on me." He rose, and then sank back down in the chair. "But we have no weapons," he reminded him. "They have been banned as well. To purchase them can be done, but 'twill cost a small fortune."

Ian nodded grimly. "I think I know just where such a fortune can be found."

While Davey took a nap—apparently hay didn't make a very comfortable bed—Ellie sneaked back downstairs and hid behind a huge barrel near the door leading to the stairs. From her vantage point she could see Ian and the burly man's intense conversation. She'd never seen Ian look so serious.

Ian shook hands with the man, opened the door for him, and then shut it firmly behind him. When he turned back, she caught her breath at the look on his face. Fury, determination, and sorrow struggled for dominance across his features. Ellie stood slowly, feeling as if she were looking at a stranger. The Ian MacGregor who had played his pipes on stage, thrilling a cheering audience, shooting them a wink and a jovial smile, was not this man.

Then his gaze met hers and he blinked, and suddenly his face smoothed into calm as one corner of his mouth curved up.

So I'm not the only one who can wear a mask, she thought.

"How did your meeting go?" she asked. He tucked his hand under her elbow and turned her toward the stairs.

"I thought I told ye to stay upstairs," he said.

Ellie stuck out her tongue, letting him guide her to the first step. "And I thought I told you that I was an adult.

Didn't you get that memo?" Even now, she could feel the tension inside of him. Something was afoot.

I have a bad feeling about this.

"Who was that guy?"

Ian stopped in front of their door, lost in thought, his gaze on the floor. Then he glanced up. "An old friend of mine named Bittie," he said. "And our meeting went well. Is Davey inside?"

"Sleeping like a baby. A big, overly intelligent baby."

He opened the door and Ellie walked in ahead of him. She gestured toward the bed, where Davey snored peacefully.

"See?" she said in feigned disgust. "Sawing logs like he hasn't a care in the world."

Ian moved to stand beside her. "Maybe he doesn't," he said.

Ellie brushed a wayward lock of hair back from Davey's face, relenting as she smiled at the man who had somehow become her friend. "He actually looks kind of sweet, doesn't he?"

Ian frowned at her. "Aye, if ye like little boys who think they know more than anyone else."

"Jealous?" she teased.

He bent down and kissed her, deeply, darkly, rocking her right down to her toes, and when he broke the embrace, Ellie was breathless.

"Just remember *that* when ye are thinking about sweet little boys like Davey." He winked at her and then leaned down and put his mouth close to the sleeping man's ear, as he began to speak in a high-pitched voice.

"Och, Davey, darlin'," Ian said lovingly, "it's time to get up for school. Change yer jammy-whammies and come downstairs for yer breakfast."

The man rolled over, one arm flung across his face. "Och, Mommy," he whined, "I dinna want to go to school."

Ellie giggled and Davey's eyes flew open. Ian's face was just a few inches from his. He wiggled his eyebrows and Davey scrambled sideways as Ian laughed. Perhaps the dry-humored, easygoing, I-love-everybody Ian was still alive and well.

"Get up, lad," Ian said. His smile faded. "It's time to get the two of ye home."

And maybe that wasn't such a good thing. Ellie drew in a sharp breath, squared her shoulders, and glared at the man she loved.

"No."

"Are we there yet?" Davey asked glumly as he paused to dig another rock out of his Nikes. If he'd known he was going to be tramping all over bloody Scotland, he'd have worn his hiking boots! Not that he *had* any hiking boots, but he could have *bought* some. If he'd *known*.

Just as he would have brought a *coat*, if he'd *known* he was going to be traveling back in *time*. Instead, he was wearing Ian's leather jacket, while the man himself wore Alex's black overcoat that he'd borrowed just before coming to their rescue.

Nearby a burn crashed over rugged rocks with such majestic beauty that Ian had insisted they take a break there, and they stood for a long while just gazing in awe at the power of the water cascading over tall boulders to the stream below. They had spent over an hour resting, splashing their weary feet in the cold water, Ellie and Ian sending burning glances at one another when they thought the other wasn't watching. Davey was about to suggest that they get a room, when Ian reluctantly called a halt to the merriment, saying he wanted to arrive before nightfall.

But arrive *where*? Ian wasn't saying.

Davey retrieved the offending pebble from his shoe and then hurried to catch up with their little caravan. Ellie sat smiling atop the shaggy red pony, intermittent sunbeams snaking out from behind the clouds to make her reddish blonde hair look like sunlight itself. He frowned at the fondness in his thoughts.

It was Ellie's fault that he was on yet another trek across

the Highlands. She might be happy to stay in the past, and he had been fine with it for a while, but the thrill of the adventure was beginning to wear thin. He had work to do back in his own time—especially now that he'd discovered the power of the spiral.

When Ian said it was time to try again at the cairn, Davey had been more than ready for their adventure to end. And he had six new hypotheses of when would be the best time and day to attempt it. It just happened that the next day would be one of his designated dates. But Ellie had refused.

Not, she had said emphatically, unless Ian went with them. And since Ian wasn't budging on his decision to stay behind, that was that. Now they were headed who knew where. All Ian would say was that it was where he had to go and he hadn't planned on taking them along; however, he couldn't leave them alone for five minutes, for no doubt they'd get arrested or hanged or beheaded if he did. Though he had scowled at both of them, his eyes gave lie to his expression, since they were dancing with happiness. It was obvious that he felt overjoyed to have Ellie still with him.

Davey shook his head as he limped after the two. Och, the two were giddy in love, and while he had all the respect in the world for love and, in fact, had once entertained thoughts of finding his own sweet lass, that kind of thing had to take a backseat to science. But he couldn't force Ellie to return to the future, and without her, his chances of getting back in one piece were slim.

He had figured one thing out with reasonable certainty—they had gone to the past together, and if the physics of energy worked with the spirals in the same way that they worked with the rest of the earth, the same amount of matter and mass must pass back through the vortex of time. Of course, he hadn't told Ellie that. He didn't want the lass to feel blackmailed into going back.

He glanced over at Ian, walking beside her, the reins in his hands. Perhaps it was just as well that Ellie had refused to return. Davey felt uneasy about leaving while Ian was acting so hotheaded about the Black Watch. If he made good on his plans to change history, there could be hell to pay.

"I love my pants!" Ellie cried, leaning back in the saddle and lifting her legs on either side of the horse, almost falling off backward.

"Whoa!" Ian said, flinging one arm out to catch her, laughing as he did. "They are not pants, lass. They are called *trews* or *breeches.*"

"Well, I love them. Things are hard enough without having to struggle with a skirt on horseback!" She grinned down at him. "Thank you for finding them for me. Did they cost much?"

"Och," Davey said, as he trudged along, "they were verra expensive. He swiped them from a clothesline behind the inn."

Ellie's mouth dropped open and she giggled. "You did not!"

Davey nodded, unable to keep from smiling as he remembered Ian's stealthy dash for the breeches hanging on the line. Ye'd have thought he was stealing the crown jewels, so carefully did he plot the caper while Ellie was taking a nap.

"Aye, he did."

Ellie gazed at Ian. "Have I told you that you are one of my favorite people?" she said. Ian lifted her hand and kissed it, making Davey feel almost ashamed for resenting their blossoming love.

Almost.

Because the truth of the matter was that the lass was headed for disaster, for if he was reading the signs right, there was no way Ian MacGregor would be returning to their time. Eventually, she would have to decide either to remain in the past indefinitely or return to her own time without Ian. Either way, there would be heartache involved. Davey sighed as they started up yet another hill, but when they reached the top, he caught his breath.

There, on top of a larger hill opposite them, sat a gray

stone castle, its parapets reaching toward the Scottish sky. He wasn't a sentimental man, but the thought of being in the eighteenth century and seeing a castle that no longer existed in the twenty-first sent a stir of excitement through his veins. He frowned, though, at the sight of gathering storm clouds in the distance, and turned up the collar of his jacket.

"Wow," Ellie said, standing up in the stirrups and echoing his thoughts. "Don't tell me that's where we're going?"

"Aye," Ian said, the sound of his voice grim. He patted the neck of the pony, frowning, his eyes downcast, as if trying to gather his thoughts; then he lifted his face to them. "Before we get any closer, there are a few things I need to tell the two of ye."

"You mean you're actually going to tell us what's going on?" Davey asked. "Gee whiz, that's kind of ye, old man."

"Oh, hush, Davey," Ellie said. "Ian has his reasons for what he does."

"Of course he does," Davey said, shaking his head.

"This is my father's castle," he said. Ellie shot him a startled look.

"Of course it is," Davey said. He should've known they'd end up here. It was only logical. This ruminating upon other people's problems was apparently affecting his cognitive abilities. He would have to school himself to keep his mind on the practical aspects of this adventure and not the emotional ones.

"My father supports the Black Watch," Ian said, "else my brothers would not be part of their ranks. My father also despises me. We will not find a warm welcome at his home."

"Then why are we going there?" Ellie asked. "Have you had a change of heart?"

Ian glanced at Davey, a warning in his eyes. "Aye, I suppose ye could say that." He shrugged. "My father is ill," he said. "'Twill probably be the last time I'll ever see him again."

"I knew you still cared about him." Ellie leaned down from the back of the pony and hugged him, resting her head on his shoulder. "I knew you didn't really hate him."

Davey folded his arms over his chest and glared at Ian. "Oh, aye," he said, his voice completely innocent. "Ian is too noble, too honorable to wish bad upon his own father." He arched one brow. Ian glared back at him.

"Ellie, darlin'," Ian said, stepping out of her embrace, "that isna the only reason I'm going to see him, and honestly, not even the main one. I want to discuss this latest ploy by the English to invade Scotland—and his role in it."

"I understand," she said, the saddle creaking as she settled back against it. "I'm just hoping you can find a way to make peace with him, Ian, before he dies." She cast her eyes down for a moment. "I'd give anything to be able to tell my mom that I was sorry about . . . so much." She rubbed one finger over a crease in the leather. "Maybe your father wants to make things right with you as well."

"And maybe not," Ian said, an edge to his words. "I'm willing to wager that yer relationship with yer mother was vastly different from mine with my father."

Ellie glanced up and reached out to him, resting one hand on his arm. "I guess I thought if you could make peace with him, maybe it would help you make peace with yourself."

A smile tugged at the corner of Ian's mouth.

"And ye dinna think I have peace?" he asked.

She shrugged again. "When you're onstage, yes. When you're laughing and joking with Quinn, maybe. But back here, in this time?" She shook her head, her tousled reddish blonde hair blowing softly against her face. "No way."

Ian held her gaze for a long moment and then nodded. "Aye," he said, "ye are right. My father disowned me. Even before I journeyed to yer time, I had to sneak around to see my brothers, and now he has turned every one of them against me, against what I believe."

Ellie lifted her hand to his face and stroked her fingers over the rough stubble on his jaw as she looked down at him. "Oh, Ian. Does their involvement in the Black Watch really make that much difference in the vast scheme of things? You've been to the future; Scotland is fine. Everything worked out."

Davey silently shook his head at her. *Och, lass, dinna go there, if ye know what's good for ye.*

Ian stared at her, and to her credit, Ellie didn't look away.

"*Really make that much difference?*" Ian finally said, his voice strained, his brows colliding above furious blue eyes.

Ellie doesn't need this, Davey thought, and stepped between the two, facing Ian, deftly plucking the reins from his hand. Ian frowned and took a step back.

"Do ye think yer father will feed us?" Davey asked. "Perhaps we can raid the fridge. Oops, there is no fridge. Ah, well." He looked up at Ellie and grinned. "Come on, lass, let's see what ye're made of!" He tugged on the leather straps and then turned and took off at a dead run.

Ellie squealed as the little horse moved into a fast trot, making her bounce up and down as Davey sacrificed the blister on his left heel to save Ellie from facing the wrath of a Scotsman on the subject of Scottish rights. He glanced back over one shoulder.

Ian strode behind them, his black overcoat swinging against his legs, an equally black look upon his face. As if to add insult to injury, it began to rain.

ten

Ian made his way down the wet green hillside dotted with pale gray stones of all sizes, as he tried to get his temper under control. The rain had thankfully been light, and the unseasonable warmth of the day kept them from growing too chilled. He kicked a stone out of the way, his hands shoved down into the pockets of Alex's overcoat. They had been able to buy or steal breeches and shirts, and he had wrapped Ellie warmly in a couple of plaids, but Ian resolved to find her a winter cloak once they reached the castle. In spite of her thoughtless words.

He couldn't remember the last time he'd been so angry from so little provocation. Ellie just didn't understand. How could she? To her, what was happening in Scotland now had ended over two hundred year ago. In her words, "Everything worked out fine."

But Ian knew better. He might not have studied their history the way Quinn had, but his friend had often told him—usually when the two of them were slightly drunk and reminiscing about their shared past—some tidbit of what he was studying.

As he walked, head down, Ian had to admit that he'd felt

strangely out of his element since returning to the past, and he suddenly knew why. He wasn't used to making important decisions. That had always been Quinn's role in their days as highwaymen and rebels. He, on the other hand, had been the sidekick, the follower.

For a moment, he wished Quinn had come with him, but just as quickly rebuked that thought. Maggie needed her husband at her side, and there was no way he would wish Quinn into this mess. Ian was perfectly able to handle things himself—wasn't he?

Ahead, Ellie had slid off the pony and was now giving Davey a ride down the steep hillside, playing like a child. In Ellie's time he had been able to play, but here, in this place, there was a sorrow hanging over him that he couldn't shake.

He frowned as a new thought darted across his mind. Quinn had called the shots in their days together, and Ellie had called the shots during his tour. Had he always taken such a secondary role in his own life? Apparently so.

Everything happened for a reason; that was what he had told Ellie. He had sounded very profound and philosophic, but perhaps he needed to listen to his own lofty beliefs. Perhaps he was here, in the past, to finally become the leader he was meant to be.

Ellie and Davey had finally run out of steam and were waiting for him at the bottom of the hill. Ellie waved, looking at him with her heart in her eyes.

When had she lowered her guard? At the Clachan, when he had almost joined her in her bed? When they touched, and he had seen the desire in her bonny eyes? There had been a spark between them ever since they first met, but Ellie had kept him at arm's length, until now.

Was she feeling the kind of freedom that he himself had experienced in *her* time? A release born of being in a different century from her own? In Ellie's time, he had felt as if the dreams he had reached for, for so long, were suddenly possible—perhaps because there was no one there to say him nay. Did Ellie feel that way here? Had she found that in this time, in this place, she could let go of her fears and inhibitions, and take hold of what she truly wanted from life?

His heart ached at the irony. It had taken a trip to the 1700s for Ellie to admit she cared for him. And now it didn't matter. They could never be together. She belonged in the twenty-first century, and he belonged here, in Scotland's past. Ian dragged one hand through his tangled hair as he trudged across the rough ground. He should never have allowed this to happen, never have let anything more than friendship blossom between him and Ellie.

In the last twenty-four hours, he had come to terms with the fact that he would likely have to remain in the past for the rest of his life. His father was dying.

As the eldest son, after his father's death, he would be in a position to help alter his family's part in Scottish history, and perhaps, at the same time, help ease the suffering of the clan he claimed as his own.

Ian stopped walking and looked up at the hazy Scottish sky. He took a deep breath, and a sweet, familiar scent made him look around, a little wildly. There! He had walked right past it—a long slope covered with deep purple heather.

Gazing down at the beautiful flower of his homeland, he knew he was doing the right thing. The thought of being apart from Ellie was almost more than he could stand, but how could he leave his family and his countrymen a second time?

He had lived a life of ease for the last year by blocking any thought of his past life from his mind. Selfishly he'd turned his back on his clan and his brothers and enjoyed being able, at last, to pursue his dream of playing the pipes—and in such a glorious way!

He'd never felt so alive! Only his days as a highwayman came remotely close. That feeling of excitement, that sense of risking all—it was the same in music or in robbery, for every time he appeared on the stage he felt as if he was taking a risk. Would this be the night that he would lose the magic? Would this be the concert when no one would show?

But most of all, it was the music that had lifted him up, over the memory of Scotland's past and her sorrows. For the first time in his life, his music had been all he had to think about, all he wanted to think about.

There was no vengeance to seek, no wrongs to make right, no injustices to wage war against. Just the beauty and the sweet pleasure of playing the pipes and writing songs—and not just for the pipes anymore but for other instruments in the band as well. The energy, the thrill, the sheer sensual surge of joy it gave him was unparalleled in anything he'd ever experienced before.

"Ian?"

Ellie was beside him, and he turned to smile at her. "Oh, wow, this is beautiful," she said, gazing down at the hillside covered in heather. The wind swept her hair upward, making it dance against her face, her blue eyes putting the sky above to shame. Ian's heart beat a little faster.

"Are you all right?" she asked, moving to his side and taking his hand.

Ellie. How could he let her go? They hadn't even made love yet. Making love to her would be like taking every concert he'd ever given, every hell-for-leather ride he'd ever taken, multiplying those by a thousand, and then injecting the feeling into his bloodstream. There would be nothing else like it, because he loved her.

He loved her.

Ian gathered her into his arms, bending his head to hers, taking her mouth with infinite care, closing his eyes and letting himself feel the magic that swept over him anytime she was near. She was wrong. He had found his peace, and it was right here in her arms. "Ellie," he began, "I—"

"In the name of the laird, cease walking!"

Ian shoved Ellie behind him and drew the sword at his side. Luckily it wasn't a patrol of the Black Watch blocking their way, but only a single man clad in a plaid usually worn by the Campbells, the cloth wrapped around his waist and held in place with a wide belt. Another wide swatch of cloth crossed the front of his fawn-colored shirt and fastened at the shoulder with a pin made from an antler or bone. Since his father was a supporter of the Black Watch, Ian assumed his men were permitted to wear the plaid and bear arms. Rough suede boots reached his knees, and a fur-covered sporran guarded the front of his kilt. He held a sword, not a true claymore, but a basket hilt, in front of him, barring the way.

The man seemed a formidable adversary at first glance, with one odd exception: He was very short.

"We are here to see the laird," he said, taking a few steps forward.

"Put down yer sword! Who are ye?"

Ian frowned. The voice was young, not that of a man. He lowered his sword but didn't drop it, then took another step forward. Upon closer examination, he saw that the stalwart defender of the keep was a lad, perhaps all of sixteen years old.

The boy's dark, tousled hair was tied back from his face and even from the twenty feet separating the two men, Ian could see his jaw was locked in determination not to let them pass.

Strange that a lad would be guarding the outskirts of the castle alone.

"Let us pass," Ian demanded.

"State yer name and business."

Soft fingers tightened on his arm and Ian glanced down at Ellie. "Stay behind me, lass," he said. He took a deep breath and spoke, feeling the heavy mantle of family responsibility settle over his shoulders.

"My name is Ian MacGregor, and Laird Campbell is my father."

The boy lowered his sword and strode forward, stopping when Ian raised his sword to keep him from getting any closer. He was pale, slight, and as he frowned at his enemy, Ian saw familiar blue eyes fringed in long, black lashes.

"Ian?" the lad whispered. "Is it really ye?"

Ian narrowed his eyes. This boy wouldn't have even been born at the time that he had supposedly died. "Aye, I am Ian. Who are ye?"

The boy strode toward him, his blue eyes bright with intention, and Ian suddenly remembered just how good he had been with a sword at the age of sixteen.

"Stay back," Ian warned, raising his sword again.

The boy stopped, then reached behind his neck and pulled a piece of twine loose, setting free a cascade of dark brown hair. A freckled face grinned up at him and Ian let the sword fall from his nerveless fingers.

It wasn't a lad at all. It was a girl.

"I'm Katie," the lass said, beaming up at him. "I'm yer sister!"

Ian stared down at Katie Campbell, stunned. After a few seconds, Ellie stepped forward and introduced herself and Davey, but the lass barely acknowledged either of them. Instead, she turned back to Ian, who stood unmoving, as if he'd been frozen in place, and began to pull him along with her, talking ninety miles an hour as they headed for the castle. Ellie and Davey quickly followed, exchanging wary glances.

Apparently, from what Ian could gather from the girl's energetic conversation, he had become quite a legend in the Highlands, and after twenty-three years, there was still speculation as to whether or not he had really died. Some said he'd been spirited away by the faeries, while others claimed to have seen his ghost walking the hills. Maybe that was why his brother Angus had believed him when he said he was a ghost.

She babbled all the way to the castle, clinging to his arm and from time to time hugging him, as if to assure herself that he was real. "I canna believe ye are here!" Katie cried, bouncing along at his side, never pausing for breath. "I've heard the stories about ye since I was a wee lassie, but everyone supposed ye were dead! I told Father that ye were too clever for that and ye and Quinn must have escaped somehow! He locked me in my room for a week with only goat milk and porridge to eat for saying that, but somehow I knew it was true!"

"Locked ye in yer room?" Ian came to a stop, anger rising up inside of him. *How dare that old bastard lock this poor child in—* He shook his head. He was already feeling protective of someone he didn't know—he didn't even know if she really was his sister. As a matter of fact, it was impossible!

"Did he lock ye in yer room when ye were a lad?" she gushed. "Och, then ye know what he's like, and Tavish just as bad, and ye know—"

"Wait a minute, just a minute!" Ian commanded and miraculously, the girl stopped talking, gazing up at him in adoration. "My mother died when I was ten years old. Ye are not my sister."

Ellie frowned at him and moved closer to the girl. Of course, she would be protective. She was no doubt missing her own sisters.

Katie rolled her eyes. "Och, verra well then, I am yer *half* sister. Our father married my mother, but she died when I was born."

"I'm sorry," Ellie said softly. "I lost my mother, so I know how hard that can be."

Katie turned and stared at her for a long moment, before giving her an appreciative smile. "Thank ye," she said. "Ellie, is it? I never knew her, but 'tis verra kind of ye." She spun back around toward Ian. "So ye *are* my brother, Ian, and I need yer help!"

She started pulling him along again and Ian realized they had almost reached the castle. A dirt road led up to a huge gate set into a wall surrounding the keep, its path dug from the wheels of countless wagons and carts over the years. The castle wasn't large in comparison to some, but it was impressive to say the least. He dug in his heels and jerked her to a halt.

"My help? For what?"

"Maybe keeping her from being locked in her room," Ellie said heatedly, her hands on her hips. He arched one brow. She'd been in such a good mood lately that he had missed the spark in her eyes when she got mad.

"Stay out of this, Eleanor."

She glared up at him, and Ian had to resist smiling.

"Och, no," Katie said, answering Ellie's statement. "I dinna mind that so much." She looked up at Ian from beneath her lashes. "No, I was thinking that perhaps ye can save me from my father's most recent punishment!" She grabbed the front of his jacket with both hands. "He's sentenced me to a fate worse than death!"

Ian sighed. What was that twenty-first-century term? Ah, yes—*drama queen*.

Ellie frowned and moved to Katie's side again. "What do you mean? Is your father mistreating you?"

Katie swept her gaze over Ellie, seemed to decide she liked her, and smiled, then turned back to Ian. "He's betrothed me to the Earl of Castlemore!" She gripped Ian's right arm. "Och, he's a horrible man!"

Davey frowned. "Betrothed you? How old are you?"

"Nineteen."

Ian raised his brows in surprise. She looked much younger. Highland lassies were usually married by the time they were sixteen or seventeen, so how had she managed to escape connubial bliss? "How is it ye are just now being betrothed?" he said. "Ye are older than most unmarried lasses, by Highland standards."

Her cheeks reddened and Ian immediately regretted his words. He had forgotten the shame placed on any young woman deemed "unmarriageable." Averting her eyes, Katie tilted her chin stubbornly before speaking.

"Aye, I know I'm a spinster, but I resolved long ago that if I canna marry for love, I willna marry at all!"

"Good for you!" Ellie said, stepping to the girl's side and putting her arm around her, as she glared up at Ian. "And you are *not* a spinster!"

"Hear, hear!" Davey agreed.

Ian shot them a look. That was all he needed, Ellie and Davey trying to convince the girl that she shouldn't marry the man her father had chosen for her. Yet, how could he make a man and woman from the future understand that in this time, Katie was practically out of the running for a husband. Women were usually married in the Highlands by the time they were fifteen or sixteen at the latest. By the time they were Katie's age, most had two or three bairns clinging to their legs.

He patted Katie's shoulder awkwardly, his anger gone. No doubt his father had found the girl a good match. "So who is this earl? Is he a good man?"

"What difference does *that* make?" Ellie asked. "She's not in love with him. She doesn't *want* to marry him."

"Ellie, leave this to me. Ye dinna ken the ways of this, er, country." He put his arm around her and smiled at Katie. "Ellie is from the New World, so ye will make allowances if she says things that are a bit strange."

Ellie stood in silence and shrugged Ian's arm off of her shoulder, her voice seething with fury.

"It isn't *strange* for a nineteen-year-old girl to not want to get married to someone she doesn't even know," Ellie declared, her eyes narrowed.

"It is *here*," Ian told her flatly. "In this—place—my father has the right to wed Katie to anyone he chooses. It's a father's duty to pick out a proper husband for his daughter." He turned back to Katie. "The laird might have his faults, but I canna imagine him betrothing ye to someone as vile as ye make this earl out to be."

Katie sighed, pulling a long lock of her hair over her shoulder. "I suppose ye're right, Ian. I think I wouldna mind so much if it weren't for the fact that he's so old."

Ian chuckled, and Ellie glared at him harder. "I imagine ye think *me* an old man."

His sister squinted up at him and then shook her head. "Nay, ye are still young."

"So how old is this earl?" Davey interjected.

"Och, I suppose not so old," Katie said, fiddling with the ends of her hair. "He just passed his sixty-fourth birthday."

Ellie's mouth dropped open. "You're kidding!"

Katie frowned at her. "I dinna ken yer words."

"You—are—freaking—kidding—me," Ellie said, slowly and distinctly. Katie shook her head and smiled.

Ian started walking toward the castle again, leaving his entourage to follow. Katie caught up quickly, and Ellie soon flanked his left side, with Davey bringing up the rear.

"Well, all that means," Ian said, trying to look at the situation based on the values of an eighteenth-century man, not one from the twenty-first, "is that the earl will be a man of wisdom and experience, just the right kind of husband for a young woman like yerself."

Katie frowned, striding along like a boy beside him. "Aye, I suppose ye are right, brother." She paused. "Did I mention that he is an Englishman?"

Ian stopped abruptly and Davey thudded into him from behind. He steadied the man, his gaze fixed on his little sister. "He is what?"

"An Englishman. King George gave the earl old MacAllister's lands after his sons fought at Sheriffmuir."

For a moment, Ian thought his brain had burst, for he truly could see nothing but the color red. Then his vision cleared and he turned on his heel, headed for the castle once more. "That traitorous son of a bitch!" he shouted, taking strides a yard long. "I wouldna believe this, even of him!"

Ellie caught up with him, grinning from ear to ear. "But like you said, Ian, he might be a good man."

"I dinna care if he is an angel or a demon," Ian said, fury coursing through his veins, "as long as he is not an Englishman! My sister is not marrying an Englishman!"

Ian turned toward Katie in time to see Ellie give her a wink, while Davey shook his head, a worried look on his face.

"Och, well, I thought ye might feel that way," Katie said.

It took another fifteen minutes to walk up the hill to the castle gates.

Katie had continued to talk nonstop, bringing Ian up-to-date on everything that had happened in her lifetime at least. He had fallen into a deep reverie, when suddenly, before he could think, several burly men clad in kilts and full regalia surrounded them, swords drawn.

The one leading the men had a craggy, weary face and

empty, sunken eyes. He looked familiar, and Ian's heart began to pound against his chest.

Katie rushed forward, her dark hair flying behind her. "Tavish! Put down yer swords!" she shouted. "They are with me! They have come to see Father!"

The leader stepped forward, his sword still raised. "Are these more of yer lame ducks, then, Kate? Have they come for a handout? If so, take them round to the kitchen and dinna be botherin' our father again."

Ian stepped forward, his face pale. "Tavish?" he whispered. "Little Tavish?"

The man glowered. "I am Tavish Campbell. Who are ye?"

For a moment Ian couldn't move, then he finally forced his feet into motion. He stopped just a few feet away from the man he had not seen for twenty-three years.

"It's Ian," he said softly. "Yer brother."

The man's gaze sharpened, but he didn't lower his sword. "My brother Ian is dead."

Katie charged forward and shoved the man backward, causing the other guards to step forward. "He's our brother, Tavish!" she cried. "'Tis Ian—the one we thought had been murdered by Montrose. He's alive!"

His brother stared at him. "Ian?" He shook his head. "It canna be possible."

"Aye," Ian said. "But it is. I have come home."

Tavish rubbed one hand across the lower half of his unshaven face and then nodded. "But take off yer sword," he said.

"Tavish!" Katie cried.

"It's all right." Ian quickly unbuckled his blade and handed it to his brother.

"Ye have been gone for a long time," Tavish said, with a frown, "if indeed ye are who ye say ye are. Much has changed. Come along, then, and I will take ye to the laird. Be advised, he is verra ill." He shook his head as he turned to lead them up the hill. "I dinna know what seeing ye will do to him."

The man seemed resigned, however, and motioned for

the group to follow. The other men fell in behind them and on each side. Ian noted that Davey quickened his pace to come up alongside of his friends.

Tavish led the visitors up the long, curving pathway winding up through the gate in the wall that surrounded the keep. As they walked, Ian felt a wave of dizziness sweep over him. His brother Tavish had been a wee lad of two when he left. Now he was grown, looking ten years older than his age.

How had his family come to this? Angus was a leader of the Black Watch, his other brothers part of their ranks as well, and his youngest sibling left to care for their dying father's estate.

Nay, Tavish was no longer his youngest. He had a little sister that he hadn't even known existed. He had seen disappointment shading the excitement in her blue eyes, disappointment that he hadn't shown more joy over meeting her, but he had been too stunned. Perhaps he could make it up to her, later on.

"Ian." Ellie nudged him, and he looked up, startled to see that they had arrived at the castle itself.

Tavish stepped forward and pushed open one of the huge twenty-foot-tall double doors leading inside. As Ian stepped across the threshold and into the foyer, he suddenly paused and glanced over at Ellie—for what, he wasn't certain. Reassurance? She looked awestruck, her gaze darting up to the carved lintels above the second set of double doors as she bit her lower lip, obviously nervous.

Och, it is I who should be giving her reassurance, he thought, and reached over and took her hand, squeezing it. She seemed surprised, but glad, and squeezed his fingers in return. He tried to give her a reassuring look as well, but knew that he failed miserably. A new sister he could accept. A dying father who had thrown away the last vestiges of honor and Scottish pride was quite another matter.

"Come," Tavish said, gesturing toward the next doorway, which led into the great hall. Inside there would be expensive tapestries hung upon every one of the tall, stone walls, sumptuous furniture—sofas and chairs, padded and brought all the way from Italy—curved to face the gigantic fireplace that took up an entire section of the longest wall in the room.

But when Ian entered the great hall, he was astounded to see that the tapestries, save one of Joan of Arc, his mother's favorite, were gone. There had once been five great tables down the middle of the hall, where meals were served for the family—the five brothers, his father, his mother—when she was alive—and any visitors. Sumptuous affairs the evening meals had been, with roast duck and steamed vegetables, puddings and cake.

Now there was one table with benches on either side, pushed down to the end of the hall. And though it was evening, there was no meal in sight. The rest of the furniture was missing as well, except for two chairs pulled in front of the fireplace. There was a roaring fire there, at least, and a man sitting in one of the chairs, his feet propped up on a stool, his body covered with a sheepskin.

Ian's throat tightened as Katie ran over to the man and threw her arms around him.

"Father! Father!" she cried, hugging the invalid. "Ye willna believe who I have brought to see ye! Look!"

Ian took a step closer. Fergus Campbell was a strong, husky man, with shoulders like an ox and the gaze of a lion. This man was old, thin, his face ashen and his eyes vacant. This stranger could not be his father. His heart began to pound faster.

The old man shrugged her off and pulled the sheepskin up closer around his neck. "Leave off, Kate," he said, his voice hoarse and gravelly. "I've told ye that I willna see the vagrants ye drag to our door."

"But 'tisn't vagrants, Father," she said, glancing over at Ian with a smile. "'Tis yer son—Ian—returned from death itself!"

The laird stared up at his daughter for a long moment and then slowly turned in his chair, his gaze bleary and unfocused, until he saw Ian. His mouth opened and closed but no words came out. He shook his head slightly and then turned back to Katie.

"Ye are a cruel child, Katherine Campbell," he said. "To bring some young buck here that resembles yer brother, in an effort to—what? Drive me mad so that Angus may take over and decide whom ye will wed? 'Twill not work."

He drew in a long, raspy breath and began to cough, the deep rattle echoing through the almost empty hall. Katie hurried to a small table sitting between the two chairs where a pewter pitcher sat. She poured what looked like wine into a goblet beside it and stood waiting until the episode passed and the old man regained his breath. She handed him the goblet and he drank greedily, almost flinging it back to her when he was finished. He shook one thin finger in her direction.

"I intend to live to see ye married to the earl," he said, new strength in his voice, "so dinna think to shock me into leaving sooner." He slumped back in the chair and closed his eyes.

Ian swallowed hard and took a step forward, moving to the front of the chair, willing the words to form, willing himself to utter them. "Father." The man's eyelids flickered. "It's Ian, your son. I've come home."

The old man's eyes flew open and he stared at the man before him for long moments; then, pushing down on the armrests of his chair, he stood shakily. Ian felt a slight twist in his belly. His father had always towered over him and all of his brothers. Now he was several inches shorter, shrunken, frail. Fergus swept his gaze over the man claiming to be his son, pausing at his face for a moment before he shook his head.

"I would say ye did well, Kate, with yer impersonator; however, ye dinna allow for the twenty-odd years since yer brother died. This man is the same age Ian was when he was fool enough to ride with Quinn MacIntyre."

"I am Ian," Ian said, moving forward before Fergus could sit again. "I may look as though I havena aged, but that is no fault of my own. I am alive and have come back."

The old man's eyes widened as Ian moved closer. "Ye say ye are my son," he said, a slight tremor in his voice. "My rebel son had a scar on his back from a bad fall he took as a child. It has an odd look to it—like a bird in flight."

Ian raised one brow. He was shocked his father even remembered that event in his life. Nodding, he turned his back toward his father, pulling up the tail of the black shirt he wore. Glancing back over his shoulder, he watched as recognition sparked in Fergus's eyes at the sight of the curved scar.

His father lifted one trembling hand toward Ian's back and almost touched the scar before letting it drop back to his side. He jerked his head up to peer into his son's face, a hardness settling over his own.

"So, it is ye. What witchcraft has kept ye lookin' younger than ye've a right to, when I stand before ye on my last legs?"

eleven

The surge of sentimental warmth Ian had felt rise up when he first saw his father quickly faded. His father hadn't changed. First and foremost in his mind was the injustice of Ian's youth versus his own elderly status.

"Happy to see ye, too, Father," he said, unable to keep the grimness from his voice. Ellie and Davey had kept back, but now they moved to stand beside him, and to his surprise, Ellie slipped her hand into his. "These are my friends, Davey Ferguson and Ellie Graham."

"And what do I care fer yer friends?" his father said, sitting back down in his chair heavily. "And what are ye doin' here? What do ye want?"

"I've come to talk to you about the Black Watch, and the MacGregors."

Fergus jerked his head toward him. "Ye willna speak that name in this house." Behind him, Katie shook her head at her new brother and frowned.

Ian smiled. "Which name? The Black Watch or MacGregor?"

"Ye know which I mean," the old man said.

"Would ye like something to eat?" Katie asked, sounding a little desperate. "Or perhaps some wine?"

"We were once MacGregors," Ian reminded his father, ignoring Katie's offer. He walked in front of his father and pulled Ellie along with him. When they reached the other chair a few feet away, he gestured toward the seat. She hesitated, but then sat down. Davey moved to stand beside Katie for some odd reason, and the girl shot him a startled look.

"Long ago we were," Fergus said, his brogue broadening. "And when the king outlawed the name, we changed it to Campbell, and Campbells we are."

Ian took a step back from Ellie's chair and folded his arms over his chest, gazing down at his father as he did. "I am not a Campbell. I am a MacGregor."

The old man's face turned red. "Aye, ye are one now, after turning yer back on yer father and yer family and yer birthright!" He lifted one scrawny fist and shook it at his son. "And ye are no more welcome here than the scoundrel who took ye away from us!"

"Are ye speaking of Rob Roy MacGregor?" Ian asked. His father didn't answer. "Perhaps I should refresh yer memory a bit, Father. 'Twas ye who turned yer back on me, remember? When I left MacCrimmons School of Piping with Quinn. Ye said if I left, ye would disown me."

"It was nonsense!" the old man cried, picking up a cane next to his chair and pounding it against the stone floor, the sound echoing through the half-empty hall. "Quinn MacIntyre's father and brother were outlaws and they deserved what they got—swingin' at the end of a rope!"

"Quinn's mother was sore ill, and their family was starvin'!" Ian shouted back, unwinding his arms and clenching his fists at his side. "Just as the MacGregors and other poor clans living on yer land and near yer land are fair starvin' now, thanks to those traitorous Scots who have thrown their lot in with General Wade and the English king."

Ian felt Ellie's eyes on him, and when he glanced her way,

she looked as if she didn't know him, as if he were a stranger. Perhaps he was. He looked back at his father.

"And do ye help them?" He shook his head. "Nay, ye do what ye have always done. Ye take care of yerself first and foremost! Ye join with the English and their bloody Black Watch instead of standing up for yer own people!"

"They are no' my people!" his father said tersely. He picked up his cane again and struck the floor over and over again, his voice rising in fury. "They are vagabonds and ruffians and traitors to the king! And so are ye!" He struggled to his feet again and shook the cane at Ian. "Get out! Do ye hear me? Get—"

His face twisted and turned a shade whiter as he clutched one hand to his chest and gasped.

"Father!" Katie cried. Ellie jumped up and flung her arm around the old man's waist, keeping him from toppling over, while Ian rushed forward and caught him in his arms.

For a split second, Ian almost began to sob. His father's flesh was all but withered away beneath his touch. He was skin and bones, as weightless as a cat. He was truly dying. Ian's throat tightened and he regretted his harsh words. There was no honor in shouting at a feeble old man.

As he lifted his father into his arms, Fergus said something, his voice so faint Ian couldn't make out his words.

"What, Father?"

Fergus opened and closed his mouth several times and then muttered, one hand plucking at Ian's chest. "I want—I want—"

"Yes, Father," Ian said gently, "what is it ye want?"

The old man's eyes searched his and then narrowed. "I want nothing to do with ye." He closed his eyes and his head fell back against his son's shoulder.

Katie rushed to Ian's side. "Lead the way to his room," he ordered. She nodded and headed up the stairs.

"I'll go up with ye and check him out," Davey said. Ian nodded and turned to Ellie.

"Ye can wait down here," he said, wishing, like a weakling, that she would come with him.

"I want to go with you," Ellie said, her blue gray eyes soft, filled with compassion.

Ian suddenly longed to take her and run from this place of death and memories, ached to hold her in his arms and simply love her. The old man in his arms groaned, loudly, and Ian nodded again and turned to follow Katie up the stairs. Ellie moved along beside him, like an anchor in a storm that was fair near to drowning him.

Ellie crept down the dark hallway from her chamber, glancing back over her shoulder as she did. Any moment she half expected a vampire to appear with his fangs bared. In high school she'd have been thrilled to find herself in such a place and would have probably asked if she could have a coffin in her room.

If it hadn't been for the lit candle she'd managed to swipe from another room, she'd be groping in the cold blackness of what Ian called home. Or did he? She couldn't imagine anyone calling this place home.

His father apparently hadn't had a heart attack, at least not according to Davey. Lucky for Fergus Campbell, in addition to the geeky guy's advanced degree in physics, the brainiac was practically a medical doctor, or at least Ellie knew he had studied at a hospital in Edinburgh.

After the laird had been made comfortable, Katie had led them each to separate chambers and brought a makeshift meal of bread and ale to their doors. Ellie was willing to bet, after seeing the downstairs, that those two items of food made up the entirety of their pantry. How had this happened? How had a man as wealthy and powerful as Fergus Campbell come to this?

During the band tour Ellie had the opportunity to stay in many castles in England, Scotland, and Ireland, and by and large they had been clean and warm, a delight. This place was the total opposite.

The stone floors were filthy and cold; the bed in her room leaned to one side, with a mattress leaking straw and only a thin coverlet for a blanket. Worst of all, there was no window and the room was eerie and silent. Even when she finally opened her door and left it that way, the only light was that of a flickering torch quite a distance down the hall.

Feeling like she'd stumbled onto the set of a very bad monster movie, Ellie had huddled on one corner of the bed, her eyes wide, for more than an hour, as she waited for bats or giant spiders or a herd of snakes to come thundering into her room.

Actually, she was waiting for Ian to come and find her. He had told her to go on to bed while he sat with his father awhile longer.

Ian's blue eyes had been thoughtful, and more than a little warm when he said he needed to talk to her before she went to sleep. Her heartbeat had quickened with anticipation, and after Katie ushered her into the cell that passed for a guest room, and left her to her fate, Ellie had waited breathlessly for Ian.

And waited.

And waited.

Finally, when she heard something scurrying in one of the corners, she'd bolted into the hallway and, after snatching a lit candle from another room, had begun her search for Davey or Ian. At this point, she didn't really care which one she found.

Either Ian is still with his father, she thought, *or he just doesn't want to sleep with me—I mean talk to me. But he did have that smoldering look in his eyes that he gets sometimes. The one that curls my toes. So why not think positive?*

Ellie smiled dreamily as she padded barefoot down the cold stone hallway, the candle's light leading her as she daydreamed about Ian. Her overactive imagination had them eloping to Vegas before she realized how ridiculous she was acting.

Good grief! Get a grip, she ordered. *You don't know that he has anything in mind but talking.*

"And you don't know that he doesn't," she said aloud, her voice echoing down the corridor.

She moved stealthily down the corridor. Surely Katie had put them all in the same section of the castle. The problem was, she'd been taken to her room first and she had no idea where the two men were. There were four more rooms on this hallway, but she had no desire to start knocking on doors. Ellie paused in the corridor, and immediately froze at the sound of footsteps behind her.

"Davey?" she whispered hopefully. "Ian?" The footsteps stopped. No one answered. Ellie pressed herself against the wall. *Anyone who thinks medieval castles are romantic should be standing in my shoes,* she thought, listening to the silence.

After a moment she released a pent-up breath. There were no more footsteps. Maybe it had just been an echo of her own. She relaxed slightly. *Sure, that's probably what it was.* Everyone was asleep. She frowned. Of course, she had no idea of exactly who "everyone" was. So far they'd seen Tavish, Ian's father, Katie, and the two men outside the castle, but surely there were others.

Ellie started walking again and soon stood in front of a large door identical to the one that had led to her room. Hesitantly—who knew what lay inside—she knocked. "Davey?" she hissed.

When she received no response, she tugged on the door handle. The door creaked open and she stuck her head inside. "Davey Ferguson, you answer me right this minute! Ian?"

Nothing.

With a sigh, Ellie shut the door and turned—only to collide with a tall, dark shadow. She screamed and dropped the candle, plunging the hallway into darkness.

"Lass, it's me!" Ian whispered loudly. "*Shhh*, ye're goin' ta wake the whole bloody castle!"

Ellie sagged, held on her feet only by his arms slipping around her waist. She dragged in a deep, cold breath of air, regained her equilibrium, and kicked him in the shin.

"Damn!" he whispered, hopping up and down on one foot and holding his leg. "Why did ye do that?"

"Hush," she said, "you're going to wake the whole bloody castle!" Then she turned on her heel and headed back down the hall toward her room, so angry even the dark corridor didn't scare her.

Ian caught up with her quickly, in spite of his limp, and pulled her to a stop. "Ellie, Ellie darlin', I'm sorry. I dinna mean to scare ye. I was trying to get close enough to whisper to ye."

"No problem," she said briskly, "I'm fine."

She turned to go, but he pulled her back and in one easy motion, picked her up in his arms. She kicked her feet, suddenly furious. "Put me down," she hissed.

"But we havena had our talk yet," he said cheerfully as he carried her back down the hallway.

Too tired to fight him, Ellie folded her arms over her chest and waited until he had opened another door and deposited her in the center of a bright, warm room. She had planned to kick him again as soon as he put her down, but she was too amazed at the sight around her.

It was a beautiful room, with a roaring fire in a large stone fireplace directly across from the four-poster bed in the middle of the big chamber, with silken burgundy draperies at the long, diamond-paned windows, and a thick, though tattered silken coverlet in matching burgundy on the bed.

Ellie's eyes narrowed. So *she* was thrown into what practically amounted to a dungeon, while Ian was given this—this—master suite! "Obviously your sister needs a few lessons on hospitality—" she began, turning to face him, only to find Ian frowning down at her, his hands on his hips. She frowned back. "What?" she demanded.

"Would ye like to tell me what the hell ye were doing out wandering alone at night in a strange castle?" He glanced down at her feet. "And where are yer shoes?" He shook his head. "Don't ye know ye can catch yer death of cold in a drafty old place like this?"

Ellie blinked at him and then crossed to the fireplace to warm her hands. "Cold? Laddie, you don't know what cold is! My room is like a Deepfreeze! I tried to go to sleep in that broken-down pile of sticks your sister calls a bed, and after a few minutes I had icicles on my backside! I have no fire, no light, no blankets, no nothing! So guess what?" She spun around. "I'm trading rooms with you!"

And with that, she flounced across the room to his bed and threw herself backward, arms spread wide. When she hit the downy mattress beneath the burgundy silk, she sighed aloud, feeling comfortable for the first time since she'd arrived in the past. But in a matter of seconds, her comfort was literally shaken as the mattress dipped from Ian's weight as he plopped down beside her.

"Oh, no, you don't!" she said, turning on one elbow to face him. "You can stay in here if you want, but you'll have to sleep on the—the—hearth thingy, or the floor. I claim the bed." He was very near, his blue eyes dark and burning with— anger? It *was* anger, wasn't it? Ellie swallowed hard as he leaned closer, his tousled blond hair drifting forward, veiling each side of his face.

"'Tis my bed," he said, his voice as dark as the corridor, but as warm as the flames dancing across the room.

Ellie ran her tongue over her lower lip and watched his eyes follow the movement. She smiled and decided she wasn't angry anymore. Remembering Davey and Ian's reaction when she stretched before, she lay back and raised her arms above her head, reaching with her fingertips for the huge headboard and with her toes for the fire.

"No, *I* claim it," she said. "I mean . . ." Her words trickled away, along with her bravado, as Ian leaned over her, his gaze fixed on her mouth.

"Ye cannot claim what is not yers," he said softly, his breath warm and sweet with the smell of whiskey.

"Yes, I can," she whispered. "I—I—"

"While I"—he slipped one hand around her waist and tugged her closer—"by right of being the eldest son of this castle, can lay claim to whatever I want." He brushed her mouth with his, lightly. She shivered, knowing it was a promise of a night just beginning. "And Ellie," he whispered, "'tis ye that I want."

Ellie started to say that was just fine with her, but he bent his head to hers again, catching her mouth half open, sliding his tongue between her lips, burning her with his desire, rendering her utterly silent. As he deepened the kiss and slid his hands upward, she suddenly felt as if time had truly stopped at this pivotal point, as if they were now suspended in a bubble, sealed away from the world and the strange reality beyond it. She felt suddenly safe.

Hungrily, Ellie kissed Ian back, her fingers curling around the collar of the rough shirt he wore. There were no buttons to open the shirt and expose his flesh, so she pulled it from the waist of his breeches. He sat up a little and she slid to her knees, facing him, sighing as he helped her remove the garment, her breath turning faint at the sight of his naked, muscular chest.

She reached out and brushed her fingers across his bare skin, trailed them over the tattoo on his right arm "Tell me about your tattoo," she said, and leaned down to lick it. Ian closed his eyes and his own breathing became ragged.

"Och, lass," he whispered, "'tis a symbol of everlasting love."

Her hand fell away and Ian opened his eyes. "Dinna be afraid."

"I'm not," she whispered, as she gazed deeply into his eyes, feeling strangely calm. This was what she'd been hoping for, ever since she first met Ian over six months ago. It seemed like years now, like she'd been waiting so very long to touch him, to kiss him, to give him every part of her. "I just wanted to do *this*."

She slid her hands up his chest to his shoulders, then trailed her fingers up his neck, and pulled him down to her. Ian knelt beside her, leaning to take her mouth again, smiling against her lips as he slipped her blouse easily down to her waist.

Katie had given her some clothes, and before she went looking for Ian, Ellie had decided to go all out. She wore what her mother would have called a "peasant" blouse, thin and cream-colored. The off-the-shoulder style and the fact that she still wore her pink bra underneath made her look extremely slutty. She hoped Ian appreciated her efforts.

She'd paired the sexy blouse with a "cincher" that made her waist look like something out of *Gone With the Wind*, and breeches, because it was just too darn cold to wear a skirt. Ellie drew in a sharp breath as Ian let his fingers drift lightly across her lacy pink bra, just hard enough that she could feel his touch as he grazed the firm peaks beneath the silk, then slid down across her ribs, to the top of her breeches.

One by one he slid the buttons out of their holes, now straddling her, kissing each spot that each button revealed, his tongue dipping lower, making her arch beneath him. She reached for him, suddenly terrified that she wouldn't know what to do, how to act, her hands closing over his shoulders, pulling him upward, back to her lips, back to something she understood.

He lay half on top of her and half on the bed. She leaned forward to bite his chin lightly as her hands slid down his back to the top of the breeches he wore. Timidly, she slipped her fingers under the edge of the cloth and he laughed and sat up, shedding the garment.

As Ellie stared at the incredible sight of Ian in all his glory, he moved back to her, his hands flat on either side of her head as he held himself above her, then leaned down to capture her mouth again. She closed her eyes at the touch of his hand on her leg, shivered as he traced the curve of her thigh and caressed her hip bone. When he moved to the V created by her unbuttoned breeches, she drew in a sharp breath, and he lifted his eyes to hers.

Ellie couldn't look away. She was sinking into the pure, liquid heat of him, drowning in those hot blue eyes, helpless as a slow, burning smile tilted his mouth and he slipped her breeches over her hips and down her legs, tossing them aside without ever taking his gaze from hers.

And when he lay down again, Ellie's breath caught in her throat as she felt the whole hard length of him pressing against her.

Her nipples pebbled hard against his chest, and he leaned away, his fingertips drifting lightly over her breasts, the look on his face one of awe.

"Och, lass," he said, his voice rough, "ye are so beautiful." He glanced up at her and the love shining in his eyes made Ellie feel that she truly *was* beautiful. Then he bent his head to each breast in turn, running his tongue across the sensitive skin, making her arch beneath him again.

His hand trailed across her stomach and down, caressing, teasing, invading, but oh, such a welcome invasion. Suddenly she wanted the man she loved inside of her, wanted to make their joining complete. Her heart pounded against her chest as she traced the curve of his neck with her tongue, then up to his ear. Her hands moved across his back to feel the sensation of taut muscles flexing beneath her fingers.

"Ian," she whispered, "I need you."

"Och, Ellie," he whispered, as he covered her with his body, taking her mouth once again as she rose to meet him, the warmth of his skin making her feel liquid inside. Then suddenly he grew still, and he stared down at her, his gaze searching hers.

We are two halves of the same whole, Ellie thought, as she trembled beneath him. *This* was the love she'd been longing for all of her life, she realized, her breath coming quickly as Ian held himself above her. This was *who* she had longed for . . . Ian.

"Eleanor," he said, his voice soft. He ran his tongue across his lips and shook his head, his eyes filled with wonder. "I love ye," he said. "'Tis never happened to me before." He smoothed her hair back from her face. "Ye are the one I've been waiting for. Ye are the lass o' my heart. I wrote that song for ye, and didn't know it."

"Ian . . ." She breathed his name and pressed herself against him, desperate for their joining, urging him to make her complete. She didn't need him to make her ready—she'd been ready for this moment for six months.

But he was trying to be gentle, and she wanted him *now*, hard and fast, rocking into her. Ellie bucked beneath him and raked her nails down his back, bit his ear, and whispered, "*Now*, laddie."

Ian groaned, the sound low and ragged, and then he thrust forward, filling her with the sweet, wonderful length of him. He cried her name. She rose to meet him, giving herself to the only man she had ever loved. He moved higher and harder, and she shook with her passion, crying out as Ian rocked into her over and over again. And just when she was about to skyrocket into space, she opened her eyes, wanting to see his face when she soared.

He gazed down at her, his eyes heavy-lidded, his face beautiful as he moved inside of her. In that moment, Ellie wanted to tell him she loved him, wanted it with all of her heart, but something held her back. Then her breath grew ragged, and coherent thought was impossible as pleasure flooded through her body, soared through her veins, rushed into her brain, and exploded in one sharp, furious blast of glorious beauty.

She shattered beneath him and Ian found her mouth, possessed it, possessed her, until she gasped again and then arched into his thrust, as they both shuddered with release. Ian breathlessly whispered her name.

Ellie floated back to earth in raw and breathless wonder. When the lazy mist finally cleared from her head, she turned on her side and stroked her hand over the hard slope of his arm, amazed at his body, already wanting him again.

"'There is always some madness in love,'" she said softly. He didn't answer. She frowned and rose up on her elbows, peering down at him. "That was Nietzsche. Surprised he knows what love is? Ian?" He lay on his back, staring up at the ceiling, looking anxious. "What's wrong?" she said, starting to feel a little worried herself.

He turned and pulled her to him, one hand smoothing the hair back from her face. "I fear that I have done something wrong."

Ellie shook her head. How could he think such a thing? "Ian, you were perfect."

"I have to ask ye something," he said.

"All right." This wasn't exactly the way she'd pictured her afterglow.

"Before tonight, had ye ever lain with a man before?"

Ellie sighed. "Did I seem that inexperienced?"

"Nay, but—so, ye are—were?"

She put her head on his chest so she wouldn't have to look at him and held up one finger. "One guy. In college. It was terrible. I swore I'd never do it again until I found the man that I wanted to spend the rest of my life with."

He grew very still beneath her and Ellie closed her eyes.

"What?" she finally said. "Are you disappointed that I wasn't a virgin?"

He tilted her face, and when she saw his eyes, tender, gentle, she almost wept with relief.

"Och, lass, no. I was afraid that ye were an innocent, and I too eager."

Ellie smiled and slid her leg across his, relief flickering through her. "*You* were magnificent," she said. "So enough about you. How was I?"

Ian laughed and rolled her to her back, gazing down at her with love in his eyes. He'd said he loved her, and she wanted so badly to say it back. Why couldn't she form the words?

"You? You were amazing," he said. "But there were a few things that I forgot to show you, you being so inexperienced and all."

Her tongue darted out and she licked the center of his chest. He shivered and she reveled in knowing she could make him tremble.

"*Oooh*, teacher," she said, "I am so ready to learn."

twelve

Davey lay down on the hard mattress in his small room and put his hands behind his head, trying to get his thoughts where they should be—on the mathematics that had to do with the cairn—but they kept wandering back to Ian and Ellie.

He was worried. From what he could tell, Ellie was head over heels in love, with Ian only moments behind her. There had to be a way to convince Ian to come back with them to their time.

Davey closed his eyes as his head began to pound. He feared that Ellie, in her euphoric state of love and freedom and partial insanity, would decide to stay in the past in some misguided attempt to sacrifice herself in the name of love. He couldn't let that happen. He had great respect for Quinn and Maggie, and was determined to bring Ellie back to them.

He had just managed to push his thoughts back to mathematics, when someone knocked on his door. He rose slowly. Who would be knocking on his door in the middle of the night? From what he'd overhead in the hall earlier, he didn't think either Ian or Ellie would be waking him up to see if he wanted a midnight snack of bread and ale. So if one of them was knocking, it must be important.

With a sigh, he rolled off the uncomfortable bed, picked up his glasses from the floor, and crossed to the door. When he opened it, he stepped back, all thoughts of sleep banished as he stared down at Katie Campbell, clad only in her nightgown.

"Can I help ye?" he asked, shoving his glasses on, ashamed to admit that he only did it so he could get a better look.

Katie glanced back over her shoulder and then without speaking, pushed past him into the room. Davey started to close the door, then thought better of the idea and left it open. He turned to find the girl frowning up at him. She was a wee thing, no more than five feet two, he calculated. He wasn't considered that tall at five foot eleven, but next to him, she was diminutive.

"Shut the door," she commanded.

"I think it best we leave it open," Davey said. "If yer brother finds ye in here, I dinna want him to get the wrong idea."

"Which brother?"

Davey thought about it, then shrugged. "Any of them."

Katie lifted her pointed chin and folded her arms across her chest. "Tavish wouldna care, nor would Ian from what I can see. I am nothing more than chattel to either of them."

For a moment, Davey felt overwhelmingly sorry for her. How awful it must be for a girl of intelligence and courage—which she undoubtedly was—to live in this time period where women were considered little more than livestock, to be traded for land and holdings and favor at court.

"Ian is not like that," Davey said. "He's just got a lot on his mind. Ye can trust that he'll come through for ye."

Her small shoulders sagged as she gazed down at the floor. For all her claim to be nineteen, she looked younger, and he felt rather perverted as he appreciated the curves beneath her soft, cream-colored gown. There were intricate little stitches around the neckline and he suddenly realized how cute Ian's sister was.

"I understand," she said. "Ian has come home to a terrible situation, and if he is the brother I think he is, he wants to set things right."

"Aye, I believe he does," Davey agreed.

Katie walked slowly toward him, her blue eyes, so much like Ian's, holding his gaze steadily. "But if he is the brother I think he is, then he will help me. He will keep my father from marrying me off to the earl."

"If he can," Davey said, "no doubt he will. But there are other, extenuating circumstances that ye dinna ken." He dragged one hand through his rumpled hair and pushed his spectacles up on his nose.

"What are those?" she asked, peering up at him. "Do they protect yer eyes?"

"What? My glasses?" He took them off self-consciously and then replaced them on his nose. "No, not protection. They help me to see more clearly." That seemed to make them of less interest to her, and she shrugged and turned away. "Look," he said hastily as she moved toward his bed, "it's late and I am extremely tired. Can we speak more about this in the morning? I assure you, if I could help prevent your marriage to the earl, I would. I'll speak to Ian of it tomorrow."

Katie stopped beside the bed and then whirled and ran lightly to the door, slamming it shut. When she skipped back to him, she was smiling, and Davey took a step back. She wasn't just cute; she was downright *pretty*.

"I have the answer!" she said, bouncing up and down on her toes.

"Uh, ye do?"

"Aye! 'Tis the perfect plan! Ye are Ian's friend, so ye must be a man of honor. Ye seem intelligent enough, though a trifle slow at times . . ."

Davey frowned. Where was she going with this? And what did she mean *slow*?

"So I know what to do!" She laughed in delight and clapped her hands together. "Why didn't I think of this before?"

"Think of what?" he asked.

Her blue eyes twinkled. "Well," she said, "the old man is determined to wed me to the earl, right?" Davey nodded. "But he canna marry me to someone if I am already wed!"

"Already wed? What do you—" Comprehension dawned and Davey began backing across the room, one hand held out to keep her at bay as she followed after him. "Oh, no, no, ye don't," he said.

"It makes perfect sense," Katie told him, following him all the way to the wall. He bumped into it and winced.

"It makes no sense at all!" Davey's heart was pounding. Did she really think—yes, he could see in the determination of her set jaw that she really did.

Anger flared in her eyes and Katie punched his arm. "Yes, it does, ye frightened weasel! If ye marry me, then my father canna marry me to the earl!"

Davey was getting a little angry. First her slur against his intelligence, and now his courage! "And why in the world would I agree to wed ye? Ye are a child."

Katie glanced away and then back up at him, a wicked grin on her petulant lips. Without warning, she grabbed his arm and jerked him forward. Davey stumbled and she spun him around, pushed him backward, and threw herself on top of him as he fell upon the bed.

"A child, am I?" she said triumphantly.

Okay, well, Davey thought, fighting sudden, inappropriate images as all of her softness pressed against him, *she is definitely not a child.*

"Marry me, Davey Ferguson," she demanded.

"Ian would kill me!" Davey cried.

"Why? Because ye bedded his sister?" Davey felt his face grow hot, as she frowned down at him.

"Oh, dinna worry. I dinna intend to truly be yer wife. I mean, I will bed ye if I *must*"—she made a face and Davey's mouth dropped open—"but once my father and my brothers are convinced I am no longer a maiden, and they see me wed to ye, and ye help me get away from them, our contract will be at an end."

"Where will ye go?" Davey asked, half admiring her determination to foil her father.

She shrugged. "If ye are willing, ye could allow me to travel along with ye until I find a place of employment." Katie gazed deeply into his eyes, and he grew very still beneath her. "Please, Davey?"

Davey sighed. It was time to put an end to this. Her lips were too full, too close, and the feel of her skin against his much too tempting.

"Now listen to me, little girl," he said sternly. "I will help ye all I can, and I know Ian will as well, but I canna marry ye. Good Lord, I'm—I'm—" he went blank. Let's see, he was twenty-two; she was nineteen. He couldn't think. Twenty-two minus nineteen was—what was it? What was wrong with him? He shook his head. "I'm *much* too old for ye."

The softness vanished from her eyes, and she rolled off of him. "Dinna be ridiculous!" she said, sitting cross-legged beside him. "The earl is forty-six years older than me, and 'tis considered a good match!"

Davey shook his head. To think that this—this—*teenager* would be given to some randy old earl and be robbed of ever finding her own true love.

"Perhaps yer father, or Ian, will find ye a different husband. One a little less—elderly."

Katie shrugged. "None of the young ones will have me. They say I'm too wild. When I was sixteen I was betrothed to an earl who was eighty-nine, but he died before we could make the agreement binding."

Davey rose from the bed and began to pace. "I canna believe that yer father would allow such a union to take place. It's—well, it's just wrong." He waved one hand, gesturing broadly. "Ye should be out having fun, dancing, singing, doing—whatever it is girls do in this day and age—falling in love and such!"

Katie jumped up from the bed and threw her arms around his waist, burying her face against his chest. "Aye, I knew ye had a good face! I knew ye were a good man who wouldna let this happen to me! Then ye will do it?" She looked up at him anxiously. "Ye'll marry me?"

Davey unwound her arms from his waist. "I will help ye," he said, feeling helpless as she continued to beam at him. "And I promise ye, I will do all I can to make sure ye dinna marry the earl. But I canna marry ye."

Her face shifted into a scowl and to his horror, she flung herself at him, knocking him backward, flat on the bed. She sprawled on top of him again, her eyes like blue steel.

"Oh, yes, ye will," she told him, as he stared at her in shock. "Because if ye don't promise to marry me, I will scream bloody murder and bring both my brothers in here, and I will tell them how ye took advantage of my inexperience and ravaged me!" She smirked down at him. "And *then* Ian will kill ye!"

"Ye wouldn't dare!" Davey cried.

"Ye think not?" She took a deep breath and opened her mouth, no doubt to let loose a scream that could be heard all the way to Edinburgh. Thinking quickly, Davey did the only thing that he could.

He kissed her.

Ellie lay in bed and looked out the diamond-paned window at the rising sun. When the sunbeams hit the window, they painted a beautiful pattern of light across the stone walls of the room, and the silken covers of the bed. She and Ian had made love again, and just before dawn, one more time. Lying in his arms, watching the sun come up, she'd never felt so happy in her life. He'd had to go and check on his father, but had kissed her soundly and promised to be back to take her downstairs for breakfast.

She stretched and smiled, trying to remember every touch, every kiss, every dazzling moment of their night together. But that made her want him again, and since he wouldn't be back for a while, she sat up and tried to think about something else. Like finding a bathroom. She ran one hand through her hair and winced as her fingers met with a mass of tangles.

With no brush and several races for their lives across the Highlands, it was no wonder she was such a mess. Ian's discarded shirt lay across the foot of the bed and she pulled it on, then headed for the huge mirror hanging on the wall near the wardrobe on the other side of the room. With a sigh, she steeled herself to face what was bound to be a disaster.

It was worse.

Her hair hung around her face in clumps. Her skin was chapped from the brisk Scottish wind of the last few days. Her nose was red. She had no makeup on and her normally pale face looked even more woebegone than usual.

Why in the world had Ian even wanted to make love to her? Good thing it had been dark in the room. Maybe Katie would lend her a brush and some clean clothes. She sniffed under her arm and shrugged. Not too bad, but a bath would be heavenly. How did people bathe in the eighteenth century? Bathtubs, or did they just jump into streams?

Ellie glanced into the mirror again and then grew still. Familiar blue gray eyes stared back at her, framed by her disheveled reddish blonde hair, but the emotions in those eyes were not familiar at all. Contentment. Happiness. Joy. Fragile, fleeting emotions.

A wave of fear rushed over her. What had she been thinking, to cast aside the shields that had served to protect her for so long? Hadn't she learned long ago not to open her heart? And hadn't she done just that when she gave herself to Ian, body and soul? So what if she hadn't said she loved him? He'd have to be a fool not to see how she felt. And she was a fool for taking this risk.

Ellie laughed, the harsh sound echoing around the room. *Risk? What risk?* It was a sure thing that she was going to get her heart broken—no, not just broken, but demolished. Ian had already said he wasn't going back with her to the twenty-first century. And in spite of this insane game she'd been playing for the last few days, pretending that Maggie and Allie didn't exist, there was no way she could remain in the past with him. She began to tremble.

Turning away from the mirror, Ellie paced across the room and back, her mind racing. She had to get a grip, to find a way to protect herself, to become the old Ellie once again. She opened the door of a wardrobe in the corner and found a good selection of breeches and shirts. Katie's? They looked small enough to be hers. Perhaps she had given up her room for her brother. Ellie chose some of the clothing, avoiding dull colors and choosing the brightest to be had.

"My kingdom for a brush," she muttered, and then spun around and crossed back to the bed. As she did, her elbow bumped a large pottery vase sitting on a small table next to the wardrobe. Filled with some kind of dried flowers that were a brilliant burgundy red, the container rocked back and forth half a second, and then, before Ellie could reach it, crashed to the floor.

She groaned and sank to her knees, avoiding the worst of the breakage as she reached out and touched one of the burgundy flowers. It crumbled and left a bright auburn residue on her fingers. She stared down at the color, and then slowly rose to her feet as the glimmer of an idea began to take shape.

After finding his father had spent a restful night, Ian had gone to the great room and sat in the old man's chair in front of the fireplace for a long time, just thinking. The bewhiskered physician had arrived at dawn and proclaimed the laird was "a little distempered in his head," and that he suffered from "ague." He prescribed whiskey and honey three times a day and left, shaking his head.

From his time spent in the modern world, Ian knew that such a diagnosis was not only wrong, but ridiculous. He had resolved to seek out Davey Ferguson that morning, to see if the scientist would give his opinion, but was told by his brother that Katie and Davey had gone to a nearby village. For what purpose, Ian couldn't imagine.

And when he went to his room to wake Ellie for breakfast, she was gone, too. An inquiry to the cook turned up the information that the "young lassie," as the cook called her, had asked for a bath. The old woman was quite put out at the strange woman's request, but had ordered her sons to carry heated water upstairs to a room reserved for that use.

The image of Ellie, relaxing naked in the large wooden tub where he'd often scrubbed as a lad, made him turn toward the stairs, only to stop before taking the first step. Best let the lass have a little time to herself. It had been scarcely an hour since he had lain with her and yet he wanted her again. But it was more than just desire. She was funny and kind and petulant and beautiful, and he loved her.

His heart began to beat faster and he backed away from the stairs, turning and half running toward the door that opened to the back of the house. He couldn't love Ellie. Och, what had he done? Now she would either expect him to go back with her or let her stay in the past with him. As far as he could see, either decision was impossible.

He wandered about the castle and the outbuildings, noting the few horses in the stable, the small amount of food in the larder, the absence of servants who had once scurried like submissive ants to do the laird's bidding. Now there were only a handful.

"So, ye were in France all this time."

He turned to find his brother Angus standing behind him wearing a dark kilt and a black shirt, a sword in his hands. Ian straightened and faced him warily. Angus was a man in his forties, second eldest, while Ian himself was the elder brother—and still only twenty-five. It fair boggled the mind.

"Aye," he said. "Boo."

His brother cut the air with the blade. "Ye always were a prankster."

"So ye dinna think me a ghost any longer?"

Another swipe. "Ye humiliated me in front of my men."

"Ye humiliated yerself when ye took a commission in King George's pack of liars and thieves."

"What did ye do in France?" Angus asked, laying his sword across his arm and balancing it there. "Conspire with the Jacobites?"

Ian gave his brother an appraising look. There was something there behind those cold eyes that made him stop and think before he answered.

"Are ye for or against the cause of the Jacobites, Angus?"

His brother's face flushed. "Against, of course!"

"Why 'of course'?"

Angus sliced the air with the sword as he spoke through gritted teeth. "Because I am loyal to the king."

"To the king? Or to our father?" Ian walked toward him, stopping a few feet away. "I thought ye were a man who followed his own heart," he said, "but I return to find that ye are simply our father's lackey."

Angus sliced the air next to Ian's ear, and then nodded with approval when his brother didn't jump. "Impressive."

Ian lifted one shoulder. "Ye always lift yer wrist before ye strike. Ye've done that since we were boys. Come over to the right side, Angus. Join me, and when Father is gone, we will take the Highlands back from General Wade."

Angus lowered his sword, his gaze distant. "Ye were not here," he said. "Ye dinna know what ye are talking about."

"I'm talking about Scotland!" Ian felt a new surge of anger rise up inside of him. "I'm talking about ye and my brothers and my father giving in to the English king, instead of rising up and supporting our own king—King James!"

Angus took a step forward, his face twisted in rage. "Ye know *nothing*!" he said, in a voice so filled with fury that Ian felt his conviction falter.

"Then tell me," he said. "Tell me what I dinna know. Tell me why ye have turned against our own clan, pillaging our people's homes in return for—what? Our father's lands?" Ian shook his head. "Is it worth yer honor?"

His brother drew in a long breath and Ian's throat tightened as he saw that Angus's hand gripped around the hilt of his sword was shaking. When he finally spoke, his voice was tight, controlled.

"I am in need of a sparring partner," he said. "Did ye practice in France, or have ye let yerself go soft, like the rest of yer kind?"

Ian smiled, one corner of his mouth quirking up derisively. "Lend me a sword," he said, "and I will show ye just how soft I am."

Ellie strode across the courtyard, feeling more like herself since—well, since she ended up in the past. She tossed her head, relishing the feel of her newly darkened hair. The cook had begrudgingly arranged for a bath to be readied for her, but even better, had concocted what passed for hair dye—henna.

She had gotten the idea from the burgundy plant in Ian's room and had remembered reading once that henna had been around for ages. The dye wasn't as good as her usual Miss Clairol Nice 'n Easy "Black Minx," but the dark, vibrant red of the henna dye had given her a real lift when she checked out her image in the mirror in Ian's room, after her bath. A little charcoal over and under the eyes and she was practically as good as new.

Raiding Katie's closet had been fun—luckily they wore almost the same size—and now, wearing hunter green breeches just a little too short, soft brown boots, a thigh-length beige shirt, and over that a long leather vest, belted at the waist with a wide belt, Ellie felt a little less panicked. Maybe it wasn't too late to protect herself from having her heart broken. Maybe she could still raise the walls that had served her so well in the past.

The cook had told her that Ian was "taking the air," so she headed out back to look for him. As she walked through the courtyard, she was so lost in thought that it took a few minutes for the distant sounds to sink in, but when they did, she stopped abruptly.

Clanging. People talking, yelling, shouting at the top of their lungs. What was going on? She headed through the courtyard at a dead run, and turned a corner to stop short as she stared down the hillside at a horrifying sight below. Surrounded by at least two dozen people—most of them women—Ian and Angus, both bare from the waist up, were circling one another, each holding a very sharp, very deadly sword.

"I swear, I can't turn my back for a minute," Ellie said. Lengthening her strides, she made it down the hillside just in time to see Ian go down on one knee and barely block the downward sweep of Angus's sword with his own. Cursing under her breath, Ellie pushed through the crowd, bursting into the clearing without any plan at all, only knowing she had to stop this ridiculous display of testosterone.

And what a display it was. As Ian stumbled to his feet, he lifted his sword above his head, his biceps as thick as tree limbs, the Trinity tattoo on his right arm almost glowing in the sunshine, his broad chest muscled, his abdomen taut. He brought the sword down against his brother's blade, and his breeches slid a little lower, revealing dusky hair beneath his navel leading downward in a V. Definitely drool worthy. It was no wonder there were so many women watching this bout.

Angus was no slouch in the body department either, though he was thicker and broader in the waist and shoulders than Ian. As he swung his sword around to block Ian's attack, the metal rang out again, and the Scot feinted to one side and sliced his brother's chest with one bold swipe.

Ellie's heart twisted in her chest. "That's *enough!*" she cried.

The crowd fell silent and the two men turned, startled enough for the moment that they both lowered their swords. Ian frowned at her, and then started to speak, but Angus beat him to the punch.

"This is no concern of yers, lassie," Angus said. He turned back to Ian. "Unless ye've had enough yerself?"

Ian shot Ellie a warning look and shook his head, droplets of sweat spinning out from him as he did. "I was just getting warmed up," he said, and raised his sword.

"Good grief!" Ellie strode across the clearing and stopped between the two men, her hands outstretched. "What are you trying to do, kill each other? Aren't you brothers? Is this what brothers in Scotland do? What about loyalty? What about family?"

Angus glowered at her. "Family doesna desert ye for twenty-three years," he said, spitting out the words. "And brothers—true brothers—dinna turn against ye."

Ellie shook her head and turned to Ian. "You made me a promise, Ian. You said you would take us back to the cairn. I'm ready to go."

She had just meant to give him an out, but when he stared down at her, looking stunned and vulnerable, she suddenly realized that if she wanted to save herself, it was time to go.

His gaze turned cool. "Ye picked a fine time to decide, but if that's what ye want, lass, then I'm happy to oblige."

Ellie's chest tightened painfully, as she shot his brother an arrogant smile. "Sorry, Angus," she said, "but I'm sure the two of you can continue hacking each other to pieces later."

"Ian!" Katie pushed her way through the crowd and stopped in front of Angus, her chin lifted stubbornly as she faced her brothers. Someone nudged Ellie, and she turned to find Davey looking at her in concern.

"What the hell do ye two think ye're doing?" Katie said, her hands on her hips. Instead of her usual breeches, she wore a skirt and blouse, both blue, with a gray bodice laced up the front.

"We're sparring," he said. "Dinna fash yerself."

"The two of ye aren't sparring—I've been watching. Ye are trying to kill each other!"

Ian wiped the blood from his chest. Ellie suddenly longed to wash that muscled skin, to bandage his wound, to kiss away his pain. Is this what remaining in the past would mean? Watching him fight and get hurt, or maybe killed? All the more reason not to stay.

"We wouldn't have killed each other," Ian finally said, his voice thoughtful.

Angus narrowed his gaze and, with an oath, sheathed his blade. "Speak fer yerself," he said. Without another word, he turned and walked away. The crowd began to wander off, now that it was apparent the fight was over, leaving Ellie and Ian, Davey and Katie, to face one another.

"So," Ian said, his eyes boring into Ellie's, "ye are ready to go home."

"Well, you know, the eighteenth century begins to pale after a while," she said.

His gaze raked over her and Ellie saw that he was just realizing she had changed her hair color and makeup. The coolness faded from his eyes and he sighed. "So we are back to that, are we?"

Ellie started to answer, to explain that she could not, she dared not, love him when he nodded.

"'Tis just as well," he said.

As Ellie stood there with her breath caught in her throat, Katie rushed toward Ian, pulling Davey behind her.

"I heard ye say ye are leaving. You can't leave, not yet!" Katie cried. "Tell him you aren't going! Not yet!"

Ian frowned and gave Davey a suspicious look. Davey responded by looking terrified.

"What's going on?" Ian demanded. "Why should ye care if Davey leaves or not?"

Katie folded her arms over her chest. "He isn't leaving."

Ellie lifted both brows, growing more alarmed by the moment. "Davey," she demanded, "what's going on?"

Davey cleared his throat. "Uh, I may have to delay my return for a bit."

"Why?" Ellie asked.

He and Katie exchanged glances, and then Davey shrugged. "Because I haven't seen all the sights?"

Ian smiled grimly as he reached out and pulled Katie away from the man. "All right, lad," he said, "now ye are safe. Tell us the facts."

"Well," Davey began, and then shook his head helplessly. "Ye see, it's like this . . ." His voice trailed away, and Katie rolled her eyes at him.

"Oh, for heaven's sake," she muttered, then lifted her chin, her eyes glimmering with defiance. "We're married!" Katie announced, and with that, she broke away from Ian, threw her arms around Davey's neck, and kissed him full on the mouth.

thirteen

With a roar, Ian jerked Davey away from his sister and followed her kiss with a hard right cross. Davey stumbled backward, and with an oath, flung himself forward, catching Ian
in the midriff, taking him down in a well-executed tackle.
The two rolled in the dirt, slugging it out for several minutes
until Katie glanced over at Ellie.

"Can ye lift a washtub?" she asked.

Ellie frowned and blinked, then followed Katie's gaze to
a round wooden tub sitting on the ground near a fence where
animals were kept. The tub was filled with water and had
two rope handles on either side. She grinned.

"Aye," she said, "that I can."

The women hauled the tub up from the ground as the men
continued to fight. When they had gotten as close as they
dared to the milieu, Katie started swinging her side of the
tub. Ellie saw her intent and laughed, swinging hers as well.

"One . . ." Ellie said.

"Two . . ." Katie cried.

"*Three!*" they shouted together. The water rose up from
the swinging tub like a gushing waterfall, rising above the

men for a split second before crashing down squarely on top of them with a tremendous, satisfying splash.

"What the—" Davey sputtered, sprawled next to Ian.

"Who did—" Ian began, then saw the women standing in front of them, legs apart, hands on their hips.

"Now," Ellie said with authority, "if the two of you are through acting like little boys, maybe we can sort this out."

"Aye," Katie agreed. "Ian, stop hitting Davey. We havena been . . . intimate, if that's what ye think." She smiled and Ellie hid a grin. The girl was obviously happy that Ian cared enough to fight for her honor.

"And I'm supposed to believe that!" Ian said as he struggled to his feet.

"Are ye calling yer sister a liar?" Davey asked, blood in his eye as he rose with slightly less agility.

"Ye know ye canna stay here!" Ian shouted in fury. "Did ye marry her just to bed her? I thought ye were my friend!"

Davey's face turned red and he took a step forward, but Ellie caught his eye and he stopped, fists clenched at his side.

"I wanted to save yer sister from the clutches of an old, nasty *Englishman*! Which is more than ye appeared willing to do."

Katie crossed to Davey's side and put her arm around his waist. As she led him away, she glanced back over her shoulder at Ian, still glowering behind them. "Thanks, brother, but dinna be hitting my husband again."

Ian watched them walk away, shaking his head.

"I'm going to kill that guy," he said.

"No, you aren't," Ellie told him. He glanced down at her, unseeing, then his eyes focused.

"So let's talk about this," he said, lifting his hand to her hair and capturing a dark red strand.

Ellie took a step back and her hair slipped from his fingers. "Nothing to talk about. You said it was just as well." She took a deep breath. "And I agree."

He took a step toward her. "I dinna mean it. I was just,

surprised, after last night. I thought we had figured out a few things."

"I thought so, too, but this morning, I figured out a few more."

He moved a little closer and this time Ellie held her ground. She was tired of running away. Ian slid both hands on either side of her face and searched her eyes.

"Tell me ye dinna love me," he said.

Ellie's heart began to beat faster and her eyes slid away from him. But she didn't move. If she moved, he might stop touching her. "I never said that I did," she whispered.

"Aye," Ian said, bending to almost, but not quite, touch her lips. "Ye did. Ye told me with every kiss"—he brushed his mouth against hers—"with every touch." He stroked his fingers over her jaw and down the side of her neck, making her close her eyes and shudder. She felt his lips against her hair and then her ear, and he bit her earlobe gently and murmured, "With all that ye are, ye told me that ye loved me as much as I love ye."

He slipped his hands around her waist and drew her against his bare chest.

Ellie shivered a little as the cold wind swept suddenly over them, and he held her even closer. He was sticky with sweat and the dirty, heady aroma of a man who has worked hard in the sun for too long. She didn't care. God help her, she was home again. And at the same time, she was so terribly lost.

"There is a place near here that I would like to show ye," he said softly. "Will ye go with me?"

Ellie nodded, wordless, and let him take her by the hand. They walked down the rocky hillside, reaching what passed for the roadway to the castle. Nearby was a forest, and Ian led her straight toward it, his long legs eating up the countryside so that she had to almost run to keep up with him.

"Where are we going?" she finally asked, when they reached the first cluster of alder and oak and she could find her voice again.

"Ye'll see," he promised. He reached out and lifted a low

limb, gesturing her to enter the shadowed realm inside the forest. A thrill rushed through her and she looked up, suddenly shy. His blue eyes burned into her. "Trust me," he said, his voice like midnight, deep and dark.

Ellie took a deep breath and nodded. She ducked under the overhanging branch he held and then found she could straighten. Ian was at her side then, and took the lead again. Without speaking they walked, hand in hand, through the trees stretching above them, tall and thick, their canopies sheltering them from the sun, or even the sky.

"Just around that old oak," he said softly. "Come."

The tree was huge, no doubt a first growth of the land, as big around as one of the cypress trees on the Guadalupe River back in Texas, but twisted, looking as if someone had carved deep waves around and up the bark, the thick ribbons of wood intertwining in curious patterns, in nature's amazing art. Ellie swallowed hard as Ian led her around the ancient tree, and then she stopped, awestruck.

There was a clearing in front of her, surrounded by trees on the edge, so large their branches stretched over and linked together, keeping it shady and cool. In the center of the clearing was a stream—a burn. It began somewhere beyond the clearing and ran through the forest, flowing crystal clear over smooth stones, down a slight slope and over a four-foot waterfall, splashing into a deep pool studded with stones before tumbling gleefully on its merry way.

But the most amazing thing was that a fine saunalike mist rose from around the stream, as if it were—hot?

"It's a hot spring?" she asked, incredulous.

"Aye," Ian said, smiling. His hand went to the waist of his breeches and in a matter of moments he stood naked before her. Ellie's mouth went dry. "I come here to bathe," he said. "I know ye already had a bath at the castle, but perhaps—"

"Never turn down the offer of a hot bath in Scotland, I always say," Ellie interrupted, and his handsome face lit up as he held his hand out to her. She reached for him, and he pulled her to his side. He began to undress her, and Ellie shivered with anticipation. He unlaced the leather vest and let it fall to the ground, then stripped the tunic over her head and tossed it to one side. She stood trembling in the cold air, clad only in her breeches as he gazed into her eyes for a long moment, then let his eyes travel downward, caressing her shoulders, her arms, her breasts. He caught his breath.

"Ye have the most perfect breasts I have ever seen," he said, and dipping his head, he flicked his tongue across first one taut nipple, and then the other. Then began to love her in earnest. Ellie let her head fall back as she clung to him, felt the ripple of muscles beneath his skin as she tried to steady herself, and then his arms moved around her, supporting her, holding her, keeping her safe.

When he had her trembling with need, Ian unbuttoned her breeches, but this time she helped, almost tearing the cloth from her legs, impatient to feel his skin against hers. And then she was naked, and they stood apart for a moment, gazing at one another, and something flashed across Ian's eyes—Regret? Fear? Some combination of the two—then it was gone and he held out his hand.

"Make love to me," she said, so softly she wasn't sure he heard, then he lifted his head and smiled.

"Yer wish, princess, is my command," he said. "Come with me."

"I thought I was the Ice Queen," she said, smiling.

He laughed and shook his head, his blue eyes hot with desire. "Not anymore."

Ellie took his hand and he led her to the edge of the spring. He stepped down into a deeper part of the stream and lifted her hand, inviting her to join him. She smiled and stepped into the spring, the water coming up to her hips, and her smile widened as the warmth rushed against her, caressing her. A large, smooth stone lay almost immersed in the water, and Ian sat down on it and gently pulled her to sit in his lap, parting her legs, letting her straddle him, pulling her snugly against him.

He cupped one breast as she gazed down at him, and he caressed her skin, his hands moved downward over her ribs, across her hip bone, and much lower, making her close her eyes and bite her lip.

"Eleanor," he whispered, and she clutched at his shoulders, letting her head fall back as his touch made her begin to melt inside. "'Tis a queen's name," he said, stroking her gently. "'Tis the name of a woman with a courageous heart."

Ellie sighed. She'd never felt so beautiful as she did at this moment, lying naked in the warm water, open to his gaze, his touch.

He stretched his lean body the length of hers, sliding his chest lightly against her, the shock of his skin sending a wave of need and heat surging through her body.

Then he lifted her, letting her find him, urging her to take her time, giving her the power as he began to lick and nibble and tease her breasts, her throat, her shoulders, her mouth. Ellie closed her eyes, embarrassed because she didn't know how to move, how to please him, but when she finally took him into her warmth, into the sweet depths of her body, and opened her eyes, she knew her fears were in vain.

Ian gazed up at her, and even she, with all of her insecurities, could not mistake the emotion in his eyes. Soft, passionate, tender, adoring. He loved her, simply, completely, without any reserve.

It was at that moment Ellie knew she was lost. In spite of her walls, in spite of anything she might try to do to resist him, she loved Ian MacGregor, and nothing could ever change that.

"Ian," she whispered, and then she had no words. She began to love him, with every fiber of her soul and her body. Her mouth upon his; her skin, hot with steam and desire, melding against his as she rose and fell; her eyes half-closed, his eyes half-closed, each watching the other as they trembled together.

Then Ellie saw his eyes quicken and burn, felt his fingers tighten against her back, and suddenly she was lost in the heat, lost in the fury of their bodies becoming one, lost in his love, as Ian met her thrust for thrust. Without warning, she broke, fast and hard and utterly breathless.

But she wouldn't close her eyes. No, as she shattered in his arms, Ellie never took her eyes from his, never stopped moving in the slow rhythm that was driving him crazy, never stopped watching as he grew flushed, his breathing ragged. He was caught in the grip of the madness she was causing. He shuddered and slid his hands into her hair, curling his fingers against her scalp, bringing her mouth down to his as he found his release.

When they could both breathe again, Ian laughed and slid down into the water, taking her with him, holding her in the cradle of his arm. The mist rose around them, and the stream eddied and swirled around their wake.

He lowered his mouth to hers and kissed her as she clung to him, her fingers clutched in his hair, feeling like she would drown if she let go.

"Dinna leave me," he whispered against her lips.

Ellie smoothed his hair back from his forehead, cupping his face between her hands. "Och, laddie," she said, "I'm not nearly as courageous as you think."

Ian fell asleep, fell into a wonderful dream. He was back in the twenty-first century and he was onstage. He was playing the pipes, looking down at his wife, Ellie. Beside her stood a little girl with his hair and Ellie's eyes, and she gazed up at him with love and hero worship in her eyes.

But suddenly he heard a loud pounding in the middle of his tune and he looked around, still playing, trying to find out where it was coming from. It was almost like a drum, but devoid of music, more like—

Ian's eyes flew open. He lay in the four-poster bed in his father's home, Ellie beside him, safe and warm in his arms. He pulled her closer to him, feeling happier than he could remember being in a long, long time.

He kissed her hair, as the pounding in his dream became

a reality. Someone was knocking on his door. He slid out of bed and into his breeches, hurrying to open it before the sound awoke Ellie. The lass had fallen into such a deep sleep that she hadn't stirred the entire night.

They had returned to the castle after their idyllic afternoon and taken supper in their room. It had been a perfect night, and Ian had almost hated to wake from his dream, from the tiny bit of respite he and Ellie had found in one another's arms.

He swung the heavy door open, and Davey stood waiting patiently on the other side. He had several bruises on his face, and Ian unconsciously lifted one hand to his own jaw. He'd forgotten about their fight. It seemed ridiculous now. Davey was a good man, and he couldn't imagine him taking advantage of any woman, let alone Katie.

"Good morning," Davey said, giving him a cautious look. "Do ye have a few moments?"

"Aye, let me grab a shirt." Ian closed the door and dressed hastily, then followed Davey down to the great room.

"I examined your father this morning," Davey said as they both sat down at the long wooden table at the far end of the hall. "He's doing better. We had an interesting talk."

"Did ye? About what?"

"First, I'd like to talk about Katie," Davey said abruptly. "Surely ye know that I would never—"

Ian waved him to silence. "Aye, I do." He looked at the other man ruefully. "My apologies. Can we speak of my sister later? I promise I willna beat ye up again."

Davey cocked one brow in his direction. "Beat *me* up? I see a few bruises on yer own face, MacGregor."

Ian smiled. "Aye. Well, then, will ye promise not to beat me up again?"

"Aye, if ye don't provoke me too much."

"Truce, then?" Ian asked.

Davey nodded. "Truce. But we do need to discuss Katie very soon."

"Aye, we will."

The cook walked into the room just then carrying a tray and gave them each a dirty look. "Good morn, mistress," Ian said. "How do ye fare the day?"

"'Twould be better if folks wouldna require supper in their rooms," she said pointedly. "'Tis fair difficult to climb those stairs."

Ian's smile widened. "My apologies. I promise it will not happen again." This seemed to please the cook, and she brightened noticeably as she placed a plate of ham on the table.

"What? Ham?" Davey asked in amazement.

The cook frowned. "Since we can no longer afford to feed the hog, the master ordered it killed and salted."

"The master is in bed," Ian said, suddenly curious. "Is he able now to give orders?"

The cook flushed as she set a plate of bread on the table and picked up the tray. "I meant, the laird's son Tavish. When the master is ill, he is in charge, ye ken."

Ian nodded. "Aye, I ken."

"This really is excellent," Davey said as he took a big bite of ham and chewed. The cook gave him what might be a smile and left the room.

"So tell me about my father," Ian said. "Is he dying?"

Davey's hand stilled, and he laid down his fork as he looked up at Ian. "Aye. From information I gleaned from the cook, and others in the castle, including yer brother, he has been slowly deteriorating over the last six months."

A muscle in Ian's jaw twitched. He'd known the truth, but to hear it spoken outright made him realize the certainty of his father's impending death. "Do ye know what it is that's killing him?"

"A cancer of some sort likely," Davey said. "I dinna think his episode last night was a result of his illness. It seemed more a nervous reaction than anything else. I expect he will be able to come downstairs by evening." He picked up his spoon again. "I'm sorry, Ian. And I'm afraid I have more bad news."

"Aye?" Ian gazed at the man steadily, his own plate untouched.

Davey nodded. "'Twould seem that yer father is completely broke. That's why he is pressing for the marriage between Katie and the earl, and why Angus is as well."

"I figured as much. The deterioration of the castle, the missing furniture and niceties, it had all the earmarks of a drastic loss of money. 'Tis hard to believe that it happened at all. He is one of the most tightfisted men I've ever known."

Davey shrugged, continuing to stuff ham into his mouth. "Times are hard," he said, "at least that's the explanation given to me by the servants. And there's been money required by the king to support the Black Watch."

"The Black Watch." Ian felt the familiar anger begin anew at the words. "I've spent enough time here," he said, every muscle in his body tense. "It's time to do what must be done."

Davey stopped eating and looked up at him, his eyes hesitant behind his glasses. "And what is that, my friend?"

"I abandoned my family," he said, his voice deceptively soft. He fixed his gaze on some distant point beyond Davey's shoulder and was filled with pain. "I was the eldest brother. Instead of taking the responsibility that position requires, I turned my back on my father and my brothers. If I had been here, I could have made my father see reason or guided my brothers into thinking rightly in spite of the old man!"

Davey shook his head. "Ian, ye did what ye had to do. Montrose was going to hang ye, isn't that what ye told me? Ye faked yer own death and even if ye hadn't traveled through time to escape, ye still would have had to leave yer family behind."

"Aye, and that's the heart of the matter." He shifted his glance to Davey. "I never should have run away with Quinn. I should have stayed here and abided by my father's wishes."

Davey put down the three-pronged fork and leaned toward the other man, lowering his voice as he spoke. "Quinn is yer best friend, and as much yer brother as yer own flesh and blood. Could ye have turned yer back on him? Could ye have supported yer father—and the English king—if ye had it to over again?"

Ian rested his head in both hands and stared down at the table. "Ye dinna understand. It wasna just for Quinn that I ran away with him from MacCrimmons and became a highwayman. 'Twas for myself. I dinna want to have the responsibility that came with being the eldest son. I knew I would have to challenge my father on his allegiance to the king, and all I wanted was to play my pipes in peace."

Davey raised one brow. "I wouldn't think being a highwayman would hold much peace for ye."

Ian lowered his hands and looked up. "Och, that was just a lark." A slight smile tilted his lips. "Two lads tearing up the countryside, getting even with the Duke of Montrose! Quinn was serious, but I"—he frowned—"I was having a good time."

"Interesting," Davey said. He picked up his fork and stabbed another piece of ham. "I canna imagine ever doing what ye and Quinn did, though I must admit, it holds some strange allure for me."

Ian grinned outright. "A hard ride through the Highlands with the English at yer heels might be just what ye need, laddie."

Davey looked up from his plate, his glasses slipping down on his nose. He pushed them up and straightened on the bench. "I dinna think so. Ye have yet to tell me what it is ye think ye must do, here, in this time."

Ian glanced away and then back again. He linked his hands together in front of him on the table and met Davey's eyes. "I must set things right, ye ken? I must undo what has been done."

Davey frowned. "What do ye mean?"

"I mean that my family will not go down in history as supporters of the English king." His mouth tightened and his voice grew grim. "And my brothers will not continue to be part of the Black Watch."

"There is nothing ye can do to change things," Davey said. "History has already been written and—"

Ian slammed his fist down on the table, cutting Davey off. "History has not been written! This is still 1734, and I can still change what happens from here on!"

Davey looked at him sadly and hesitantly shook his head. "No, Ian, I fear ye cannot."

fourteen

"So then what did he say?" Ellie asked as she ate a piece of the ham Davey had brought her.

He spread his hands apart. "He wouldn't listen to me. He got up and stormed off!"

"Do you think he means to stay here? In the past?"

Davey leaned back in the brocade chair in Ian's room. He thought full well that was what Ian had planned, but since he didn't know which way the wind was blowing in Ellie's life, he hesitated to say. "I dinna know for certain," he replied at last.

She sat yoga-style on the edge of the four-poster bed in a too-large shirt, probably Ian's, with her knees akimbo, devouring the ham as eagerly as Davey had. Her legs were bare, at least to the knee, which was as far as the shirt reached. He cleared his throat and quickly glanced up to find the woman's stricken gaze upon him.

"So what does that mean, to you and—and—to me, if he doesn't return with us? Will it mess things up?" she asked.

"I've been doing a lot of calculations since we arrived in the past," Davey said. "With the notes I had with me, and those in my head"—he reached into his pocket and pulled

out the little notebook he always kept with him—"I've figured out why we could not return to our own time when we
tried before."

Ellie leaned forward, her eyes filled with hope. "Well,
that's good news, isn't it? That you know what was wrong?"

He nodded. "Aye. I think that we simply did not use the
spiral at the right time."

Ellie frowned. "What do you mean?"

Davey began pacing around the room, his eyes on the
ceiling.

"I think there was something that determined whether
the spirals worked or not—like a light switch. When it's 'on,'
it works, when it's 'off,' it doesn't. It worked when we came
back in time, and when Ian used it, so all I had to do was
figure out what those two instances have in common."

Ellie's eyes lit up. "They were both at night!"

"Exactly. But not just any night—on a night when the
moon was full."

"So you think the moon has to be full before we can return?"

He nodded. "Aye."

"That's great!" She bounced a little on the bed. "So now,
when we finally talk Ian into coming back with us, we'll
know when it will work! Davey, you're a genius!"

"Aye, but there's something else that's not so great." He
took a deep breath. This was the hard part.

Ellie picked up another piece of ham. "I knew there had
to be a catch."

"I believe that the amount of mass sent back in time must
equal the mass which will return."

"In English, Davey, please."

He nodded and began to pace again. "Because ye and I
journeyed through time together, one of us cannot return to
the twenty-first century without the other. Two bodies must
return at the same time. However, Ian journeyed alone, so he
must return alone."

"So if you and I don't return together, we can't get back
home?"

He frowned thoughtfully. "Excuse me. What I should have said is that it is *dangerous* to change the amount of mass traveling through time, but not impossible."

"Oh, gee, thanks. That makes me feel a *lot* better," she said.

"Well, er, it does leave us with a problem."

"What problem?" Ellie asked, and Davey hated to tell her, but she needed to know.

"Uh, well, it means that you won't be able to leave anytime soon."

"Well, I'm not planning to go without Ian, but why not?"

"Because I have to figure out what to do about Katie."

Ellie's despair changed to amusement. "Oh, that. I forgot to say congratulations. You are such a marshmallow."

Davey's mouth dropped open. "Marshmallow? Why would ye say that?"

"Because you let that girl coerce you into marrying her. Ian wouldn't have let her marry the earl—there was no reason for you to tie the knot!" She shook her head, presumably at his foolishness.

Davey stared back at her grimly. "Are ye so sure of that, lass? Appears to me that Ian has his mind on one thing and one thing only—the Black Watch."

"Well, I wouldn't say *that*," Ellie murmured, glancing thoughtfully toward the rumpled sheet behind her.

Davey blushed and hurried on to his next point. "I'm just saying that I'm not certain he even realizes the seriousness of Katie's plight," he said. "I wanted to make sure."

"Why?" Ellie leaned forward, her gaze curious. "What's it to you?"

Davey blinked and pushed his glasses up on his nose. "To me? Well, 'tis nothing to me, personally, but I couldn't let a young girl be sentenced to marriage with some old codger, could I?"

Ellie raised both brows and nodded. "Ah. Of course." She glanced away and smiled a knowing little smile that Davey did not care for. "You were just being chivalrous."

"Aye."

"A hero of sorts."

He shrugged, uncomfortable with the words. "Not exactly . . ."

"A saver of damsels in distress." She winked at him. "I've got you figured out now, Davey Ferguson." She slid off the bed and padded over to a pile of clothes on the floor and began sorting through them. "So is that it? All the bad news?"

"No."

She looked up at him, startled.

"Remember, we started this conversation about Ian and his plans to change history?"

"Oh, yeah, I forgot." She sighed and flounced back on the four-poster bed. She pulled her legs underneath her and knit her brows together. "Okay, so Ian wants to fight the Black Watch. I mean, he's a Scot and he's come back in time and wants to fight against injustices. He thinks maybe he can change things, make a difference."

Davey shook his head. "It's pointless."

Ellie sat up a little straighter. "What do you mean?"

"I mean that what he does here willna change a thing—barring, of course, the possibility of something huge, like his building an army of a hundred thousand men and leading them at the Battle of Culloden Moor—which doesna happen for another eleven years—and that might have been possible, if it weren't for the fact that his father, or someone, has squandered the family fortune."

"What about *Terminator II*?"

"Beg pardon?" He pushed his glasses up on his nose. He knew the movie she was referring to, of course, but what did it have to do with—

"In *Terminator II*, Sarah Connor and her son are trying to change what happens in their time to prevent the catastrophe of Judgment Day in the future."

"Oh, aye, and that's correct"—he smiled—"in the movies."

"You're saying that everything that's ahead of us is set in stone? It's predestined to happen a certain way?" Ellie shook her head. "What about free will?"

Davey waved one hand impatiently. "It has to do with mathematics, lass. Probability. There is a very low chance statistically that Ian can change the course of Scottish history by his actions. It would take an extremely large fluctuation in the equation. And of course, it could be very risky, even if he *could* cause such an event. What if history, and by extension, the future, is changed for the worse by what Ian does? His actions could actually be disastrous."

Ellie stared at him for a long moment and then Davey saw comprehension dawn behind her eyes. "So you're saying that no matter what Ian does here, in the past, it's not going to make a difference to Scotland's future unless it's something huge?"

"Aye," he said. "But what he does could change Katie's future."

"I don't get it. Why isn't her future predetermined?"

"I was speaking in terms of history," he said. "The likelihood that the history of the world would be altered by the actions of one person is very small. However, the life of one person may very well be altered by the actions of another person."

"Okay, that makes sense, I guess." Ellie frowned. "Did you tell him all of this?"

He nodded. At last he'd gotten through to her. "He's risking himself for nothing," he said. "I thought perhaps ye could talk to him, keep him from throwing his life away for naught." He shook his head. "God only knows where he went and what he plans to do."

Ellie grew very still. "What do you mean?"

"Och, I told ye—he took a horse from the stable and rode away."

"No, you did not tell me!" she cried, jumping off the bed and starting to pull on her clothes. Davey turned his head to give her some privacy, but she was so intent on her task he doubted she noticed. When Ellie was completely clothed in breeches, leather vest, tunic, and a cloak Katie had found for her, she grabbed Davey by the hand and dragged him with her out the door.

"Wait a minute," he protested as she stalked forward. "Where are we going?"

She shot him a steely-eyed look and Davey gulped. "To find Ian," she said.

To anyone passing by, the Clachan Inn appeared to be closed. The shutters had been fastened, the candles and lanterns extinguished, and the front door locked. Ian watched from an upstairs window as the autumn sky rapidly grew dark and a cold wind swept through the town, bringing the promise of snow. There was only a gibbous moon tonight, cutting the moonlight by a third, granting more shadow to those who dared to venture forth.

Ian stood with his arms crossed over his chest and waited. Bittie had sent out word to the MacGregors and the MacIntyres, and anyone else who were allies to those two clans to come to a secret meeting and plot the demise of the Black Watch. He had no idea if anyone would come to hear the words of a man who had disappeared from their midst twenty-three years before and never looked back, but he knew he had to try.

The room the innkeeper had provided—he was a staunch Jacobite—was his largest, and held a long table with benches on either side. There were several chairs as well. The window had been covered with black cloth, allowing a lantern to be lit and placed in the center of the table, and it cast an eerie light against the walls.

Ian paced the room, his hands clasped behind his back, feeling a mixture of impatience and nervousness that in themselves were against his nature. As footsteps sounded on the stairway, he turned to greet the first of the men, and then scowled as he saw not a man, but Ellie.

"What are ye doing here?" he demanded, as she walked inside and swept the room with her long-lashed gaze. Having taken stock, she turned her eyes to him and raised both auburn brows, then leaned against the wall, her arms folded under her breasts.

"I might ask the same of you," she said.

With an exasperated sigh, knowing he might as well tell her the truth, now that she was there, Ian started to explain. Then he stopped and simply stared, his jaw dropping, his pulse racing.

The cream-colored, V-necked shirt she wore with dark brown breeches was a little too big, and the black leather vest laced over it a little too tight, accentuating what Ian considered one—no, two—of her best features, as her defiant stance pushed her lovely breasts together in a delightful décolleté, rendering him suddenly speechless. Heat flared inside of him and he walked toward her, coming to a stop only inches away.

Ellie's eyes widened and then she smiled, an answering fire in her gaze. He leaned down to touch his lips to hers and she lifted her face to his, when the sound of heavy, booted feet tromping up the stairs made Ian jerk back and turn in irritation toward the door. It was Davey, holding his chest and panting like a dog.

"Good Mother of Mercy," he gasped as he stumbled into the room.

"What are ye doing here?" Ian said, regaining his equilibrium as he glared at Davey. He gestured toward Ellie. "Why would ye bring her here?"

"I dinna bring her anywhere, believe me!" the man said, collapsing onto the bench. "She brought me, bouncing across the Highlands on horseback!" He took a deep breath. "Do ye have anything to drink?"

Ian pointed to the corner of the room where a tray of pewter mugs sat, filled with ale. Davey rose and staggered toward it. Part of Bittie's entreaty to the clans was a promise of free ale. Ian hoped there was enough for everyone.

When he turned his attention back to Ellie, the fire in her eyes was gone, and in its place, suspicion. "What are you up to, Ian?" she asked.

"I'm having a—meeting of sorts."

"Oh." She straightened from the wall. "What kind of meeting?"

"I've invited a few acquaintances over to seek their investment in a business venture," he said vaguely. "So go back to my father's house."

"Ohhh, a business venture! Awesome." She moved across the room slowly, like a cat, her fingers trailing across the top of the long table in the middle of the room until she stopped in front of him. "What kind of business? Amway? Tupperware? Mary Kay? Will there be door prizes?"

Ian shook his head. "I have no idea what ye just said, but I need ye to get out of here. Now."

Ellie glanced over at Davey, who was sitting on the bench once again. He tilted the mug to his lips, drained it, and then leaned his head back with a sigh.

"I don't think so," Ellie said. "Davey's tired. It was a fast, bumpy ride."

"I dinna care if Davey is dead," Ian said roughly, striding away from her. He stopped at the doorway and spun around, trying to look as fierce as he could. As much as he loved her, he couldn't take a chance on Ellie—or Davey—saying the wrong thing in front of the men he had summoned. "I want the two of ye out of here!"

Davey blinked, looking owl-like behind his glasses. Ellie shook her head.

"Now, that's not nice," she said. "Davey, he didn't mean it. He's just upset." She frowned thoughtfully. "Why are you upset, Ian? Oh, yeah, because Davey told you that whatever it is you're about to do won't make a bit of difference in the outcome of Scottish history."

Ian tightened his jaw. This meeting could mean the difference in his family's legacy being one of heroism and Scottish pride, or one of treachery. He had no time for Ellie's well-meant concern. He started to tell her so, but the sweet, open caring he saw reflected in her eyes sent a sudden wave of calm over him, and he sagged against the wall, his anger disappearing.

"Ah, lass," he said, "this is something I have to do. I need ye to understand."

Ellie crossed the room to slide her arms around his waist as she looked up at him. "I do," she said, "but I'm not going anywhere." She slipped her hands up the front of his linen shirt and linked them behind his neck, her body soft and warm against him.

"If you want me to sit in the corner like a good little girl, well, okay, for now. But I'm not leaving." She leaned her head back and smiled, daring him to challenge her.

Ian gave up. "Fine. Sit down and stay out of the way, the both of ye. And dinna speak."

"I may just go and find a bed," Davey said with a yawn.

"Great idea," Ellie murmured, and rested her head against Ian's chest, making him ache with wanting her.

Was that her plan? To seduce him away from the meeting? But before he could accuse her, she slid out of his arms and turned to Davey.

"Unfortunately, we've got to stay here and look after this madman so he won't get himself killed."

"I dinna need looking after!" Ian said, irritated once again.

Ellie snapped her head around, and her dark hair fell in tousled curls upon her shoulders. "Look, I know what you're up to. You're planning some kind of resistance or rebellion against the Black Watch. But Davey's already told you that it's not going to change anything, so why are you doing this? It's pointless!"

Ian ground his teeth together, feeling like his jaw was about to crack. How could the lass be so obtuse? He took several deep breaths before he had himself under control enough to answer without taking her head off.

"Eleanor," he began, only to be interrupted by the first of the real guests to arrive. Two tall men, one dark-haired, walked in. With effort, Ian turned his attention from Ellie and held out his hand to the first man.

"I am Ian MacGregor," he said. "Welcome."

fifteen

An hour later Ian sat on the bench beside Davey, leaning his head against the wall.

"I canna believe it," he said, feeling stunned. "I canna believe that neither the MacGregors nor the MacIntyres are interested in joining me."

"I can't believe it either," Ellie said from where she stood beside Davey, and the tone in her voice made him turn and look at her.

To give her credit, she hadn't uttered a word while he had told the representatives of the clans his proposal. Now she sat staring at him, looking equally disturbed. Maybe the lass was finally starting to understand. Then she spoke again.

"I can't believe that you think that you're going to single-handedly start another Jacobite uprising! You don't have to do this, Ian! Scotland is going to end up just fine. Maybe not the Scotland you envisioned, but fine nevertheless—without you killing yourself!"

"Davey doesna know everything," Ian said as he rose and began pacing around the room. "Ye dinna understand, lass. This isna just about the future of Scotland. This is about the future of my family! Ye saw the condition of the castle, and my brothers are out doing King George's bidding, terrorizing their fellow countrymen instead of helping Tavish take care of my father's affairs! *And* 'tis only *yer* opinion that Scotland is 'just fine,' as ye put it." He stopped pacing and shook his head. "If we are yoked with England, we are no' 'just fine.'"

"You didn't seem to feel that way when we toured England last month," she reminded him.

"Aye, I know." Ian released his breath explosively. "I blocked out my past, my heritage, because I so enjoyed being able to play my music. It was all that mattered."

"Oh, Ian," she said, shaking her head. "There was nothing wrong with you finally being able to do that. What's happened to your family—and Scotland—is not your fault."

He met her stricken gaze. "I know 'twas not my doing that I have been away from my family for twenty-three years. 'Twas not my doing that I have not been here to fight for Scotland. But I am here now."

Davey, three sheets to the wind, lifted another tankard of ale to his lips and drank deeply, then shook his head. "'Twill make no diff—diff—it won't change anything. I'm sorry, lad, but the future is set. And ye may try as ye like, but 'tis not going to change, unlesh"—he cleared his throat—"unless, as I told ye, ye can raish—raise an army to march against the English and con—con—" He took another drink. "Defeat them."

Ellie shot him a startled look. "Don't tell him that! You'll just encourage him!"

New hope quickened in Ian's veins. "What would happen if I could do that?" he asked.

The scientist frowned, lost in thought for a moment. "Well, it could consheivably change the course of English history. And Scottish, of course. If the Scots con—con—defeated the English, if the second Jacobite uprising was successful, and James was placed on the throne, with Princsh—Princsh—oh, hell—with Charlie in line to inherit, Scotland could very well end up as the superpower England later became." He ran one hand over his rumpled hair, looking a little dazed. "But that would mean"—he shook his head—"that *everything* would change."

"Then that's what I have to do," Ian said, his heart beating faster.

"No, Ian," Ellie said, coming to her feet and crossing to him.

"Aye. I must find a way to raise an army."

Davey shook his head as Ellie sat down beside him, her heart in her eyes. Ian steeled himself against her fear.

"'Twould take a for—a for—a lot of money," Davey said, and then drained the tankard he held and put it down on the table. "Ye'd have to hire mershenaries to build a big enough armly—amry—army."

"Shut up, Davey," Ellie said, her gaze still locked with Ian's. "You're drunk. Ian, tell me you aren't considering this insanity? Where would you get that kind of money? Be reasonable. You had your meeting. They aren't interested. Now forget this nonsense!" She turned and walked away from him, her arms folded tightly across her chest.

Ian couldn't speak for a moment because it was suddenly clear to him what she was trying to do. She was trying to convince him to give up the fight so that he would return to the future with her. Hadn't he made it clear to her that he wasn't returning to the twenty-first century? And hadn't she said she would stay with him, no matter what he decided? She was staying here, with him, to fight at his side for Scottish independence—wasn't she? Then her words sank in.

"Nonsense?"

"Oh, boy," Davey muttered and picked up another mug.

Ellie whirled around, her blue eyes impatient. "Yes, nonsense! You can't single-handedly change history! You can't save Scotland, Ian. But you can save us." Tears flooded her eyes. "I was willing to stay with you when I thought you had a fighting chance to make a difference, but now I've realized that by doing that, I'm just aiding and abetting this suicidal obsession!"

Her voice softened and she sat down beside him, one

hand on his arm. "We can go back home now, Ian. I can see my sisters again. You can have your music again. You can come back with me and have a life—with me!"

Ian stood, his worst fears realized. "I thought ye understood. I thought—" He broke off. He wasn't going to encourage her to stay behind with him. This was a dangerous time and with what he had planned—she needed to go back to her own time, where she'd be safe.

"It's time for ye and Davey to go back home," he said softly. "I'm sorry, Eleanor. I wish things could be different." He dragged one hand through his hair and shook his head. "We can stay here the night, but tomorrow we'll get some supplies and I'll take the two of ye back to the cairn. It will be safer for ye to stay there until the spiral deigns to work again. The room at the end of the hall is yers, Ellie, and the one next to it yers, Davey."

"Where are ye shleeping?" Davey asked, his eyes half closed.

"Downstairs." He let his gaze flicker to Ellie. Her face was like stone and her tears were gone.

"And if the spiral doesn't work like last time?" she asked dully.

"I'll check back in a few days." Ian crossed to the door, the wooden floor squeaking beneath his boots. He flung it open, fighting the urge to turn back and take her in his arms, and drew in a ragged breath. "If it hasn't worked by then, we'll have to figure things out from there."

"And if I want to stay here, with you?" She lifted her chin, her body rigid, her fists clenched.

Ian leaned against the open door, his eyes closed as a wave of longing flooded over him—a longing for his life in the future as a piper, a longing for his carefree days on the tour, a longing for Ellie. He opened his eyes, schooling them not to betray him as he shook his head.

"I'm sorry, lass, but I dinna want ye to stay." He walked out and closed the door behind him.

* * *

Ellie had stared at the ceiling of her room for hours. She'd hoped that Ian would come knocking on her door, begging her forgiveness, or declaring he didn't mean a word he'd said. But the moon was beginning to set before she finally gave up and fell into a restless sleep, to dream.

The car was going too fast. Her father always drove too fast. But he and her mom were laughing, glancing back at her to bring her into their happiness too, as they sped down the interstate. Allie was at a friend's house and it was the first time in a long while that Ellie could remember having her parents all to herself. She was drawing on a sketchpad to amuse herself when her mom started singing a song about unicorns. It was a song her mom used to sing to them when they were little, and Ellie joined in.

Her dad laughed. His dark, shaggy hair was a direct contrast to her mother's smooth red hair. Ellie felt her heart swell up with love for them and finished the picture she was drawing. "Look!" she said eagerly, holding it up for them to see. Her mother glanced back at her and smiled and told her it was beautiful. Then the world exploded.

Everything went black and suddenly a scream from far, far away echoed into her head, getting louder and louder until she thought it would shatter her brain, until her eyes flew open and she found she was the one screaming. Ian burst through the door, his eyes wild, his sword in his hand.

"Lass," he said, laying the sword aside and taking her in his arms. She stopped screaming and really woke up then, her heart pounding. "'Twas just a bad dream, that's all."

She clung to him, tears running down her face. "No," she whispered, "no."

"Come," he said gently, "let me lie with ye a while, and hold ye 'til ye go back to sleep."

Ian pulled her down beside him and cradled her against him. She twisted her fingers into the fabric of his shirt, trying to erase the dream from her mind along with the memories it had evoked. She had slept in her clothes, but the room was so cold that she was shivering. Ian drew the thin blanket on the bed up over her shoulder and she sighed.

He shifted beside her, one hand stroking down her arm and up again, and she lifted her face to his. His tawny brows collided over distraught blue eyes.

"Eleanor," he said, and then slid his hand to her face and brushed away the moisture from her cheek.

"What?" she whispered, hoping against hope that he would kiss her, would tell her that he loved her, would say that he'd never leave her. His eyes searched hers, and then he pulled her close again and rested his chin against her hair as he held her tightly.

"Go to sleep," he said. "I'll keep the bad dreams away."

If only you could, Ellie thought, but obediently closed her eyes, just grateful for the respite she had been given. Apparently the joyride was over.

Ian stood restlessly outside Rob Roy's home, near Craigrostan, pacing back and forth, pounding his fist into his palm. He had taken one of the horses that Davey and Ellie had borrowed from his father's stable and ridden to see Rob Roy MacGregor. When he first reached the small cottage, he'd been surprised to see a gathering of men outside. He knew many of them, but brushed aside their surprise and their questions in order to find out why they were all there. When he found out, he felt as if he'd been punched in the stomach.

Rob Roy was dying.

As he walked a groove outside the whitewashed cottage, the men who had gathered murmured loudly, and Ian knew full well they were discussing him. It took everything inside of him not to turn and speak to them, to recruit them for the plan still forming in his mind, but his respect for Rob Roy held him back. This was not the time or place. Still, he had to see the man.

The door to the cottage opened then, and Ian looked up. Mary MacGregor, Rob Roy's wife, walked outside, her face weary as she wiped her hands on the apron tied around her waist. Her red hair had faded, Ian saw, and the years of fighting had taken more out of her than he'd ever imagined possible.

"Mary," he said, from his vantage point beside the door, "may I have a word with ye?" She looked up at him with no recognition in her eyes, and then grew pale.

"Ian MacGregor," she said softly. "So ye have returned at last."

Mary and Rob had been two of the few who knew the realities behind his and Quinn's "deaths" at the hands of the Duke of Montrose twenty-three years before. He took her hand and brought it to his lips, then held on to her tense fingers as he straightened, his heart aching. "Aye," he said. "I'm sorry it took so long."

"And Quinn?"

"He's alive, but not here. He's married, a child on the way."

She nodded and looked away. "I'm glad," she said simply, then shot him a sharp look. "Ye have stayed away so long, Ian. Rob needed ye. Why have ye come back now?"

"I couldn't return until now," he told her, shame washing over him. He should have been here. But now it was too late.

She frowned up at him. "Ye look"—her eyes widened—"ye look the same. How is that possible? Ye havena aged a day!"

Ah, sweet Mary, but ye have, he thought sorrowfully. The years had taken their toll upon her beautiful face, leaving fine lines spidering out from the corners of her eyes, and deep grooves around her mouth. But she was still Mary MacGregor. Still lovely and strong.

"Good genes," he said without thinking.

"Good what?" Her frown deepened and she suddenly looked wary. She pulled her hand from his. "Why are ye here?"

"To see Rob," he said. "I dinna know he was ill, and I am sore sorry to hear it. But I must speak with him about the Black Watch."

She shook her head. "What is there to speak about? I

canna have him disturbed for such things." She took a step forward as other men and women began to draw closer to the two. Ian moved to block her way and her eyes flashed up at him.

"Mary, please. I need his endorsement," Ian said hastily. He glanced around at the suspicious glares of the people around them and took her hand again, gently. "If I could just speak to ye for a moment, in private?"

A tall, russet-haired man stepped forward. "Leave my mother in peace," he said, his voice and his appearance so much like Rob Roy's that it brought tears to Ian's eyes. "She is tired."

"Aye, I know," Ian said, his gaze searching the young man's. "Is it Coll?" he said, recognizing one of Rob's sons. "I'm an old friend of yer father and mother's."

The man shook his head. "Ye are no older than I. How could ye be an 'old' friend?" He took a step forward, his hand going to his waist, and then back to his side as he stiffened. "If the cursed English had not taken my sword, I would challenge ye properly, but know this—if my mother doesna wish to speak to you—"

"Whist! Whist!" Mary said sharply. "Ye make too much of things, laddie." She glanced back at Ian and turned to open the door behind her. "Come inside, Ian. We will speak."

Inside, the cottage Ian had once thought spacious for a Highland home now seemed tiny, dark, and dank. He swallowed hard as Mary led him over to a bench and sat down beside him.

"Speak quickly," she said. "I have much to do."

"I want to raise a group of men who will fight the Black Watch with me as their leader," he said, trying to condense the plans that had been forming in his mind into one sentence. "And I want Rob Roy to tell the rest of the clan to follow me," he added.

Her mouth slipped into a humorless smile. "Och, is that all?"

"Mary," he said, "my father has done a great injustice to

the MacGregors by supporting Wade and his men. The English king has set these loyalists upon our clans, with carte blanche to do as they wish!"

"And how do ye know this, Ian? Ye have been away for over twenty years." Her voice was flat, weary.

"As soon as I arrived I learned of it. General Wade must be stopped! I ran into one of their patrols, led by my own brother Angus. I must save my family from this path, undo what my father has done—"

"It is too late," Mary said, cutting him off. "The English have grown too strong in the Highlands, their number too many." She arched one auburn brow at him. "Why do ye think they brought the roads into the hills? To bring their men in as well—hundreds of them. There is no way to fight them anymore."

"I dinna believe that."

She rose. "Well, believe it," she said. "There is nothing that can be done. Rob knew it in 1724 when he made an agreement with General Wade to cease his outlaw ways. He grew weary of running and fighting, and his wife and family even more so!" She turned to face him, fire in her eyes. "And I willna have ye comin' round, tryin' to stir things up! I will not have Rob disturbed!" Her anger faded and she shook her head at him. "Go home, Ian, wherever that is now. Find a good woman and make the best life that ye can."

Her eyes were like stone and Ian knew there was no way to make her understand. "I will honor yer wishes, Mary. But may I just see him—for a moment?"

She hesitated, and then nodded. "If ye dinna badger him to 'endorse' ye." With a snort of contempt, she led him to a door at the end of the room. She opened it and ducked under the low eave, with Ian close behind. It was a small room with a fireplace and a bed barely large enough for two people against one wall. Lying upon it was an old man.

Rob Roy.

Ian almost turned away, but held himself in check. How could Rob Roy MacGregor be old! A year ago he'd been

strong and vital and—and—his shock faded as he drew
nearer the bed and stared down at his hero. But it hadn't
been a year, but three and twenty. The once-infamous outlaw's face was ashen, his breathing labored, his eyes closed.
Deep lines creased his face, his hawklike nose still promi-
nent, still strong amid a sagging façade.

"Rob," Ian whispered, when he finally found his voice.
"Rob, can ye hear me?" He took the sick man's rough, cold
hand between his.

Rob's closed eyelids flickered and then slowly opened.
The piercing hazel eyes Ian remembered so well were now
muddled with illness, the whites around them yellowish. Ian
took a deep breath to fight back the sob welling up in his
throat.

"Ian?" Rob Roy whispered, his voice hoarse and cracked.
"Am I dead, then, and ye here to welcome me to heaven?"

"Och, no, Rob," Ian said, his own voice trembling. "Ye
remember, 'twas all a ruse—me and Quinn dying—to escape Montrose's dungeon."

Something flickered in the man's eyes. "Oh, aye, aye,"
he said. "Now I remember." His eyelids slid half shut, then
opened again. "Ye have been gone a long time. Why have ye
returned?"

Ian struggled for a moment. He wanted so much to ask
Rob Roy why he had made a deal with General Wade, why he
had given up fighting the English and the Scots who put their
own fortunes before that of their country. But he couldn't.

"Och, my friend, I just wanted to see ye again," he finally
said. "Ye are like the father I never had, ye ken?"

Rob Roy nodded and squeezed the hand holding his. "I
am sore glad that ye came," he whispered. "Many the night
I have longed to hear ye and Quinn play the pipes again." He
took a deep breath and his chest rattled, making Ian swallow
hard. "Will ye play them for me, lad? One last time?"

Ian nodded, too choked up to speak, and turned to ask
Mary where he might find a set of pipes—but she was
standing there already, at the end of Rob's bed, shaking
her head.

"My love," she said to Rob, "ye remember, they took our pipes, and they are outlawed for such as us."

Ian closed his eyes against the pain that twisted Rob Roy's face as he remembered and nodded. "Aye, aye, I remember."

Ian opened his eyes and clasped the outlaw's hand more firmly. "Dinna fash yerself, Rob," he said, "for I will find a set of pipes, and I will return to play them for ye."

Mary frowned at him, her hand on her hips. "Aye, and bring the wrath of the Black Watch down upon as well no doubt," she muttered.

Hesitantly, Ian glanced back down at Rob Roy, and the man winked. He nodded and then smiled at Mary MacGregor.

"I will be back," Ian said, feeling a new strength rise up within. "With my pipes."

He turned and walked out of the room, out of the cottage, back into daylight, blinking at the sudden brightness and shading his eyes. More than three dozen men stood there, women and children in the background, staring at him. This was his chance.

"I am here to talk to ye of something verra important. Something that could change yer lives forever."

He needed to say something profound, something that would gain their attention. Suddenly he remembered a poster he'd seen back in the twenty-first century that had given him pause. He lowered his hand from his eyes and took another step forward.

"I am Ian MacGregor," he said loudly, his hands on his hips, "and I am looking for a few good men."

sixteen

"I've been thinking. Is this thing even actually a horse? Or is it some kind of Scottish imitation?" Ellie demanded as she bounced along on top of the shaggy pony. Ian had taken their other horse, leaving the two of them to share.

Davey winced. "Do ye have to talk so loudly?" he asked. "'Tis bad enough that I have no sunglasses to stop the glare." He shaded his eyes and looked up as he walked beside her. The day was bright—unusually bright for Scotland. He shook his head and winced again.

"And dinna disparage the pony," he said. "If ye dinna like her, I will be glad to exchange places with ye."

"You are being punished for getting drunk and putting the idea of raising an army in Ian's head," Ellie said, pulling back on the reins.

She slid one leg over the pommel of the saddle and jumped down, handing the reins to him.

"Here," she said, "it's your lucky day. I'm ready for a break. Are you sure he's gone to see—see Rob Roy MacGregor?" Even with her limited knowledge of Scottish history, Ellie knew that infamous name.

"Aye," Davey said as he leaned against the horse, looking a little green. "If Ian is thinking of engineering a new uprising, he would go to Rob Roy first, for his blessing and his help."

Ellie shaded her eyes and looked across the misty green hills ahead of them. "So how much farther do you think we have to go?"

They had paused on the crest of a low hill and below was a dark loch that stretched across the valley. Somewhere, nearby, Ian was taking steps to alter not only his life, but the lives of everyone in Scotland, perhaps the world. They had to find him.

Davey took a few steps forward and surveyed the countryside, then shook his head. "Katie told me that we should look for the standing stones of Dunham. She dinna say anything about a loch near the MacGregors'. It must be a ways more."

Ellie pushed her bangs out of her eyes and sighed. "*A ways more*. I just love Scottish accuracy. Why didn't you get Katie to come with us and show us the way?"

"I dinna want her to come with us."

"Why not?" she asked, irritated. "Afraid she'll look at one of the big MacGregor lads instead of you for a change?"

Davey gave her an uncharacteristically fierce look from under his auburn brows. "I dinna want to involve her in this. The MacGregors have always been hotheads—Ian being a perfect example—and Katie is equally volatile. I dinna think would be wise to bring her along."

"I knew ye dinna want me to come!" cried a petulant voice behind them.

Ellie and Davey turned to find Katie, riding toward them astride a beautiful brown gelding.

"Ye said that I shouldn't come because my father might need me!" she said, pulling the horse to a stop and glaring down at Davey. One gloved hand slapped against her thigh in rhythmic frustration.

"There's no need to shout," Davey said, his eyebrows crushing together. "My head is killing me."

"That's not all that will be killin' ye, if ye leave me behind again!"

"Ye should have stayed with yer father," Davey said crossly. "What are ye doing here?"

"Proving that ye canna tell me what to do!" she said. She threw her left leg over the saddle horn and slid off the great beast to hit the ground, her knees bent. She wore the same clothes she'd had on the day they'd met her on the hillside—brown breeches and tunic with the addition of a waistcoat of sorts and a dark green cloak flying behind her in the cold breeze. She straightened and put her hands on her hips as she faced Davey.

"Aye, I can tell ye what to do," Davey said, holding his head with one hand. "I'm yer husband."

"In name only!" she reminded him. "I never said ye would be my lord and master!"

Davey pretended to think, tapping one finger against his chin. "Hmmm, if memory serves, I believe the kind priest who joined us made you swear to do exactly that. It came under the heading of 'love and obey.'"

"Davey!" Ellie said, suddenly weary not only of the petulant exchange, but the reminder that a marriage was something she would likely never experience. "We need Katie to take us to the MacGregors'. Quit being such a chauvinist pig and get out of the way!"

Katie's face brightened and she glanced back at Ellie. "What does that mean? *Chauvinist pig?*"

"It means that he thinks a woman is less of a person just because she's a woman," Ellie said flatly, her arms folded across her chest.

Davey's mouth fell open. "I do not think that!" he said.

Ellie shrugged. "Could have fooled me," she said.

"And me!" Katie said, moving to stand beside Ellie. "Ye chauvinist pig!" She grinned up at Ellie.

Ellie grinned back. "Ready to take us to see an infamous outlaw?"

"Ye mean Rob Roy?" she said. She gave Davey a haughty

look—the equivalent of sticking out her tongue—then returned to her horse, mounting again with ease. She held out her hand to Ellie. "Aye, I will show *ye*. Come on up. Just put your foot on top of the stirrup."

Ellie stared up at her. "Uh, that horse is kind of tall, isn't it?"

"Och, he's an old sweetie." Katie leaned down and patted his neck. "Come on, then, up with ye."

Risk, that's what this new adventure was all about. Risk and living life to the fullest. Ellie swallowed hard and nodded.

"Okay. Thanks." Taking a deep breath, she took Katie's hand in her right, put her left foot on top of the stirrup. Katie tugged, and suddenly Ellie was sitting on top of the huge horse behind her, gazing out at the Scottish countryside. "Wow."

"And what am *I* supposed to do?" Davey said.

Ellie clung to Katie's waist, but dared to look down—way, way down—at the scientist. "You can ride Sorbet."

"Sorbet?"

"That's what I named the pony," she said.

Davey shook his head. "Why?"

She cocked her head at him. "Because every time I ride her, I get a Sore-butt. Get it?"

Katie glanced back over her shoulder. "I dinna get it."

Davey gazed up at her, his glasses perched on the end of his nose. He shrugged. "I dinna get it either."

Ellie rolled her eyes. "You two were made for each other. Can we just get going, please?" She stopped smiling as she remembered why they were heading for the MacGregors'. "We've got to stop Ian."

"Stop him from what?" Katie asked as she nudged the horse into a walk. Davey had mounted the pony and was bumping along behind them.

Ellie sighed. "Stop him from trying to be a hero."

They rode for another hour, away from the loch, before Katie finally stopped beside a narrow river. The ground sloped upward from the river to form a low, rolling hill, and at the top was a thatch-roofed cottage made of stone, looking over the river below.

A large crowd of men and women were gathered outside the cottage, and as Ellie and her two companions made their way up the knoll, she could see that the crowd was gathered around someone standing on a large stone—a man speaking so fervently that his voice carried all the way to the three on horseback.

Ian.

"Oh, great," she said. Katie clucked to their mount, and they moved toward the cottage. "Leave it to Ian to find a stage."

"So will ye simply lay down and dee?" Ian was saying, his brogue broader than she had ever heard it. "Will ye give up? Let the English tell ye what to do and what to say and wear—down to the very music ye will play?"

"He's right!" A teenaged boy pushed through the crowd, his hair standing wildly around his head, his face twisted with passion. "Why do ye not hear him? We have let the Black Watch overrun our valley, order us around in our villages! Why do we not fight back?"

"Come up here, lad!" Ian called. The boy ran lightly up the craggy stone to stand beside him. Ian put his arm around his shoulders. "Now here is a man! A Scotsman, who puts the rest of ye to shame!"

"And that Scotsman will soon lie in an early grave if he listens to ye, Ian MacGregor!"

Ellie caught her breath as a woman with faded auburn hair stalked up to the stone and glared at Ian and the boy.

"Get down from there, Murdoch!" she ordered.

"Och, Grandmither," the boy began, only to be cut off when she grabbed him by the arm and jerked him off the impromptu platform. Then she mounted the rock herself and stood glaring down at the rest of the people as well.

"My Rob has fought the English for nigh onto forty years and what has it ever gained us? What has been the outcome? Only death and sorrow and grief." Mary pointed toward the cottage. "Now he lies inside dyin', and I willna have the lives of my children and grandchildren taken with him." She lifted her chin and gazed down at the crowd haughtily. "Ye all know Rob's wishes. Ye all know what must be done. Now see to it!"

She flounced off the stone and then whirled around and pointed at Ian. "And ye, Ian MacGregor—dinna meddle in what ye canna understand! Ye are not welcome here, so go back to where ye've been hiding for the last twenty years!"

The look on Ian's face made Ellie almost cry out, and when his gaze lowered to the ground, she couldn't bear it. She slid off the giant horse and rushed to Ian's side.

"Wait a minute!" she said. Ian jerked his head toward her in surprise and she patted his arm with one hand. "I'm not from Scotland, but I've been told all of my life what big, bold warriors the men here are."

"Ellie, dinna do this—" Ian said, his voice low.

"But I don't see big, bold warriors," she went on. "I see a bunch of sniveling cowards unwilling to defend their women and children from the scourge of the countryside, from the lowest scum ever to walk the face of the earth—"

"Ellie, stop, I tell ye!" Ian ordered, but Ellie was on a roll now.

"—from the scurviest knaves, the slimiest devils, the stupidest, most lame-brained, *ball*-less half-wits ever to draw breath! So are you with Ian—or are you with *them*—the traitorous dogs who have taken your homes and your swords and your beloved *pipes*?" She took a deep breath and put her hands on her hips, tossing her head.

There! Let's see what they have to say about that!

"Eleanor," Ian said softly, "I am beggin' ye. Dinna say anything more."

"Why?" she asked, lifting her chin the way Mary MacGregor had. "They need to hear this!"

"But they are not the only ones hearing it, lass," he said.

Ellie followed his gaze and then froze, her breath leaving her in one big rush. Angus Campbell sat on horseback behind the people gathered, glaring fiercely in her direction.

"Uh-oh," she said.

Ian stepped in front of her to face the fire as Angus swung down off his horse and strode through the crowd.

"Are ye out of yer minds?" he shouted.

"So, it's you again, is it?" Ellie demanded. "Back to slice and dice your brother a little more?"

"Whist," Ian said, pulling her back behind him again. "Pay no attention to her. She's daft."

"Daft!" Ellie struggled against Ian's grip. "I am not daft!"

"Why are ye all standing here listening to a traitor?" Angus roared. His gaze pierced the crowd and then his eyes widened as they stopped on Katie. "Katie? What in God's name are ye doing here?"

"Uh-oh," Ellie said again.

The big man strode over to his sister, his gaze flashing to Davey and back to her. "Why aren't ye home with Father, taking care of him?"

"Because I've run away from there and I'm never going back!" she cried, clinging to Davey.

"Big uh-oh," Ian muttered under his breath.

"As long as she doesn't tell him—" Ellie began, only to wince as Katie spoke up again.

"This is my husband," she said, patting Davey's arm. "I'm married now, and neither ye, nor father, nor Ian, nor *anyone*, can tell me what to do!" She lifted her petulant little chin, and Ellie squeezed her eyes shut.

"Not the chin, don't use the chin," she pleaded.

"Husband?!" Angus lunged for Davey and would have slammed his big fist squarely into his face if Katie hadn't jumped in front of him, a small *skean dhu* in her hand.

"Stay back, brother," she said.

Angus staggered in his rage, but did as she said. Ian and Ellie jumped down from the rock and hurried to her side. Angus's eyes shifted furiously to his brother.

"So—this is how ye repay my kindness of lettin' ye stay in my home," he said. "Ye undermine the wishes of both our father and myself, and help yer sister—whom ye've never seen before—run away and marry this"—he glared at Davey—"this spalpeen who hides behind a woman's skirt!"

Davey stepped out from behind Katie and shrugged. "I dinna know what a spalpeen is, but if it means a man who ducks a punch instead of taking it—then, aye, I'm a spalpeen."

"Ye are worse than that!" Angus said. "And ye"—he whirled on Ian— "do ye know what ye've done? Ye've ruined everything. Katie's marriage to the earl was *necessary*!" He turned back to Katie. "Ye knew this, and yet ye would selfishly turn yer back on yer family."

"I haven't turned my back on ye," Katie said, her eyes blazing. "I just refused to be traded like cattle to an auld man with no teeth!"

You go, girl! Ellie stepped up to her side and put her arm around her. "You had no right to force her into marriage," she told him. "This is your fault—yours and your father's. If she hadn't felt so desperate, she never would have married Davey."

"Uh, thanks," Davey muttered.

Ellie shot him a half smile. "You know what I mean."

"And who are ye to say such things?" Angus demanded.

"Then I will say them," Ian said.

Ellie suddenly felt her heart begin to pound. This "new" Ian, with his chiseled jaw and fire in his eyes, stirred her just as much as the old Ian ever had.

"Ye should have protected her from Father's edict," Ian said, his fists clenched at his side. "She's yer little sister, man! And ye know that he cares more for his place at court and these lands than any of his family."

"That is not so!" Angus cried. "And who are ye to speak of protecting anyone in our family?"

"I know. I wasna here, but I am here now!" Ian reached out and pulled Katie to him. "I have lost my brothers to the Black Watch," he told him. "I willna let my sister be sold into marriage to an Englishman! For as surely as the sun comes up in the morning, if ye had married her to that knave, she would have been lost to us forever."

Angus narrowed his eyes. "It was not yers to decide."

"No," Ian agreed, "it was hers. And she has made her decision."

His brother's hand went to his sword hilt as he looked back at Davey. "I can unmake it, if I choose."

"Ye touch one hair on Davey's head and I'll murder ye in yer sleep!" Katie cried.

Davey's brows darted up. "Really?"

Ian rested his hands on her shoulders. "No, Katie, ye will not. He is our brother. Angus, I am sorry I was not here when ye needed me, and all I can tell ye is that I couldna return before now, and I regret it with all of my heart. Can ye no' believe me? Can ye no' forgive me and join me? Lead our brothers back to fighting on the right side once again?"

Angus met his eyes for a long moment, and then turned to let his gaze travel over the people assembled. "I heard what ye were saying to these men." He gestured toward the crowd, now murmuring and shooting all of them wary glances. "I was behind the cottage, but yer voice carries." He nodded toward Ellie. "And I heard what this one said." Shaking his head, he turned and moved away from the four, then paused and faced them again, his face like carved granite and his eyes just as cold.

"I am no brother nor friend to traitors."

He turned on his heel and strode away from them, the crowd parting around him as he headed for his horse. He swung up on the well-groomed mount and lifted the reins, his eyes hard as he turned them on his brother.

"If ye truly still care about yer family, ye will cease this treachery and leave us be."

He laid the reins across his horse and turned it sharply in the opposite direction, leaving Ian to stare after him. "Well," Ellie said softly, "now what?"

"I hope ye are satisfied," Mary MacGregor said, walking toward them, her weary gaze unyielding. "'Tis bad enough that ye have to come to our home and stir up trouble, but to drag poor Angus into it as well . . ." She shook her head. "Do as he says—leave us be!"

She glanced around at the uneasy crowd. "Go home, all of ye! Rob needs his rest, and so do I!" She stalked past them and back into the cottage, slamming the door behind her.

Ellie sighed and then turned to the rest of their little band of "traitors." Katie looked as if she was about to burst into tears, Davey was patting her back, and Ian stood staring into space, looking like a statue.

"Gee," she said, "that went well."

"So now what?" Davey asked, having apparently grown bold enough to put his arm firmly around Katie's shoulder to comfort her. "Where do we go from here?"

"We'll camp near here until morning," Ian said, too weary to even contemplate riding anywhere. "Then I'll lead ye to the cairn."

Ellie folded her arms across her chest, and the look in her eyes told him it wasn't going to be as easy as that.

"Okay," she said, "maybe I screwed up back there, but I'm not going anywhere without you. So why don't you just let us help you with your plan?"

"Aye," Katie said, her eyes bright in the fading sunlight. "Let us help!"

"Ye canna help," Ian said. "And with or without the aid of the MacGregor clan, I'm going to do my best to fight back against the Black Watch, and I dinna want any of ye to get hurt when I do." He looked out over the valley. "Perhaps if I spoke to the rest of my brothers, some of them would join me."

Ellie laid one hand on his arm, her touch gentle. "Don't shut us out," she said.

"Please, Ian?" Katie begged.

Ian closed his eyes briefly and then waved one hand toward Davey. "Will ye explain to them why they canna be part of this?"

"Because we're women?" Ellie stepped back and narrowed her eyes, darting a warning look at Davey. "I wouldn't advise you to do that, laddie!"

"Wouldn't dream of it," Davey said hastily. "And being women has nothing to do with it. In fact, I don't agree with Ian. There might very well be something ye could do to help that no one else could."

Ellie and Katie exchanged glances.

"Like what?" Ellie asked, her gaze suspicious.

"Aye, Dr. Ferguson," Ian said, folding his arms over his chest as he glared at him. "Like what?"

"Well, if ye'll give us some details of what ye have in mind, maybe we can figure out how we can help."

"I hate to point it out to you, laddie," Ellie said to Ian, "but we're all you've got."

Katie nodded and Davey gave him a halfhearted grin. Ian dragged one hand through his hair. It was true. He couldn't do what he planned without more than one person. But he'd be damned if he'd put Ellie and Katie in danger.

"Bloody hell," he swore. He stood with hands on his hips for a long moment, staring at the ground, then released his pent-up breath and looked up. "Let's find a place to camp for the night, then we'll talk."

"So you're saying that no matter what I do, my efforts will be futile."

Davey glanced uneasily across the campfire at Ian and Ellie and then nodded. They had made camp near a burn and close to a large wooded area, giving them wood for their fire and water to drink. The sun had seemed to drop out of the sky at sunset, and night had fallen cold and crisp.

"Aye," Davey said. "I mean, unless, as I told ye, ye could raise an army, or something monumental, like killing the king and putting a Jacobite sympathizer on the throne." He laughed and reached into his pocket. He took out his small notebook, squinting at it in the firelight. "But even then, ye have to take into account the machinations of the English court and the Scottish aristocracy, and och, so much more. The mathematics dinna lie."

Ian fell silent, his mind racing.

"Ian," Ellie said, her voice fearful, "what are you thinking?"

"What do ye mean, what am I thinking?" he pulled himself from his reverie. "I'm just thinking."

She frowned. "Don't do anything crazy," she said.

"Crazy? Me?" Ian gave her a lazy smile, hoping that she only *seemed* to be able to read his mind. "I'm the staid, sober one of this bunch."

"Right." She shook her head at him. "Please. Don't even think about it."

"I'm hungry," Davey said.

"Drink some more water," Ellie advised, her own stomach rumbling.

"So tell me," Katie said, "what do ye plan to do to aid those who are against the king?"

Ian stared into the fire for a moment and then shifted his gaze to Ellie. "I suppose there is nothing I can do," he said.

"But what about yer plan?" Katie frowned. "And what did ye mean, Davey, when ye said it would make no difference? Even the effort of one man makes a difference in any endeavor."

"Don't encourage him," Ellie said, her head on Ian's shoulder. He put his arm around her and let his fingers caress the side of her neck. He could feel her pulse pounding rapidly against her skin.

"The clans won't back you, Ian." Davey took a swig of water and looked up at the stars. "So let it go, please. Come back with us and live your own life."

"And what about me?" Katie asked. "Will ye take me to France, as Angus ordered?"

Ian shook his head as he poked the fire with a long tree branch. "Angus's orders dinna come into this one way or another. But I'll talk to him, and to our father. They willna be kicking ye out of yer home."

"But I dinna want to go back home," she said, shaking her dark mane of hair back from her shoulders. "I want to go with all of ye. I want to help put King James back on the throne where he belongs."

Ian stared at his sister and then laughed outright. "Och, a little Jacobite in our midst."

She shrugged. "We all were until about five years ago," she said, "though we kept it secret."

Ian froze. "What do ye mean?"

"I dinna know what happened," she said, her face growing shadowed. "I remember some men coming to speak to Father and there was a lot of shouting and threats. And then General Wade himself came, and he and Angus had a long meeting. Not long after that, Angus told us he had been commissioned into the Black Watch. I tried to argue with him, remind him that we were loyal to King James, but he told me to never, ever say that again, that King James had turned his back upon Scotland and we were no longer supporters of his cause."

She frowned. "I think that he had to make some sizeable contributions to the king's coffers to get the commission, because that was when our furniture disappeared and we fell on hard times." She leaned against Davey and he put his arm around her.

"Angus became part of the Black Watch," Ellie said softly, "to prove that his father was still faithful to the king."

"I dinna want to go back there," Katie insisted.

"We can talk about it in the morning," Davey said with a yawn. "I'm so tired I fear I may fall over at any moment." He glanced over at Ian sympathetically. "What do ye say, Ian? Ye must be exhausted as well."

"In the morning we will head back to my father's house."

Ian didn't miss the worried look between Davey and Ellie.

"Ian—" Katie began, only to be cut off by her brother's abrupt voice.

"Go to sleep, Katie," he ordered. "Mary did deign to give me some plaids for us to use as covering so we willna freeze to death." He stood and crossed to the pony where the bundles were tied. He tossed each of them a bound blanket and then walked away from the fire.

Ellie followed. When he was a few yards away from the camp, he stopped and stared up at the stars. She walked quietly up to him and laid her hand on his arm. Ian glanced down at her, then returned his gaze to the sky.

"Do you remember when you told me that everything happens for a reason?" she asked.

He nodded. "Aye."

"Do you really believe that?"

"Aye."

She tightened her hand on his arm. "Do you remember when I told you that I couldn't be your tour manager anymore?"

He met her eyes on that one. "Aye."

"Do you know why?"

Where was she going with this? She frowned back at him, drew in a deep breath, and tugged on his arm, making him turn to face her.

"Because," she said, "I was falling in love with you and I couldn't risk your rejection. If I walked away, I could control what happened. That's what my whole life has been about since I was twelve years old—controlling everything around me so I wouldn't get hurt! But now I know it isn't up to me to keep the world spinning, or to keep Allie and Maggie alive. I can't do it. I can't." She paused and then her voice grew more fervent. "And neither can *you*."

Ian turned away from her, back to the stars.

Ellie circled around to stand in front of him, but he continued to look over her head. "And even if you could do something huge and sweeping, like Davey talked about, even then, you might set in motion things that would change *my* world, and that's not fair." She took a deep breath. "Your time made its choices, Ian, and it isn't right that my world should suffer because you think yours deserves a second chance."

He lowered his eyes to hers, anger in his gaze.

"Ian," she whispered, one hand upon his chest. "Let's go home."

In that moment he wanted nothing more than to do exactly

what she asked. He closed his eyes and somehow found the strength to refuse. "I left my family once, abandoned them. I canna do it again," he said.

"So you're going to abandon me instead?"

He closed his eyes. The thought of being without her was as painful as the blade of a sword piercing his heart. "I'm sorry, Ellie," he said. "Ye must go back where ye belong."

Without a word, Ellie slipped her arms around his neck. Ian sighed and leaned his head against hers.

"Oh, laddie," she finally said, "I don't belong anywhere without you."

seventeen

"I'm worried," Ellie said.

Davey nodded. "Aye."

She and Davey had both refused to go to the cairn, and Ian had finally given up and taken them back to his father's home. After a little judicial gossip with the cook, Ellie learned that although Fergus Campbell had told Ian not to come back home if he helped his friend Quinn and had said he would be disowned, his father had never legally done so.

Apparently, Ian knew this as well, for when they returned to the castle, Ian basically took over, making his brother Tavish furious. Angus had come home several times over the next couple of weeks to threaten and argue with his un-yielding brother.

So Ian had turned to other endeavors. Using the castle as a base, he continued to try to raise his army. She thought he was doing more than that, but he refused to discuss any of it with her, telling her the less she knew, the better. Then he had somehow managed to talk all of his brothers into a meeting at their father's home, and since many of them had not seen their father since he had fallen so ill, they had agreed. That morning, the three brothers who had been out on patrol, Alastair, Finley, and Collin, had arrived and had assembled with Tavish and Angus to listen to what Ian had to say. The laird had not awakened for several days and his death appeared imminent.

By the time luncheon was served, the arguing and shouting had become so intense that Ellie and Davey had left the great hall, and Katie had fled to her father's room.

Ellie and Davey took a walk to a stream that ran near the castle gates, and sat beside it as storm clouds gathered above them. It was November, and gone was any inkling of warmth from the air. Ellie snuggled down into the cloak Katie had lent her and wished suddenly she was home, in her apartment with Allie or in Maggie's cozy cottage, curled up on the sofa with a cup of hot tea in her hands.

She shook the thought away. She was just tired, that was all, exhausted right down to the marrow of her bones. Which was strange because for the last two weeks she had not done much of anything as Ian plotted and schemed and hid whatever it was he was doing from all of them.

At night he came to their bed and was her Ian again, and though there was many a day when she planned to turn him away, she found she could not. He was in such pain, and she loved him. Every night she welcomed him back into her arms.

Right now, she wanted nothing more than to go to sleep, but it seemed lazy to lie abed when it wasn't even sundown yet. "It's too cold," she said, rising from the stone she'd been sitting on. "Let's go back."

"Och, I canna bear to hear the shouting."

"We'll sneak in and go upstairs," she suggested, and shrugged. "I doubt Ian will even notice us." She turned and started walking, only to stop and look back when Davey spoke.

"He needs to play his pipes," Davey said, as he came to his feet, his eyes thoughtful.

Ellie gathered her cloak around her and waited for him to catch up with her. "His pipes?" she asked.

They began to walk quickly as a burst of cold, arctic air

swept suddenly over them. Davey shoved his hands down in the pockets of Ian's black overcoat and nodded.

"Aye. The Ian we know was a piper, a musician, a poet. Now he thinks he's a warrior. He needs to play his pipes again."

Ellie came to a halt and stared at Davey for a long moment, and then grabbed his face between her hands and kissed him soundly on both cheeks. He blinked up at her in confusion and she smiled, feeling the first glimmer of hope.

"Davey Ferguson," she said, "you are brilliant!"

"Aye," he agreed, "but dinna kiss me in front of Ian. I dinna need another punch in the eye."

His brothers had walked out, their faces like stone, leaving Ian to stare after them, stunned. They would not listen to him. Not one of them. Nor would even one of them admit that up until five years ago, the Fergus Campbell family had favored the Jacobite cause. Now only Angus remained behind, and Ian turned to him, trying to keep his voice calm in spite of the raging fury inside of him.

"And so that's it," Ian said. "Ye have turned them all against me."

Angus shook his head. "Ye turned them yerself, twenty-three years ago." His brow darkened. "And more recently, when ye began to destroy General Wade's roads."

Ian schooled his features carefully not to react to the accusation. His scheme to disrupt the work of the English in the Highlands was something he had not shared with anyone, not even Ellie.

"I dinna know what ye are talking about," he said.

"Of course ye would lie about it!" Angus scowled. "Ye seek only to enact yer own revenge and give no thought to what yer actions bring down upon us. But why should ye care? Ye abandoned us all long ago."

"Must ye continue to see it as such?" His heart ached at the thought of his brother viewing him in such a way. Yet, how could he explain that where he had been, only one year's time had passed? He would be thought insane, and Angus might use that information to have him stripped of his rights as his father's heir. That power was all he had left to use against the king and his men.

"How else can we see it?" Angus said. "Ye faked yer death to escape the wrath of the duke, then disappeared with Quinn MacIntyre never to return."

"I have told ye—all of ye—that I couldna return!"

"But ye willna tell us why." Angus sighed. "If ye would only offer some explanation, some reason—"

"I know how it seems." Ian faced his brother, blue eyes meeting blue. "Can ye not trust me enough to accept that there are reasons I canna tell ye the whole story?"

Angus held his gaze for a long moment and then looked away, his jaw set. "Nay," he said. "I wish that I could."

Ian released an explosive breath and turned and paced across the room. He paused in front of the huge tapestry of Joan of Arc that his mother had loved and tried to gather his thoughts. What would make Angus admit that he had once supported the cause of the Jacobites? For if he would admit that, Ian felt sure he could convince Angus to return to the fight.

"Angus," he said, "do ye truly not believe that what the English king is doing to Scotland is wrong? That the Black Watch seeks to usurp our rights? If King James is restored to the throne—"

Angus's face went ashen and he took a step toward him, shaking his fist. "Lower yer voice!" he hissed. "And dinna speak that name in this house! I have fought long and hard to keep this family safe, and ye willna come into my home and undo all I have done!"

Ian stiffened. "It is my home as well."

"No, it is not!" Angus said sharply. "Ye gave it up when ye threw yer lot in with Quinn MacIntyre. Instead of coming home and fulfilling the duties of an eldest son, ye were out seeking to destroy Montrose, one of our father's closest friends!"

"What do ye know of it?" Ian narrowed his eyes, feeling the anger mounting again inside of him. "Ye were not there when I was arrested and incarcerated in Montrose's dungeon!"

Angus spread his hands apart, his voice exasperated. *"Because ye were a highwayman!* Even then ye were a rebel!"

"Ye dinna know what drove me," he said, the memory of Quinn's stricken face when he learned of his father's and brother's murders, as clear as if it had happened yesterday. "Montrose was far from innocent!"

"I know that Father wept when ye wouldna renounce yer affiliation with MacIntyre and the MacGregors," Angus said. "I know that the king's soldiers came and tore our home apart. I know that they beat him within an inch of his life!"

Ian grew still. "I dinna know that."

Angus's eyes were like blue glass. "Nay, ye dinna know. If it had not been for the intervention of Montrose himself, our father would have been hanged because of what ye did! Father did what he had to do, to save our home, our lands—our heads!"

"And ye are doing the same, aren't ye, Angus?" Ian said softly. "Ye are trying to sell yer little sister to the highest bidder and yer honor to the king."

Angus closed his eyes briefly, and when they snapped open, there was such sorrow there that Ian almost took a step back.

"Ye will never understand. I love Katie," he said. "I dinna want her to marry the earl, but she is such a spitfire. She has been linked with known Jacobite sympathizers! I thought if she was married to the earl and if he took her to his home on Skye, that it would protect her as well as Father." He picked up his gloves from the table and slapped them down again, the sharp snap echoing in the near-empty hall. "But yer friend took care of that. The only way now for Katie to be safe is if I make her a widow."

The sympathy that had been glimmering inside of Ian disappeared with Angus's words. "If anything happens to my friends," he said, his voice low and tense, "ye will live to regret it."

Angus shook his head. "Yer family still means so little to ye."

Ian walked away from him and back. "Och, Angus, listen to me, please! I have been talking to people, learning what has happened since I left. George Wade invaded the Highlands, bringing with him martial law. Martial law, Angus! The orders from the king told him to confiscate all weapons, and if any Scotsman resisted, to *make an example of him*! The king has taken not just our pipes and our plaids and our swords—he has taken our dignity! Why can ye not see this?"

"All I can see is yer determination to destroy what I have spent my entire life defending!" Angus said. "Because Father did not have the heart to officially disown ye, I canna keep ye from being here. But know this—if ye use our father's home as a place of dissention and rebellion, we will all end up in prison or dead, and the destruction will be on yer head!"

Angus turned and, pausing only to pick up his cloak tossed across a chair near the fire, stormed out of the room and the castle.

Ian crossed to the fireplace and stood staring into the flames, his hands on his hips, more confused and frustrated than he'd ever been in his life.

"I've got to find a set of pipes," Ellie said, as they reached the huge double doors of the Campbell castle. "Where would I find a set of pipes?"

"Ask Katie," Davey suggested, helping Ellie tug on one of the huge brass handles.

"Another brilliant idea!" she proclaimed, as the doors swung open.

She paused outside the entrance to the great hall and whispered over her shoulder. "Okay, now, remember, head straight for the stairs and go to my room. We have plans to make." She slipped into the room, with Davey close behind, only to find the great hall deserted. "I wonder how it went."

"I wonder where Ian went," Davey said, sounding worried.

Ellie nodded, and suddenly realized how much she had grown to depend on Davey and his friendship.

"Davey, can I tell you something?"

"What?" he asked, his voice suspicious.

She wrapped her arms his waist and leaned her head on his chest, grinning as she felt him stiffen and lean away from her.

"Thanks, Davey, for being such a good friend." She smiled up at him. "I don't know what I would have done without you over the last couple of weeks."

Davey patted her on the back, obviously stricken by her display of affection, his face beet red, but he was nonetheless smiling. "'Tis all right, lass," he said. "I always wanted a little sister."

Ellie laughed. "Big sister, you mean."

"Davey Ferguson! What do ye think ye're doin'?"

They both turned toward the irate voice to see Katie coming down the stairs, her dark brows knit together.

"Why are ye kissing my husband?" she demanded, as she stood on the last step and looked down at Ellie.

Ellie glanced back at Davey and laughed. "Well, I'm not kissing him; I'm hugging him. Even if I were, it's not like he's really your husband," she said, only to see Katie's eyes flame with anger.

"He is my husband! We were joined by a priest!"

Well, well, well. Ellie slid a knowing smile toward Davey. *Katie is jealous!*

"I'm sorry," Ellie said, crossing to the fireplace and holding out her hands. The heat flooded into her chilled body, and she sighed. "I was just excited because he gave me an idea about getting Ian back to his old self. So tell me, do you know where any bagpipes are?"

Katie moved to stand beside her, still sullen. "Ian left his pipes here, when he—feigned his own death."

Ellie exchanged a delighted look with Davey. "Wonderful! That's even better, for it to be his own set of pipes! Where are they?"

Katie's face darkened. "Father gave them to General Wade."

"What?" Ellie's mouth fell open, and she sank down on the ledge of the hearth. "Why in the world would he do that?"

Davey spoke before Katie could. "To prove that he was a fervent supporter of the king. Bagpipes were outlawed for all save the loyalists, but Fergus took it a step farther and gave up his family's pipes to show his loyalty to the king meant more than his loyalty to Scotland."

"Aye," Katie said, "but how did ye know?"

He shrugged. "'Tis logical."

"Great," Ellie said. "So where are the pipes now?"

"At Fort William, I suppose," the girl said. "At least that's where General Wade has made his headquarters since he started building the roads."

"The roads?" Davey asked. "What roads?"

"The roads that made it easier"—Ellie corrected herself—"*make* it easier for English troops to invade the Highlands and put down any uprisings."

"How do ye know that?" Davey said.

"My sister was—is—a history teacher." A wave of homesickness washed over her.

"Who does she teach?" Katie asked with interest.

"Oh, anyone who will listen," Ellie said affectionately. "She used to drive us crazy with the history of Scotland. She was obsessed." Ellie shook her head. "We need those pipes," she said.

"Fort William is a long ways away, lass," Davey said. "And dinna fool yerself into believing that simply giving Ian back his pipes will change him. They aren't magic."

Ellie rose from the hearth. "They might be," she said softly. "At least where Ian is concerned."

* * *

Ellie spent the next week trying to figure out how she and Davey could get to Fort William to steal Ian's pipes, or find another set somewhere closer. Ian spent his days riding to clans close by, talking to his kinsmen, and came home at sunset or sometimes the next morning weary and discouraged. Except for a few small groups of Jacobite supporters, he was met with closed doors and closed minds.

Davey spent his time with Katie, and Ellie watched the two—doing chores together, laughing together—and began to worry. What if Davey decided to stay in the past with Katie forever? She still had hope that she could convince Ian to return, but if Davey didn't, what would that mean to their chances of ending up back in 2009?

She had too much to worry about, she decided. So when Ian asked her and Davey to join him in his chamber one day for a private meeting, Ellie found herself praying he was finally giving up on his plan to change Scotland's past.

No such luck.

"I am leaving the castle," he said, standing in front of the tall, narrow casement windows, his hands clasped behind him. "It is time for me to take more drastic measures, and I willna bring more trouble to my family than I already have."

"Where are we going?" Ellie asked, already envisioning more cold, wet nights spent in caves and out under the stars.

"Ye two are going home," he said, his eyes empty of emotion.

Ellie sighed. "Haven't we been over this enough times?"

Davey stood in front of the fireplace, the light from the flames casting shadows on his frowning face. "I canna leave," he said, affirming Ellie's fears. "I canna leave Katie."

Ian's mouth flattened into a grim line. "Katie will be fine."

"No," Davey said, and stared into the fire.

Ian turned to Ellie, his frustration evident. "Then ye will go home alone," he said to Ellie. She moved to stand beside Davey.

"Can't," she said with a shrug. "Davey says if we don't go back together, it could be dangerous."

Ian strode across the short space between them and grabbed Davey by the arm, jerking him around to face him. "Take her back!" he demanded. "I will see to Katie's safety!"

Davey simply shook his head again, and Ellie laid one hand on Ian's arm. "Ian, let him go," she said softly.

He closed his eyes for a moment and then opened them, the fury gone, resignation in its place. He released the man's arm and stepped back.

"Davey isn't going anywhere, and neither am I," Ellie said. "At least not without you." She shrugged. "We're all stuck here together. So you might as well take us with you, wherever you're going, and let us help you."

Ian shook his head. "No. If ye refuse to go back to yer own time, ye must stay here."

Ellie shrugged again and cocked her head to one side. "Who's going to make us? You'll be gone, wreaking havoc somewhere. Maybe Davey and Katie and I will wreak some havoc of our own." She turned to Davey. "What do you say, pal? Katie's all set for some Jacobite rebellion stuff. Should we help her?"

Ian's eyes narrowed. "Ye wouldna dare." He shot a swift glance at Davey. "Ye said ye wanted to keep Katie safe."

"Aye," he agreed, "but ye know how these fiery women can be. Short of tying them up, I'm no' sure how I can stop them."

"Then tie them," Ian said shortly. "I will supply the rope."

"Or you could take us with you," Ellie suggested, moving to put her arms around his waist. He didn't respond at first, but after a few seconds, he sighed and put his arms around her. "Just think," she went on, "more nights under the stars and the moon, camping on rocks. Such fun!"

"Lass, I canna take ye with me."

She took a step back and gazed up at him, her voice firm. "Then I'll follow you. Davey isn't going to tie me up," she said, "because he knows if he tries, I'll truss him up like a Christmas turkey. I'm going with you, one way or another."

"Ye might as well give in," Davey said, pushing his glasses up on his nose. "But we can leave Katie here. I'll tell her that the three of us are going to visit an old friend of yers, Ian." He glanced at Ellie. "This one, I canna control, but Katie is my wife. She will do as I say."

Ellie smiled. *Right. In what universe?* she thought, but kept her mouth shut, as it seemed Ian might be about to agree.

"On one condition." Ian's eyes were fixed on her, and Ellie tried to look innocent.

"Of course, just name it," she lied.

"Ye have to do as I say. Ye must promise to obey my commands."

Ellie raised one brow and narrowed her eyes. "Commands?"

The tension suddenly faded from Ian's face, and he grinned and pulled her to him, giving her a hug and a quick kiss. "Ah, there's my girl. Aye, commands! Promise or I swear I'll tie ye up myself and leave ye in what passes for a dungeon in this place."

Ellie glared up at him but was so happy to see him more like his old self that she had to agree. "All right," she said. "I'll obey you—within reason."

He frowned. "What does that mean?"

"It means she'll do what ye want when she agrees with it," Davey said. He yawned. "Come on, Ellie, give him yer word."

Ellie rolled her eyes, but Ian's arms around her and his mouth against her cheek were very convincing arguments. "Oh, all right," she said, pushing away from him and giving him a stern look. "But you have to promise to remember that just because I'm a woman, that doesn't mean I can't help. Remember all those booking agents I sliced and diced when we were on the road?" She shook her finger at him. "I'm not afraid to fight at your side!"

And suddenly Ellie realized it was the truth. What had happened to her fear of dying? Her fear of losing the ones she loved? Something had altered inside of her, giving her new strength, and she was no longer afraid.

"Aye, lass," Ian said, slipping his arms around her again.

"I know it. I will agree to remember yer courage, but I am still in charge, agreed?"

Ellie sighed. "Agreed."

The sound of someone pounding down the hallway made Davey jump, and they all turned toward the door as it burst open and Katie staggered into the room.

"Katie!" Davey cried, rushing to her side. "Are ye all right?"

"They've taken Angus!"

Ian crossed the room to his sister, his face grim. "Who? Who has taken Angus?"

She lifted her frightened gaze to his. "The king's soldiers," she said. "He's been arrested!" Then she threw herself into Davey's arms and began to sob.

It took all of Ellie's pleading and Davey's logic to keep Ian from dashing out the door and catching up with the soldiers who had arrested Angus. They managed to talk him into sitting down in the great hall to discuss what had happened, but he was tense and ready to bolt at any moment.

"Dinna be rash," his brother Tavish added to their arguments. "If ye try to free him now, he could be killed in the struggle." He frowned down at his brother. "Or is that what ye are hoping for? With Angus out of the way, do ye think to sway the brothers to yer side?"

Ian stared at the man, horror-stricken. "Ye cannot believe that," he said.

Tavish shrugged. "I dinna know what to think about ye anymore. 'Tis ye who have brought this upon us. Do ye think Angus dinna know about yer activities? And more important, did ye think that 'twould have no effect on the rest of us? As far as General Wade is concerned, Angus is the head of this family and is held accountable. He doesna know ye exist." He turned and walked away.

Ian sat staring into space. He was conscious of Ellie and Davey on either side of him, and Katie across the table from him. They were all thankfully silent. He rose and Ellie jumped to her feet, one hand on his arm. He turned to her, his jaw set.

"I'm sorry, lass," he said. "I need to be alone, to think." He strode out of the room and up the stairs.

As a child, Ian had often felt the need to be alone, to play his music, or simply to think. In a busy household, this was not always easy, but one day he'd discovered the high tower, long abandoned by the inhabitants of the keep. With its ramshackle stairway and wooden floor studded with holes, he had daydreamed of being the piper of the clan and hidden from his father's rages. Over the years, he had made repairs to his hiding place, and now, as he mounted the narrow stairway, he felt, in a sense, that he had truly come home.

The turret had three broad casement windows, and he opened them, standing to gaze out across the lands owned by his father. Ben Lomond stood in the distance, a silent sentinel guarding the Trossachs, and Ian felt his heart swell with true love for his country.

His country.

When he had returned to the past, his only thought had been to find Ellie and Davey and return to his comfortable place in the twenty-first century. His encounter with Angus and the Black Watch had changed all of that.

He frowned and leaned against the iron bar that divided one of the windows. His headlong quest to change Scotland's history had been born from his need to assuage his own guilt. He saw that now. If he could change Scotland's future, he had thought, perhaps he could live with the past. But instead, his need to prove himself to his brothers, even to his ailing father, had placed his family in danger, and his pride had kept him from admitting it.

Now Angus was under arrest, and it was his fault. There was only one thing to be done. One way to set things right.

"Ian?"

Ellie's voice stirred him from his reverie, and he turned, his gaze softening as she stood uncertainly at the entrance to his fortress of solitude. Her eyes spoke of her love for him, of her fear, and of her compassion. He held out his hand, and she crossed the small circular room to his side.

"Och, lass," he said, holding her tightly in his arms, "I have made a mess of things."

"It's all right," she told him, her face pressed against his chest. "Angus hasn't done anything wrong. They'll see that and let him go."

Ian cupped her face between his hands and bent to kiss her, gently, tenderly, with all of his love and all of his heart. And as his lips touched hers, she grew still, and when he lifted his head, there was sorrow in her eyes.

"What?" she whispered. "Why are you telling me good-bye?"

"I must go to Fort William," he said. "That's where they will take him. I must confess what I have done and save my brother."

Ellie stared at him for a moment and then smiled. "Och, laddie," she said. "We can come up with something better than that."

"Tell me again what this has to do with rescuing Angus?" Davey said.

Ellie scowled at him. "We're going to blow up a road and prove to General Wade that the leader of the growing rebellion isn't Angus."

"Oh."

"Which you know, because you're the one who helped Ian make the gunpowder from Angus's storeroom into explosives."

Davey scowled back at her. "Aye. Against my better judgment."

She glanced over at Ian but saw he was focusing on the road below, his shoulders tense. "Well," she said, "he ran out of the batch he'd been using, the stuff that Bittie's friend had made, and he trusted you to make a better bomb anyway."

"Och, lass, that makes me feel so much better."

Ellie, Davey, and Ian sat huddled behind a large grouping of stones on a rise just above beside the sleek and beautiful road recently built by General Wade around Loch Ness.

The sixteen-foot-wide highway, built in layers of stone and topped with a final layer of gravel, led from Fort William to Inverness. Across the loch, on the north side, Urquhart Castle, a ruin even in 1734, perched upon a rocky outcropping, overlooking the dark waters below. Beyond it, Ellie knew from her travels during Ian's tour, was the town of Drumnadrochit. A brisk wind swept over the stones and Ellie shivered and pulled the cloak she had borrowed from Katie more securely around her shoulders.

"All right," Ian said, "look lively." He disappeared around one of the large stones. Ellie watched him go, nervously smoothing the legs of her breeches. Ian hadn't allowed them to make a fire while they waited, and she was freezing. Winter had arrived in the Highlands.

"This is not like Ian," Davey said. "He is not a violent man."

Ellie pushed away the feelings of guilt his words brought to the surface. "No one will be hurt," she said.

"Ye dinna know that for certain."

"Look," she said, her teeth almost chattering, "it was the only way I could talk Ian out of turning himself in! Come on, we can do this! If the bombings of the road continue, Wade will have to let Angus go free!"

"Or he'll simply think that Angus's men are continuing to fight the good fight that he began."

Ellie stared at him, unable to speak for a moment. "You couldn't have mentioned that *before* we started bombing Loch Ness?"

The moon was practically full now, giving more than enough light to see well ahead of them, or gaze upon the reflections of Urquhart Castle and the moon itself, gleaming in the dark waters of Loch Ness. It had taken them the better part of a week to reach this part of the Highlands, taking little time to stop along the way. They were near Fort William, where Angus was being held.

Completely exhausted on that last day of the journey, Ellie had been overwhelmed with relief when Ian announced it was time to dismount and make camp. They hadn't rested for long.

Suddenly Ian came running back around the stones, a long string gripped in his hand and trailing after him. "Come on!" he whispered, and ran past them.

Ellie and Davey scrambled to their feet and ran, bent over in the moonlight, imitating Ian. When they reached another outcropping of stones and hid behind them, out of breath, Ian turned to Davey.

"Have ye got the lighter?" he asked.

Davey dug in his pocket and pulled out the lighter Ian had brought back with him and handed it over. "Are ye sure no one will get hurt?" Davey asked.

Ian held up one hand. "Listen!"

The sound of horse hooves striking the hard surface of the road echoed down to them as Ian flicked the lighter's switch several times before it suddenly flamed to life. He held the fire to the end of the string, waiting patiently until it ignited.

The flame licked along the string as it disappeared around the side of the stones. Ellie ran to the last stone and peeked around it. The flickering ember danced across the ground and up to the roadway like a sparkler after its sizzle is gone.

"Ellie, get down!" Ian shouted, just as an explosion ripped apart the silence of the night.

eighteen

Ellie dove for cover and hit the ground hard.

"Keep yer head covered!" Ian shouted, and seconds later a shower of small rocks rained down on them, striking her cloak with rapid fire.

When the deluge stopped, Ian grabbed her by the hand and dragged her to her feet. "Come on!" he said again. Pulling her after him, with a dazed-looking Davey following, they ran away from the road, down a sloping hillside.

"Was that the Black Watch?" Ellie asked breathlessly as they ran.

"Aye," Ian said, "a new regiment is being mustered out tomorrow. They are on their way to Fort William. Were on their way."

Ellie slid to a stop and faced him, her heart pounding. "Ian, we didn't kill them, right? That wasn't the plan!"

"Och, we just blew up the road in front of them. Now come on, let's get to the horses while the men are confused and disorganized. We've got to reach the next vantage point." He pulled her along by the hand, and Ellie stumbled after him, only slightly relieved.

* * *

For the next several days, the three followed General Wade's highway as it led up and around Loch Ness. They traveled as far as Inverness but never entered the city, to Ellie's disappointment. She got used to being tired and dirty and hungry.

We'll get Angus out of jail, and then everything will be all right, Ellie told herself. *Ian will have saved his brother and then we'll live happily ever after. Somewhere.* She had to keep remembering that or she'd lose hope entirely.

Glancing over where Ian waited, half-crouched behind yet another stone, about to set yet another explosion off, she wondered if they were just fooling themselves. General Wade had not set Angus free yet. Perhaps Davey was right. Perhaps these endeavors were useless.

"All right," Ian whispered, bringing her back to the task at hand. "Pay attention." Davey leaned closer and Ellie tensed as she always did before Ian lit the fuse. "I've found a good place to hide once the powder explodes. Just stay close to me and be ready to ride as soon as it blows. In fact, go ahead and mount yer ponies now."

Ellie had barely swung into the saddle before the explosion rocked the countryside. Before the smoke cleared, a patrol came out of nowhere in the darkness.

"Go on! Go on!" Ian shouted, running toward his horse. Davey and Ellie turned the heads of their ponies and kicked them into a dead run.

As they tore across the land, Ellie glanced up at the sky and saw that Ian's usually impeccable timing was off. It was almost dawn. In another few minutes, the patrol would be able to see them clearly. She put her head down, swallowed, and rode faster, silently thanking her sister for all those riding lessons back in Texas.

They reached a rise where the patrol could not be seen behind them, and Ian pulled up his horse to a stop and searched the horizon. For what, Ellie had no idea. But he must have found it, because he smiled and turned to call out to them.

"Follow me!" he cried. He rode as if every demon in hell were chasing him, and Ellie felt jarred to the core of her backbone. As Ian zigged and zagged across the Highlands, she tried to follow him.

She glanced back and saw that Davey was having as much trouble as she. Ian finally slowed, waiting for them. He grabbed her reins as she came alongside and pulled her after him to charge around a large outcropping of stones, and then down the sharply sloping hillside toward a glen; beyond that was a craggy mountain that appeared to be hewn out of solid rock.

After they reached the flatter land, Ian rode straight for the mountain, with Ellie at his side and Davey lagging behind. The Black Watch was still nowhere in sight, but Ellie knew it was only a matter of time. Ian swerved to the left, riding between huge boulders that had created a long, narrow pathway to the mountain. The horses were lathered when he finally pulled back on the reins and leaped out of the saddle.

Ellie sat stunned as she stared up at the sheer, stark face of a cliff. Ian had led them into a dead end!

"What the hell?" Davey cried as his mount slid to a stop.

Ellie dismounted and ran over to hold Davey's reins, helping him slide out of the saddle to the ground. "Ian!" she shouted. "What are we doing?"

Not answering, Ian grabbed the reins of his horse and pulled it after him, gathering the reins of Davey's and Ellie's horses as well. As Ellie and Davey watched, dumbstruck, he led the mounts a few yards down the stone-rimmed corridor and then slapped one of them on the rump. The horse jumped and tore off down the pathway, with the other two running closely behind. Ian whirled around and ran back toward the mountain, rushing by Davey and grabbing Ellie, pulling her behind him.

"*Come on!*" Ian shouted, waving one arm toward the great steep face of the cliff.

Come on where? Ellie wondered as she stumbled along beside him. *Into the side of the mountain?*

Davey swore, but followed. A few seconds later, they both collided with Ian as he stopped abruptly in front of a thick copse of bushy trees.

"Bushes?" Davey cried. "Is he daft?"

Ellie was too scared to wonder. Ian lifted a branch and ducked under it, then held it up for her as she followed him. She straightened and looked around in surprise. The branch ricocheted back and hit Davey squarely in the face.

"Ow! Thanks a lot, Ellie!"

"Sorry," she said, but her attention was on the space in which she stood—a cave about six feet wide and six feet high. The trees had hidden the entrance.

"Bloody hell!" Davey grumbled as he pushed the branch out of his face and stumbled into the cave, blinking at their surroundings. "Another cave? Crickey."

"Come on!" Ian said, his voice low and sure. He turned and led them out of the small cave and into what appeared to be a tunnel. Ellie followed him, her throat tight, the acrid smell of dirt making her cough.

Where did the tunnel lead? Would they end up in a larger cave, or go on like this 'til they reached the other side? She hated small, dark places. Even as a child she had been afraid of the dark.

Don't be a wimp, she ordered. *You're tougher than that!* Her head bumped against the "ceiling" as the tunnel began to get smaller.

Maybe.

Ellie kept moving forward, keeping her eyes on Ian's back as he kept a steady pace. Her heart was pounding so hard she thought surely the Black Watch would be able to find them just from the vibrations.

But at last the tunnel grew wider and taller, and Ellie began to relax a little. Ian led them into a bigger cave, and she stood stock-still in the center of the huge cavern, looking upward, her eyes wide. Davey stopped beside her, his face reflecting the same awe Ellie felt. The ceiling of the cavern was covered with some kind of phosphorescent moss.

"Good glory," Davey said aloud, and the sound reverberated around the cave.

"Dinna stop," Ian said. "Time isna on our side."

"Irony," Ellie said. "I love it." She trudged after him.

At the other side of the large cavern was another opening about eight feet tall. Beside the "doorway" was a torch, fixed into the stone with a metal ring. Ian took it down, and using the lighter once again, he lit the brushy, charred end of it. Ellie took a deep, steadying breath. The light made her feel a little better.

But after a while, as one cave led into another and there seemed to be no end in sight, Ellie began to feel the panic begin again.

Finally, they reached what Ian told them was the last of the interlocking caverns leading through the mountain. When she saw daylight streaming in through the opening that led outside, Ellie released a breath she hadn't known she'd been holding.

Ian stopped her before she could rush out of the musty cave and into the sunlight. "We've come out on the other side of the mountain, far from the place we entered," Ian said. "These caves twist around for miles. My brothers and I used to play in them when we were children, when my mother would come to a little town near here to visit her sister. Outside, we will still be hidden from anyone below. There's a small clearing with the mountain surrounding it, creating a sort of bowl. I'll climb up the side and take a look around."

"Whist!" Davey whispered suddenly. "I hear something!"

"Quick! Back into the other cave!" Ian tossed the torch to the floor and stamped the flame out, then took the lead. Soon they were back in the smaller, narrower cave, which had led into the larger one. "Follow me!" he said, and headed for a dark corner, where a large, flat rock seemed to be part of the "wall" making up the "room."

Ellie blinked. One moment Ian was there, and the next he

wasn't. Then she saw his hand waving from behind the rock and breathed a sigh of relief. The stone looked as if it was embedded in the wall, but there was actually a space behind it wide enough to let a person stand, or in this case, walk through the hidden opening behind it.

"Where does this lead?" Davey asked as they ducked under an overhanging rock and followed Ian.

"To a small room that has no outlet," he whispered. "Be silent and follow me."

Ellie hurried after him. The farther they went, the more claustrophobic she became. She'd never shared with anyone how absolutely terrified she was of small spaces—not even her sisters.

The tunnel grew smaller and smaller as they walked, until finally they had to get down on their hands and knees and crawl, then—to her horror—lie down flat and slide on their bellies.

"Come on!" Ian encouraged from ahead. "We are almost there!"

As Ellie inched forward, trying to keep from breathing in the acrid air, her heart began to pound as if it might burst out of her chest. She saw flashes of black in front of her and she closed her eyes, coming to a stop. Davey was behind her, Ian ahead, but she couldn't move. She couldn't breathe. She needed to scream; she needed to—

"Ellie?" Ian called back to her. "Are ye all right?"

"Ian—Ian!" she cried, her voice weak with fear. "I can't do this—I can't do this!"

"It's just a few feet farther," he called back to her. "I promise, love, it's just a wee bit farther."

"I—can't," she whispered, her cheek flat on the dirt and stone beneath her, her arms outstretched in front of her. "I—can't."

"What's happening?" Davey said from behind. "Why have ye stopped, Ellie?"

"I can't—" She squeezed her eyes together more tightly. She couldn't do this. Why had she thought she was strong? She wasn't strong. She was weak and fearful and a complete coward. And now Davey would have to back out of the tunnel and would likely get caught, all because she didn't have a brave bone in her body!

"Ellie!" Davey called, but she couldn't answer. "Just close yer eyes and keep moving forward!"

"Ellie."

Her eyes flew open at the sound of Ian's voice. She must be hallucinating now, because she thought for a second that she felt his breath upon her brow.

"Ellie," he said again, and she turned her head toward the sound.

Somehow he had turned around and was facing her, and it was all Ellie could do not to grab on to him and never let go.

"Ye see?" he said gently. "We are so close I was able to reach the cave, get up, turn around and crawl back. Come, love, ye can do this."

"I'm a big, fat fraud," she whispered, his face so close she could kiss him if she just scooted forward an inch. But she couldn't move.

"Shhh . . . take a deep breath. 'Tis all right."

"I act all tough and brave," she said, "but I'm a coward."

"Och, lass," Ian shook his head. "Ye are no coward. Come now, 'tis just a few feet more, I promise."

"Ellie!" Davey whispered again, and this time he grabbed her foot. "I hear voices."

She kicked her foot and he let go. "Well, that's nothing new," Ellie muttered, trying to keep up her nerve.

"Whist!" Ian called back to Davey softly. "Sound travels! Ellie, look at me." His fingers were warm against her arms now, and she felt the sheer strength of his hands.

"I can't see you," she said.

"Ye can do this. Ye could do it without me, but I'm here, so why should ye? Just hold on to me and I will pull ye out."

Her throat was growing tighter. Davey was muttering about voices. "No, no, I can't."

"Ellie." The calm of his voice forced her to listen. "Ye are not the kind of person who would jeopardize someone else's life. If ye dinna move, we will all be found, for I willna leave ye, and if Davey must back out of the tunnel, he will surely be caught."

She started to close her eyes, but his hand slid to the side of her face and his fingers tightened in her hair. "Listen to the sound of my voice. What do ye hear?"

She ran her tongue over her dry, cracked lips. "Strength," she said.

"Do ye know what gives me strength?"

"No," she whispered.

"Ye give me strength. The love ye give to me, the joy ye give to me. Ye are my strength, Eleanor Graham. Ye can do this. Do it for Davey. Do it for me, for I canna live without ye, and if ye stay here, I will stay here with ye, forever, if need be."

His hands moved from her hair to her shoulders, and then down to clasp her hands. Suddenly, Ellie found the strength to bend her knees slightly, to dig her toes into the dirt and stone beneath them, and to move forward just an inch.

"That's my girl," Ian said softly. "Come on, now."

After the first few inches it got easier, and after a few more, she began to move without any help from Ian. In a matter of moments, the tunnel opened to a cave about eight feet tall and ten feet wide. Ian stood and reached down for her hand, pulling her to her feet and into his arms.

Davey crawled out just behind her, white-faced beneath the dirt, but he patted her on the back. She reached out and gripped his hand tightly.

"I'm sorry," she said.

Davey squeezed her hand and then laughed. "Och, dinna fash yerself. 'Tis good for a scientist to experience many different facets of nature. Now I know what a sardine feels like."

She smiled, but couldn't summon the strength to laugh with him.

"We'll spend the night here," Ian said, holding her close. "By tomorrow, they'll have given up."

A sudden thought made Ellie jerk her head up from his

chest. "And then we'll have to go back through the tunnel," she said, an echo of terror in her voice.

Ian cupped her face between his hands. "Aye," he said, one thumb caressing her cheek as he gazed down at her. "But this time, ye and I will go last, and I will back my way out, and we will talk to one another all the way. All right?"

Ellie's lips trembled as he leaned down and kissed her. "All right," she whispered.

Ian lay in a soft bed next to Ellie with his eyes still closed, trying to summon the nerve to open them. Once he did, everything would be different. They had left the cave and walked to the small village of Maryburgh outside Fort William. There they found rooms at an inn run by a Jacobite sympathizer, ordered a meal and devoured it like animals because they were so starved, then stumbled to their rooms.

In the comfort of their bed, Ian had made love to her gently, lovingly, and she had arched beneath him, soft and giving, and when he looked into her eyes, burning with passion, he had fallen in love with her all over again. It seemed now that he had always loved her, from the moment they first met. But afterward, she had clung to him, silent and withdrawn.

After she fell asleep, he had met with Davey to ask him more questions about time travel and the implications of changing the past. The more they had talked, the more he had realized that the man was probably right. Unless he could recruit an entire army of men to rise up in revolt against the king, it was unlikely anything would change. Look at his and Quinn's highwaymen activities—the Duke of Montrose had continued despite their attempts to wreak havoc upon him.

Unless I can alter something big in history—something important—nothing is going to change.

Davey also believed that their attempts to convince General Wade that Angus could not be responsible for the bombings were failing, and Ian feared he was right. He couldn't continue to drag Ellie around the countryside indefinitely. She didn't belong here in this age of violence; she belonged with her family, with Allie and Maggie, and Maggie's new babe. He selfishly had hoped she would stay with him, and she had been willing, but now, after their harrowing escape from his enemies, he knew that if he truly loved her, he would send her home.

nineteen

"He is discouraged," Davey said. He and Ellie sat at a table in the great room of the inn, drinking ale and watching Ian across the room as he spoke once again to Bittie.

"How many more roads does he have to blow up before he realizes this isn't going to work?" Ellie asked, her voice filled with anguish as she gripped the pewter mug in front of her as if it were a lifeline.

Davey glanced around the inn anxiously. When would the lass remember to lower her voice? Thankfully, besides Ian and Bittie, they were the only ones in the inn. He turned back and raised one auburn brow, giving her a knowing smile. "Och, ye are just frustrated because it was yer plan in the first place."

She glared at him, and he was glad to see she wasn't completely in despair. "Well, it seemed like a good idea at the time."

He nodded. "Aye, and it was. But now we need a better idea."

Ellie shook her head and laced her fingers through her hair at the temples, leaning against them. "I'm fresh out. What about you? You're the genius, remember?"

Davey nodded. "Aye. I'm a bit frustrated with myself these days. I don't seem to be able to come up with anything brilliant. 'Tis unusual for me."

She lifted her head from her hands and grinned. "You're the only person in the world who could say something like that and not come across as a pompous ass."

He smiled, frowning slightly. "Thank ye. I think." Picking up his own tankard, he took a sip. Ever since his disastrous drunken episode, he'd kept his drinking under tight control. "He is desperate to redeem himself in the eyes of his family, but everything he does just pushes them further away. If only we could do something to make him remember that this is not his world any longer, because truly, it isn't."

"His pipes!" Ellie said, leaning toward Davey across the table. "Everything got so crazy we forgot about getting back his bagpipes! And now here we are, practically in Fort William, where the pipes are likely being held!"

Davey laughed. "Ye make it sound as if they'd been kidnapped."

Ellie shook her head, and her dark hair danced across her shoulders. "No, it's more like they were sold into slavery, you know? Ian's father gave them to General Wade as a kind of payment, as a gift declaring their loyalty. But the pipes didn't want to go. The pipes wanted to stay with the person who loved them—Ian."

"They are not alive, lass," he said, unable to keep from smiling at her fancy.

Ellie rolled her eyes at him. "Duh. I know that. It's a metaphor. Okay, so let's get going!"

"Get going where?" The woman jumped from one subject to the next like a hoptoad.

She leaned her elbows on the table and folded her arms across it, then rested her chin on top of them, gazing up at him, a sparkle in her eyes. "To Fort William," she whispered, glancing toward Ian. "To steal back Ian's bagpipes!"

Davey frowned and leaned forward, lacing his hands together atop the table. "'Twould be too dangerous," he said.

"The last thing Ian needs is for ye to go running off half-cocked and get into trouble."

She narrowed her eyes and straightened. "I am *not* running off half-cocked! We're going to make a plan, and it will go off without a hitch, because you are brilliant and I am determined. Now come on, get off your duff and start using that brain you brag about so much."

Davey sighed as she slipped off the bench and hurried up the stairs to the room she shared with Ian. He was almost certain that he was going to regret this. But he rose and headed after her all the same.

Davey and Ellie waited until a few days later, when Ian was out scouting their next target, to implement the plan they had painstakingly devised. Fearful that someone might recognize stolen ponies, they had walked to the huge fort, and the sun was halfway up in the sky before they finally reached the front gates.

"I am starving," Davey said as they stopped outside the gate, both panting like dogs. "Did ye bring any money?"

Ellie moaned. "No. Ian has all of it. I'm hungry, too."

"Dinna fash yerself. I have an idea." He pointed in the direction of a woman standing near the gate talking to one of the guards. She held a basket of bread. Davey waited until she walked away from the soldiers and then approached her, flashing his most winning smile.

A few minutes later he stumbled back to Ellie, one hand held to his jaw. "Saint Christopher's medal! I truly do not understand women!"

"What happened?"

"I dinna know. I simply told her I was hungry and that I'd love to get my hands on her luscious round rolls, and she slapped me!" He rubbed the side of his face and Ellie laughed.

"Oh, Davey, you are such an innocent."

He sighed. "I suppose I am."

She patted his hand. "That's not necessarily a bad thing."

"Ha. Right. Well, now, are ye ready to do this?" Ellie, instead of being eager as he'd expected, looked troubled. "What is it, lass?"

She shook her head. "It's strange. We're about to do something that's pretty risky, and I'm not afraid." She turned her head to look at him. "Don't you think that's strange? I mean, especially after the way I freaked out in the caves."

Davey shrugged. "I dinna know. Perhaps after all ye have been through, ye have learned how to deal with yer fears a little better."

"Maybe. I just—" She broke off, her face growing pink and tears glistening in her downcast eyes.

Touched by her sudden vulnerability, he rested one hand gently on her shoulder. "What is it, Ellie?"

She shook her head, still staring at the ground. "It's just that I feel the way I used to *pretend* to feel, after my parents were killed."

"And how did ye pretend to feel?" Davey asked, his voice soft.

"Like I was strong and confident. Like there wasn't anything I couldn't handle." She looked up. "Now I really feel that it's true."

"Och," he said, "I'm glad to hear it, for I am absolutely terrified." He grinned, and Ellie grinned back, a kind of joy rushing over her as she turned toward the gates.

It was no problem getting into the fort. The guards barely looked at them as they passed through the huge arched gateway. The gates were left open during the day, Davey had learned, and were only closed at night.

In the broad courtyard within, flanked by a dozen or more buildings, there was a wealth of vendors with their wares set up. Davey's mouth watered again at the sight of breads and cheeses spread out upon the makeshift tables.

While Davey searched his pockets for something he could trade for food—he still insisted on wearing his own trousers—Ellie stood in the center of the courtyard, a frown on her face. She had been wearing breeches and a shirt during their "bombing" missions, but had the foresight to snag a skirt and blouse from a clothesline in the village. A woman wearing breeches would have brought unwanted attention from the residents of Fort William.

She'd pinned her short hair up again, diminishing the strangeness of its length in this time and place, and her new, darker color helped her blend in quite well with the Scots who made up most of the population. She'd laced up the vest she usually wore with her breeches over the blouse, giving her just enough cleavage for the job at hand.

In spite of how she had worked to blend in to her surroundings, the way she stood appraising the perimeter of the fort itself would have made Davey wary had he been a military man. He hurried over to one of the tables, pulling his wallet out of his back pocket. Better get food now before they were both thrown in the brig.

He rummaged through his wallet and found a business card he'd picked up once. It had a picture of a huge yellow sunflower on it. When he handed it to the old woman behind the table of bread and asked if she would take it in trade, her face lit up. Amazing how the simple little things the people of the twenty-first century took for granted were practically miracles in this day and age!

Gathering up the three loaves of bread and a block of cheese—he patted himself on the back for his astute business sense—he hurried back to Ellie, only to see that she was talking to one of the guards!

"Och, Davey! Ye're just in time," she said in a convincing Scottish accent. She hugged his arm. "This is my brother," she explained. "This kind man was telling me that General Wade will be back in a few minutes and that we can wait in his office."

Davey schooled his features not to show any surprise, but he was very surprised. Though this was part of their plan, it was the part he had secretly doubted would work. What kind of general allowed the riffraff off the streets to wait in his office? And he hated to say it, but Ellie looked extremely riffraffish.

"That's grand," he said, and Davey smiled as comprehension dawned. The "man" was no more than seventeen and gazed up at Ellie in besotted admiration.

"Would ye mind taking us to his office, Richard?" she asked, her answering gaze filled with mutual admiration.

"Oh, yes, miss," the boy said, in a proper English accent, "I'd be happy to do that! And you won't forget about, er, later?"

She swept her eyelashes down and then up again and—no, she wasn't . . . oh, yes, she was—batting her eyelashes! "Och, of course not, Richard." She leaned closer to him and whispered in his ear, loud enough for Davey to hear. "Tonight at midnight." Then she patted his cheek, and he closed his eyes in rapture.

Davey hid his smile with his hand as the lad stumbled across the courtyard, taking them to the largest building inside the fort. *Apparently security isn't that tight at Fort William,* he thought, as they were led into the barracklike building and then into a fairly small room. There were no guards inside. Come to think of it, there weren't that many outside either. Richard ushered Ellie over to a chair and beamed as she sat down.

"You can wait here as long as you like," the young man said.

"And can you wait with me?" Ellie said, giving him a coy look.

Don't overdo it, Davey thought, and then realized there was no danger there. The boy was positively smitten.

"Uh, yes, I suppose I could," he said, glancing over one shoulder toward the door. Obviously there was somewhere else he was supposed to be. Davey moved to stand in front of the door and then leaned against it and surreptitiously slid the bolt that locked it from the inside.

"Richard, you're so sweet," Ellie said. "I was just wondering, have you ever seen a set of bagpipes in General Wade's quarters?"

"Oh, yes, I have," he said.

"I have quite a—*passion* for bagpipes," she told him. "They make me feel all, oh, I don't know, all *soft*, and *hot*, inside."

"Would you like to see them?" he asked eagerly.

"I would!" she said, gazing at him with admiration. "You are so wonderful! Where are his quarters?"

"Right up here!" he said, pointing to a stairwell at the back of the room.

"Lovely. Davey, you can stay down here for a while."

Davey raised one brow in question, then saw the stunned look on the young guard's face. He definitely thought he was about to get laid. Without another word, Richard charged up the steps, no doubt thinking of what might happen when he got there.

Ellie followed him, lifting her skirt as she stepped upon the bottom step of the narrow stairway. She paused and looked back at Davey, then pointed to a small iron shovel beside the equally small fireplace on the other side of the room, and then gestured for him to follow. She disappeared up the steps and Davey stomped across the room and picked up the shovel.

"The things I do for Scotland," he groused, and headed for the stairs.

"I'm surprised a garrison of this size doesn't have more soldiers," Davey heard Ellie say as he started up the stairs with the shovel.

"Oh, it's because of the king, you know," Richard said, still smiling at Ellie.

"The king? What do ye mean? What does the king have to do with it?"

Davey froze and he heard the same panic filter through Ellie's question.

"Oh, because the king is coming to Fort William, and most of the men have been sent to guard him on his way here."

Davey found movement again and reached the top of the stairs. He peered around the doorframe into the room and saw the lad boldly bring Ellie's hand to his lips. Ellie was facing the stairwell, and Richard had his back to it. As Davey moved toward the two, he saw Ellie's face had gone white.

"The king?" she said softly. "Here?"

Davey knew she was thinking the same as he. If Ian heard this news, what would he do? They had to get out of here and find him.

"Yes." The boy smiled at her, his freckled face soft with love. "I myself have been given the task of preparing General Wade's bedroom for His Majesty." He gestured toward the big four-poster bed in the center of the room, and Davey blinked as he saw a set of bagpipes in a glass case sitting on the mantle of the fireplace.

Ellie saw it, too. She turned back to Richard. "Grand. And when will the king be arriving?"

"Tonight, around eventide. You know, I just remembered that General Wade will not be here for several hours. He is riding out to meet the king's escort. You might as well not wait." He stood uncertainly.

"But we're just beginning to get to know one another," she said, moving closer, her eyes half-shut, her lips puckered. The boy leaned forward for his kiss and behind him, Davey lifted the shovel—and hesitated.

twenty

Ian had returned to his room at the inn after his scouting trip to find a piece of paper torn out of Davey's notebook saying that he and Ellie were taking a walk.

Taking a walk?

With all the hiking they'd had to do since their arrival in the past, why in the world would they be taking a walk for pleasure? He shook his head, crumpled the note in his hand, and then tossed it aside. Dragging his shirt over his head, he tossed that aside, too, and then stretched out on the bed. Closing his eyes, he tried to ignore the thoughts tumbling through his head. He was so weary, and sleep called to him like a siren's song.

But after tossing and turning for half an hour, he finally gave up. Instead, he lay staring at the ceiling, trying to make a decent plan for rescuing his brother. If he broke him out of the jail, which he knew he could do, then Angus would indeed be a wanted man. If he continued to bomb roads in the hope that General Wade would finally realize that someone else was responsible for the attacks, there was no telling how long Angus would remain incarcerated. If he turned himself in . . .

Aye. If he turned himself in, Angus would be released. Simple. Easy. What was not so easy was the thought of leaving Ellie to fend for herself in the past without him.

Ian sat up and laced his hands around his knees. He had to get Ellie and Davey back to the cairn. He had to make her understand that she had to return. Perhaps he could use the birth of Maggie's baby as leverage. Making Ellie feel guilty was the last thing he wanted to do, but perhaps it was the only way to coerce her into going back to her own time. Back to safety.

Och, but the lass is stubborn. What if she willna agree?

He was revisiting his opinion on ropes and willful women when a knock came at the door. Irritated by the interruption, he slipped out of bed and opened it only to find Bittie standing there. Ian frowned. The man looked as though he had aged since they'd last met. His lined, beefy face sagged, and his eyes were troubled.

"I have news," he said softly.

Ellie leaned over the young man and kissed his forehead. In spite of the gag in his mouth, and the fact that he was tied up with a bruise on his head, he still gazed up at her with stars in his eyes.

"You're a good lad," Ellie told him, "but just remember that you can't trust everyone." She patted his face. "Now, remember the story. We hit you over the head and dragged you up here. No one will blame you for being overpowered by three large men, right?"

He nodded, his eyes blinking up at her like a kitten's.

"Ye are an evil woman," Davey said, shaking his head. "That lad will be dreaming about ye for the rest of his life."

"Yeah, well, what about Katie?" she said. She didn't like the guilt trip Davey was laying on her, even if he was right. The poor kid. She just hoped he didn't get in trouble. But there was no time to spend worrying about poor Richard. "You haven't got any call to talk, boyo."

"Boyo?" He frowned. "That's an Irish expression."

"Okay, then, *laddie*." She stared up at the case, her hands on her hips. "That girl is in love with you. At least I didn't marry Richie and then abandon him."

"I'm not abandoning her. I'm—"

"Come on, help me get this off the wall. We don't have time to argue. If the king is due here tonight at sunset, we still have time to find Ian and stop him. Maybe."

Together they lifted the case down and set it on the floor. There was no latch, no door on the case, and finally in frustration Ellie took the shovel Davey had tentatively tapped the boy with, and slammed it down on the rippled glass. Davey helped her carefully pick out the larger pieces of glass until finally she could grab the pipes without getting cut. She picked them up and shook off the tiny shards still clinging to the bag, and released her pent-up breath.

"Okay. Let's go." She tucked the instrument under her cloak and headed for the stairs.

"What about your boyfriend?"

She stopped and looked back at the boy on the floor, trussed up like a heifer in a rodeo back in Texas. "Bye, bye, Richie," she said, and blew him a kiss. He closed his eyes, looking like he was imagining the kiss wafting across the room and settling upon his brow. "You'll find the right girl someday. Don't dream of me, because I promise, I won't be back!"

She hurried down the stairs with Davey close behind.

"That was lovely," he told her.

"Do you really think Ian may try to kill the king?" she said, ignoring his dry attempt at humor.

"I dinna know. I wouldna have thought so a week ago, but now . . ." His voice trailed off.

"Yeah, that's what I was afraid of!" She stopped beside the locked door to the outside.

"When we get outside we'll split up. You go to the left; I'll go to the right."

"Ellie, I'm not sure ye should go alone."

"I'll be fine. Just hurry!"

She slid the bolt back and walked down the few steps

leading to the graveled courtyard, then hesitated. The court-yard had been practically deserted when they went inside General Wade's office. Now there were probably a dozen soldiers milling about.

Ellie looked back over her shoulder to see that Davey had obediently turned to the right. He stuck his hands in his pock-ets and started whistling as he strolled down past the ven-dors. She grinned and turned back, only to collide with someone tall and broad with such force that it knocked her backward. She fell flat on her rump and the bagpipes flew out of her arms. As she lay gasping, trying to catch her breath again, the man walked over to the pipes, bent down, and picked them up. Then he crossed to her.

"What the bloody hell are ye doing?" the heavyset man asked.

Ellie glared up at him. Leave it to some fat soldier to spoil her getaway. "I'm General Wade's niece, and he sent me to fetch his pipes. Who the bloody hell are *you*?" she demanded.

He glared back. "*I* am General Wade."

Ian sat upon the back of the black horse he had stolen and followed the king's caravan. He had a distinct feeling of déjà vu, remembering his highwayman days with Quinn, know-ing that his black garb and mask let him blend in perfectly with the night as he stalked his prey. Ahead, the king's car-riage had bright lanterns hanging from its side.

As he had arranged, the destruction of the roads near Fort William had slowed the king's arrival and had forced the royal party to travel at night. There was a full moon to-night, the brilliant orb casting a bright light across the coun-tryside, but mostly creating more shadows into which Ian could disappear in a matter of seconds. Still, he hung back, waiting for the right time for his plan to unfold.

He'd hated bringing Bittie further into this mess, but the old man had been eager to help, and without his help, Ian's plan wouldn't work. Ellie and Davey had not returned and there was no way he could set two charges and be ready to attack the carriage at the same time. It was better this way. He could not imagine either of them agreeing with what he planned to do.

He had, at least, refused to let Bittie actually take the risk himself. This was a gambit for younger men. Instead, he'd managed to get the names of two young Jacobites eager for the chance to fight against King George.

Someone ahead cried out for the carriage to stop, and Ian turned his attention back to the matter at hand. The road in front of the carriage had been blown up about thirty minutes before, and now, as the soldiers gathered atop the rubble to see what had happened and what could be fixed, Ian prayed that his new allies would not let him down.

The sound of a mighty explosion proved they had not.

The blast rendered most of the soldiers either unconscious or moaning on the ground. Ian had planted the explosives far enough ahead of the first impact that he had hoped there would be no deaths, and he was relieved to see that was the case as he strode toward the carriage.

The two men aiding him ran toward the fallen and quickly began tying the hands of the conscious but stunned ones. They had pistols loaded and stuck in their belts. Ian hoped they wouldn't have to use them.

What a hypocrite ye are! that dratted voice shouted inside his head. *Ye are glad that the men did not die, but ye plan to kill a man in cold blood?*

This is different, he told himself. *This isn't personal, not really. This is for the good of Scotland and all of her people.*

He strode quickly toward the carriage. The explosion had knocked it on its side, and he hoped the king had been knocked unconscious. He wrenched the door open and drew the sword he had taken from his father's house.

The sovereign of England, His Royal Majesty King George II, cowered inside like a rat trapped by a lion. *What a coward,* Ian thought, his mouth twisting in a sneer. *I bet he will not even fight me.*

Coward? But ye are not a coward for hoping he was un-conscious? Ye are not a coward for hoping ye could kill him in cold blood, without having to look him in the eye?

"Get out of the carriage!" he commanded the man who was, in the eyes of England, his liege lord. Trembling, the man climbed out and fell to his knees in the dirt. His long, curling white wig was askew, and his white satin knee breeches and long matching coat were dirty, his cravat turned sideways and his beady little eyes as wide as a reptile's.

Because the man *was* a reptile, Ian reminded himself. He and his father, George I, as well as the Williams before them, had taken it upon themselves to try to eradicate the Highland Scots from the face of the earth! He leveled his blade across the man's throat. He deserved to die.

This was the huge change in history that Davey had said would make a difference. All he had to do was kill the King of England. All he had to do was avenge the lives of hundreds of Scots. That was all.

"Please . . ." the man on his knees said, his hands clasped together.

"Well, well, George the Second on his knees, beggin' for mercy," Ian said. "Who would have believed it? Oh, aye, except myself and a thousand other Scots!"

His words seemed to shake the king from his terror. Slowly the man stood, straightened his silk coat and his ruffled collar, and stared at his captor balefully.

"Who are you?" the king asked. "How dare you accost your king?"

"Ye are not my king," Ian said, his fingers tightening around the hilt of his sword. "I swore my allegiance to none but King James."

"A Jacobite." King George spit the word out. "You will hang for this!"

A sudden idea sparkled in Ian's mind, and he grinned. Perhaps there was a way out of this mess with Angus after all. "*I* will hang? But my liege, ye have already arrested a man for my crimes, one Angus Campbell."

Ian began walking around him, twitching the blade of the sword close enough to make the king blanch.

"I arranged for certain evidence to point to Campbell, never daring to hope that his own commander would believe it of him. When I heard the news of Campbell's arrest by General Wade, I was thrilled beyond words. The man is one of yer staunchest allies!" He shook his head and chuckled. "How rich that Wade will hang one of the captains of the Black Watch. Och, what that will do to his credibility in the Highlands." He faced the king once again and lifted the tip of his blade to the man's throat. "What it will do to yers."

The king's eyes narrowed. "Why would ye tell me the truth about Campbell, if General Wade has apparently played right into yer hands?"

Ian held his gaze. "Och, my liege, I confess that my need to brag about my cleverness outweighs my need for blood. It is more benefit to me to let ye know how able I am at outwitting those under yer command." He shrugged. "Besides, ye will not live to tell anyone else."

"You pompous blackguard!" The king's face darkened, and even in the pale moonlight Ian could see the veins in his forehead rise in fury. "Campbell will not pay for your crimes, you Jacobite scum! I will see you in hell first!"

Ian inclined his head. "Dinna wait for me," he said, pressing the point of his blade against the man's throat. A drop of blood trickled down his neck. "For ye will be there long before I."

"Papa? Papa!"

A quavering voice drifted up from the overturned carriage, and stayed his hand. Startled, Ian took a step back, his gaze never leaving the king. King George's face twisted in alarm as someone called out again.

"Papa, where are you?" The girl—woman—whoever it was—began to cry.

The king fell to his knees and clasped his hands together, no longer a monarch, but simply a man.

A father.

"Don't hurt her," he begged. "Kill me if you must, but don't hurt my daughter."

Ian turned cautiously toward the sound of bitter weeping. One of the lanterns that had hung on the side of the carriage was still burning, and he could just make out someone's head sticking out through the window in the caved in door.

"Dinna move!" Ian ordered. "Stay in the carriage!"

"Please . . ." the king whispered.

"Quiet!" Ian cried, and pressed the tip of his sword into the man's shoulder. "Lie down on the ground."

The king shook his head. "Promise that you will not harm her, and I will do whatever you ask."

Ian felt the fury rising inside of him. Even in this situation, the usurper was giving orders! "Very well. Tell her to come out."

"You promise you will not harm her?"

"I swear upon the souls of Quinn MacIntyre's father and brother—which yer friend Montrose sent to heaven at a very young age." His mouth twisted grimly. "I will not harm yer daughter."

"Louisa," the king called softly, "come to me if you are able."

In the dim light it was hard to see, but Ian could make out someone clambering over the side of the overturned carriage—someone very short. She ran to her father's side and threw her arms around his neck, burying her face against his shoulder, not uttering a sound.

Ian took the few steps necessary to reach the lit lantern and picked it up, then brought it back and raised it over the king's head. "Stand up," he told the princess of the realm. "Let me see yer face."

She looked up, pale and frightened, her eyes round in the lamplight, tears brimming on her lashes. Slowly, she straightened away from her father, standing erect as she stared back at Ian. Her bottom lip quivered. Ian lowered his sword.

"How old are ye?" he asked, the question a whisper.

"Ten years," she said, "and four months."

* * *

Ian could not remember the last time he'd been so drunk.
He was not a drinking man, normally, but now, perhaps he
would be.

"Laddie," Bittie whispered to him, "what happened?"

He didn't answer, just picked up the glass of whiskey in
front of him and drained it. Again.

As he had looked down into that little girl's eyes, he suddenly wondered what his child, a child born of he and Ellie,
would look like. And suddenly he knew he was not going to
kill the King of England. He could no more murder that
man in front of his daughter than he could drown a basket of
kittens.

He had stared down at the sword in his hand, sickened by
the thought of what he had planned to do, of the bloodshed
he had already caused with the explosions—hopefully none
of it resulting in death.

Who had he thought that he was? Robert the Bruce? William Wallace? He was not a warrior; he was a piper, a bard,
a—his lips curled up derisively—a Celtic rock star, as Ellie
used to say. He was not going to change what happened to
Scotland. He picked up the bottle of whiskey and poured the
last of it into his glass.

"Get me another bottle," he told his friend.

"Ian, lad," Bittie begged, "please stop drinkin'. Go upstairs and go to bed. The longer ye sit here, the more chance
there is of the king's men findin' ye."

"Let them find me."

He had tied the king and his daughter's hands behind
their backs and left them sitting against the overturned carriage. Then he had walked away. Somehow he had made his
way back to his horse, feeling dazed, as if he had been
caught in the blast of the bomb himself. He and his cohorts
had disappeared into the night before anyone was the wiser.

He arrived back at the inn in Maryburgh at dawn, and
though he assumed Ellie had returned, he could not bring
himself to go upstairs. The image of her face, twisted in

disgust at what he had planned to do, had been responsible for the first bottle of whiskey. And half of the second.

He had passed out, sprawled upon a bench against the wall. When he awakened, Bittie was still there, watching over him amidst the clatter and noise of breakfast being served around him. News of the attack upon the king traveled quickly, and as he tackled the remainder of the second bottle, Ian learned that the soldiers at Fort William, and two other garrisons, were presently tearing up the countryside looking for the three traitors who dared attack the king's convoy. With his masked face, his black clothing, and the faintness of the moon that night, Ian doubted the king or his daughter could identify him, and his two helpers were already likely back in Balquhidder, raising a pint in their own town pub.

He had no regrets over his confrontation with George the Second, and hoped the man would make good his threat to release Angus. It was the memory of the king's daughter's horror-stricken eyes that filled him with remorse and made him reach for the bottle again.

Ah, it was empty.

Ian slammed the bottle down on the table. "Another bottle," he ordered.

Like most inns in this part of Scotland, the King's Pride, so named because the king had once stayed there in an emergency, had a large pub that took up the first floor and rooms to let upstairs. The irony of the inn's name had not escaped Ian, even as drunk as he was. Outside, lightning cracked across the sky, while the wind and rain pelted against the rippled windowpane.

The door to the inn crashed open, but for a moment Ian wasn't sure if it was the door or the thunder, as he looked up blearily. Davey Ferguson stood staring across the room at him, soaked to the bone.

Ian rubbed one eye. Bittie was right. He'd drunk far too much. Or perhaps not enough, he thought, as the hallucination walked toward him. He stumbled to his feet, suddenly much more sober.

"Davey? What are ye doing out in this storm? I thought ye were upstairs asleep."

"Ian!" the man grabbed him by both arms and shook him. "God in heaven, tell me ye aren't drunk!"

He blinked at him. "I'm not drunk."

"Yes, ye are!"

Ian sat back down, unsteadily, and picked up the fresh bottle Bittie had just brought him. The stablemaster frowned at Davey.

"Leave him be," he told the scientist. "He has a great sorrow in his heart."

"Well, he's going to have a greater one if he doesn't listen to me!" Davey said, bending over his friend. He lowered his voice. "Ellie is in gaol," he said.

Ian had the drink halfway to his lips and stopped. The fuzz around his brain tried to tell him that Davey had just told him Ellie was in jail. What year was it? For a moment he couldn't remember if he was in 2009 or 1711 or 1734. His head began to swim.

"Do ye hear me, man?" Davey said again, his voice fierce. "Ellie is in *gaol*!"

Ian set the drink down and stood, reaching out for Davey's shoulder. He found it, and straightened, then pulled the redheaded man closer.

"Where is she? Where is Ellie being held?"

"At the fort."

"What's the charge?" He staggered slightly and threw his arm around Davey's shoulder for better support.

Davey gagged and pushed him away. "Good Lord, how much of that stuff did ye drink?"

"What's the *charge*?"

"Theft."

"What?" Ian sat back down, heavily. "What did she steal?"

"Yer bagpipes."

"My—my what?" He dragged both hands through his ragged hair.

"Bagpipes. Seems yer father gave them to General Wade as a show of good faith."

"That son of a bitch," Ian muttered, and then looked up. "And ye helped her I suppose."

Davey looked toward the ceiling. "Aye."

Ian shook his head and then winced and grabbed it to keep it from falling off. Bittie had been standing nearby, simply watching the proceedings, but Ian motioned to him and he hurried over..

"Bittie, my good friend," he said softly, "what will get me sober the fastest?"

The man thought about it for a moment. "My old grandmither's recipe was a cup of goat's milk, a teaspoon of honey, and a dollop of sheep urine."

"A dollop of *what*?" Davey asked, horrified.

"Bring it on!" Ian cried. "Ellie needs me."

twenty-one

Ellie paced the confines of her cell, pausing in the center to scratch yet another fleabite.

"By the time I get out of here, I'll probably have the Bubonic plague," she said grumpily.

"Och, dinna say such a thing," a voice said from outside the door. She paused to look out the tiny barred window and saw a towheaded young man. His name was Timothy, she'd learned, and he guarded her during the day. He genuflected and then kissed his thumb. "'Tis bad luck."

Ellie noted the blatant symbol of Catholicism and tucked the information away for future use. Hopefully.

"You're so right, Tim," she said. "I should have a more positive outlook. Have you been saying prayers for me, as I asked?"

He looked shamefaced, but nodded. "Aye. I'm that sorry, lass, that ye are still stuck inside this hole. Is there any word on yer release?"

"No," she said, trying her best to sound weak and feminine. "Maybe you could ask around for me. I don't know why they won't let me go." She coughed delicately into her hand. "My cough is getting worse."

His eyes widened in alarm. "Aye, lass, as soon as my shift is over, I'll see what I can find out."

"Thank you, Timmy," she said, letting her voice caress his name. He blushed, and she turned away from the door, feeling just a wee bit ashamed.

It had been three days since General Wade had arrested her. Her initial fear was that Ian would try to break her out and get arrested himself. But he hadn't showed up, thank goodness.

Okay, if she were honest, she'd have to take the "thank goodness" off that statement. Even though she didn't want Ian to risk his life for her, she had to admit she'd expected him to do exactly that.

When she was first thrown into the eight-by-eight-foot cell, she'd shuddered and felt a wave of fear unparalleled except for her time spent stuck in the caves. The tiny room with no windows and a rotting door with only a tiny barred window near the top gave her a smothering sense of claustrophobia. It was filthy, with bugs crawling across the floor, dirty hay for a bed, and a bucket of dirty water for drinking and washing.

Not usually the kind of woman to use her wiles on men, she quickly added up her chances of survival and found they were next to nothing, unless she got some immediate help. Luckily, Timothy had been the first guard she met, and after she had lied, explaining that the bagpipes belonged to her father and that he was dying, and after a judicious amount of flattering and flirting, he had become her staunchest supporter.

Within hours he'd had her cell cleaned and fresh hay put down, and had even procured her a meal of bread and cheese, and a worn blanket. After the first day he'd trusted her with an oil lantern and a tinderbox to light it, so that she didn't have to be in the pitch-black darkness the whole night long.

The other guards hadn't been quite so forthcoming, but she thought they all felt a little sorry for her at the very least. She'd convinced Timmy to let her walk outside in the courtyard that abutted the jail when the captain of the guard was gone, and her days got easier.

The nights had been the worst, especially the first one.

As she'd lain on the worn blanket, Ellie had turned on her side and tucked her knees to her chest, refusing to give in to the panic welling up inside of her, nor the tears that threatened to send her into hysteria. Instead, she had forced her mind to think about her future with Ian, back in her own time. Because deep in her heart, in spite of what he'd said and what she'd said, Ellie believed that after Ian settled all of this with his brother, he would return with her to the twenty-first century.

Once they were home, they'd get married, of course, and she spared a good half hour planning that grand event. She'd pick up the reins of managing Ian's career again, and they'd take the band on a UK tour for a few months, and then, if she could find a way to forge a passport for him, they'd take the band to the United States.

After a couple of years of touring, with some time off along the way, they'd find a cottage near Maggie's, maybe not in the same village, but somewhere nearby. She'd paint the outside a creamy white and the shutters emerald green, and plant roses around the doorway. Ian would play gigs closer to home for a while, and they would start their family.

That was her favorite part of the daydream. Two boys and two girls would be ideal. She imagined one of the girls with Ian's beautiful white blond hair and the other with her auburn tresses. The boys would have dark hair like Ian's brothers, and of course, they'd all have bright blue eyes.

The bright and sunshiney future she was entertaining was as far removed from her former dark and moody self as the moon from the Earth. And it was all because of Ian. He had brought sunshine and laughter into her heart and her life, and she wasn't going to let anything take that away from her. As she had lain there, staring at the stone walls encompassing her, the wooden door with its bars, Ellie had felt a strange peace settle into her heart.

I will survive this. Ian will come for me, and we'll return to the place we belong and have the incredible life together we're destined to find.

She had risen the next morning with a new determination to survive. Not long after that, she found a brand-new reason to survive.

The bathroom situation had been the most urgent worry on her mind when Timothy reluctantly closed the door behind her that first day. Prisoners were expected to make use of a bucket in the corner. Ellie had done some quick calculations to figure out when her cycle was due, terrified at the thought of such an embarrassing situation, and as she arrived at the right date, she had grown suddenly still.

She was late. By about two weeks.

After more frantic figuring, she realized that the first night she and Ian made love would have been right when she ovulated. She'd always been as regular as clockwork, and there was no doubt in her mind that she was pregnant. That would explain the extreme fatigue she'd been having. She remembered Maggie talking about how she'd been tired in her first trimester.

Somehow, in the middle of her surreal adventure, she'd forgotten something as important as birth control. This experience had been a dream, not reality. In the back of her mind, Ellie had known she would wake up someday and be back in her own time and all of this would fade away.

Only it wasn't a dream, was it? And if she was pregnant, there was a helpless little baby who was going to be very, very real about eight months from now.

If she had still been lost in her old outlook of cynicism, her first thought would have been, "It figures!" Instead, she was thrilled. No, it wasn't the best situation, but—pregnant with Ian's child! How wonderful was that?

Now, on her third day in jail, Ellie paced the cell, trying to keep her focus on her pregnancy, knowing the joy of that thought would keep up her spirits, in spite of Ian's refusal to show up and save the day! She drew in a ragged breath and laid one hand gently upon her belly. Ian's baby. She closed her eyes and sat down on the hay, not even feeling the prickles.

Ian had made her feel like no one ever had before. He had changed the way she thought about herself and life and, most of all, love. He had taught her how to love, how to trust. And he would understand why they had to return, that she couldn't let her child be born in a time and place devoid of doctors and antiseptics and good medical care. Her heart began to beat faster.

Ian *would* understand, wouldn't he? And he would want to go back with her, to be there with her for the birth of their child. *Wouldn't he?*

But what if he didn't? What if his need for revenge and recompense was greater than his love for her? For their child?

Tears gathered in Ellie's eyes, and she covered her face with her hands as she began to sob her heart out—for Ian and his pointless quest, for the sisters she missed so terribly, for the new baby inside of her, for the decision she knew she must make, no matter what Ian's choices.

Footsteps walked rapidly down the hallway outside her door, and Ellie grew still. She had discovered, through Timothy, that there were three other prisoners in this jail. Two had had visitors earlier in the day, and now, as she listened, it seemed the third had company, too. She sighed and leaned her chin on her hand.

"Angus?"

Ellie sat up straighter. Angus was a common name in Scotland, but—

"Aye, Gordon—thank God ye have come!"

It was Angus Campbell's voice. Ellie jumped to her feet and hurried to the door, putting her ear as close to the little window as she could.

"I have bribed the guards to give us a few minutes," the one he called Gordon said. "Does Wade know, then? Is all lost?"

"Shhh. Keep yer voice down. Nay, not all. Their proof is the word of one man."

"Lachlan?"

"Aye. We suspected him but couldna prove anything. Well, now, they canna prove anything against me. Unfortunately, that hasna stopped them in the past."

"Is it the road bombings they are trying to pin on ye?" Gordon asked.

Ellie's ears perked up.

"Nay." He chuckled. "But 'tis amusing, for it is my brother who is responsible for that blow against the monarchy."

Ellie's eyebrows went up.

"Tavish?"

She could hear the disbelief in the man's voice. She didn't blame him. She couldn't imagine Tavish doing anything risky. That was probably why he hadn't been included in the Black Watch along with the rest of the brothers.

"Nay, not Tavish. My eldest brother, Ian. The one who supposedly died back in 1711. He has come back."

"But—but—how?"

"Dinna fash yerself about the hows and whys; just know this. My brother is a brave lad, but he doesna know of our plans. He thinks I am a loyalist and has apparently taken it on himself to fight the whole of England!" He laughed, and Ellie's eyes widened.

Not only was Angus showing signs of having a sense of humor, but he'd actually sounded proud of Ian! And what did he mean, Ian thought he was a loyalist. He *was* a loyalist, wasn't he?

What gives?

"Unfortunately," Angus went on, "he doesn't know that he's ruining our own very carefully laid-out plans."

"Ye could turn the suspicion on him," Gordon said. "Angus, ye are too valuable to the Jacobite struggle to—"

"Bite yer tongue!" Angus's voice was harsh. "He is my brother. I may not have seen him in the last twenty-odd years, but he is my brother still."

Ellie breath caught in her throat. Their voices grew softer and Ellie leaned against the door, feeling stunned.

Angus was a Jacobite.

* * *

"Hold yerself still if ye dinna want this needle to end up in yer leg."

"Not so loud," Ian said. "Or I'll fall on ye."

Bittie's "remedy" had made Ian so ill that he spent the next three days flat on his back.

He had spent those agonizing hours worried sick over what Ellie might be enduring inside Wade's prison. As soon as he could lift his head without vomiting, he and Davey had devised a plan. Now, as he stood on a chair wearing a woman's skirt in his room at the King's Pride, he realized it probably wasn't the best of plans, but apparently it was the best they could do.

"Ouch! Damn it, Davey, I'm warnin' ye!" Dressing like a woman was bad enough without being jabbed with a needle every other minute!

"I canna believe this is the plan ye came up with," Davey muttered.

"Well, I dinna hear ye thinking of anything different!" he said crossly. "Ellie's been incarcerated now for four days and I am sick with worry. We have to get her out of there."

Davey shook his head. "I have a verra bad feeling about this. If ye had just listened to me about trying to change history, none of this would have happened."

Ian scowled. "And if ye hadn't helped her try and rob the commander of the king's army, maybe none of this would have happened!"

"Aye, but—bloody hell—hold still!"

"Damn it, man, stop poking me."

Davey sat back on his heels and was silent for a long moment. "Do ye think Ellie is all right?"

Ian went very still. "Why do ye ask such things?" In spite of numerous tries, Bittie had been unable to find anything out about Ellie's condition.

"Where did ye get these clothes?" Davey asked, changing the subject with the deftness of a bull in a parlor, but Ian was thankful for the question. He couldn't bear to think what might be happening to Ellie, much less entertain the thought that she had been harmed in any way.

"Bittie 'procured' them for us, from the cook."

"Humph. 'Tis why it is made for the girth of a cow." Davey grew still and jerked his head up. "Ye dinna take him into yer confidence?"

"What do ye take me for? I wouldna risk old Bittie's life in that way. He's sweet upon the cook and stole the skirts from her chambers after, er, spending a long evening with her."

"What did ye tell him ye needed the skirts for?"

"He dinna ask. Bittie knows not to ask too many questions," Ian said grimly. "Dinna fash yerself."

"Dinna fash yerself, dinna fash yerself." Davey jabbed the needle through the hem and Ian jumped. "'Tis all ye ever say."

"Ye missed me that time," Ian said.

"It will still be too short, though I took out the entire hem. Lucky for ye that I went to theatre camp." Davey thrust the needle through the cloth again. "I wonder if Katie knows how to sew."

"Now that, I canna imagine."

"Well, that just goes to show how little ye know about me, Ian MacGregor!" a voice said from behind them.

Davey turned. "Katie!" he cried, and jumped up from the stool.

"Ow!" Ian cried as the needle raked across his leg. He grabbed his shin and clambered down out of the chair. "That's enough! I'll wear it as it is, ye thick-fisted dolt!"

"What the hell are ye doing here?" Davey said. "I left ye at home!"

"Aye, that ye did!" Katie Campbell said, her hands on her hips. "And it's taken me this long to track ye down! I knew, when I heard the news of the attack upon the king, that the two of ye would be somewhere nearby."

She wore dark burgundy breeches and a blue and burgundy brocade bodice over a white silk shirt with billowing sleeves. The garments clung to her body like a second skin and Ian frowned at her complete disregard for propriety. A slim sword hung at her side, and her dark hair was tied back in the fashion of a man. Ian turned to tell Davey to send her home and caught him with his mouth hanging open. Ian jabbed him with his elbow, bringing the other man to his senses.

"What are ye doing here?" Davey said again, but Ian could tell he was glad to see her.

"I dinna think ye would be such a coward as to sneak away in the middle of the night!" she said angrily.

Ian turned to his red-faced friend. "I thought ye said ye told her what we were doing and she agreed she should stay home?"

"And ye believed that." Davey shook his head. "Just goes to show, ye dinna know yer sister."

"Go home, Katie," Ian said.

"Uh, I can pretty much promise ye," Davey said, "that isna going to happen."

Sighing, Ian looked down at the bright blue skirt he was wearing, and then the green one Davey had on. "I suppose we have to tell her."

Davey frowned in confusion but straightened beside him. "Aye."

Ian put his arm around Davey and looked at his sister with a perfectly straight face. "Katie, Davey and I are girly men. Go home and leave us to our rendezvous in peace."

Her mouth dropped open and then she laughed, the sound filling the room and giving Ian an odd sense of comfort.

Davey stared at Ian in outrage. "Bloody hell!" he said. "'Tis not the sort of thing a man wants his wife to think!"

Katie laughed again. "Dinna fash yerself, husband. I think ye are a fine man, and it would take more than the sight of ye and my brother in skirts to change my mind." She sobered abruptly. "So what are ye doing? This is some plan to get Ellie out of Fort William, I am supposing."

Ian stared at her. "How did ye know about that?"

"Tavish?" Davey suggested.

"Aye. General Wade sent word to Tavish asking if Eleanor

Graham was his guest. Of course, he dinna want to be linked with her and said she was not. How are ye going to rescue her?"

Davey sat down on the end of the bed and sighed. "We're going to dress up like women, get inside, and sneak her out."

"How are ye going to get her past the guards?"

Davey raised one eyebrow at Ian and smiled. Ian glowered back at him.

"We'll find a way," Ian said. "A solution will present itself."

"I saw that movie," Davey murmured.

"I had a little plan of my own that I put into action today." Katie pulled the chair Ian had vacated over to the small fireplace in the room, where a tepid fire burned.

Ian moved to her side, holding the skirt up with both hands so he wouldn't trip, ignoring how ridiculous he felt. "What have ye gone and done now?"

She shrugged and sat down in the chair. "I dinna like the tone of yer voice, Ian Campbell," she said. "I dinna think I will tell ye anything."

"Ian MacGregor is my name," he reminded her. "I refused to give up my heritage, unlike our father." He loomed over her, his hands on his hips. "Now tell me what you have done."

"Ian," Davey said from behind him. Ian turned, surprised to find the man had shed his skirt and was standing very close, a tight look on his face. "Let me handle this."

Ian frowned and started to tell him to stay out of it, but something in the man's eyes stopped him.

"I am her husband after all," he said, "even if it is in name only. She is bound to obey me."

Katie smiled up at him. "Och, if ye think that little fact will make me tell ye, ye truly dinna know me, Davey Ferguson."

Davey returned her smile and then knelt down beside her, bringing his face level to hers.

"I know that ye are a woman of yer word," he said. He

nodded at Ian. "And I know that ye care for yer brother. He's been half out of his mind with worry over Ellie. Dinna give him more cause to fret. Tell him what ye have done." He rose and then folded his arms over his chest, waiting.

Ian stood back, impressed by Davey's firm hand with the lass. Too bad the lad was in denial about his feelings for her. The two actually made a good match. Katie pouted for a moment and then flounced out of the chair.

"Fine! Ye two are no fun at all." She glanced at Ian's skirt and giggled. "Well, perhaps behind closed doors ye have some fun that I'd rather not know about."

"Katie . . ." Davey said, a warning in his voice.

She rolled her eyes. "All right. If ye hadn't been such an ogre, Ian *MacGregor*, ye would already be knowing that Ellie is just fine and has not been harmed."

"What?" Ian said. "How do ye know this?"

"Oh, I just did a little flirting with one of the soldiers guarding the gate to the gaol, and found out all kinds of interesting things." She fluttered her eyelashes dramatically. "But why should I tell ye anything, brother mine? When ye treat me so ill?"

Ian stiffened and was about to turn her over his knee, when Davey intervened again. "Flirting? Ye are a married woman!"

"In name only, remember?" She smiled broadly at him.

"Only because—" He darted a swift look at Ian. "Please, Katie, tell Ian what ye know about Ellie."

Katie stuck out her tongue and then sat down in the chair once again. Davey gave her a stern look, and she sighed. "I'm sorry, Ian," she said. "But sometimes ye make me so mad!"

Ian held on to his patience and tried to follow Davey's example. "I'm sorry, lass. Please, tell me what ye learned."

She leaned back in the chair and sighed. "Well, all right. The guard said that she had quickly won over all the men, and that they practically jumped to do her bidding. Apparently she's got them all convinced that she should never have been arrested in the first place."

"Och," Ian said proudly, "that's my girl."

"Ellie is in good health," Katie went on, "though being confined makes her nervous. The guard said they often sneak her out for a stroll when the captain of the guard is out on patrol."

Ian glanced over at Davey and smiled, then turned back to his sister. "Tell me, Katie darlin', do any of these guards happen to be Scots?"

Ellie lay upon the prickly hay and tried to sleep.

Day four, and counting.

Where the heck was Ian? She'd even asked Timmy if a man of his description had been arrested, but he'd said no, only a Scottish aristocrat. That was Angus, she supposed.

She was making headway with Timmy and her own escape plans, but she still wondered where Ian could be. She was anxious to tell him what she'd discovered about Angus! The thought that he had abandoned her had cropped up only once and she had met it with the scorn such a thought deserved.

Quick footsteps hurried down the corridor outside her cell, and Ellie was on her feet. Moving cautiously to look out the small window in the door, she had to duck back as General Wade walked past. She peeked back out in time to see a tall, distinguished-looking man wearing a long, curling wig and a pale blue silk ensemble that made her think of pictures she'd seen of Louis VIII, right down to the white hose and gold-buckled shoes. He moved regally, and suddenly Ellie realized who he was.

"Your Majesty," General Wade said with a bow, "are ye certain that ye will not allow me to handle this situation?"

The king—for that was surely who it was—waved a delicate hanky in the other man's direction, the foppish gesture belying the iron in his eyes.

"Apparently you are not capable of handling the situation, General," he said icily, "else this innocent man—one of your own captains—would not be incarcerated with common criminals."

Hey, watch it buddy, Ellie thought, narrowing her eyes. *Just who are you calling* common?

"Open the door," the general commanded, and Ellie stood on her tiptoes to try to see who was coming out of the cell. There was a murmur of voices overlapping one another; then the door of the cell slammed shut, and she shrank back as the men walked past again. They stopped just past her door, and she took a chance and peeked out.

Angus Campbell stood rigidly beside the king, with General Wade scowling on the other side of him.

"I regret that this has happened, sir," King George was saying, "but rest assured I shall get to the bottom of it!"

"Thank ye, Yer Majesty," Angus said, bowing slightly, as there was not much room for movement. "I remain yer faithful servant."

The king nodded and then turned his gaze upon the general. "Perhaps General Wade can now turn his efforts toward bringing in the real criminal, the one who accosted us upon the road and had the audacity to place a sword at my throat! At my throat, sir!" His pale hand moved to his throat, and his eyes narrowed. "Ye should have heard him. He looked like a highwayman, dressed in black, wearing a mask. He laughed at you, General, for putting an innocent man in prison. He said the crimes this man had been arrested for were his own! Find him, General. Tell your men that he is to be shot or quartered on sight! Find him, or reap the consequences!"

He turned on his heel and walked away, leaving the general and Angus bowing behind him. When the door slammed at the front of the jail, the two men straightened and glared at one another.

"So if it was not ye," Wade said, "who is the viper in yer nest?"

Angus met his steely eyed gaze and then without a word, walked past him, toward freedom. General Wade cursed and slammed his fist against Ellie's door, making her fall to the floor, her heart pounding. When he slammed out of the building and she could breathe again, she sat up and shook her head.

Ian had tried to kill the king? But he hadn't—that was the important thing—he hadn't! And he was still free, though she'd bet that every soldier in Scotland was looking for him. That was why he hadn't been able to rescue her, or even get word to her yet! And now, if he showed up, he wouldn't just be arrested; he would be killed on sight!

"Are ye all right, lass?" Timothy's voice jarred her from her reverie. "I've brought ye a wee bit of cheese and bread."

She rose and crossed to the door to take the food from him. "Thank you, Timmy," she said. "You are a saint."

"Is there anything else I can do for ye?" he asked softly.

Ellie hesitated, then pressed one trembling hand against her stomach. It was time to quit waiting for her knight in shining armor.

"Yes, there is. You see, Timmy, I need your help."

twenty-two

Katie talked Ian and Davey into dressing in their full costumes so that she could take a look at them. As they stood in front of her, waiting for inspection, she shook her head at them woefully.

"Aye, this would work if yon fort were filled with Vikings! Then no one would think a thing about the height and breadth of women who look like the two of ye!"

Ian looked down at his costume again. The cook's clothing covered him generously, though as Davey had predicted, the skirt was too short by a good four inches. Katie was right. It was evident they would have to do something to further disguise themselves. He was too tall, too big, and too broad to pass as a lass.

As he considered the problem, Davey turned and picked up a cane that Bittie had included with the clothes for some reason. He bent over and started waddling across the room toward Katie, who sat on the bed shaking her head at them.

"Weel, now, lassie," he said in a high-pitched voice. "Come and give Grandfather a kiss."

"Hey!" Ian pointed to the pile of clothes. "See if there's an extra shawl over there, and, Davey, give me that cane."

"But I like being a dirty old man," Davey complained.

Katie shook her head again and slid off the bed to rummage through the clothes stacked on the end. "Ian needs it more than ye do, Davey mine. Ye are prettier than he."

"Thanks," Davey said. "I think."

She pulled out a large woolen shawl the color of heather and handed it to Ian as Davey begrudgingly gave him the cane.

"Now, watch this." Ian draped the shawl over his head and bent his long frame almost in two, leaning on the cane. "What do ye think? Could I pass for Ellie's poor auld withered grandmither?"

She gave him an appraising look, one finger resting against her chin. Finally she nodded. "Perhaps. If ye keep yer face well covered."

"I think I might be able to actually hide a weapon under this," Ian said.

"It might just work," Katie agreed. "There's only one problem."

"Only one?" Davey asked as he sprawled on top of the thin bedclothes and put his hands behind his head. His skirt billowed up to his knees and Katie smiled at him, a glint in her eyes. Ian tensed. Something was afoot.

"How are ye planning on getting one of the guards to help ye?" she asked. "Ye dinna dare show yer faces inside the fort to ask, and besides, ye dinna know which ones to approach." She sat back down on the bed, curling her legs beneath her as she gazed first at Ian and then at Davey, looking as smug as the cat that licked the creamer dry.

Davey frowned at her. "But ye said that ye knew a guard who would likely help."

"Aye," she said, "I do."

Ian folded his arms over his chest, knowing what a comical sight he probably presented, trying hard to keep the sternness in his gaze. "All right, Katie, what is it ye want?"

Davey raised both brows, and then comprehension dawned in his eyes. "Och, ye little vixen!"

She smiled complacently. "I want to go with ye and help save Ellie."

"No way!" the two men said in unison.

Katie folded her hands neatly in her lap, trying to look demure and failing utterly. "Then I won't tell ye which guard will help."

Davey sat up and gazed down at the scruffy boots he still wore. "She's bluffing, Ian," he said. "She wouldna let Ellie rot in jail just to get her own way."

Ian laughed without humor. "Och, laddie, ye have a lot to learn about women." He fixed Katie with a steely eye. "And just what part would ye be playing in our scenario?"

The girl sat up on her knees, her eyes flashing with eagerness. "Here's what I was thinking—" she began.

Davey shook his head and sighed. "Saints preserve us."

After brainstorming 'til the wee hours, the three had arrived upon a plan they could all live with—just barely. It took another full day for Katie to find the guard she had flirted with—Malcolm MacReynolds, a distant cousin of Ian's father's mother—when he was off duty, and set things up. She assured Malcolm that they would make it look like he had been overpowered, and thus save him from any repercussions.

Ian hoped it worked out that way. He didn't want to bring misfortune down on anyone else in his family if he could help it. The plan was for Katie to take Davey's place.

Davey had tried to talk Ian into staying out of it altogether, but he had refused. Dressed as an old woman, Ian would be escorted by Katie, who would answer any questions that might be asked of them before they reached the jail. Their cover story would be that "Grandmither" was there to see one of the prisoners. Once Ian was inside the jail, Katie would keep the outside guards occupied.

Once inside, Malcolm would release Ellie, and then Ian would tie up the guard and don his uniform. When he brought

Ellie out of the prison unit disguised as the "grandmither," Katie would keep the other guards distracted until the two made their escape. As soon as possible, Katie would bid the lads outside a fond farewell, and hurry to where Davey waited with the horses.

Ian had to admit it was a better idea than having Davey ride shotgun, but letting Katie take part in the danger put a different spin on things. He didn't like it, but the girl had adamantly refused to tell them the name of the guard they could trust until Ian gave his word to include her in their plot.

Now, after a good night's sleep, Ian was waiting for Katie to show up and approve his costume. He went over the plan again in his head and was just beginning to grow impatient when the door to the room opened and Katie stuck her head inside.

"Are ye ready?" she asked, sounding excited. Ian hoped she wouldn't give them away with her exuberance. "Where's Davey?"

"He's already gone to take his position with the horses."

"Good," she said, but looked disappointed. "I dinna want him fussing over me. There's a big storm headed this way. Perhaps it will help hide us during our escape."

"If we are caught," Ian reminded her, "ye must act as shocked as the rest. Ye dinna know I was not some poor laddie's grandmother. Ye felt sorry for the auld woman and took pity upon her, asking the guards if she could visit. Do ye understand?"

"Aye, Ian," she said, "dinna worry so much. We won't be caught."

"And Malcolm is apprised of everything, aye?" he asked.

"Aye," she said.

"And ye feel certain ye can trust him?"

"Oh, aye," she said impatiently. "If he could, he'd marry Ellie himself!"

Ian frowned down at his skirt as it slipped over his hip. He straightened to adjust it, his eyes on the cloth. "But he knows that isna part of the plan, right?" His sister didn't answer and he jerked his head up. "Right?"

Katie bit her lower lip and Ian straightened. "Katie . . ." he began, unable to keep the growl out of his voice.

She shrugged and looked away. "Och, well, I had to promise him something, didn't I?"

Ian closed his eyes and then opened them again and glared at her. "And just what did you promise him?"

"That we would meet him at the stream just outside the village, tomorrow morning—but dinna worry, we'll be long gone by then."

Ian shook his head. "Have ye no sense of honor, child? That poor man—"

Katie interrupted him, her face flushed. "I think ye are living in a fool's paradise, Ian," she said. "In the real world, ye must sometimes get yer hands dirty to accomplish what needs to be done!"

Ian couldn't speak for a moment. When he did speak, his voice was brusque. "Dinna speak of what ye dinna know. Are ye ready?"

Katie reached up to adjust the shawl over his shoulders and sighed. "Aye, brother, that I am."

Ian bent over and leaned on the knob-headed cane. Katie patted him on the back and opened the door. He shuffled after her, his heart pounding in his chest like a druid's drum.

He couldn't wait to see Ellie again. For a moment he pictured her—her bright blue eyes, her smile, her laughter. Soon she would be in his arms again. He could hardly wait.

"Now," he said in a high, crackling voice as they approached the stairway, "gae us yer arm, dearie, and take me to see my poor wee lassie." He sobered and added under his breath, in his own voice, "Before it is too late."

It took some time to ride from the inn and then walk into the fort with Ian hobbling along, but at last they drew near the jail.

"What's in that bag?" Katie asked softly.

"A dagger," he said. "Courtesy of our dear father."

"Ye are too hard on him, I'm thinking."

"How is he?"

"He woke up finally," she said. "He asked for ye."

Ian stopped and straightened enough to look her in the eyes. "For me?"

"Aye. He is dying, Ian. Will ye no' forgive him?"

"He never forgave me, now did he?"

She pulled her cloak more tightly around her. "Och, is it hard-hearted ye have become, my brother? I heard ye were a kind man."

Ian pushed away the sorrow that suddenly filled his heart. "I canna speak of this now," he said, more sharply than he intended. "We must focus on the matter at hand."

"Aye," she said, "but he wants to see ye."

Ian was silent as they made their way toward the small building. It was a square, squat structure. The crescent moon was bright above them and two lanterns hung on the posts holding up the roof of the jail's "porch," where two men stood.

They moved slowly toward the guards, and one walked toward them. Katie waited until he was a few feet away and then spoke in her Scottish brogue.

"Hello, is it Donald?"

"Katie Campbell?" The man smiled as he held up the lantern and let it shine upon her face. "What are ye doing wandering about so late?"

She patted Ian's arm. "This is the grandmither of one of the lads in yer jail," she said. "She came to me requesting that she be allowed to see him tonight." She whispered her next words. "She's sore worried and hasna slept for several nights."

"Och, I'm sorry, lass, but ye must come back tomorrow morning."

Ian began to moan and sway from side to side. Katie put her arm around him. "Please, Donald. I promise she won't stay long." She smiled up at him. "While she's visiting, I'll stay out here and talk to ye and—is that yer brother, Aidan?"

"Aye." He rubbed his jaw thoughtfully and then nodded. "All right, then, come along. We'll see what Malcolm says." He walked ahead of them and Ian felt Katie breathe a sigh of relief beside him.

"I thought 'twas all arranged," he whispered.

"I canna work miracles," she muttered. "The guard inside is the one who is on our side."

He kept silent, still bowed over, until they reached the door of the gaol. Donald opened it with a large key and pushed it open. "Malcolm," he called out, "there's a visitor for one of yer lads."

"What? This time of night?"

"Aye, and ye so busy. Come and take Grandmither inside."

A few seconds later, a very anxious young man arrived at the door. "It's too late," he said, his eyes darting from one side to the other. "Come back tomorrow."

"Oh, please, Malcolm," Katie said, stepping forward and laying her hand on his arm. "Poor Grandmither has traveled a long way today to get here. Please let her see her grandson for just a moment."

The man licked his lips and his gaze shifted from Katie to Ian to Donald. "Aye, aye," he muttered, opening the door wider. "Come on in."

"I'll just stay outside, Grandmither, and talk with these two fine, upstanding men," she said, with a teasing glance toward Donald and a warning one at Malcolm.

The nervous man let Ian hobble past him before closing the door, and then led him down the hallway to the last door on the right. The guard's hand was shaking as he inserted a key into the door and turned it, then looked up, startled, as Ian's hand came down over his.

"So what's the matter, laddie?" he said as he straightened and with a hand to his back groaned. " 'Tis harder to be an auld woman than I thought." He towered over Malcolm, searching the man's face. "So tell me, what's gone wrong?"

The lad had solid Scottish features, square jaw, large nose, and while he was much shorter than Ian, he was still well-built. He took a deep breath and opened the door. Inside, a man wearing only a cloth around his waist sat at a table, five cards in his hand. He blinked up at Ian.

"I think," Malcolm said, "there's been a wee bit of a miscommunication."

Ellie hugged the bagpipes to her as she stood outside the gates of Fort William. Bless Timothy's heart. The bagpipes were being held as evidence for her trial in a locked box in the jail. He had kicked it in and given the pipes to her. She wished she could find a way to thank him.

She had planned to steal a horse once she got outside the jail, but everything was locked up tight in the courtyard, and she was forced to venture outside the gates. Clad in Timothy's uniform and cloak, she gauged the distance from where she stood to the village of Maryburgh. It didn't look too far.

She started walking just as the first snowflakes began to fall.

Ian tied the leather satchel stuffed with Katie's warm cloak, a flask of whiskey, half a loaf of bread, and an extra plaid behind the saddle, as snow flurries danced above him. His face felt chapped and cold in spite of the half bottle of whiskey he had put away himself before he poured the rest into the flask.

"Let me go with ye," Davey said, standing behind him, the snow already up to his ankles. He stamped his feet, his breath making soft clouds around his face.

"No," he said. "I want ye to take care of Katie. When I find Ellie, I'm taking her to the cairn. In the morning, ye and Katie must get there. Here"—he thrust a handful of coins into his hand—"buy a horse, hire one, whatever it takes, just get there."

"Ye want me to bring Katie to the cairn?" Light dawned in his eyes. "Ye mean to take her back to—to Ellie's time?"

He shrugged. "I canna think of any better idea, can ye?"

"No. At least, not yet." He scratched his head. "I'll have to do the math, though. I'm not sure just how many people from the eighteenth century can come to the twenty-first without there being repercussions."

"Repercussions." Ian shook his head. "Life is just one repercussion after another, isn't it? What does it matter?"

Davey stared at him. "Aye, there's one hypothesis."

Ian swung up into the saddle, the leather creaking, the horse whinnying, the sounds harsh in the stillness of the night outside the inn. "Meet us at the cairn by tomorrow afternoon."

"Godspeed," the scientist said.

Ian headed into the wind, the snow whirling around him as he rode. He had waited at the inn until midnight, hoping that Ellie had found out, somehow, that they were there. When she didn't show up, he knew she was simply running and that he had wasted precious time.

Perhaps she had tried to reach Maryburgh. That would make the most sense. He would ride through the streets before turning to the hills. If she wasn't in the town, the only other place he could think that she would go was to the cairn. But surely she wouldn't strike out on her own in the middle of the night, in the middle of a snowstorm, to find a place a good fifty miles away!

No, she must be somewhere nearby. He just had to find her.

"Ye ride west and I will ride east," one of the soldiers said to another. "She's hiding somewhere in the village."

"Aye, no wench would dare go across the countryside on a night like this!"

The other man laughed and they parted, riding in opposite directions.

Ellie glared impotently at the two, so cold it was a wonder

they hadn't heard her teeth chattering. It was only a matter of time before they found her. Or she froze to death. Maybe she should have had a contingency plan, but who knew it would snow like this in November in Scotland? It never snowed in Texas. Maybe she should move back there, after this was all over.

After she was back in her own time.

Alone.

Without Ian.

But she wouldn't be alone. She'd have her baby. She took a deep breath that felt like ice in her lungs. No freezing to death. That wasn't in the cards. Her baby was going to be born and have a wonderful life. With or without Ian MacGregor.

Timothy had given her a cloak before she made her break, and his uniform was made of wool, but she was still cold. She shivered. There was a long, narrow alley ahead. Maybe the wind would be less fierce between the stone walls.

She hurried across to it, ducking her head, hoping no soldiers would ride by. The alleyway was even narrower than it had seemed, and instead of keeping out the wind, it acted as a funnel, sweeping the wind in with even greater velocity, almost knocking her off her feet. Ellie turned and started back toward the street, when she heard someone cry out.

"Stop! Stop in the name of the king!" Shots rang out, different from any she'd ever heard on TV or in the movies. Some kind of ancient gun, no doubt.

Clutching her cloak around her, she turned, and ran. When she reached the end of the alley, there was nothing beyond but the open Scottish countryside. Snow covered the land, the rolling hillside in front of her and the woods beyond, glistening in the moonlight. Hesitating only a moment, she plunged forward, away from the buildings, and out into the icy wilderness.

"Help me," she prayed, one hand pressed to her stomach. "Dear God, please help me."

* * *

Ian grabbed the end of the cloth with his teeth, making it tighter around his upper arm in an effort to stop the bleeding. The shot the soldier had fired had only grazed him, and he had been able to throw himself back into the saddle and ride in the opposite direction, out of the village.

He had seen a mound of something beside an ash can that looked like a person. After dismounting, he soon learned it was just a pile of discarded rubbish, not Ellie. Apparently the soldiers from Fort William had pursued the lass into Maryburgh, and had taken a potshot at him as he stood in the shadows.

He'd spent hours searching the town. Ellie had either found a place to hole up for the night, or she had done something foolish like head into the Highlands. If she'd seen the soldiers, though, she might think that the safest place for her to be was in the hills.

He shivered beneath the thick cloak he wore, wondering if Ellie had something to keep her warm. He rode around the edge of the village, his gaze on the ground. Perhaps he should have brought Davey. Together they could have covered a bigger area. If only it wasn't so dark. If only the soldiers would give up and go to bed so he could call out to her. If only he could find her!

When the sun came up, he would be able to see better, and he would find her. But even as the thought came, another followed. By the time the sun came up, it might be too late.

Up ahead was a mound in the snow. Ian dug his heels into his horse's side and slid out of the saddle when he reached it. He had no gloves, and using his bare hands he dug into the deep snow, shoveling it out, his desperation growing as he met only snow and finally rock. The wind rose up around him and howled, as more snow began to fall.

His hands were numb, and his feet were frozen. He looked up into the falling snow. Once he had been a man of prayer. Long ago, before his father kicked him out, before he'd turned highwayman with Quinn MacIntyre. He fell to his knees and clasped his hands together.

"Father God," he whispered, "help me find her. Keep her safe until I do. Please . . ."

Another sharp-edged wind swept down, and Ian stumbled to his feet, knowing if he didn't, he might not be able to in another minute. Snow whirled around his face, and blindly he reached out for the side of the black gelding he had taken from his father's stable. In some befuddled part of his mind, he realized he didn't even know the horse's name.

He managed to climb back up into the saddle, and rode on, hoping God had heard the prayer of a would-be murderer such as he. He turned the collar of the cloak up to protect his neck, hoping that Ellie had something to protect her from the elements.

If he found her, he would never again leave her side. If he found her, he would stay with her, go back to her time, whatever she wanted. If he found her, he knew their future would be bright and beautiful and—

Like a light breaking through the darkness, suddenly Ian saw the truth. The history of Scotland was finished, written up by great men in books of wisdom, and while there might be something he could do to change the outcome, he was not willing to pay that price.

The cold wind swept over him, freezing his face beneath the hood of his cloak and his thoughts, growing more muddled by the moment, shifted back to Scotland. The bloodshed and turmoil in Scotland had been set in motion long before he had ever been born. Now he had been given the rare gift of seeing ahead, of knowing that, in spite of the sacrifice of life and land and joy, Scotland had one day found a kind of peace. All was as it should be.

But his history with Ellie was only just beginning, and if he found her—*when* he found her—he could change their future, their future that was, as yet, unfinished. His heartbeat quickened and he prayed harder as he drove his pony

forward, through the three-foot snowbanks. He didn't know
where he was going, but he knew he was headed for Ellie,
wherever she was.

He rode for another hour, knew his horse would not make
it much longer, when all at once, up ahead, he saw a light.
No, a star. Ian urged his mount forward.

"Come on, Snowflake," he said, "we'll be home soon."
The horse whinnied in the cold emptiness around them, but
Ian kept his eyes on the star ahead.

When he thought he could go no farther, and Snowflake
was stumbling to stay on his feet, Ian saw another light. This
one was on the ground. He swung down off of the horse
and began leading him, digging a path with his own body
through the snow, pushing forward toward the light.

Ian stopped in his tracks, and for a moment he thought he
was dreaming. Ellie stood inside a cave, little more than a
deep overhang sheltered from the storm, beside a campfire.
He stumbled into her arms as Snowflake gratefully moved
closer to the fire.

"Ellie," he whispered into her hair, "darling Eleanor.
How—how—"

She pulled him down to her and pressed her face against
his, trembling as he wrapped the cloak he wore around her
body and pulled her into his heat.

"Oh, Ian! Ian!" She slid her arms around him and laughed,
the sound making him feel a joy he'd never known existed.
"I thought I'd never see you again! I thought—I thought—"

"Whist, lass, did ye not know that there is nowhere ye
can go, where I cannot find ye?" He gazed down at her, her
face between his hands. "How did ye make a fire?"

"The guard who helped me escape gave me his cloak by
mistake." Ellie held up a small metal box. "A tinderbox was
in the pocket. I guess everything *does* happen for a reason,"
she whispered in wonder.

"Och, lass." He closed his eyes, gratefulness flooding
through him.

"I got you something," she said, so sweetly that he felt

tears burn into his eyes, but brought them under control and laughed instead.

"Did ye now? And what did ye get me, my love, out here in this icebox?"

She hurried across the cave and the loss of her body against his was painful as he watched her pick up something behind a rock and run back to him.

"Here," she said, shoving something large and bulky into his arms, "and don't you dare say you don't like it! I went to jail for that present."

His hand closed around the bundle, and he slowly unwrapped the cloth from around the bulky object. "My bagpipes," he said, in disbelief. "Katie told me that Father gave them to General Wade." He looked up, shaking his head. "Eleanor, I dinna understand. Why would ye risk yerself to get these back?"

She gazed up at him, shivering. He moved forward and opened his cloak again, enfolding her. "Because," she said, "I hoped they would help me find you again."

"Find me?"

"Find the real Ian. The Ian I fell in love with so long ago."

"Och, lass"—he leaned his head against hers—"I am found."

Ellie searched his face, uncertainty in her eyes, but he smiled and suddenly her face split into a beatific smile. With a squeal, she threw herself into his arms and then kissed him, and Ian fell into the warmth of her lips, so happy he could scarcely breathe.

"Oh, Ian," she said, when at last they came up for air, "is it real? Are you truly ready to give up this fight?"

"'Tis not my fight," he told her, knowing in his heart it was true. "Not anymore."

"Then—what's next?" she asked, her voice shaking slightly. "What do you plan to do?"

"First, I must make sure that Angus has been released and—"

"He has been! I was there when the king came and demanded his release! Was that your doing?"

Ian closed his eyes and clutched her against him. "Och, lass, then I am truly free!" He tilted her face to his and kissed the tip of her nose. "Now I can take yer wonderful gift and put it to good use, and then we will go home."

Ellie rode in front of Ian, leaning back against his broad chest, feeling more content than she ever had in her life. She no longer felt that she had something to prove or that she had something she needed to run away from. Heck, she had traveled through time, endured an eighteenth-century jail, and survived a blizzard—what else could life throw at her that she couldn't handle?

Her hand covered her stomach, and her cockiness slipped a little. Okay, so maybe she had been thrown for a loop after all, but now she knew she could handle this little loop. She smiled softly at thought of holding Ian's baby in her arms.

He was going back with her, right? He'd said he was *taking* her home. That meant he was going, too. Didn't it? But it had to be his choice, his decision, his *free will*, as to whether or not he would come with her. That's why she hadn't told him about the baby. There was no way she would use her child as some kind of inducement or blackmail to force him into making the right decision. Because of course the right decision was to travel back to the year 2009. Of course it was.

She only hoped he realized that, too.

But before they could go to the cairn, Ian had said he had two other stops to make first. As Ellie rode in front of him, she decided that once she got back to her own time, she was never traveling anywhere again. She'd had enough traveling to last her a lifetime. Okay, she'd have to tour with Ian, but other than that, she was going to be a homebody, Suzy Homemaker, Supermom.

She closed her eyes and thought again about what their baby might look like as she snuggled warm and safe in Ian's arms. Now if only he and his brother could—she sat up a little straighter.

"I forgot to tell you," she said.

"Forgot to tell me what?" Ian drew her back against him, and she relaxed and smiled.

"Oh, just a little something about Angus." She began to tell him all about his brother, the Jacobite.

There would be time later to talk about another little something.

twenty-three

When Ian stopped outside of Rob Roy's cottage, he felt a surge of joy, knowing that at last, he could do something for his friend, his mentor, the man who had been more of a father to him than his own ever could. He slid off the horse and then grabbed Ellie around the waist and swept her from the saddle, spinning her around in a circle before placing her gently on the ground. Then he unstrapped the bundle behind the saddle and, taking her hand, headed up to the door.

Mary answered, looking so tired that Ian's heart ached for her. There was a spark there, for a moment, a gladness that they had come, but then it was like she had to cover it up, to not let them see. He hoped what he was about to do would change her mind, would make her—and Rob—love him again.

"Mary," Ian said softly, "may I see Rob? I am leaving Scotland, but before I go, I have something for him."

She hesitated, then nodded. "But no talk of rebellions or reiving or—or"—her eyes filled with tears—"or anything else he loved." She wiped the tears away with the back of her hand and lifted her chin. "I mean it, Ian MacGregor," she said. "Mind yer ways."

"I promise, Mary."

They followed her into the small bedroom, where someone, probably one of his sons, had cut a large window in the
wall. Rob Roy sat up in his bed, propped up against a pile of
pillows, looking out his window at Loch Lomond below,
and Ben Nevis in the distance. Ellie hesitated, but he drew
her into the room with him. She was part of him now, and he
wanted to share this moment with her as much as with the
MacGregors.

"Hello, Rob," Ian said. The sickly man turned toward him,
his eyes distant and bleak. "I told ye I would be back." He
placed the bundle on the end of the bed and opened it, then
lifted out the set of pipes Ellie had given him—no, stolen for
him. Ah, what a wife she would make. His pipes.

Mary stood in the doorway, her hands clasped together,
tears streaming down her cheeks as Ian lifted the slim reed
to his mouth, filled the bag with his breath, and began to
play.

First he played the sunrise, just coming up over the distant purple mountains, shining down on Ben Nevis with its
snowy peak, then he slid down the mountainside and slipped
over the lilting roll of the meadows and dells before climb-
ing the lower mountains, making saucy sheep cavort upon the
craggy hillsides and the burns chortle and laugh across the
deep emerald grass and the lavender heather; he painted
the deep, dark lochs below and the bonny blue sky above,
and the midday and the soft rain, the rainbow over the glen
and the evening in the woods; and then finally, Ian made the
sun set and made the birds sing, and with all of his heart, he
played the song of the Highlands for his friend, his mentor,
his father.

When he finished and lowered the pipe from his lips,
Rob Roy sat smiling, his lips trembling, his translucent
skin bright again, his faded eyes sparkling with joy, tears
flooding down his cheeks as he held out his arms to Ian
MacGregor. When he finally released Ian from his tight
embrace, Rob turned his head slowly toward his wife.

"Tell him," he said, his voice hoarse.

"But Rob—"

"Tell him," he said again.

Mary shook her head at him. "Well, and haven't I been saying all along that ye should tell him? Foolish old man."

"Tell me what?" Ian asked. Ellie stood beside him, wiping away her own tears. He held her close, half-fearful of what Mary was about to say.

"Yer brother Angus."

"Aye?"

"He is no loyalist. Nor are the rest of yer brothers."

"Aye," Ian said, with a glance toward Ellie. "I have heard something about that. But ye canna blame me for thinking the worst. He's a captain in the Watch, and seemed to be thick as thieves with General Wade."

"Aye," Mary said, "and because of this, we will eat this winter. Did ye never consider that perhaps yer brother was simply pretending to go along with the king's men in order to aid his clan, his friends and family? And did it never occur to ye that perhaps by doing so, he was placed in a position through which he would be able to help those who were planning the next uprising?"

Ian shook his head, wordless for a moment because her words made so much sense. "No," he finally said. "It did not. But why did he not tell me?"

"Perhaps because he dinna know if ye could be trusted," she said. "Ye turned yer back on yer family, Ian, and that is a shame ye must live with for the rest of yer life."

Ian felt his heart constrict, and he bowed his head. "Aye. I owe Angus a great apology, for many things."

He felt her hand on his face and lifted his head to find her gazing at him. "Well, then, perhaps there's another home ye should visit before ye take yer leave of Scotland."

"We've almost come full circle," Ellie said, as they walked through the two huge doors that led into the castle.

"Almost," Ian agreed, "but not quite." He looked around for Angus, and then his mouth dropped open at the sight of Katie and Davey sitting in front of the fireplace. "Katie! Davey!"

"Hello, Ian." Davey sat in front of the hearth, a book in his lap, smoking a pipe. "Welcome back."

Ellie grinned and then shook her head, trying to look innocent. "Don't look at me! I didn't know they'd be here."

Ian crossed to the fireplace as Katie rose from her chair.

Katie ran across the wide room and threw herself against her brother. "Ian!" she cried. "I'm so glad to see ye! I was so worried about ye!" She turned to Ellie. "And about ye, too! Thank God ye are both all right!"

"I told ye they'd be fine," Davey said.

"But what are ye doing here? I thought I told ye to meet us at the cairn?"

Davey carefully put the book aside and stood, lowering the pipe from his mouth. "Yes," he said, "ye did. But ye know—and I may have given ye a wrong impression up to now—but the truth is, I don't always do what other people tell me."

"But I dinna understand," Ian said, frowning. "Why didn't ye go to the cairn? Why are ye here?"

"Well, about that." His gaze flickered to meet Katie's smiling one. "I decided that yer brother Angus and I needed to have a little talk. I had figured out a few things, and once he and I had a meeting of the minds, Katie decided she wanted to stay here." He pushed his glasses up on his nose. "And so did I."

Ian nodded, and then doubled up his fist. "Ye dirty little man," he said. "Ye plan to defile my sister as soon as I'm gone! I knew it would come to this. I knew—"

"What?" Davey stared at him, and then comprehension dawned and he turned bright red. "Oh, no, no!" He looked down at Katie, clinging tightly to his arm, and shook his head even harder. "We're just friends. Right, Kate?"

"Oh, aye," she said. "How did ye put it?" She frowned slightly. "The best of buddies."

"You're staying here?" Ellie said, her voice distraught. "I can't believe it. What about your work? Your research? What about me needing your mass to get back home?"

Davey smiled. "Ian's mass isna so different to mine. Ye'll be fine. And I can keep researching, keep working, keep making new discoveries about the cairn. I'll send my notes forward—er, that is, I can still stay in touch with all of ye."

Ellie shook her head. "I don't understand. How?"

He glanced at Ian and jerked his head to one side.

"Katie, darlin'," her brother said, "come over here and tell me why in the world ye want to stay married to this atom splitter?" He led her to the fireplace, giving Davey a narrow look over his shoulder.

Davey turned back to Ellie. "I will send word to ye, and to Alex, simply by placing my notes inside a protective covering and burying them in the cairn. Remember the stone with the ogham carved upon it?" She nodded. "I'll leave messages buried behind that stone. The dirt is softer there. And maybe someday, who knows? Maybe I'll return."

"Oh, Davey," Ellie said, reaching out to hug him. "I'm going to miss you so much."

"Aye, lass," he said, "as I will miss ye."

Ellie turned away so that Davey couldn't see her tears and saw Ian gazing at her, his eyes soft with love. She smiled, knowing that she had to ask him, had to *know*, if he was going back with her or not.

"Ian," Katie said, pulling his attention back to her, "Father has been asking for ye." She shook her head. "We dinna expect him to last much longer."

He didn't move or speak, and Ellie crossed the room to his side. "Ian, aren't you going to see him?"

"I don't know," he said, his hands tightening around the bundle in his arms. "I thought I would, but now . . ."

"Ian," Ellie said, her voice firm as she laid her hand over his, "he's your father. I'd give anything in the world if I could speak to my father one more time. Go upstairs, and tell him good-bye."

Their eyes met, and his anger was gone. "Aye," he said.

As Ian walked into his father's chamber, he steeled himself against what was to come. No doubt Fergus wanted to rake him over the coals again about his disappearance twenty-three years before. Or about his affiliation with the MacGregors. Or any number of things.

The laird's bedroom was large, elaborate, and vastly different from the rest of the austere household, and as Ian and Ellie, Katie and Davey all filed in, there was still plenty of room to spare. Fergus Campbell lay in a huge four-poster bed carved from ebony wood, so large that his shrunken body seemed small and insignificant in the middle of it.

Sumptuous burgundy and gold curtains hung at the windows and from the canopy of the bed, matching the silken bedclothes pulled up around the frail man's neck. A large fireplace graced one wall, vivid tapestries lined two others, and on the last a portrait of a beautiful woman hung.

Ian drew in a sharp breath. His mother. He'd forgotten how beautiful she was. Her pale blonde hair was pulled up in an artfully careless knot atop her head, with long tendrils hanging on either side of her face; her skin was like porcelain. Her eyes were large and blue, her smile soft and tender, and tears burned into Ian's eyes as he gazed up at the only person in his life who had ever truly loved him. Until now.

"She's lovely," Ellie said softly from beside him. "She must be your mother. You look just like her."

Ian glanced down at her, and something inside of him let go. "Thank ye. Her name was Lenora."

"Ian? Is that ye?" came a weak voice from the bed.

Katie gave Ian a push, and he was almost grateful to look away from his mother's eyes. Instead, he turned toward his father, expecting to see the same anger and disgust in his gaze that had been there since Ian was fifteen years old.

"Yes, it's me," he said brusquely, moving toward the bed, only to stop and stare.

Fergus Campbell smiled up at him with warmth in his eyes. Gone was the hatred, the bitterness, and Ian suddenly felt as if a hand had tightened around his heart and squeezed. How could he have forgotten? Forgotten that once upon a time, his father had loved him. That once, long ago, before MacCrimmons School of Piping, before everything had gone so wrong, his father had looked upon him with pride and affection.

"Ian," Fergus said, extending one trembling hand across the covers toward his son. "What are ye doing here, laddie? I thought ye still were at MacCrimmons! What a delight to see ye."

Ian sat down beside him, stunned, and Katie bent over to whisper in his ear. "He's been asking for ye, Cook told me, for days. It's as if he doesna remember any of the bad times. He thinks ye are still at the piping school, still his fair-haired boy."

"Dear Lord in heaven," Ian said, and automatically took his father's hand, his heart thudding painfully inside his chest. Ellie came and stood behind him and put her hand on his shoulder. He took a deep, ragged breath.

"Hello, Father," he said, and took another breath. "I have missed ye."

The last note of "MacGregor's Lament" vibrated in the air, and Ellie sat beside the fireplace in Fergus Campbell's room, tears streaming down her face. She stood and walked across the room to Ian's side. His father lay with his eyes closed, a peaceful, contented look on his sleeping face.

"That was beautiful," she said softly.

Ian laid the pipes at the foot of the bed and gazed down at his father. "He never asked me to play for him before. Never once."

"Until now."

"Aye, until now."

"Ian," Ellie said softly. "I know you want to stay here, with your family. You don't have to leave him. I understand."

He turned and shook his head. "Och, lass, ye dinna understand. I want to go with ye. I finally have faced the fact— I no more belong here than ye do."

Ellie felt the dormant hope inside stir. "What do you mean?"

"I think," he said slowly, "that I have always been something of a misfit here. As a child, I only wanted to play my pipes. I cared only for my music. Then, when that dream was crushed, I found pleasure in raising hell with Quinn, my best friend." He dragged one hand through his hair and laughed softly. "Now, my music, my best friend, and my love—all wait for me in the future."

"But what about changing the future of Scotland?" she said, the small voice inside her head telling her to shut up. But she had to be sure. She didn't want him to regret coming with her, later on.

Ian looked up from his father and turned shame-filled eyes her way. There was such sorrow there that she reached out for him, and he walked willingly into her arms. He held her close, his face pressed against her hair.

"Och, love, I had the chance to change the history of Scotland, once and for all."

"The king," she said, and his eyes widened in surprise. "I heard about it, when I was in jail."

He nodded. "I could have killed him and changed the course of history."

"But you didn't."

"No, I did not. His daughter was with him, and as I looked into her eyes, I knew I couldna bring such unspeakable horror into a child's life. I could not do it. Afterward, I felt weak and cowardly, and wondered if I had done the right thing, but I knew that I had."

"Oh, Ian." Ellie pulled away so she could look up at him. "I'm so proud of you." He stroked his hand across her cheek and cupped her face, smiling down at her.

"And now that I know about Angus and my brothers, I know the fight for independence will continue, led by better men than I. My presence here has caused nothing but trouble."

"I wouldna say that," a deep voice said from behind them.

Ian turned. Angus stood in the doorway, his eyes suspiciously bright. He walked toward his brother and stopped a few feet away.

"How are ye, Angus?"

To Ian's surprise, Angus gave him a brilliant smile. "Never better," he said. " 'Twas a bonny tune ye played the laird."

Ian put his arm around Ellie, drawing comfort from the way she leaned against him. " 'MacGregor's Lament,' " he said.

"Appropriate." Angus glanced down at Ellie and then back to his brother. "Could I have a private word with ye?"

"Anything ye can say to me, ye can say to Ellie," he began, but Ellie kissed him on the cheek, surprising him into silence.

"Don't be silly," she told him, shooting a smile toward Angus. "Talk to your brother." She motioned to Davey and Katie, and the three left the room, closing the door softly behind them.

Silence descended between them as the two men stood and gazed at one another. Then Angus spoke, and Ian released a breath he didn't know he was holding.

"Ye saved my life," he said.

"I?" Ian shook his head. "I dinna think so."

"And ye saved George the Second's life as well." Angus rubbed his chin thoughtfully. "Although since ye were the threat to his life in the first place, I dinna think that counts quite the same."

Ian's reticence broke, and he laughed. "So, ye know."

"Aye, just as I suppose ye know now about me and my bonny little secrets."

"I'm sorry—" Ian began, only to be waved to silence by his brother.

"Dinna apologize. 'Tis I who am sorry. I should have taken ye into my confidence earlier, but—"

"Ye dinna trust me."

He nodded.

"And why should ye?" Ian said. "As far as ye knew, I had brought nothing but trouble upon yer family, then disappeared for twenty-three years, only to reappear and cause more."

"But ye are my brother," Angus said. "And I should have given ye a chance. Now, thanks to ye, I have the king's favor. If anything suspicious should surface about my activities again, I doubt General Wade will have the courage to arrest me again."

"But if it was not for me, ye would not have been arrested in the first place."

Angus frowned slightly and smiled. "Is that what ye think?" He shook his head. "I was arrested because of my own mistakes, not yers. We had a spy in our midst, and he gave Wade certain information that led to my being thrown in jail."

Ian stared. "Ye are kidding me."

"Kidding? What do goats have to do with anything?"

Ian laughed in relief. "Never mind. I thought—"

"That it was yer fault. Nay, in fact, ye have prevented a very important network of Jacobite sympathizers from being discovered, laddie," his brother said solemnly. "For all ye know, ye have changed the course of history."

Ian sobered. "Nay, 'tis just the way things were meant to be."

Angus frowned then and reached inside the velvet vest he wore.

"Yer friend Davey has been speaking to me of strange things for the last few days. He spoke in terms of hypothetical reasoning, spoke of strange possibilities like . . . traveling through time, and how a person might, in a sense, lose years of his life."

Ian drew in a sharp breath and then released it. "Did he now?"

"Aye. Do ye believe in such things?"

He hesitated and then nodded. "I do."

Angus withdrew his hand from his vest and held something out to his brother. Ian blinked down at Davey's calculator. "Do ye know what this is?"

"Aye. 'Tis a calculator. A way to do mathematics without paper or pen."

"'Tis more than that," Angus said. "'Tis an *invention*. It has a *light* inside of it. It practically thinks for itself! Davey let me borrow it." He shook his head, amazed. "There is nothing like this in our world."

"Well, there is now." Ian bit his lip. Perhaps he shouldn't have said that. What, he wondered, would his brother think about a home computer or a movie? He smiled. The same as he had, he supposed.

"Aye, there is now." Angus tucked the calculator back inside his vest. "Ye are leaving us, so I hear."

"Aye."

He nodded again and stared at the floor for a long moment before looking back up. "Ian. I dinna know where ye are going, or . . . how, but I want ye to know that I no longer hold yer absence against ye."

A wave of relief washed over Ian like a summer's breeze. "In truth?"

Angus held out his hand, and Ian automatically clasped it. "In truth," he said. "The name of Ian MacGregor will no more be maligned. I willna allow it. Ye saved my life, and I know that if ye could have returned sooner, then ye would have. Perhaps, after all, this is why ye came, though ye did not know it at the time."

Ian couldn't speak for a moment but continued to grasp his brother's hand until he could find his voice. "Thank ye," he whispered. He took a deep breath. "I canna return again, ye ken? The risks—" He broke off.

Sadness flickered across Angus's eyes. "Aye," he said, "I ken." He released Ian's hand and stepped forward to throw his arms around his brother. Ian's heart pounded inside of him, feeling as if it would break. He could not even tell his brother that all would be well with their family. He did not know, but he had faith.

"Scotland's future . . ." Ian began, as he wiped the moisture from his eyes with the back of his hand.

"Whist, laddie," Angus said. "All will be as it should be." With another pat on his brother's back, he turned and left the room. Minutes later, Ellie came in, her beautiful face wreathed in concern.

"Is everything all right?"

He put his arm around her. "Aye, lass, everything is wonderful. My brother has forgiven me, my family is well, and if Scotland's history canna be changed, well, then it is as I told ye: everything happens for a reason, aye?"

"Can you walk away from all of this, truly? I know how much it matters to you." Ellie whispered, lifting her face to his.

"Ye are all that matters to me now," he said, and kissed her with all the gentleness and love in his heart, feeling once again like her poet, her piper, her Ian, her love. She leaned against him, her face nestled against his chest.

"And you're sure that you want to go back with me, to my time, and live there for the rest of our lives?"

"Aye."

Ellie took a deep breath and released it, and it was as if, in that moment, she could feel every fear, every pain, every nightmare, every ounce of tragic melancholy she had ever embraced, slide away, leaving only joy behind. She trembled with the power of it and then lifted her head to smile up at him.

"Well, in that case," she said, "I have another little surprise for you."

"More bagpipes?" he teased.

She leaned up for a kiss. "Not exactly."

epilogue

Ellie held her newborn daughter in her arms, while Ian stood beside her and beamed. In a few minutes, Maggie and Quinn and eight-month-old Robert Roy, along with Allie and Alex, would be at the cottage to celebrate the arrival of Mr. and Mrs. Ian MacGregor's first child, but for now, this special moment was theirs and theirs alone.

It hardly seemed real at all now, traveling back in time, but Ian was the daily proof that she had, indeed, taken the risk, embarked upon the grand adventure of a lifetime, and lived to tell about it. Owing to the uniquely unstable power of the spiral, they had returned only days after the date they had journeyed back in time. Ellie had made up a story for Allie and Alex about Ellie eloping to Paris with Ian. In truth, they had been married in a tiny church in Edinburgh the day after their return. Maggie knew the truth, of course, and when Allie saw how happy Ellie was, she forgave her for making them worry.

Ellie had been overjoyed to be back in time for the birth of Maggie's baby, which had been a joyous time. Ellie had managed to keep her own news a secret until a week after Maggie delivered her baby. She and Ian had spent the next four months on tour with his band, Outlaw, and then had hunkered down to get ready for the arrival of their new daughter.

Ian had almost stopped worrying about Scotland; however, he was thinking of running for Parliament someday. Ellie had stopped wearing eyeliner, though she did still dye her hair; but she dyed it red, not black, with occasional streaks of blue.

Everyone missed Davey. Alex told Allie, the only one in the group still in the dark about time travel, that he had returned to Edinburgh to do more research. Exactly one month to the day after Ian and Ellie arrived in the present, the first of Davey's notes arrived as well, buried beneath the ogham stone in the cairn. Alex was thrilled. Ellie wept when she received her own letter, full of jokes and indiscernible scientific jargon and a tiny drawing of a baby wearing a kilt.

"She looks like ye," Ian said softly, his voice bringing Ellie back to the precious bundle in her arms. He gently smoothed the soft reddish blonde hair on her downy head with one finger.

"She has your eyes," Ellie said. "So that makes her perfect."

"*Ah, bonny lass,*" he sang to his daughter, his low voice sending a rush of love and happiness through Ellie's soul, "I dinna know yer name, but now that ye are with me . . . Ye are my heart, my life, my all . . . my love forevermore . . ." He paused and leaned down to kiss Ellie's forehead. "Ah, ye are my bonny lass," he said softly. "Ye are my heart, dear Ellie."

"And you, mine," she whispered, tears brimming in her eyes. After a few kisses, Ellie took a deep breath and brought up the subject she'd been putting off.

"Speaking of names . . . Ian, I know you wanted to call her Eleanor, but I have a new name I'd like to suggest."

Ian leaned down and kissed her cheek, his long blond hair caressing her face. "Whatever ye want, darlin'," he said.

"I want to name her after my mother . . . and yours. I want to name her Sunshine Lenora."

"Sunshine." Ian straightened, one corner of his mouth twitching in amusement. "Yer mother's name was Sunshine."

Ellie frowned. "She was a hippie. It's not my fault. We could call her Sunny, or Lenora, your pick."

"You want to name our child Sunny," Ian said, leaning closer, his mouth scant inches from hers.

"Yes," she said.

"You're sure?"

"Positively."

He chuckled and brushed his lips lightly across hers. "Och, Mrs. MacGregor, ye make me believe in miracles."

Ellie stroked her hand down the soft, sweet swell of her baby's cheek, and then looked up into the shining eyes of her husband, feeling so full of joy she thought she might just explode into a billion brilliant rays of light.

But not yet. Because right now, in this perfect moment, she was about to nurse Miss Sunshine Lenora MacGregor for the very first time.

"Nothing wrong with sunshine and miracles," she said, and smiled down at the sweetest little miracle of all.